"A sexy cowboy with bite."   —⸻ *Reviews*

"Rural romantic fantasy fans w⸻ ⸻e."

—*Midwest Book Review*

"*Jared* shows that Sarah McCarty is ⸻ author you want to read . . . [She] definitely pushes the imagination with the deviousness of the vampires from Sanctuary. *Jared* will suck you in with its captivating characters, dramatic plot, and tempting love scenes!"   —*The Romance Studio*

Promises Reveal

"Few writers can match the skill of Sarah McCarty when it comes to providing her audience with an intelligent, exhilarating Western romance starring two likable protagonists. The fast-paced story line hooks the audience."   —*Midwest Book Review*

"Entertaining . . . Kept this reader turning the pages. I've got a soft spot for Western historicals, with their hard times and smooth-talking cowboys. Ms. McCarty delivers on both of those fronts."

—*Romance Reader at Heart*

"I absolutely adored the chemistry and witty banter between these two spicy characters, and the sex, as always, was titillating, sizzling, and realistic . . . I don't know how she does it, but I want more and more and more. You will too once you read this fantastic tale."

—*Night Owl Romance*

"A must-read . . . Enticing and erotic . . . I am already craving more!"

—*Romance Junkies*

"Highly entertaining . . . Plenty steamy . . . and a great complement to the series."   —*A Romance Review*

"A delightful tale with lots of intense passion . . . Outstanding! Not to be missed by fans of historical Westerns who enjoy a strong dose of erotic fiction."   —*The Romance Readers Connection*

continued . . .

Running Wild

"[Sarah McCarty's] captivating characters, scorching love scenes, and dramatic plot twists kept me on the edge. I could not put it down."
—*Night Owl Romance*

"McCarty . . . skillfully brings out her characters' deepest emotions. Three strong heroines and three mouthwatering heroes . . . will tug at your heartstrings, and the well-written sex scenes will not disappoint."
—*Romantic Times*

"Sarah McCarty entices and enchants . . . and has taken paranormal romance to a whole new level."
—*Romance Junkies*

"You are going to love this . . . Entertaining and passionate . . . Fast-paced story lines and super-hot sex scenes . . . Sarah McCarty definitely takes you on a wild ride and . . . weaves a fascinating paranormal."
—*Lucrezia*

"This one is a scorcher. If you're looking for a romance to raise the temperatures, then look no further than McCarty's *Running Wild*!"
—*Romance Reader at Heart*

"Provide[s] werewolf romance fans with a strong, heated collection. Fans will be *Running Wild*."
—*Midwest Book Review*

More praise for the novels of Sarah McCarty

"[A] pulse-pounding paranormal."
—*Road to Romance*

"Masterfully written."
—*The Romance Readers Connection*

"Powerfully erotic, emotional, and thought provoking."
—*Ecataromance*

"Has the WOW factor . . . Characters that jump off the pages!"
—*Just Erotic Romance Reviews*

"Toe curling."
—*Fallen Angel Reviews* (Recommended Read)

"Ms. McCarty is a genius!"
—*Romance Junkies*

THE SHADOW WRANGLERS

JACE

Sarah McCarty

BERKLEY SENSATION, NEW YORK

THE BERKLEY PUBLISHING GROUP
Published by the Penguin Group
Penguin Group (USA) Inc.
375 Hudson Street, New York, New York 10014, USA
Penguin Group (Canada), 90 Eglinton Avenue East, Suite 700, Toronto, Ontario M4P 2Y3, Canada
(a division of Pearson Penguin Canada Inc.)
Penguin Books Ltd., 80 Strand, London WC2R 0RL, England
Penguin Group Ireland, 25 St. Stephen's Green, Dublin 2, Ireland (a division of Penguin Books Ltd.)
Penguin Group (Australia), 250 Camberwell Road, Camberwell, Victoria 3124, Australia
(a division of Pearson Australia Group Pty. Ltd.)
Penguin Books India Pvt. Ltd., 11 Community Centre, Panchsheel Park, New Delhi—110 017, India
Penguin Group (NZ), 67 Apollo Drive, Rosedale, Auckland 0632, New Zealand
(a division of Pearson New Zealand Ltd.)
Penguin Books (South Africa) (Pty.) Ltd., 24 Sturdee Avenue, Rosebank, Johannesburg 2196,
South Africa

Penguin Books Ltd., Registered Offices: 80 Strand, London WC2R 0RL, England

This book is an original publication of The Berkley Publishing Group.

This is a work of fiction. Names, characters, places, and incidents either are the product of the author's imagination or are used fictitiously, and any resemblance to actual persons, living or dead, business establishments, events, or locales is entirely coincidental. The publisher does not have any control over and does not assume any responsibility for author or third-party websites or their content.

PRINTING HISTORY
Berkley Sensation trade paperback edition / May 2011

Library of Congress Cataloging-in-Publication Data

McCarty, Sarah.
    Jace / Sarah McCarty.—Berkley Sensation trade paperback ed.
        p.   cm.—(Shadow wranglers ; 3)
    ISBN 978-0-425-24089-2
1. Vampires—Fiction.   2. Shapeshifting—Fiction.   I. Title.
    PS3613.C3568J33   2011
    813'.6—dc22   2011000497

PRINTED IN THE UNITED STATES OF AMERICA

10 9 8 7 6 5 4 3 2

❋ 1 ❋

MIRI was here.

Anticipation thrummed along Jace Johnson's nerves as he stood outside the Sanctuary stronghold; his fangs cut through his gums; bloodlust filled his veins. The bones in his face ached in pre-morph exhilaration. After a year of hell, he was close, very close to finding her. His mate. Adrenaline surged through his body, both from the battle about to begin and from the hunt about to end. A year ago she'd disappeared. He'd come home from a mission and found her gone, and no one, pack or vampire, claimed to know where she'd gone. It wasn't until his brother Jared had brought home his mate, a pretty little vamp who they'd all had reason to hate, that Jace had discovered she'd run from him, pregnant, straight into a Sanctuary trap. They'd taken her, kept her prisoner, experimented on her until Miri said there wasn't much left of the woman he remembered. And what was left, Miri said, she wasn't sure he'd want. Not after what had been done to her. Things she was sure no wolf mate could get past.

Jace slid along the stone wall leading to the bolt-hole from the Sanctuary compound, motioning Derek forward on the other side.

Miri had an annoying habit of forgetting she wasn't mated to a werewolf. There was nothing that could change what she meant to him, and if she had scars, they had forever left to get past them, and they'd do it together. Jace pressed his hand to the wood door, illusioned to look like solid rock. He mentally scanned for energy on the other side, any flicker of light or change that would indicate Sanctuary vampires. He didn't find any, but that didn't mean anything. He tightened his grip on his gun. Hell, with the new cloaking devices that Sanctuary had invented, there could be a whole army of Sanctuary vampires on the other side of that door and he wouldn't know. He smiled as adrenaline rushed through his system like a good friend. He hoped to hell there was. After a year of searching and worrying, he had a ton of frustration to vent.

He glanced over at Derek. The powerful werewolf wore the same smile he could feel on his face. Nothing like the potential for a good fight to perk a man up. Derek jerked his head and raised his eyebrow. Jace shrugged. He didn't know what they were going to find on the other side of the door. He touched the side of his nose with his finger. Weres had a much better sense of smell than vampires. A second later, the wolf also shrugged. Jace nodded. So be it. Tonight they were going in blind. He scanned again, this time looking for another type of energy. The video feed was easy to find. He mentally threw a subtle cloak of energy over the area before carefully opening the door. It swung soundlessly on its hinges.

The corridor beyond was dark. Not surprising. Vampires didn't need light to navigate. He sent another tendril of energy through the opening. Still nothing. A quick glance didn't reveal anything untoward, just a dark corridor stretching into the bowels of the mountain. The slight scrape of claw over metal disturbed the silence as Derek shifted his grip on his gun. It was the only sign the were shared his unease. There should be at least one sentry. Either the Sanctuary vamps thought no one knew about this little bolt-hole, or it was a trap. Either way, they didn't have any more time. Once his brothers and the Renegades launched their assault on the front of the compound, the chances of getting caught in the bolt-hole by fleeing Sanctuary vamps grew exponentially with the number of cowards in the place. He was betting there'd be a lot of cowards.

Derek gave him the thumbs-up. Jace went in first, and Derek slipped in behind him, a silent, deadly ghost. The wolf was a good man. A McClaren to the bone, which meant he had a very black-and-white philosophy about right and wrong, which probably explained why Jace and his brothers had taken up with the McClarens when they'd turned. The alliance might have evolved by accident when Caleb saved Derek's life, but it had grown out of respect for the values each held, until now, two hundred and fifty years later, the McClaren pack was family. And in some ways, the Johnsons were pack. The relationship might defy description, but it worked.

Jace paused just inside the door and mouthed, *You can still go back*.

Derek flipped him off.

Jace shook his head. There was just no talking to some men. And deep inside, he admitted he was glad of it. With Derek along, this mission might work out to be more than glorified suicide. The McClarens were hell on wheels when it came to a fight, and more than a match for most vampires. With Derek along, he might just get his wife back. And his child, who he only found out about days ago. He shook his head at that. Jace Johnson, a family man. It didn't hit his funny bone as hard as it could have. Over the last few days he'd grown rather attached to the notion.

They made their way soundlessly down the dark corridor. Processed air blew past. A few feet beyond the opening, his night vision kicked in, casting everything in shades of gray. He blinked. He'd never quite gotten used to the switch. Night vision was as detailed as day vision, but he still had the hardest time getting used to the lack of color.

Truth was, he liked color. He liked laughter. Hell, he even liked life as a damn vampire. Of all the Johnson brothers, he was the only one who'd welcomed Caleb turning him. He couldn't imagine being left behind. It'd always been the Johnson brothers against the world. And when push came to shove he didn't see the sense of losing his brothers for want of turning. Being immortal definitely had its advantages. He was stronger and faster, and he could fight better and love longer. It had pretty much been wine, woman, and song interspersed with an occasional battle for two centuries. Until Miri. Miri D'Nally, with her witchy eyes, sunny smile, and soft-as-summer-rain ways, had turned the fun into something much more serious. He tightened his grip on his gun. Much more welcome.

They came to a split in the corridor and another camera. He shimmered an illusion of the surrounding wall over himself and Derek and quickly passed beyond its view. Video devices were good against weres and they were good against humans, but they were pretty useless against vampires.

He scanned again. There were people in one of the rooms ahead to the right. Not moving. Prisoners? He was too far away to tell and the energy too weak to read. No telling whether they were wolf, vamp, or human, but his gut twisted with a hard clench. It had to be Miri. He signaled for Derek to cover him and pointed down the corridor. Derek nodded. Jace moved forward, curling his finger against the trigger guard, itching for a target. He wanted to kill someone for burying Miri in this glorified grave. Just being this far beneath the earth must have driven a woman like her mad.

Miri was a woman of laughter and joy, a werewolf who loved to run in sunlight and dance in moonlight, who gloried in her connection to nature. Forbidden to him by her pack law, given to him as a mate by fate, he remembered her as he'd last seen her: relaxed and sated from his lovemaking, her lips parted and swollen, her breath panting, her long black hair a fan of contrast against the white sheets. She'd stared at him as he'd told her he was leaving, disbelief slowly replacing the bliss in her soft golden-brown eyes when he'd told her he was coming back the following week, creating a nagging unease that he was missing something. An unease he'd ignored. To their detriment. Truth was, if he'd spent more time understanding her out of bed, he'd have known how devastating his casual announcement that he was leaving had been to her, but he'd been thinking as a human and she'd been thinking as a wolf. Not a good combination in any circumstances. Damn near terminal when it happened in the beginning of a relationship. It'd taken longer than a week to come back. Civil war had a way of messing with a man's schedule, and when he had returned, Miri had been as gone as if she'd never existed. And there hadn't been a whisper as to where. And when all his efforts to find her had come up empty, he'd braved direct confrontation with the D'Nallys. While he'd accepted the D'Nallys' right to put a bounty on his head for touching a were female, he hadn't accepted their statement that his Miri was dead. Not when his gut told him she wasn't. Not when, every time he closed his eyes, he went quietly crazy because her cries haunted his dreams. And then Raisa had come to the compound and he realized those nightmares were real. For a year, his wife had needed him, called for him to save her, believed he would come. Goddamn! For a year she'd suffered while he'd hunted in all the wrong places. For a year she'd kept believing until, Raisa said, she finally couldn't believe anymore and she'd given up, forced by Sanctuary plans into a final act of desperation to save their child. Something that had her living on borrowed time. And now the clock was ticking.

Rage flared as he moved deeper into the mountain. If her pack hadn't been so insular, so stuck on tradition, Jace might have found her sooner, but the D'Nallys were real particular about their women and no doubt one of their women hanging out with a vampire from the wrong side of immortality did not float their boat. He moved down the corridor, studying the energy coming from the room, slowing as it became more distinct. He couldn't afford a mistake. Derek growled a low warning. He was flaring out of control. Jace stopped, taking a breath, steadying the wild fluctuation of

energy that surged at the thought. Legend was, vampires were
sterile beings that could only be made, not born, but apparently
the Johnsons were the exception to the rule, because Caleb's wife,
Allie, was pregnant and he . . . Shit! He had a child.

The wonder of that tempered his rage, giving him something
positive on which to hook his excess emotion. Once again under
control, he moved on, logging the information coming at him as
he did. About a hundred feet ahead, the corridor veered off. He
probed the left hall. There was the hollow thunk of machinery and
the consistent hum of fans but no sense of life. Maybe a security
room? If there was one, the occupants were cloaked or it was unmanned. He was betting unmanned, since the hairs on the back of
his neck weren't standing on end. Derek paused against the opposite wall, his eyebrows raised, gun sitting easily in his hand, the
butt resting against his hip, looking for all the world like he was
out for a picnic, while from somewhere down the maze of corri-
dors came the muffled sound of a single shot and an explosion. Vibrations from the blast vibrated through the floor and wall, adding
to the tension in Jace's muscles. They only had a short time to find
Miri and get out. Sanctuary leaders were notorious for blowing up
compounds if the battle went south. And this battle was definitely
going to go south. The Johnsons had a score to settle.

Don't be influenced by what you see. Use your senses.

Caleb's words came back to him. Jace closed his eyes, going
deep into his vampire senses. Instinct told him this area was where
he needed to be and the direction he needed to go was . . . right.
He needed to go to the right. The walls came alive with echoes of
the past as he concentrated, expanding and contracting with the
embedded energy that only came from extreme suffering, seeming
to writhe with the agony of the screams of those who had suffered
in the Sanctuary's bid for power.

He closed his mind to the empathic pulse, not wanting to know,
now, what had been done to Miri, what he had allowed to be done
to her because he'd assumed that while he was away she'd be safe

with her pack. Though he blocked out the remnants of screams, the memories haunted him, dogging his steps, just waiting for a break in his concentration to pounce. Ten seconds later, he felt it. The subtlest of vibrations. Just twinges on the edge of his consciousness, but everything in him snapped to attention—Miri.

Instinct demanded he charge down that connection and wrap her safely in his energy, hold her the only way he could, tell her he was coming, that she wasn't alone.

Another growl from Derek, rumbling over the impulse. He nodded, stifling the urge. If Miri wasn't alone, if he betrayed his presence with his energy, if Miri showed any sign, to whomever was with her, that he was coming, the rescue might be over before it began. It was doubtful all of them were going to get out of here alive as it was, but he was determined that one of the survivors would be Miri. She had to live.

He signaled to Derek. Corridor on the right. Approximately thirty feet. His normally steady heartbeat, the one that didn't elevate even in the tightest situations, picked up speed. One by one, his senses focused on the woman just a minute away. He hadn't seen her in over a year. Hadn't caressed her face, hadn't loved her body or restored himself with the touch of her soul in too damn long.

Another explosion shook the walls. Derek made the motion to hurry. He nodded. It did sound like the boys were having just a bit too much fun with Slade's toys. And that much boom meant they were fighting hard to buy him time against some ugly odds, but the Renegades didn't have an endless supply of weapons. He picked up speed. Derek followed. Calm and steady, with a vicious side most didn't see coming until it was too late, Derek had saved all their asses more than once. The day Caleb had saved Derek's life and forged the pact between the McClarens and the Johnsons had been a good one for the Johnsons.

The next corridor was short and unremarkable. Two doors on either side with a steel door at the end. The one at the end was an impressively thick device, with one of those mechanical locks they didn't have a prayer of opening without five hours and Slade sitting there working his magic with technology. That is, if someone hadn't already opened it for them. The heavy door was jammed open about fourteen inches with a metal bar. Not big enough for a man to get through, but it might just be big enough for a small woman to squeeze through. Miri was small. Jace glided to the opening. Miri's scent reached out, flowed around him in a silent caress. Subtle, light, enticing, cinnamon spiced with bitter fear. A red stain on the door drew his hand. Blood. He rubbed the residual smear between his fingers, keeping his expression impassive as his vampire howled in recognition. Miri's. He brought his fingers to his mouth, refreshing his memory with her taste as he reached out carefully with his mind.

Derek, following his actions, frowned. Jace didn't have an answer for the question in his eyes. He didn't know how badly she was hurt. From the standpoint of Miri's rescue, it didn't matter. They'd planned for the worst, hoping for the best. He looked through the door. The room was large, with computers and gadgets around the perimeter. It looked a lot like the lab that had held Caleb for a time. In the middle stood a stainless steel table. Restraints made of the same stainless steel gleamed ominously in the sterile white light. A dark liquid spread over the bottom of the table and dripped off the edge. Two bodies lay crumpled on the ground, shards of glass sparkling around them. No energy came off the bodies. Looked like the worst hadn't happened. Miri was ambulatory. Jace smiled. And kicking ass.

He backed up, linking to the faint trail of energy that lingered in the aperture. Derek stayed put, covering him as he searched with his senses. She hadn't gone past them to the exit—he would have felt her if she had—so she had to be in the compound somewhere. Probably not far. She was covering her energy, as he'd taught her, but she couldn't hide the scent of her blood. Not from any vamp, but especially not from him. Not from her mate.

He ran his tongue over his lips, refreshing his senses, and back-tracked slowly. Not the first room. He moved across the corridor, sending his mind into the space beyond, tuning in to her unique vibration. Not there. But across the hall, at the third door, some-thing was different there. There was a heaviness that didn't belong. He let his rifle lightly touch the metal surface. A start of feminine fear, overridden immediately by a heavy surge of male energy.

He motioned to Derek. Miri was in there, and she wasn't alone. He made the sign for "vamp" and then the sign for "kill." Derek nodded. Jace braced his back against the wall, reached for the knob, paused, gathered his muscles, and pushed the door open.

Blinding light burned his eyes. A bullet whined out of the room. With super speed, he leapt between the bullet and the echo of the gun's report, diving into the room, taking in the scene as he rolled. In the back right corner of the room a male vamp held a naked Miri against his chest. One hand was around her throat, his nails pressed to her jugular. And in his other hand he held a gun.

Shit. Not good.

Through the violence of the scene his vampire senses hyper-focused on Miri, taking in all that he saw, all that was different. The straggly hair, the sleek beauty of her small body, the blood on her thighs, the jagged scars on her cheek. The fury in her eyes. He came to his feet smiling. That was his girl. All spit and vinegar. All heat and laughter.

He brought his gun up as he reached his feet. The vamp's at-tention was split between Derek, dead ahead of him in the hall, and Jace to his left. "You've got nowhere to go."

The vamp smiled, revealing his fangs. "Just out the door."

Jace shook his head. "Not an option."

The Sanctuary vampire jerked Miri forward a step. "Something tells me I'm holding my get-out-of-jail-free card."

He was an ugly son of a bitch, with his torn, half-morphed face and ragged sneer. Jace met Miri's gaze, the hand at her throat re-maining at the periphery of his gaze.

"I got your message."

"What took you so long?"

The naturally husky tone to her voice strained to hoarseness under the pressure the vamp was applying. "Things kept getting in my way."

A tiny jerk of her chin indicated the man hiding behind her. The move put a nick in her skin. A drop of blood welled. "Things are still in your way."

Out of the corner of his eye he watched that bright red drop swell and quiver, holding one instant before it grew too big and began its slow, inevitable surrender to gravity, sliding down her neck, almost glowing in intensity. "Not for long."

"Just long enough," the vampire snarled, pressing those nails deeper, sending more droplets of blood chasing the first in a splash of color. A little more pressure and those razor-sharp talons would sever her jugular.

Jace brought his revolver higher, sighting it dead center between the vamp's eyes. "So you say."

The vamp focused on him, reaching out with his energy. Not for the first time, Jace wished he had his brother Jared's ability to turn people's energy against them, to manipulate their minds. It would come in real handy right now. "Miri, sweet?"

"What?"

"Drop."

She didn't question, didn't blink, just held his gaze and took the leap of faith he needed. He was moving before her weight shifted, springing across the distance between them. Derek's shot came at the same second. Blood exploded into an arc, filling his vision. Miri's scream ended in a gurgle. Bastard, she better not be hit. Jace's hand closed over her upper arm, sinking into the resilient flesh. A flash of recognition shot to his soul, staggeringly strong. He grabbed the vamp's slack fingers, yanking them away from her throat as he tossed her back toward Derek.

And then there was just him and the stunned vamp. The shot

had been too high to scatter his brains. The caliber too high to have the bullet just ricochet around inside the skull. But, still, he should be out. He should not be blinking the blood out of his eyes and snarling. He should definitely not have the strength to lash out.

"Fuck!"

Jace went flying backward and slammed into shelves. Glass vials fell, exploding by his feet in glittering shards. His vampire rose at the challenge. His fangs cut through his gums; his talons stretched; bloodlust rose. This vampire had threatened Miri. Drawn her blood. Hurt her. There was another scream as the vamp launched at him, fangs and talons bared. Jace met him in midair, holding his red-rimmed gaze with his own, snarling back. The vamp was strong. Very strong. Enhanced maybe. Jace twisted away from the swipe of his claws, using the vamp's momentum against him, sending him into the same shelf he'd just left.

"Stop playing around, Jace, and finish it," Derek snapped from the doorway. "You're needed over here."

Derek never used that tone unless things were bad. Jace risked a glance over, tracking the vamp's next advance from his peripheral vision. Derek was holding Miri. His hand pressed to her neck, blood was spilling through his fingers as she struggled to get free, her gaze locked on him with a desperation he couldn't fathom.

The vampire hit him with a shoulder in the gut, overconfident in his strength. Jace pulled his revolver. He placed the muzzle against the vamp's side and pulled the trigger. The vamp jerked in shock a second before the paralyzing agent went through him. Jace pushed him off. "I don't have time to wrestle with you."

Leaning over the prone man, he drove his hand through his chest and removed his heart. The vamp's eyes closed. Jace tossed the organ to the floor and torched it with the sunlight replicator attachment from his gun; a damn handy gadget.

The whole thing took about fifteen seconds. That was fourteen too long. The one more required to get to Miri's side, a lifetime.

Derek, his eyes narrowed, handed her over before Jace could make the demand. Jace checked her heart rate, her blood levels. She was bad.

"Has she lost too much?" Derek asked.

Jace placed his hand over the wound, reaching for the knowledge he instinctively knew was his. "I don't know."

Miri bled for desperate seconds as he came up empty. He searched harder, delved deeper into instinct, and then he felt it. A warmth in his hand. A link from his life force to hers. He followed the trail deep into her mind, then out into her body, down to her wound and the torn tissue that screamed with agony.

Jace.

The sound of her voice in his mind was shock enough that he lost the connection. Her lips shaped his name again. No sound followed.

Derek growled, "Focus, damn it!"

He didn't need the wolf to tell him that.

Jace refocused his energy. As soon as the link re-formed, so did that husky feminine whisper. She was using his link to communicate.

Jace.

Right here, baby.

You have to save her.

He didn't care about anyone but Miri. He frowned, working at the edges of the tear in the artery. *In a minute.*

They'll hurt her.

She was talking about his daughter. Their child was a girl. He kept working on her injury as he absorbed the knowledge.

Leave me.

No way in hell.

I'm too hurt.

Shut up.

You have to leave me.

I said shut up.

He wasn't leaving her. He began repairing the artery wall as fast as he could, starting with the outside of the opening, wasting precious seconds before he realized his mistake. Jace swore mentally and then changed his plan, working from the inside out. He echoed Derek's sigh of relief as the repair held and the blood flowed within the artery.

"We've got company coming," Derek warned, touching his fingers to the transceiver in his ear.

Jace concentrated on a weak spot in the repair. "You're turning into a nag."

"Must be my age."

He sealed the last edge of the artery. He didn't have time to close the wound. She needed blood fast. He sliced his chest open, bringing her mouth to the wound. They'd never done this. As she always had, she resisted now, obviously still believing taking blood from him to be taboo. He didn't give a fuck. "Drink."

Go to hell.

"I think we've both already been there." He rubbed his fingertip over the back of her head. "And I for one don't want to go back."

The smallest of hesitations, the shakiest of breaths, and then her teeth scraped his skin. Her breath covered the sensitive spot, raising goose bumps and lust. He cupped her head, cradling her close, tenderness, lust, desire blocking out the danger, narrowing the focus to this one moment, this first moment of bonding.

Feed, sweet.

The endearment welled from his soul, slipped past his guard. In a life filled with temptation and opportunity, she was the only woman he'd ever wanted to keep. The only woman he'd ever failed to protect, and it didn't matter if that failure was his fault or not. All that mattered was that she'd suffered. Miri hesitated, not taking that final step, wavering between fear and trust, needing an incentive to go over the edge. He gave it to her.

Without you, our child dies.

Bastard!

You've only just figured that out?

With a husky snarl, her canines sank deep, the bite no doubt meant to hurt, but all that poured over him was a pleasure so intense, a culmination so complete, he cried out. Out of the corner of his eye, he saw Derek cast him a shocked look before quickly averting his eyes. The power of the connection draped over Jace, hazing his good sense. His mind tuned to hers, his body to hers, his focus concentrating on her need.

It was unthinkable that she be so weak. He needed to make her strong. He needed to give her what she required. Whatever it was. Whatever the cost. His head dropped back as he pulled her close. He gritted his teeth and found his voice with the last bit of reason he had. "Derek, don't let me give her too much."

The look Derek cut him was dry. "How do you suggest I stop you?"

He anchored his fingers in her hair. "Remind me what's at stake."

He would do anything for Miri. Anything for his child. Anything except give up this moment of richness after a year of desperation and barrenness.

Miri's claws dug into his back as her mouth worked erotically against his chest, her torso sliding against his in a languorous twist of need. His clothes chafed his skin, an unwelcome barrier. He needed to feel her against him. To hold her tightly, to feel her heat merge with his.

Derek's hand on his shoulder prevented him from shrugging out of his shirt. "You get naked with her and I'm not going to be able to stop anything."

Jace snarled but returned his hand to Miri's head, supporting her, feeling the power flow from him to her, feeling the strength return to her with a bone-deep sense of satisfaction. It was right that he give this to her.

"That's enough," Derek ordered.

Not yet.

The whisper came into his mind. Jace's vampire surged to the fore, snarling at Derek in warning. The wolf would not take him from her.

"Son of a bitch." Derek stood over them, his natural drawl shortened as he snapped out, "Miri Tragallion-D'Nally, as a pack Alpha, I order you to stop."

Miri shuddered. Jace's vampire snarled. No male but him commanded his mate. Not even one invoking the universal superiority of being an Alpha.

Derek grabbed Miri's shoulder. Jace lashed out. Derek leapt back, his voice maintaining the hold he relinquished. "Obey, Miri."

With a moan, Miri released Jace. He breathed deeply as the connection was severed, closing his eyes against his own instinct to bring her back, to give her everything she needed, wanted.

Miri moaned again. When he opened his eyes, she was holding both hands over her mouth, staring in horror at the blood flowing down his chest. He wiped his hand over the wound, sealing it, nodding to Derek. "Thanks." He cut a glare at Miri. "When this is over, we're going to talk about your snapping to at anyone's orders but mine."

He shrugged out of his jacket and wrapped it around Miri's shoulders.

"A were woman is raised to obey her pack male," Derek explained.

"You'll pardon me, but to date I haven't seen much of this so-called obedience." He caught Miri's hand when she would have reached for him, redirecting it into the sleeve of the coat. "And, she's my mate. There's no such thing as a pack male for her."

"She's were. There will always be pack loyalty."

Jace made a grab for Miri's other hand, gritting his teeth when she moaned and swayed toward him. The blood exchange should have been private, the sharing one of commitment rather than necessity. "Uh-huh." He yanked the sleeve up over her hand. It immediately fell back down. "You keep believing that." He closed the coat over her chest, working the buttons with deft precision. "Come on, Miri. Stand up."

She did. Slowly, languorously, the subtle flex of her muscles playing hell with his libido. He couldn't resist. He cupped her cheeks in his hands and kissed her full lips, the edges of his clinging to the softness of hers. Damn, he'd missed her.

Another explosion shook the walls. He tapped her cheek with his fingers. "Snap out of it, baby. We've got to go."

She blinked, those big golden-brown eyes that haunted his dreams slowly coming back into focus. She stepped back. He kept his hand on her shoulder until he was sure she was steady.

He dropped his hand as Derek said, "Time's a-wasting."

"You okay?" he asked Miri. She nodded. Jace glanced down at the dried bloodstains on her legs and feet. "Can you run?"

She looked around, distaste twisting her features. "Try to keep up."

He smiled. "I'll do my best."

Derek took the lead, Jace the rear. Miri, as protected as they could make her, ran between them. The ground beneath their feet vibrated with an explosion unlike the others. This was stronger and came from beneath rather than above. "Shit."

That about covered it. They were out of time. "They're blowing the place from within." Jace turned on the transceiver in his ear and sent a signal to his brother. If the Sanctuary were blowing the place up, there wasn't any need for secrecy. "I've got her. We're coming out."

As soon as the words left his mouth, the walls exploded in a hail of rock and dust. "Shit!"

Jace grabbed Miri, throwing her down, covering her with his body as boulders spewed like water droplets.

"Shit" didn't begin to cover it.

✤ 2 ✤

THE first thing he heard in the wake of the explosion was a ringing in his ears. Shrill and high-pitched, coming in an odd rhythm.

It wasn't ringing. It was screaming. A woman was screaming.

Miri heaved beneath him. "Oh, my God! She's alive."

He braced himself on his palms. "Who's alive?"

Miri scooted out from under him.

"The human woman. I thought they'd killed her."

Derek cast a wary eye at the cracking ceiling above them. "Why would they kill her?"

Her face twisted. "Because of me."

"Explain."

It was almost a snarl from Derek, who never lost control, and it reflected the strange tension in his muscles. Keeping an eye on the powerful were, Jace shifted so he was between Miri and Derek.

"They needed someone new to force my cooperation."

Jace glanced at the blood on her thighs. "Cooperation for what?"

"They've got it in their heads I can control conception."

"You can't."

She shrugged. "Logic doesn't have any bearing on their beliefs."

He just bet it didn't. The Sanctuary vamps were a fucked-up bunch.

Derek held out his hand, his attention clearly centered down the hall. Miri took it briefly, standing steadily amid the rubble in her bare feet. Shit. No shoes. That was going to be a problem with the ceiling lying on the floor.

The scream came again. High-pitched, terrified.

Jace's first priority was Miri, but leaving a woman alone here . . . he couldn't do it. He shoved Miri at Derek.

"Get her out of here."

The wolf had a strange look on his face. "No."

The walls around them groaned. Derek ran for the opening, Miri right behind him, her long silky hair swaying as she darted through the debris.

Jace followed. "And everyone says I'm insane."

"Not insane," Derek muttered as he helped Miri over a slab of concrete. "Just unpredictable." There was a protectiveness in the way the were held Miri's hand. The growl rumbled out of Jace's throat without conscious thought. Derek steadied Miri as she jumped over, flashing him a warning look. "Especially this last year."

With an easy leap, Jace landed on top of the pile, beside Miri, shouldering the were out of the way. Miri shook her head as he slid his arm around her waist.

"You are as possessive as any wolf."

There was no indication in her tone as to how she felt about that. "Make no mistake about it: I'm worse."

The far side of the pile was pointed steel and sharp edges. He tucked his arm behind her knees and lifted. Her arms went around his neck and her scent enfolded him with the same intensity.

"I can walk."

"I just made an executive decision."

Her eyebrows raised. "Since when do you know anything about being an executive?"

"There's a lot you don't know about me."

She just stared at him for the three steps it took him to get through the debris. "Maybe it's better that way."

He let her slide down his body, enjoying every soft sigh of contact. Ignoring their differences was what had caused the problems between them in the first place. "No, it's not."

Derek was already moving ahead. It wasn't hard to figure out which way to go; the woman's scent came strong on the reconditioned air, tainted with fresh blood, soured with desperation. Another scent blended with hers. Vampire. Jace thrust Miri behind him. "Keep up."

"No problem." There was a tug on his belt.

He glanced over his shoulder. She had one of his guns in her hand. "You know how to use that?"

"I think so, and if not, I'll just wing it."

He smiled at the sheer grit in her voice. "Just remember to flip off the safety before you start threatening people. It's on the side."

She tipped the gun and flipped the switch. "Done."

He reached over, his fingers gliding over hers, his starved senses relishing the contact. He tilted the barrel away from his midsection. "It's there for a reason."

"Not a good one."

He slid the switch back. "Trust me and leave it on."

Her mouth twisted. He placed his finger over her lips, cutting off the retort he knew was building. The support to the right groaned. "Bitch at me after we're out of here."

She flipped her hair over her shoulder, a totally feminine gesture of anger and challenge. A stray tendril fell forward, ignoring her want, feeding his. "Count on it."

Despite the danger, her sass made him smile. He pushed her hair back. Derek disappeared around the corner. He tucked the stray strand behind her ear. "C'mon."

* * *

DEREK knelt in what remained of a doorway. The frame listed heavily to the right, leaning against a fallen beam. The whole place was unstable. Derek's gun lay discarded beside him. He was hunched over something.

Another groan from the steel beams set Jace's teeth on edge. "One more blast and this whole place is coming down."

Derek didn't respond, just reached out as if in a trance and touched something with a tenderness Jace had never seen him offer anything before. A few steps closer and he knew why.

There was a woman trapped in the debris. Probably the one who'd been screaming, though she wasn't making a sound now. Even from here he could see she was tiny; so small, Derek's hand against her cheek dwarfed her face. Her features marked her of Asian descent. Blood trickled from the corner of her mouth. Another step and he could see the male body trapped on top of her, his head level with her chest. No energy came off the body. "Guess we found the missing sentry."

Derek nodded.

Jace holstered his gun. Miri came up beside him, her fingertips resting on his arm, her energy snuggling into his.

"Is she okay?"

The woman didn't look good. He wasn't even sure she was alive. "I don't know. Derek?" Another warning vibration shook the floor. Jace touched Derek's shoulder. "Derek. We have to leave."

The were shrugged off his hand and reached for the concrete slab compressing the woman's chest, shoulder, and arm. He moved it carefully aside. The vampire's blood-spattered shoulder came into view. Beside him Miri aimed her gun. With her thumb, she switched the safety off. Her hands were shaking.

"He's dead, Miri."

She shook her head. The gun stayed pointed. "They never die."

"This one did."

She didn't look convinced. He didn't argue. Another piece of debris came off. The woman gasped and choked; blood sprayed from her mouth. Jesus.

Derek caught her head before it could slam back onto the concrete. "Shh, just lie still."

His voice was as soft as his hand on the small woman's skin. Her almond-shaped eyes opened, then stared vaguely a second before they focused on the man above her. She blinked once and blinked again. Mesmerized by terror or something else—probably the first, for, sure as shit, waking up to find Derek glaring down at her like he wanted to commit murder would be enough to give any woman nightmares.

Her breathing increased to shallow pants. Her scent was tainted with fresh fear and fresh pain.

"Hush, baby," Derek murmured.

Baby?

The cold muzzle of the gun was thrust into Jace's hand before Miri sank to her knees at the woman's side. "It's all right, Kim. He's a friend."

Jace switched his grip to the handle, warm and damp from her nervous grip. He flipped the safety on before putting it back in his belt.

After a slow blink and a series of shallow breaths, the woman managed one word. "Alive?"

"Yes." Miri's hands fluttered over the debris where the woman's hand should be. "And I'm glad to see you are, too."

"Sor-ry."

Miri's soft face went hard as she moved another chunk of concrete off the woman. "I'm the one who should be apologizing to you. They hurt you because of me."

The woman shook her head, the movement shallow but emphatic. "No."

Derek moved more debris off her torso. Immediately, her eyes flew wide and fixed on a point high above, and a violent trembling seized her. Jace's senses, so tuned to the emotions in others, registered the blood loss going on inside the woman's broken body; registered the anguish coming off Derek and the horror off Miri. Above him the hall structure shuddered with a violence almost matching that racking the woman. They didn't have much time.

Vampire instinct said to get his mate the hell out of there and leave everything else to its own fate. Tiny rocks pinged down on his head, emphasizing the need to hurry. Miri reached back, her hand searching for his. He caught it and held it. Her energy reached up his arm, soft, strong, determined. She wanted him to save this woman. He owed this woman. Jace glanced at Derek. He owed this man. He owed his child. Shit, he must be losing his mind. He didn't have time to get all human.

"Help her," Miri whispered.

Apparently, he wasn't going to have a choice.

Kneeling beside Derek, Jace put his hand over the were's when he would have removed the last piece of debris compressing the severed artery he could sense in her arm. Derek slashed at his arm, drawing blood. There was only one thing that could inspire such a reaction in a wolf. The discovery of his other half. "Your mate's dying, Derek."

"No."

Jace understood that instinctive terror. The soul-deep rejection of the possibility of never feeling the brush of that person's hand again.

"She's human. She can't regenerate. If you remove that slab of concrete, she'll bleed out in seconds." The big wolf shuddered. "If she's going to stand a chance, she needs to be converted," Jace continued.

Derek blinked. Awareness came back to his eyes. His canines flashed as he snarled. "There's not enough time for a were conversion."

Which was going to complicate things. "Do you think she can be converted?"

Jace didn't know how one assessed that sort of thing. It'd never been an issue in his life.

Derek's "Yes" was immediate and strong.

"What makes you so sure?"

"She's my mate."

Which meant they were going on faith, but at this point, did it really matter? Jace brushed a smear of dust from his eyes with the back of his hand. "It's not too late for me to convert her."

Beside him, Miri gasped. Her hands squeezed his. Derek was a pack leader. He had responsibilities. Pack leaders could not mate with vampires.

Derek touched the woman's cheek again, his fingers a delicate brush on the bruised and bloody flesh. His voice was a gravelly husk of regret. "Do it."

"If her conversion is anything like Allie's, she'll be unconscious for a few hours, but then she's going to hurt like hell."

Derek made room for Jace at the woman's side. "She already hurts too much."

"Conversion will make this feel like a picnic." He leaned over the woman. The comforting words he meant to say stuck in his throat. Her face was white, her lips just one shade darker with a bluish tinge around the edges. She was too far gone to hear them. "We'll need to get her to a safe place before she wakes."

"I'll take her to the D'Nally stronghold."

He glanced at Miri. She shook her head. He couldn't take Miri there. "Can you get her there alone?"

Derek nodded, not questioning the why. "Yes." He slipped his big hand under the woman's head, arching it back, presenting her to Jace. "Do it."

Jace shifted forward, feeling the weight of expectation upon him. It was harder than it should be to muster the enthusiasm. He'd never fed from the innocent before. Never tried to convert someone before, didn't have a clue how to do it correctly. Didn't know how he was going to face Derek's devastation if the woman died.

Miri's hand withdrew from his. He didn't blame her for the lack of faith. He hadn't done much to prove to her he was a man to count on. His fangs, partially retracted, extended as he gathered his strength, his energy, and sent it forward into the woman, searching for her life force. Needing to hold it as the transition was made. He came up hard against a wall of nothing. He closed his eyes, searched harder. Again nothing. "Damn it."

"What's wrong?"

He wasn't aware he'd spoken aloud. "I can't feel her. It's too late."

"Like hell it is." Derek's wrist was in front of his mouth. "Bite me."

A vampire that bit a were had access to his thoughts. A were connected to a vampire could be ostracized from his pack. It was a hell of a risk to take for a woman who was probably already dead. "It might already be too late."

Derek didn't waver. "It's not."

What the hell, someone had to be right today. Jace bit, taking in the were's blood, feeling his power go through him. A lot of power. Along with that power came the vibration of an external connection. The woman.

Jace followed his instincts, following that vibration to deep inside Derek's core. Things got more confusing there, thoughts and emotions a careening, jumbled chaos. Unlike Jared, who could move in and out of another's mind like a whisper of a memory, Jace wasn't so skilled. His talents lay in other directions.

Here.

The whisper came into his mind, Derek guiding him through the chaos with a surety that made Jace wonder if he'd done this before. The *Here* came again. Stronger, louder, giving him a point of focus. He flowed along it, following it toward that black wall of nothingness, feeling the prod from Derek as he did.

Hurry.

Seconds stretched like hours as he searched for a crack, Derek's implacable resolve shoving him onward until he found it. Right there. A weakness. He burst through, flinching back as he got to the other side, unable to absorb in one breath all the information coming at him.

Damaged. She was so damaged, the energy coming off her little more than a silent scream. Too late, he tried to block Derek from following him in, but it was no use. Nothing came between a wolf and his mate, and Derek was one particularly stubborn wolf. His energy passed in a powerful force that bruised as it surged by, surrounding that stuttering life force with all the strength he had, covering it, sheltering it within his power.

Can you hold her without me? Jace asked.

The answer came in a snap of impatience. *Yes.*

Good.

He took a mental breath and glanced over at Miri.

"When I tell you to, slice my wrist."

Her lips set in a firm line. She nodded.

"And then you get the hell out of here."

Her hair slid over her shoulders. Her energy convulsively reached for his in instinctive denial. "No."

He met her gaze, unable to pull his will from the woman to enforce it on his mate. "One of us has to get out of here for our child."

Miri bit her lip. Her eyes filled with tears, but not one fell. Her shoulders squared. She nodded again.

He wanted to touch her so badly it was a live ache inside him, but he couldn't. Physically and mentally he was tied to the woman they were trying to save. Miri's hand touched his shoulder. Her energy smoothed over him. Chaos stilled, leaving only purpose behind. He lowered his head, scraped his teeth over the other woman's delicate skin, gauged the depth, and then bit down.

There was a moment of total disorientation as her life force flailed. Derek was there, strong and implacable, quelling the instinctive rebellion with the ruthless efficiency that made him such an invincible enemy and invaluable friend. Jace pulled the last of the woman's blood into him. They only had seconds. *Now!*

He grabbed the woman's mind as Miri's claws cut through the artery in his wrist. Blood sprayed. He forced his wrist against the woman's mouth.

Drink.

The woman resisted. He didn't give her an option, overriding her revulsion with force.

Derek's snarl snapped his head around. The few remaining lights flickered, strobing white slashes of light over his bared fangs. Jace hesitated, sensing the precarious hold the were had over his instinctive need to protect his mate, even against the vampire trying to save her. Then Derek shook his head. With a jerk of his chin, Derek motioned Jace on.

Swallow.

Jace gave the order. The woman didn't obey. He didn't have time to fight with her. He probed her mind, skating by her will, honing in on reflex. *Swallow.*

Her lips moved, her throat worked. After the first few swallows, her will to survive took over and resistance turned to demand, increasing their bond, draining his strength. As she fed, he focused on healing the worst of her injuries.

Derek growled a warning. Around them the teetering mass of debris shuddered. Behind him, Jace heard the scrape of feet over rock. Miri leaving. Good.

Seconds dragged as Derek's mate fed. He could feel her body absorbing his strength, the collapsed arteries expanding with renewed life, the blood seeping around the spike puncturing her abdomen.

Faster. She had to feed faster, and he had to heal her faster. Otherwise they were all going to die.

As he worked, he tracked Miri with his mind, unable to disconnect from her after so recently finding her. She was working her way up, systematically testing tunnels and pathways for a clear one, following the scent of fresh air to freedom. Fear, tension, and desperation drove every step, claustrophobia threatening her sanity. He sent a thought after her.

It's all right, Miri.

A thought came back, awkward and weakened by distance, but very Miri in tone. *It'd better be. I don't want to die down here.*

You're not going to die.

You can't promise that.

No, he couldn't. But he could lie. *Yes, I can. Just keep climbing and I promise you, it will all be okay.*

I'm holding you to that.

You do that.

She was almost to safety, but their situation was precarious.

The woman's heart rate steadied; her breathing regulated. As soon as Jace pulled his wrist from her mouth, Derek snatched her against his chest, his breath coming in hard draws, his grip tender as he took her moan against his neck. His gaze met Jace's. "Thank you."

Jace closed the wound on his wrist. "Anytime." He motioned to her. "She's going to get very sick before the change completes."

"I know."

"She's going to need blood for her first feeding."

"I'll give it to her."

"More than you can probably spare."

"I'll take care of it."

The set expression on his face didn't give Jace a warm fuzzy about the ware's ability to let another man around her long enough to fulfill her first bloodlust.

"You might have to let her go."

"I don't have to do shit."

He didn't suppose he did. Lord knew, if it came to a choice between life without Miri or death with her, he'd take the latter.
"Let's get her free of this mess."

Together they lifted the concrete slab. It immediately became
clear that the rebar that had punctured the vampire's heart, stopping it, was the same rebar that pierced her chest.

Jace took a breath, fighting the dizziness that came from giving too much blood and expending too much energy. "Pull it off
slowly."

Derek nodded.

With every inch that rasped free, precious blood flowed. Jace
worked feverishly. As the last inch cleared, he sealed off the wound.

Looking up, he saw the dead vampire hadn't been just guarding
the woman and subsequently caught in the collapse. If his undone
pants were a clue, he'd been intent on having sex with her. Derek
took the heavy body and hurled it, concrete and all. As the body hit
the wall, Jace looked at the woman. There were some very distinct
bruises on the woman's body that had nothing to do with falling
objects. Some were old. Some were new.

"The bastards."

Derek didn't say a word, just shrugged out of his heavy coat
and carefully wrapped it around the woman. The heavy shearling
all but swallowed her, with just her slender calves emerging. Growls
rumbled from his chest as he buttoned it closed.

Jace traced Miri's progress. Clever little wolf. She was almost
out.

Jace touched the woman's shoulder. "I did the best I could, but
some of it's fragile."

Derek nodded and slid his hands under her shoulders and legs,
her bare feet dangling. "Understood."

Jace stood with him, those bare feet bothering him. "Until her
conversion is complete, she can't regulate her body temperature."

Derek took a breath, every one a struggle for control. He glared
at the corpse in the corner. "Get the boots off the bastard."

Jace admired Derek's ability to think rationally with emotion pounding him. Jace didn't know if he could stand to see anything of his woman's rapist on her body. He made short work of stripping the boots and socks from the body. The socks slid easily over the woman's feet and calves, but there was no way to keep the huge boots on her tiny feet. No matter how tightly he tied them, they fell off.

"You're gonna have to make do with the socks."

Derek nodded. He turned to leave, then stopped and stood there, feet braced. "Thank you."

Jace pulled his gun, unlocking the safety. "You'd do the same for me."

In fact, he already had by coming to help rescue Miri.

"I just wish I knew how to save her without converting her. Being vampire isn't going to make things easy for you."

"Her being vampire gives me a chance. I don't need more than that." Derek's expression was so cold it appeared set in stone. "Your woman's almost out."

"Yeah." Jace headed down the corridor, trailing Miri's mental path rather than her scent.

Derek was right behind him. "You've got a long row to hoe with that woman."

Jace shrugged. "I've got forever to do it in."

"If she'll continue to accept you."

He frowned at Derek. "What in hell do you mean?"

"Weres don't convert to vampires. Once mated, their longevity depends on their continued intake of vampire blood."

Son of a bitch! He'd let Miri go on ahead of him because he thought she was immortal now. He put on more speed, going so fast debris seemed to fall in slow motion. "How long does the effect last?"

Derek kept pace. "It depends, from couple to couple."

"Tell me more than ten minutes."

"Okay. More than ten minutes."

He did not need Derek's levity right now. He cut him a glare. "Now tell me the truth."

Derek paced him easily, not breaking stride or breath. "There haven't been that many were/vampire couplings, and as blood exchange is normal on a daily basis we don't have a lot of cold hard facts."

Jace took a sharp left, hunching to avoid the low-hanging brace beam. Miri had been converted when she'd taken his blood. There was no going back. "I'll take speculation." Hell, at this point, he'd take anything.

"About a week."

The knot in his chest loosened. "Thanks."

"Of course, that was only after the couple's bond had been reinforced multiple times."

Jace cut Derek a glare. "You just had to add that."

"You asked."

So he had. "What do you know about were/vampire children?"

"Enough to know that you-all are in one hell of a fix."

"Yeah."

"On the bright side, you have a child to be in a fix about. Not all such pairings are fertile."

He knew Derek was thinking about the impossibility of completing his mating to the woman. Weres lived for family and pack, desired children more than anything. Cherished them. Converting his potential mate to vampire might have robbed Derek of every werewolf's dream, but Derek hadn't even hesitated in making the decision, any more than he would hold back from his commitment to her. The woman, whoever she was, was a very lucky one.

An explosion lower down shook the ground beneath their feet and sent debris crashing around them. Derek, running beside him, hunched protectively over the woman. With his forearm, Jace blocked a falling chunk of concrete from striking the were's head. He continued tracking Miri, fumbling with the connection, finding the link, surging along it until he saw what she saw. She was at the opening, scenting the air as she pulled rock away, getting ready to dash across the open field.

No!

All his order did was fuel her desperation and make Derek flinch. His projecting needed fine-tuning.

Damn it, woman, don't you move.

Her *Don't tell me what to do!* came back in a succinct denial of obedience.

Jace swore.

Derek's shoulder bumped his as they took another left. "I take it she's not listening?"

"She's thinking of dashing across the field."

"Not good."

"No shit. Where the hell is pack obedience when I need it?"

"You're not pack."

"I'm her mate. I rank higher."

Miri's scent came to him, along with the clean scent of the night. They were almost upon her. One more turn and he saw her. She spotted him at about the same time. One quick glance over her shoulder, and she frantically dug at the opening. Derek saw the same thing he did. And damn him for the smile. "Looks like you've got some work ahead of you convincing her of that."

Miri dove for the opening. She got as far as those luscious hips of hers and then hung up. The view had Jace hard in an instant, despite the danger, despite his anger. "You goddamn well better have your eyes closed, Derek."

"Not likely."

If his friend hadn't been holding the small woman, Jace would have shoved him into the wall. Miri kicked and wiggled. Along with her scent came the odor of fresh blood. His vampire instincts homed in on the source immediately. She'd cut the bottom of her foot.

He dropped beside her. She kicked back hard when his fingers encircled her ankle. He went with the momentum, sitting back, dragging her out of the hole. She emerged, a snarling, twisting ball of fear, talons outstretched, canines flashing. Jace caught her hands before she could find his face. Fury radiated off her, bathing him with the heat of her emotions. She squirmed on his lap, igniting his lust. Damn, she was something. Her lips drew back from her teeth, her eyes narrowed. Bending his head, he put his neck within reach as he whispered for her ears alone, "If you bite me, I'm going to come."

She went absolutely still. Very slowly, as if she was afraid any motion was going to set him off, she raised her eyes to his. The hint of vulnerability deepened the normally soft brown color. "You are such a pervert."

A smile tugged at the corner of his mouth. It was all he could do to suppress it. "You're just remembering that?"

Miri in a snit had always been the hottest thing he'd ever seen. Something she'd often used to get her way, because he was very susceptible to her charms.

The sound of rock tumbling against rock drove play from his mind. He shoved Miri at Derek, who dragged her beneath the breadth of his shoulders, shielding both women as best he could with his bigger body. With all the strength he had, and some he hadn't realized he possessed, Jace tossed debris from the pile, widening the hole. Derek's curses and Miri's gasps drove him on past weariness to sheer determination. Another curse from Derek and something slipped beneath him. Miri.

"Get the hell clear."

"Shut the hell up."

She grabbed a rock and tossed it back, reaching for another.

"It's too dangerous."

More rocks came down. "Appears to me, either way, I'm in danger of being buried alive."

"Less likely to happen over there."

He hauled a boulder back.

She slipped under his arm and worked her way into the hole.

"Pardon me, but if I'm going to get crushed by a pile of rocks, I don't think it particularly matters where it happens."

She wiggled back, dragging rocks with her, squealing as the dirt poured down on her head. He grabbed her feet and hauled her out. "How the hell can you do something so incredibly brave and then squeal like a girl when it gets you dirty?"

She shoved the dirt out of her eyes. "Probably because I'm a girl."

He tugged the jacket he'd given her to wear down over her thighs. "So we can all see."

She rolled her eyes.

"Miri," Derek called.

"What?"

"Come here and care for this female."

It galled Jace to no end that Miri stood immediately and headed toward the were. Jace caught her hand. She jerked around, her hair swinging around her face. He motioned to Derek. "We're going to have to talk about that."

"What?"

"Your instant obedience to Derek."

She frowned. "He's Alpha."

"And I'm your mate."

She yanked her arm free. "He's earned my respect."

"Let her go, Jace."

Jace had no intention of doing anything of the kind. "Stay out of it, Derek."

"As an unmated were, Miri's my responsibility."

"We're mated."

"The union wasn't sanctioned. It's not recognized."

Miri jerked her hand free and headed to Derek's side. "We don't have time to waste arguing this."

She knelt by the woman Derek held and took her head into her lap. Derek touched the unconscious woman's cheek, brushing the dirt from the edges of her eyelashes before standing and coming over to grab the rock Jace handed him. He couldn't keep his eyes off the woman. "If you're so gone over her now, what in hell you going to do when she wakes up?" Jace asked as the were went to work beside him.

"Bear it."

Jace yanked a hunk of rock free. "You could just marry her."

"Were law is very specific on that. Mating is a woman's choice."

"And I'm willing to bet were males have been getting around the specifics of that law since the day after it was made."

"Maybe."

Jace sighed. "But not you?"

"No." He tossed a rock back. "She's been tricked enough."

Jace threw the rock behind him. It bounced off the floor before rolling up against the wall. "One of these days you're going to realize pack law is made to be broken."

Derek looked over at the woman, regret in his eyes. "Maybe." He turned back, his expression as barren as the cavern behind them. Derek was pack to his bones. What part of his soul that wasn't claimed by his mate was owned by his pack. Breaking pack law would break him. Surrendering his mate would kill him. Nothing of the bleakness of his choice was reflected in Derek's tone as he motioned toward the night beyond the opening.

"The hole's big enough. Let's go."

❧ 3 ❧

THEY were running out of time. Jace grabbed Miri's shoulders and pulled her, and the unconscious woman tied to her back, out of the hole. Using Miri as a makeshift sled for Kim had seemed the safest way. He steadied Kim, catching her when she slid to the side as Miri stood. Kim was incredibly light and tiny. It didn't take any effort at all to hold her. With an explosion of energy, Derek surged out of the hole, not even pausing to brush the dust from his clothes before taking Kim from Jace.

The werewolf studied her with an intensity that was unnerving as he shifted her in his arms. Kim's head lolled over the crook of his elbow, her long black hair falling straight toward the ground. Derek looked at him. "How much time do I have?"

Jace didn't really know. He and his brothers weren't in the habit of converting humans. "Judging by what happened to Allie, about three hours."

"Shit." Derek swore, glancing at the sky. There were only about two hours until dawn. "Can she stand the sun before she's converted?"

Jace caught Miri's hand, keeping her at his side. "I don't know, but Allie couldn't stand any light on her eyes."

Derek took a breath, stroked the woman's cheek with that foreign tenderness. "Then I'll have to make do."

"You're a good four hours from the D'Nally compound."

"I know."

"You could hole up until tonight."

Derek was shaking his head. "No. I want her safe."

Jace pulled Miri closer, squeezing her fingers when she tugged at her hand.

"I can't go with you," Miri said to Derek.

Derek's slate gray eyes fastened on Miri. "No. You can't."

The little bit of hope Jace clung to that the wolves would accept their union died.

Derek lifted his head. Jace didn't need to hear his "Company coming" to know the Sanctuary thugs were closing in. He could feel them like an itch under his skin.

"Good luck."

"I'll catch up to you later."

"I'll be watching for you."

Derek took off across the barren clearing, reaching the scraggly pines in a blink of an eye before disappearing into the shadows of the rocks rimming the base of the bluff.

"Do you think he'll make it?" Miri asked.

Jace glanced down at her face. The scars down both her cheeks glowed brilliantly white in his night vision. He reached up and touched them. "If not, he'll die trying."

Her eyes narrowed. "I'm not so pretty anymore, am I?"

The scars were perfectly smooth, perfectly symmetrical. They had to have been done on purpose, and, to become permanent, they had to have been inflicted when she was near death. It took one hell of a lot to put a were near death and then keep him or her there long enough to scar. "You're beautiful."

The enemy was getting closer. So was the dawn. He hooked his arm around her waist and lifted her up.

Miri wrapped her arms around his neck. "You lie."

He levitated them across the packed snow and frozen ground. "No, I don't."

"You lied in the cave."

"When?"

"When you promised I'd be all right."

He cocked an eyebrow at her. "Aren't you?"

"But you couldn't know I would be."

"But you are, so I didn't, and your argument is empty."

"Hrrmph!"

It wasn't as easy as it should have been carrying her. He'd given her too much blood, weakening himself. She frowned up at him. "I can walk."

"You'd leave footprints."

"You could erase them."

"That would leave an energy trail."

Her claws dug into his nape. "You could leave me."

He ducked under a branch. "Never again."

A disturbance in the energy to the left raised the hairs on the back of his neck. Miri opened her mouth. He put his hand over it. Something was wrong. She didn't move, just froze, absolute and complete terror staining her scent, startling him. He smoothed his thumb over her cheek. His lips over her brow, wrapping a thread of energy around hers. As much as he dared.

You're safe.

She didn't relax, and he guessed he couldn't blame her. They were out in the open, and she had only him to rely on. Their brief time together hadn't allowed him an opportunity to play knight to her damsel in distress.

Stay quiet.

Her eyes widened. The nod of her head was almost imperceptible.

Jace crept forward. Ahead of them, at the opposite edge of the field, four Sanctuary vamps searched. He leaned back against the tree, blending his energy into it, covering Miri's with an additional layer. Unfortunately, there was nothing he could do about the scent of fresh blood clinging to her.

If the wind shifts, I want you to run that way. He gave her a mental push to the northwest. *Hide with Derek and the D'Nallys.*

It won't be safe.

Those were mean-looking vamps. His energy was depleted. He could take them out, give Miri time, but he wasn't sure he'd survive it. *It will by then.*

Miri's instinctive *No* screamed through his mind. He cut it off. *Yes. With me dead the weres will let you live. Derek will take you to the Circle J. My brothers will get our daughter.*

Again that shake of her head.

I thought you wanted me dead.

The patrol was moving on.

Yes, but I wanted to be the one to kill you.

His eyebrow raised. *I'll keep that in mind.*

The vampires passed the point where Derek had moved off. They hesitated. One man separated from the patrol, disappearing into the shadows. Miri watched. Jace felt her fear.

Derek can handle him.

She didn't look convinced.

Jace was more worried about the three men who still hunted the edge of the clearing. They weren't bothering to hide their energy. It came off them in powerful waves, a statement in itself. The vampire inside him rose to the challenge, wanting to take them on; the human side considered caution; the mate side of him cared about only two things: keeping Miri safe and finding their daughter. An image teased his mind, coming from Miri to him. He closed it off before it could coalesce, the ache in his chest expanding. He didn't want to know what his little girl looked like. Not yet. Not until he found her. Right now, Miri's pain was all he could handle.

The attempt at connection fizzled out. Behind it rose Miri's pain at the rejection. Goddamn, he was a coward, but he'd just found out that Miri was alive and he had a daughter. He wanted his first knowledge of his little girl to be a good one, not a panicked sharing that only conjured dread.

The patrol moved on. Lifting Miri, shadowing to the right, moving from energy field to energy field, Jace circled behind the patrol, scanning for others, wishing they had Raisa with them. She could sense any energy, even that blocked by the Sanctuary shield.

Against his side, Miri stiffened. This echo of thought was too hard and fast to block. Sharing minds was going to take some getting used to.

Raisa?

He shook his head, unwilling to be distracted by an explanation. His transceiver was blank, no static, nothing; the way it had been since the walls had come down. He didn't know if it was being monitored or being blocked, but he couldn't chance using it. Couldn't check to see if Derek was okay. Couldn't call his brothers. Couldn't rely on them to back him up. At least not today. And today was what he had to focus on. Today they needed to get clear of Sanctuary patrols and find shelter. At the south point of the clearing there was a separation in the rock. Barely narrow enough for a man to get through. He probed. There was an opening on the other side. He would have to put Miri down. That would leave her scent behind. She shivered. The odor of fresh blood tickled his nose. He checked her neck. It wasn't coming from there. He glanced down. Bright red smeared her thighs.

"Miri? Sweet?" he whispered against her ear.

The glance she cast him was anguished. She shook her head and clamped her legs together. He knew it wasn't that time of the month. Menstrual blood had its own unique scent; this was different. This spoke of injury, but also something else. The vamps were getting closer, the anguish in her eyes stronger. He didn't have time to question her now. And her condition didn't leave him any choice.

He levitated her through the opening, sweat breaking out on his brow with the effort. He needed to feed, needed strength. As soon as he had her through the crevice to the cavern beyond he set her down, sliding in after her.

What had felt like a clearing was actually a wide opening in the cavern. The opening high in the rock wall above gave it a sense of space. There was no back exit. They were trapped.

"Shit."

It would have felt a lot better if he could have shouted it rather than breathed it.

"Jace?"

Miri swayed. He set her down, his hand over her stomach. "Why are you bleeding?"

Again that anguished look. This time backed by fear.

He sent his energy within, and while he struggled to come up with the answer to his second question he had the answer to the first. *Miscarriage.*

"You were pregnant?"

She swallowed. Her expression went completely blank, but the razor-sharp edge of her fear sliced over his nerve endings. And then he had the answer to his first question. Were males were very territorial. There were some instances that triggered their primitive instincts and they could go into a killing rage. Circumstances like evidence their mate had slept with another. Cupping Miri's chin in his hand, Jace lifted her face. "I asked you a question."

She licked her lips and seemed to stop breathing altogether. Her hand slipped behind her back.

"Have you gone all quiet because you think hearing you were pregnant by someone other than me is going to upset my delicate sensibilities?"

She blinked, narrowed her gaze, and then nodded. He eased her up, reaching over and removing the rock from her grip. "I'm not pack, Miri." He set it aside. "I don't go loco just because I'm pissed."

"What do you do?"

Lingering damage in her throat hoarsened the whispered query. He stroked his thumb across her voice box. "I get furious and scared."

Her eyebrows went up. "Why scared?"

He pressed against her abdomen. "I want the bleeding stopped."

"It's not like I can make it stop."

"But I can." It would cost him more energy than was safe, but he hadn't found her just to let her bleed to death. He pressed with his fingers, struggling to find the path to the wound, reaching inside, locating it through the heat. He found the tear inside and frowned. It had a familiar feel. Like a wound from a knife or a gouge from . . .

This time he bit off a swear word. Abortion. Her baby had been aborted.

He pulled her against him, pressing his lips to her hair. "Ah, Miri, I'm sorry. So very sorry."

Her tears wet his shirt as he healed the wound. Her fingers dug into his forearm. "It wasn't yours."

He drew back to see her expression. And wished he hadn't. Pain, brilliant and cutting, glimmered among the shattered edges of her control.

"I know. I can do the math." A fresh tear hovered on her lash. He watched it swell, then caught it before it could fall on his thumb, rubbing it between his fingers until it was gone. If only he could remove the memories of the last year so easily. "But it was yours, and I'm sorry."

She blinked uncomprehendingly, as if he spoke a foreign language. Her mouth opened, closed. On the next attempt she found her voice. "You left me, our daughter. You left me and they—" She bit off whatever she was going to say. Her arms wrapped around her torso. She finished the brief outburst with the same abruptness with which she'd begun. "You left."

The biggest crime a were could commit against a mate. "Listen to me, Miri."

The order fell on deaf ears. She struggled out of his arms. "I can't."

Jace grabbed her hand, tugging her back. "You have to."

Her chin came up and the gold in her eyes grew more pronounced, seeming to light them from within. "No, I don't. Not now. Not ever."

She had another think coming if she thought he was going to leave that subject standing between them forever. He could, however, drop it for now. "Fine, but there is something we do need to talk about."

She seemed to almost pull within herself, her eyes becoming as blank as her expression. If the moisture of her tear hadn't lingered on his fingers, he might have been fooled into thinking she was calm. She was a very strong woman, but beneath her outer mask, he could sense her control splintering, piece by piece, layer by layer. He didn't wanted to see her shatter, but he had to know. "Do you know where our child is?"

Her lids lowered. Her lips firmed. And she didn't answer. He cupped her cheek in his hand, running his thumb along her lower lip, pulling it away from the edge of her teeth. "I can take the information from your mind."

That chin came up another notch. The golden-brown eyes flared with wolf rage. "So why don't you?"

Because it would hurt her. "I will if you force me to."

She shrugged as if she didn't care. "It won't be the first time I've been forced."

More blame at his feet. "You have to trust someone, Miri, and right now, I'm all you've got."

YES, he was. Miri stared up at Jace. Hating him for looking so much like she remembered—so strong, so in control, so damn unchanged—as if the last year that had done so much to her had passed him by. Reinforcing her growing conviction that she'd done this to herself—to her daughter—by mating outside pack approval, and now she had only him to trust to make it right. "I should never have trusted you."

He didn't flinch or give any sign that her words hurt. "But you did. You did even more than that. You chose me for your mate."

She felt her eyelashes flicker. "Mating is not a choice."

"And neither is accepting my help now."

She pushed his hand away from her stomach. God, she wished she could say she didn't need him. Her daughter's face flashed before her, tiny little features, all red from the stress of childbirth. She'd only seen her for a brief few minutes. Long enough to know she had black hair like hers, the changeable between gray and blue hazel eyes like her father's, and the sweetest little expression. She'd only had that brief time before sending her off with strangers, out in the human world, hoping she could hide in plain sight. Hoping her ancestry wouldn't show before she could get help for her. "There's nothing saying I have to like it."

His thumb pressed on her lower lip, sliding inside. His taste flooded her mouth. As if her very soul had been starving for this moment. The hunger rose.

"No, there isn't."

Against her will, her tongue touched his skin. The inner cry of bliss rolled through her. Her lids dropped as she shuddered. Cells that had lain dormant, parts of her she thought long past the point of demise, rose and screamed in happiness. Everything in her said to lean in to Jace, hand him her cares, her worries, the responsibility for their daughter. Fall into his arms and just let him hold her until all the trauma of the last year went away. She shoved at his hold. "Let me go."

He did, getting to this feet with that smooth grace that used to make her heart flutter. She was used to coordinated men, but Jace moved differently from weres. There was a lightness to his movement that made her think of cats rather than canines. From this angle, he looked so much bigger, so much more lethal. So damn invincible.

"I'm going to feed."

"There are patrols all over the place."

"That's what I'm hoping."

Good God, he was going to feed from the Sanctuary! "You'll be killed!"

"Then that should save you some trouble."

"But it won't save our daughter."

"Then I guess you'll have to pray I live a bit longer."

She had been. Every day since she'd met him, she'd prayed for that. Even after she'd been taken and it had become clear that rescue wasn't imminent, she'd prayed until she'd been ashamed of herself for clinging to hope. "I guess I will."

"Soon you're going to go through conversion. We can't stay here and I'm too weak as I am to get you to a safe place. I need to feed."

"Don't let me stop you."

His gaze took in her appearance. She felt every new imperfection, every mark left on her from the last year. "You're the only thing that could."

She tried a different tactic, unwilling to just let him go out there into danger. "I'm a were. Weres don't change."

"What makes you so sure?"

She didn't have an answer.

He tucked her back against a far wall. "That's what I thought. The way I see it, there has to be something more than just leadership succession and pack hierarchy that has weres stressing about their women mating with vampires, and whatever it is, I don't want you exposed and vulnerable when it occurs."

Great. More trouble. Stress drove her talons into her palms. "I could have done without that piece of knowledge."

"I imagine you could, but you wanted to know."

"No, I didn't."

He moved toward the entrance. "Well, that's what happens when you argue. All kinds of unpleasant things get brought up."

How had she forgotten how irking his sense of humor could be?

He looked back over his shoulder. "You seem to have forgotten a lot of things."

He'd read her mind. She'd heard that happened between mated vampires and weres, much easier than the practiced links some weres could make. It wasn't at all convenient to know it was working that way between them. Not now. "Not on purpose."

"You sure?"

No, she wasn't. She folded her arms across her chest.

A smile tucked into the creases around his eyes. "You can get back to me with that answer."

It was a rhetorical statement. She found herself nodding anyway. Damn, was she really that programmed?

The hint of a smile had slipped to a frown by the time Jace got to the opening. His energy reached out and pushed against her, a mental order to stay put that he backed with a low verbal order. "Remember, if I don't return stay put until just before night and then head to the D'Nallys'."

"What makes you think I'm going to stay here?"

He cut her a glance. "You're not a day walker anymore. Leave now and the sun will turn you into a crispy critter before you make it halfway anywhere."

He disappeared through the opening.

You're not a day walker anymore.

He seemed awfully sure of that. It could be a trick to make her stay put, but Miri didn't think so. One thing about Jace: he never lied about important things. Just always delivered the blunt, unvarnished truth no matter how much it hurt.

She placed her hand over her abdomen. Inside, she could feel the lingering heat of his healing. And beneath it, a disturbance that shouldn't be there. She closed her eyes and focused inward, trying to identify the source, but there wasn't just one spot. The discord was more generalized than localized. She spread her fingers wide in an attempt to encompass the whole of what was happening. Understanding was slow in coming, but when it did, she had to sit down. She was Jace Johnson's mate. And it was changing her.

JACE slipped back into the crevice, energy vibrating within him. Sanctuary vamps might be on the wrong side of right, but they had potent blood. They also had vindictive natures, and it wasn't going to take the patrols long to find the bodies of the two men he'd fought and then fed from. He needed to get Miri out of here.

Miri.

He called mentally again. Nothing. The same nothing he'd run up against every time he'd probed for her. Either the woman had learned to block him or she was in trouble. As much as he wanted to believe the former because it would mean she was safe, Miri was too smart a woman to endanger them all with a tantrum.

As soon as he entered the cavern, Jace knew Miri was in trouble. She lay curled on the ground, hands over her abdomen, face as white as a sheet. Her ribs heaved with short pants of breath. The two steps it took to get to her were two steps too many. He dropped to his knees on the dirt floor.

"Shit."

"That's my word."

"Wolf females don't swear."

"I've decided to pick up your bad habits," she whispered in a strained voice.

"Because we're mated?"

He lifted her off the cold ground. She whimpered and shivered. Neither sound nor motion was as strong as he thought they should be. The way she collapsed against him told him more than words about how bad this was.

She turned her cheek in to his throat. "Because I'm sick of being nice. Nice people get squashed."

He brushed his lips across her forehead. "I like you nice."

"I rest my case."

She was determined to hold on to her grudge. Another shudder rippled through her. The change was beginning. Ah, hell. He opened his palm across her back as her teeth bit into the tough leather of his jacket. "I know you're hurting, sweet, but we've got to get out of here."

She tilted her face up. He caught her head on his palm, supporting her when she would have overbalanced. "You're done ticking off the Sanctuary?" she asked.

"For the moment."

"Okay, then." Bracing her hand on his knee, she levered herself up. Without the support of his hand in the middle of her back, she wouldn't have made it. She was that weak.

She bit her lip and swayed. "I'm ready."

The overpowering nausea rolling through her spilled over onto him. "How long has this been going on?"

She swallowed hard, once, twice. If anything, she got a bit greener. "Since about ten minutes after you left."

Damn. He tucked his hand under her chin. Lifting her face. "If you need to puke, you might want to do it now."

"I'm not vomiting."

"I'm going to have to carry you over my shoulder to get where we need to go."

"Where are we going?"

"To a safe place." At least, he hoped it was safe. And that it was still there.

She glanced over at the crevice. "What's wrong with here?"

He pointed up to the aperture in the ceiling. "The sun will fry us."

Biting her lip, she looked around. "It might not reach the corners."

Like he would chance her to a "might" and a glimmer of hope. He shook his head. "We're leaving."

"And for that I need to vomit?"

"The only way I can move fast enough to beat the sun is to carry you over my shoulder."

Her hand clutched her stomach, her eyes widened, and she looked at him again. "I . . . can't."

Because he was there. "This is not the time for modesty."

"Tell my modesty that."

He stood, holding her hand, drawing her with him. Her flesh was too cold. Damn it, he didn't know how this would go for her, but if it was anything like what he had gone through when he converted, he wanted her surrounded by the best of medical knowledge. He wanted her safe, coddled. He wanted that haunted look out of her beautiful brown eyes. He wanted the last year back.

"You going to puke?"

"No."

"Good enough."

He scanned outside the door. Still nothing. It was now or never. "C'mon."

He went through the opening first, holding her hand in case she got stubborn, mildly disappointed when she didn't. As soon as he broke free from the crevice, Jace scanned again. To the left about a hundred feet the patrol was coming back. Fast. With a "Hold tight" he had Miri out and into the clear. As she stumbled forward he bent down, placed his shoulder in her abdomen, straightened, and took off.

It was natural that his palm fell to her buttocks. The desire that surged through him at the contact wasn't. They were in danger. If he didn't get them both away now they were going to end up as Sanctuary dog meat. And yet, right alongside the adrenaline that came from danger rode the hot lust only she inspired.

Miri swatted his back. "You're sick."

Obviously, some thoughts he wasn't good at concealing. He patted her buttock. "Only around you."

He angled down the mountain, heading toward home and safety. She dropped her head against his back. "Lucky me."

✻ 4 ✻

THEY'D found a new way to hurt her. She frowned. Before there'd never been any malice in what they did. She was just another experiment to be brought to its conclusion. They applied force when necessary to get the compliance they needed, but it had never gone deeper than that. It had never been personal. This, however, felt very personal. The fire burned up from her gut, spreading outward, a living, breathing agony that fed on itself in an ever-growing twist of agony. Enough so, dear God, that she wished she knew what they wanted so she could give it to them.

She cried out. There was no reason not to. They'd know all they needed about her level of pain from the electrodes attached to her skull. It fed reams of biofeedback into the machines lining the room, to the point that hiding her distress didn't prove anything. They didn't care if she screamed blue murder. All they cared about were the readouts on their screens. Though, if she screamed so that it grated their nerves, they might gag her. But it was never the first scream that did it, or even the fifth.

The next agonizing burn brought out more than a whimper. It brought out her frustration, her helplessness, her sheer fury at being trapped, unable to escape, unable to let anyone know she needed to escape. Just trapped.

Endlessly trapped. She tilted her head back and screamed. As loud as she could, with everything she could.

A hand clamped over her mouth. "Shh, Miri."

Her eyes flew open. Jace's face filled her vision. This close she could see the flecks of blue in his gray eyes and the tiny flickers of vampire power lighting the edges. And deep within her, that irrational stupid part of her she'd tried to kill off surged to greet it.

"You've got to be quiet, princess."

With a start she realized she was still screaming. She might not care if the Sanctuary scientist saw her scream, but it mattered that Jace just had. She caught her breath and inhaled slowly through her nose, but the tears that spilled over her cheeks were beyond her control. A dream. It had been a dream. She wasn't trapped there anymore. She was free. She closed her eyes and struggled with the breadth of that reality.

"Miri?"

She opened her eyes. Jace frowned down at her, his hand going to her stomach. She felt the press of his energy, the warmth from his touch, and the pain abated. The crease between his brows deepened. The lights in his eyes increased to golden swirls. His muscles bunched. Understanding came quickly. He was taking her pain into himself. She grabbed his wrist and pressed his hand away from her mouth. She managed an inch. "Stop it."

The growled order didn't even cause his brow to flick. The rough pad of his thumb smoothed along her jaw as he asked in a soft whisper, "Now, what would be my incentive to do that?"

She followed his example and kept her voice barely audible. "You wouldn't have to feel the pain."

Another stroke along her jaw. "Not much of an incentive from where I'm sitting."

The muscles in her stomach contracted. A bead of blood—vampire sweat—formed on Jace's temple. He had no right to make this sacrifice for her. She didn't want to be obligated to him. "I don't want this from you!"

52 Sarah McCarty

"Tough."

His voice echoed in the small chamber. A look around showed they were within a shallow cave formed by an overhang of rock. A rotting tree that had fallen years ago from the looks of it, covered the access point. If it shifted just the slightest they'd be trapped. His grip on her jaw tightened. Like she was.

"I don't need this." Yanking on his wrist, she snarled, "I don't need you."

He didn't flinch, just stroked his thumb along her jaw again, reminding her of happier times before she'd known how differently he saw her than she saw him. "You need me to find our daughter."

She slowly closed her eyes. Yes, she did. And she needed to keep that in mind when dealing with him. She couldn't afford these rushes of emotion, the bursts of anger. "I'm sorry."

His curse disturbed the hair on her head, creating an annoyance that welled much larger than it should have. His grip tightened before gradually relaxing. "I think I'd rather have you mad at me than—"

"Than what?"

This time his fingers closed around the point of her chin, bringing her gaze to his narrowed one. "Than sucking up."

She threw his own word back at him. "Tough."

A blinding flash of pain shot through her, catching them both by surprise. Another curse from Jace and then the agony ceased.

He released her chin. "Sorry."

He was sorry? It took her a minute to figure it out, her mind preoccupied with the expectation of agony and the hope it had ended, but when logic kicked in, it wasn't difficult to do. Jace was a man who did things one way and one way only. The right way as he saw it. The lapse in concentration that let that brief agony through bothered him. He, no doubt, saw it as a failure. A break in his control. And he was a man who valued control. Her stomach muscles contracted again, her body tensing at the vaguely disconnected feeling, but the promise of pain never materialized. At least not for her. More blood beaded on Jace's face. She wanted to wipe it away. She wanted to slap him. "Why do you have to be so noble?"

"My dad raised me right."

"Your father died when you were young."

"He was the kind of man who left a legacy."

Her father had been that kind, too, before he'd been killed by humans. Her mother had followed quickly as all bonded mates did. And then she'd been all alone. Without the support of her pack, she would have gone crazy when faced with such crushing loneliness, maybe even taken her own life.

"Am I dying?"

He didn't answer right away.

Fear became the only truth. "You have to tell me."

His lips firmed to a flat line. "No."

"No, you won't tell me, or no, I'm not dying?"

Another of those pauses that made her uncomfortable. He shifted her against him, blood from the pain he was taking for her dripping to her shoulder. "Just no."

Fear spread to panic. If she died, no one would get Faith. No one would know where she was. No one would care, and her little girl would live all alone with no family, no pack, no protection. And when her heritage made itself known, the Sanctuary would find her very easily.

Faith was already five months old. Anytime now, the people taking care of her would begin to notice her differences. The glowing of her eyes when she got angry. Her need for red meat. Or maybe even blood, she realized. Faith was half vampire. Miri closed her eyes against the overwhelming panic. Were or vampire, it didn't matter. Whatever traits Faith exhibited would mark her as different and call attention to her. Miri couldn't let that happen.

She clutched Jace's hand. "If I die, you have to promise me you'll get Faith."

A strange looked crossed his face. His thumb brushed across

her knuckles, settling into the middle hollow. "Faith. Is that what you named her?"

He didn't know their daughter's name. The enormity of what that implied floored her. If she died, Jace wouldn't know what their daughter looked like, wouldn't know who to look for, wouldn't recognize her if he saw her. Miri was the only one alive who knew who Faith was.

"You can't let me die."

"I hadn't planned on it."

He didn't understand. "You can't die, either."

"The most I figured was that we're going to spend a damn uncomfortable day."

"Promise me I'm not dying."

"I promise."

He said that too easily. Too fast. This time the burn seared deep, past his block. Her canines cut into her lip. The scent of blood lay heavy between them. His. Hers. Familiar in an elusive way. She dropped her head to his chest, grinding her forehead against him. "We smell like Faith."

His laugh strained the silence. "I've never heard it described that way."

He still didn't understand. She took the blood from her lip, smeared it across his temple, and then held it under his nose. "Our daughter smells like this."

He went rigid, not breathing in, not breathing out. She rubbed the mix of their blood against his upper lip, pressing hard with her hand, her mind. "This is who our daughter is."

A shudder went through his big body. He grabbed her hand, breathed deep, and then drew her fingers into his mouth, licking the blood off, his gaze never leaving hers, his energy threading through hers in heavy tendrils. His gaze lit the dark with pinpoints of gold. "Tell me about her."

The shake of her head was at the pain that stole her voice. He took it as something else.

"It's going to be a long time until night, Miri."

"So?"

"So you can spend it making me pay, or you can spend it sharing memories of your daughter with the one person in the world who's as desperate to hear them as you are to share them."

Desperate? "Don't you think that's laying it on a bit thick?"

"I've been looking for you for a year, Miri. I didn't know if you were alive or dead, and then I find you covered in blood and our daughter missing. If you think I'm anything close to stable, you're in for a surprise."

"You left."

"No, I didn't."

Anything that she would have said to that was lost as the burning agony spread through her. All she could do was dig her talons into his muscle. The coppery aroma of fresh blood scented the air. She had to be hurting him. He didn't say a word, just held her closer as she rode it out.

"Is it supposed to be like this?" she gasped.

His gaze never wavered. "I don't know. I've never converted a wolf before."

"Weres don't convert." The elders always hammered that fact to the young of the pack. It was an absolute.

"They apparently do something. I just wish I could control it."

The scent of blood grew stronger. His, hers—there was no sorting it out anymore. The pain twisted deeper. "Oh, God, I want to scream."

Jace placed his palm over her mouth. "Scream away."

She shook her head, the darkness pressing in as his shadow fell over her. She couldn't make out anything around her, but she knew he could see her and she wouldn't scream in front of him. She bit his hand instead. His cheek dropped to hers, the skin sliding on her tears and his sweat. "Tell me about our baby, Miri."

She had to wait a minute to get her breath. And then she had to wait to get past the agony in her soul to bring the memory forward. "She was so little. I only had a few minutes to get her out."

His mind touched hers, asked permission, entered. "What did she look like?"

"Like a . . . red, wrinkled version of us."

He kissed her cheek. "She damn well better look like you."

"She has black hair and my mouth, but . . . your eyes."

Even with him taking most of the pain from her, it was bad.

He jerked. "There's really something of me in her?"

How could he doubt it? She felt his mental probe and was helpless to refuse the need within him to know something of his child. She mentally shared with him her first glimpse of her daughter's face, her first impression of her personality, the one touch she'd allowed herself of that super-soft skin, the one kiss she'd permitted herself before she'd sent her away.

As he pulled the image she gave him into that fierce well of emotion she could sense seething beyond the calm he gave her, she stroked his neck, sliding her fingers around the back to his nape, stroking the spot she knew soothed him. "Judging from the way she fussed when she wasn't held the way she wanted, she got a lot of your personality."

He flinched away. His hand caught hers, but not before she felt the irregularity. A scar? "What happened to your neck?"

"Nothing to worry about."

She yanked her hands free of his and scooted up. He blocked her with an arm across her shoulders. Her back scraped against something spongy. The scent of wet wood overcame the scent of blood and—she leaned closer—burned flesh. "Oh, my God!"

He'd been burned. And only one thing burned a vampire like that. "You were in the sun."

"For a bit."

For a bit. As if that was nothing. Any sun was devastating to a vampire. How long had it taken him to find this spot "How badly are you burned?"

"I'll heal."

"That wasn't what I asked."

"I know." He folded her arms against his chest, holding them with one hand surrounding hers. She wiggled her thumb free, checking the back of his hand. The skin was rough there, too. She'd assumed he'd gotten her here before the sun had come up. "You were burned because of me."

"I was burned because of bad timing."

"How long were you in the sun?"

"Not too long."

She told herself it didn't matter, that it changed nothing, but that was a lie. "'Not too long' meaning not long enough to kill you?"

She felt his smile against her hair. Only Jace would smile now. "Pretty much."

He would think that way. Jace and his brothers defined "tough." "When we were together before, did I mention how much I hate the big macho-man thing you and your brothers have going?"

His lips brushed her hair and his tense laugh vibrated through her. "I think you were too distracted to bring it up."

She rolled her eyes. "I would not have been that distracted."

Which wasn't exactly true. From the moment she'd seen Jace standing in the moonlight by the pool where she was bathing eighteen months ago, she'd been drawn to him. So much so that she hadn't called for help when he approached, hadn't resisted when he'd drawn her into his arms, hadn't protested when he'd kissed her. Just responded with that instinctive drive to submit to him that a female wolf experienced with her mate. To give him whatever he wanted. Being with Jace had been addictive. When he'd asked her to meet him again in secret, she had. When he'd asked for her virginity, she'd given it, so caught up in him that she'd ignored all caution and tradition. Way too sheltered to understand what she was doing, she'd opened her heart and mind to Jace's, welcoming him as her mate with total abandon, assuming he saw her the way she saw him. Assuming that "mate" meant the same thing to him as it did to her. Nothing had mattered but being with him, being his.

She'd wanted to give him her mark, the final act of commitment for a wolf, the final act necessary to complete a vampire/were mating; and she had intended to take his blood in return. She'd thought it so fitting, an act so perfect its symbolism rose in her mind more powerfully than the taboo of a wolf woman doing such a thing.

And then Jace had announced he was leaving, as if it were nothing, taking her joy, leaving her with pain. Right up until the moment he'd walked out the door to go on his mission, she hadn't truly believed he'd do it. True mates didn't separate—but he had. And her pain had begun. Pain worse than what now consumed her, because illusion died hard, and when it was gone there was no avoiding reality. She loved more than she was loved and nothing could close that inequality.

And yet today, the man she thought didn't care for her the way she cared about him had faced the sun for her. For duty? For love? For something else? Miri grazed her fingers over Jace's, skimming the edge of the burned flesh. It was no small thing. Burns were the worst thing for a vampire. The only thing that didn't heal at their normally rapid pace. Which was why all vampires feared them. "You must be in so much pain."

"Will pity for my suffering soften a bit of that anger you're feeling toward me?"

Yes. No. She shrugged. "Probably."

"You don't sound too happy about it."

"I told you, I'm working on not being so nice."

With a flex of muscle, he cradled her closer. "I told you before, I like you nice."

"Everybody likes me nice because that gets them what they want. The only catch with that is everybody but me is happy and when things go wrong, I'm the one who suffers."

The glow in his eyes deepened. "I didn't mean to make you suffer."

"I know." She understood that now. "The misunderstanding was my fault for taking up with a man who's not pack."

"How the hell would taking up with pack have been any better for you?"

She let go of his hand. He didn't let go of hers. It didn't matter. His holding on now wouldn't mitigate the differences between them. There was no returning to innocence lost. "Weres don't leave."

WERES *don't leave.*

Three words said with such acceptance and the grief of one who mourned a death. Three words that marked the differences in their philosophies. Three words that emphasized the cultural chasm between them. It wasn't that he was vampire that upset Miri. It wasn't that her pack would ostracize her for marrying him, which, alone, would cripple most wolves. What had shaken Miri to the core was not that he had left her, but that he could. One security a wolf always had was a pack to come back to and a mate always at his or her side. Wolves lived to find their mates. Sometimes lived hundreds of years before they did. Once they found them, according to the wolf lore Derek had shared with him, they would never know loneliness again. A mate was the other half of a soul. An inseparable other half. He remembered how he'd kissed Miri and smiled that day before he'd left. He'd been looking at her, thinking how beautiful she was and how wonderful it would be to come back and find her waiting. Derek had been quite explicit in that tidbit of were mating when Jace had thought to ask, after Miri's disappearance.

Once bonded, werewolves could not conceive of separating from their mates, and they suffered physically if they did. Miri had grown up secure in the belief that once bonded with her mate, he could never leave her. But she'd bonded with him, and he'd left her as easily as he would have any human woman, comfortable with the parting because he'd known he would return. He touched his finger to one of the white lines of strain bracketing the sides of her mouth, eyeing the drop of blood on her lower lip. The smile he'd meant to be shared must have seemed so cavalier to her, mocking even.

"My leaving really shook you up, didn't it?"

Her gaze ducked his and her lips pressed together, flattening the drop of blood. She was embarrassed about how she'd been back then. "That was my fault. I was naive and I didn't think."

Neither had he, too caught up in the passion and miracle of finding the woman who fit him. He'd just wanted to clear everything out of his way so he could be with her. In his rush he'd just managed to trample all over her giving nature and make her ashamed. "And I didn't know."

"It doesn't matter."

"Yeah, it does."

He wiped the smear of blood from her lip, remembering the unique taste of their blood together, thinking of his child out there somewhere, her only protection being that, supposedly, no one knew who she was. The fragility of Faith's safety drove him crazy. She should be at the Circle J, protected by her family, surrounded by love. Not out there somewhere facing Lord knew what. Miri shifted against him. A long hank of hair fell over her face. Jace smoothed it back, using the pressure of his hand to keep her cheek against his chest, holding her to his warmth. "I never thought to ask if matings were different for weres."

"Whereas I've lived my life knowing the fickleness of vampires."

Of that he had no doubt. The other thing he'd learned from Derek was the deep-seated prejudice most weres felt toward their companions in immortality. One of those prejudices was the ludicrous belief that vampires couldn't be faithful. "I guess, to you, it looked like I fell right into the stereotype."

"You left."

She kept holding that fact out like a talisman.

"I won't leave you again."

"Yes, you will." Her hand opened over his chest as the pain left. "You won't be able to help it."

Her gaze didn't waver from his, the deep brown of her eyes near black in his night vision, devoid of the softness he was used to seeing there. A shiver shook her. Damn, she was getting cold. No matter what he did, her body temperature kept dropping. "We can fight about the semantics of that statement later."

"When it's dark?"

He forced a smile. "That'd be preferable to now."

She blinked once, twice, making him think his smile came across more real than it felt. Then she shook her head. "Are you ever serious?"

"Yes." The scars on her cheeks drew his eyes; bright slashes against her skin, glowing in a ghostly reminder of what she'd been through. "And always about you."

Her response died an ignoble death as another wave of pain swept over her. He quickly siphoned it off, gritting his teeth as it immediately felt like a gallon of acid poured into his gut.

It was almost too much for him to bear, and he was a big man used to being hurt. He didn't know how Miri withstood it. She felt so fragile to him. Her bones much finer, wonderfully feminine. How the hell was she supposed to endure this? He rubbed his chin against her cheek.

Leaning his head back against the rotted trunk of the tree they were hiding within, he said, "Tell me more about our daughter. Please."

Her talons nipped his wrist. "Why?"

"Because we could both use the distraction."

He had to wait through three steady breaths. Memories flashed in her mind just out of his reach, flitting, teasing touches of emotion. Wonder, stress, agony, hope, and then absolute despair. He changed his mind as that last skimmed his consciousness. Maybe he wasn't ready for this.

"She was so tiny," Miri began in a soft voice, as if she, too, was afraid of what would happen if the memory was made real. "Premature, because we had to do a C-section in order to sneak her out, but her lungs were good." Her talons sank deeper. "She screamed when they took her away."

"Jesus."

He knew for sure he didn't want to hear this now, but he had to. This was the kind of pain a mate shared. "Who took her away?"

"The tech."

"Which tech?"

"The one working for the Renegades."

As far as he knew, they didn't have any Renegades that deep in the Sanctuary structure. Shit. "Why?"

"I had to get her out before they could get her blood, before they could experiment." Her head ducked lower and she held herself perfectly still. "It was my only choice."

It dawned on him that she was braced for criticism. Because she'd risked everything for their daughter. She had done what he hadn't been there to do—gotten their daughter to safety. With his finger under her chin, he lifted her face back to his. His mate was a very strong woman. "You did what you had to. That took guts."

She licked her lips. "Thank you."

No moisture remained in the wake of the gesture. Damn, she was dehydrating. "Where is Faith now?"

She shook her head. "I don't know."

He took a slow breath, dread hollowing out a hole in the layers of agony consuming his strength. Or was it her strength, or maybe theirs? His, hers, he was beginning to understand it didn't matter anymore. They were two halves of a whole. Mated, according to legend. According to choice.

Mating is not a choice.

He still wasn't sure he believed that, but it was damn powerful.

In his arms, Miri tensed. Sliding his energy over hers, Jace pulled her in to him with everything he had as she arched beneath the lash of pain he couldn't control. The conversion was intensifying. "What was the name of the tech who took her?"

She didn't answer. Her energy changed, became discordant.

It was the only warning he had before her body jerked, spasmed within his grip. Convulsions. Son of a bitch, she was convulsing. Tension wrenched through her muscles, snapping her violently back and forth in a grotesque dance. No matter how hard he held her, he couldn't prevent the vicious contortions. Jace lay Miri on the ground, pinning her with his greater weight, narrowly avoiding the snap of her teeth. Her canines flashed white. She was changing. He didn't know what would happen if she changed mid-conversion, but it couldn't be good.

Thrusting his mind into hers, Jace searched for the cause of the convulsions, pulling back when he found it, shocked. Her systems were in total meltdown, changing without direction as energy scrambled for purchase, fought for control, ricocheted off receptors no longer tuned to receive it, giving birth to chaos. He pressed her down harder, mentally swearing, struggling to forge paths inside her mind to carry the imbalance away. After endless minutes, the violent jerking tightened to steady vibrations until all she did was shudder in his arms. He took advantage of the misleading calm, weaving more and more mental bonds between them, immersing himself deeper into her psyche, holding her with everything he had. Just holding her, because the alternative was not acceptable.

A break appeared in the chaos. A small, dark concentration of energy. He lunged toward it.

Jace.

He was floored that she could even communicate. *What?*

Her energy was weak and fluctuating, but she was there. Thank God.

Bring Faith home.

"I will." He eased her upright. She panted, holding on to him as she quivered from the residual force of the attack. "We both will."

He wouldn't accept anything less. His Miri was a fighter. So was he. They'd beat this.

The shake of her head was more thought than action. *This is killing me.*

"Nah." He kept his tone deliberately unconcerned. "It's just a son of a bitch." Then:

Don't you fucking give up on me, sweet.

The thought spilled beyond his ability to contain it. Miri wavered on the verge of unconsciousness, her energy flagging. She couldn't pass out. Not yet.

Turning, he kissed her temple. His lips lingered on the erratic pulse pounding there.

"Stay with me."

Her fingers pressed into his back. That spot of energy wavered, grew stronger. She was fighting.

"That's my girl."

"Trying," she whispered.

With everything she had, he knew. And with Miri, that was one hell of a lot. "Who has Faith, Miri?" he whispered, aware of the patrols looking for them outside their very vulnerable hiding place.

She shook her head, her lower lip slipping between her teeth as a bead of sweat trickled down the side of her brow. "I don't know, but the tech said he'd leave me a clue."

"What kind of clue?"

"I don't know."

That sick feeling of dread spread. Jace had always assumed, when he found Miri, she'd have the information he needed to find their daughter. It was inconceivable that she didn't. "Where did the tech take her?"

Damn, she had to give him something. Again that mental shake of Miri's head. He eased her up in his arms, locking his mind to hers, probing so deeply that there was no disbelieving her softly repeated, "I don't know."

She twisted in his arms as the burning agony escaped his control and attacked her again, rapidly depleting the last vestiges of her energy. "But," she gasped as her energy winked away, "I think the Sanctuary might have figured it out."

❧ 5 ❧

"I'M never going to find the clue if you keep wiggling."

Miri pulled her long black hair over her shoulder, the unaccustomed weakness that had been with her since the previous day's conversion hampering the move. She braced her hand against the tree trunk that composed one side of their shelter. "Sorry."

"No need to be sorry." Jace pressed his fingertips against her bare skin with subtle pressure. "You, sweet, could tempt a man into forgetting what he's supposed to be doing."

"You're just a pervert."

There was a pause in which his energy rippled over her flesh in a tender stroke. Goose bumps sprang up as her nerve endings reached for more. "Nah, just a normal vampire with a healthy appetite for his mate." He caught her eye. "But if there's some perversion you want to explore . . ." The quirk of his lips belied the seriousness of his tone. "I'd be happy to accommodate you."

Standing naked before him was something she'd done many times before. It was ridiculous to feel so insecure. But she did. Insecure and vulnerable. This wasn't the same body he'd known before. It wasn't perfect. It wasn't only his any longer. And that made her angry for a lot of reasons, most of which she didn't want to explore. "There's no accommodating anything," she snapped, hating her anger almost more than she wanted to hate him. "I just lost a baby, and our daughter is still missing."

Nothing was softer than his "I know all that" and that just made her madder.

"Then why are you so . . . happy?" For lack of a better word.

His fingertip settled in the middle of her spine, on the nub of a vertebra, in a ghost of sensation that sank deeper than her skin. His expression sobered. "Because I have you, and that's definitely a sign that things are picking up."

There was no mistaking the glow in his eyes. Desire. For her, when her hair was greasy and she smelled of old blood and sweat. He was insane. "I'm a mess."

A smile ghosted his lips with the same delicacy of his touch. "You look pretty damn gorgeous to me."

"You need glasses."

"Or maybe you need to give me more credit than you'd give a wolf."

She wasn't going there. There it was dangerous. There she was vulnerable. His finger drifted lower. A shiver of sensation snaked down her spine. She shifted her feet at the discomfort. She didn't want this awareness between them. She didn't want to want him. She didn't want to want anyone. She just wanted her daughter and some peace. She shook her hair out of her face and redirected his attention. "Do you see anything?"

"Nope." The tips of his fingers grazed her buttock. "If that Renegade put a clue to Faith's location on your body, he hid it well."

She already knew that. The Sanctuary vamps had searched her from head to toe.

"Keep looking."

"Yes, ma'am." Pressure between her shoulder blades tipped her forward. "It might have been easier if you had let him tell you a hint as to where he put it."

She braced her hands on the side of the tree and shook her head. "The Sanctuary would have forced the information from me. I couldn't take the chance."

Behind her, Jace stilled.

She twisted around, trying to see what had his attention, hope surging. "What is it? Did you find it?"

He cleared his throat. His big hands cupped her buttocks as he crouched behind her. "Sorry. I got distracted by the view."

All the awareness she'd been trying to suppress flared with white-hot heat as his breath teased the surface of her thighs, sensitizing the nerve endings in an area she'd thought had become pretty immune to temptation.

"Just keep your mind on what you're doing." And she'd try to keep her thoughts where they belonged, too.

He parted her cheeks, then moved lower, more sensuality in the gesture than efficiency. "I'm doing my best, but it would help if you weren't so beautiful."

She didn't feel beautiful. She felt old and used up. And desperate. Incredibly desperate.

Jace's mouth touched her right buttock, his lips firm and yet somehow soft at the same time, lingering in a hot kiss, his hands holding her steady for the caress. "When I get you to someplace safe, I'll show you just how beautiful you are."

The promise, pressed so intimately, sent shivers down her spine and a warning to her core. As if she need reminding how devastating Jace could be to her good intentions. Clearing her throat, she growled, "Stop playing around and focus."

It came out more throaty than imperative so she wasn't surprised by his chuckle. "I'm focusing. There just isn't anything to see but you."

Her desperation grew. "There has to be something. He said he'd put a clue on me while I was unconscious for the C-section."

"I'm not doubting he said it." Jace's fingers skimmed down her thigh to her calf, circled her ankle, lifted her foot. "I just can't find it."

She dropped her forehead to her hands. "It *has* to be there."

He lifted her other foot. "I'm sure it is, but anybody smart enough to sneak our daughter out of the Sanctuary is smart enough to make sure the clue isn't easy to find."

"We have to find it."

He stood, grazing his hands up her sides, following the flares and hollows of her figure, not coming near anything private, yet the touch seeming so much more intimate than a blatant caress. She shook her head. Nothing was ever simple between her and Jace.

His body pressed hard behind her, big and so warm. "We will."

She'd never really been cold before the Sanctuary had started with their experimenting. As a werewolf, she had a natural resistance to temperature extremes, to the point that throwing a coat on made the most bitter cold bearable, but the Sanctuary's numerous efforts to get her pregnant again had her system so messed up that the slightest shift in temperature affected her badly. Taking Jace's blood seemed to have thrown things even more out of whack. Another shiver, another moment of self-pity. She pushed it back. This momentary discomfort didn't matter. Even if it became permanent, it didn't matter. All that mattered was finding her daughter.

Jace's arms came around her. His chin rested on top of her head. His insistence on treating her as if her anger weren't a barrier really annoyed her. She wanted to annoy him in return. There was one guaranteed way to do so.

"Have I mentioned lately that I'm divorcing you?"

"Nope."

He pressed her back against him, his energy reaching out and surrounding her in a hug stronger than muscle could deliver. She glanced down at his forearms, lightly dusted with hair, delineated with the strength common to vampires, yet somehow more vivid in him.

Something disturbed her hair. From the way her nerve endings leapt and tightened she recognized it as a kiss. The man had spent the last twenty-four hours holding her, hugging her, kissing her. Sneaky little kisses that didn't give her anything to fight with. And the tiny space they were crammed into between the shallow cave and the rotting tree didn't allow for distance.

"You might want to keep drilling it into my head if you want it to stick," he told her.

She definitely wanted it to stick. It was different for him. He could leave, while she couldn't. She couldn't live with that—the loving more than being loved, the needing more than being needed. It went against every certainty she'd held dear as a wolf.

His lips skimmed her temple. "But I've got to warn you, there's no way it ever will."

"Why not?"

"Because I claimed you and I have a tendency to hold on to what's mine."

She elbowed him in the stomach. "I'm no longer yours."

Not by a whisper of breath did he indicate that the blow affected him. "I hate to break it to you, sweet, but in the last year I did a lot of research in my free time."

"Into what?"

"Pack law."

Shoot. "So?"

"So, I know there's no divorce in pack law, and separations can only be instigated by a male."

"When I get home, I'll have my cousin do it."

"Hmm." The tantalizing brush of his lips traveled down her cheek, approached her mouth. "But we're not home."

"So, what will that get you?"

The kiss on her lips was quick, efficient, not the lingering exploration her body hungered for.

"Time to change your mind."

She turned to see his face, angry at herself for responding, angry at him for teasing. Her elbows bumped the wall and his chest, one after the other, in a discordant awkwardness that only increased her frustration. His gray eyes glowed in the darkness of their safe place, not flinching from hers. His confidence irked her more than it should. She grabbed his coat off the floor. "Then I guess that also gives me time to change yours."

His "You're welcome to try" was slightly muffled by the whisper of leather over her skin.

She pulled the long swathe of her hair free of the collar. "Thank you. I will."

While she was off balance, Jace tucked his fingers under the lapel and lowered his head, drawing her up on tiptoe as he did. His breath stroked her lips, his energy smoothed along her nerves, and that fast desire flared between them. "You do that and see what it gets you."

She had to concentrate very hard to find her voice. "Is that a threat?"

If it wasn't, her knees were quaking for nothing and the shewolf in her was getting all aflutter for no reason. "Nah, just something to keep you thinking."

There was nothing to think about. "We're not compatible."

He lifted her a little higher, stretched the tension between them a little tighter. "You feel damn compatible to me, right now."

"That's just hormones. That doesn't mean anything."

His laugh was a caress unto itself, spreading over her hungry senses, feeding her his breath and his scent. "Just nothing. Another thing I discovered in my research is those hormones mean everything in were mating."

Miri dropped her forehead to Jace's hard chest, removing the temptation of his lips from her sight. As if her body could be fooled by so paltry a move. Her mate was standing before her and all it would take to meld their bodies was for her to rise up onto her toes and press her mouth to his. Judging from the heat arcing between them, she wouldn't even have to do the pressing. He'd handle it for her. The weakness that spread through her wasn't entirely due to her illness. "Not this time."

He released the right lapel. The small change in pressure tipped her off balance. Cupping her head, he steadied her. His eyes glowed. "I can wait."

"Huh. You have no patience."

"When it comes to you, I have all you need."

She severely doubted that. She'd changed so much, felt so broken inside. "You're wasting your time."

The glow in his eyes intensified. "It's mine to waste."

There wasn't much she could say to that. Jace wasn't the type to be dissuaded by words.

"So while I'm waiting," he continued, "why don't you tell me all you remember about that day."

She didn't want to. Didn't want to relive the loss. But there was no help for it, so she leaned in, letting him support her. "Where do you want me to start?"

He rubbed his thumb across her cheekbone, an abstract gesture of a distracted man. "Where did all this take place?"

"At one of their compounds."

"I mean, what kind of room."

"A surgical room. I was supposed to be going in for my daily exam."

"Describe it to me. Everything you can remember."

She did, closing her eyes, picturing the bright light gleaming off the polished equipment. She'd been in it so many times, lain there helplessly while they performed their tests, with nothing to do but count the tiles in the ceiling. She knew it down to the smallest detail. She described it to him, taking him through the sterile room, starting at the far corner and working him back to the middle, where the big cabinet was.

"What do you see on the cabinet?"

The mental image blurred. She couldn't remember.

"Easy, sweet. Just take your time and walk me through it."
Walk me through it.

He was in her mind and she hadn't even known it. "If you're going to intrude, you might as well be useful."

"Sorry. It just happened."

"Invading someone's mind just happens?"

"With you it does. You invite me in, and I go."

"I did not invite you in!" Had she?

"Not knowingly. I'm beginning to understand that." He pushed her hair off her face, his eyes kind, his expression hard. "But I still need to know that room and everything in it."

"Why?"

"It might give us a clue as to what we're looking for."

She'd do whatever it took to find the clue that would link her to her daughter. "How do I do it?"

"What?"

"How do I invite you in?"

"You just did." His smile softened the planes of his face but the wildness inside him had never been more evident. She immediately had second thoughts.

"Too late," he whispered.

And it was. He was in her mind, her memories. The pressure was incredible. She grabbed his hand and held on, understanding, even as she did it, how irrational it was to seek comfort from the person scaring her.

It's not irrational at all. I've got you.

She certainly hoped so, because she felt like she was coming apart as, minute by minute, piece by piece, he dismantled her memory.

Please, she whispered to whomever was listening. *Let him find a clue.*

SIX hours later she stood with Jace at the back entrance of a veterinary office. "Hurry up."

He didn't glance up. "I'm picking the lock as fast as I can."

She rubbed her arms as the wind bit with icy teeth into her legs. "I thought you'd be better at this."

He cocked an eyebrow at her. "Why? Because I'm a vampire?"

"Because you used to be an outlaw."

He cut her a glance. "I wasn't technically an outlaw, and even if I was, locks back then didn't look anything like this."

She glanced around. The alley behind the clinic was isolated and cluttered with huge trash containers and boxes that could hide anything.

"Just break it."

He didn't look away, just kept manipulating the mechanism. "I'm not leaving any sign we were here."

"What possible harm could it do?"

"Think on it a minute."

She did, and then swallowed. A break-in would be reported. Anyone could pick up the notice. "Even if the Sanctuary guessed it was us, they wouldn't know why."

"All they'd have to do is inventory the lab room and they'd have a clue."

"You don't know that."

The latch clicked. He turned the knob and stood, a big dark shadow blending with the night. "I'm not taking the chance."

Holding the door open, he motioned her through. The excitement she'd been trying to contain danced past caution, dragging hope onto the floor, picking up the rhythm of her pulse.

"What about the alarm?"

"That I handled the vampire way."

"Which would be?"

"I'm keeping the circuit connected."

She stepped into the dark room. Light glowed eerily off all the stainless steel. "How?"

"Think of it as copying the energy."

"You can do that?"

He closed the door. "I can do a lot of things."

And he wasn't just talking about electronics. She stepped back, the sexual tension between them crowding her more than his entrance into the small room. She crossed her arms over her chest and looked around. "So where do you think they'd keep a black light?"

"Somewhere around the exam table."

He kept coming toward her, a small smile on his face. It took her two seconds to figure out why. The exam table was the flat shiny thing she was leaning against. Just before he got to her, she ducked under his arm. "I'll check the drawers over there."

His chuckle followed her. "Chicken."

"I prefer to think of it as being efficient."

His hand ghosted her right buttock. "I just bet you do."

She swung at him. Naturally she didn't connect. Jace was incredibly fast, even for a vampire. His hand caught hers. "Hold up."

He took his gloves out of his pocket. "Put these on. No sense leaving prints."

They were way too big for her hands and made things awkward, but she didn't want to leave a trail any more than he did. "What about you?"

He motioned to the drawer. It slid almost soundlessly open. "I'll make do."

"Show-off."

He cocked that left brow. It was a habit all the Johnson brothers had, but on him it was unbearably sexy. Especially when that slight quirk of his lips joined it. Oh, why did she have to be so attracted to him?

"Are you impressed?" he asked.

She slid open the drawer in front of her. "Not in the least."

The drawer held an assortment of things, but nothing that looked like a light. She pushed the pen and batteries aside. "Do you have any idea what this thing looks like?"

"Nope. But I figure if it has a switch and a bulb, it's a candidate."

"Sounds good to me."

She reached into the back of the drawer for a black rectangle and pulled it out. It had a long bulb that covered one side and a switch on the other. For a second, she couldn't move. In the next, she couldn't breathe. A fine trembling shook her fingers. Sweat broke out on her brow. This could be it. She flipped the switch. The small light cast a purple glow. She pulled off a glove with her teeth. Her nails glowed a dramatic white. She turned her hand over, ran the light over her palm. The calluses were whiter than the rest, but nothing untoward jumped out and said *notice me*.

"Miri?"

She tugged off her other glove. It hit the floor with a soft plop. It had to be here. The clue had to be here. In a flurry of dread and excitement, she ran the light over her hand—back, front, and then back again. Nothing. Nothing at all. A sob broke past her lips. A second tried to follow. She bit it back. It had to be here. Tattooing the information on her in glow-in-the-dark ink was the only logical thing, based on what she knew of the equipment they had. She didn't look at Jace as he covered her trembling hands. "It's not on my hands."

JACE had never heard a calm so badly faked. Miri stood there, all five foot six inches of terrified woman, clutching her pride like it was her last defense. And maybe it was. He couldn't imagine all she'd been through in the last year, but he'd heard enough from Raisa, and seen enough, to know that hell didn't begin to cover it. He reached to take the light. "He wouldn't have put it any place obvious."

She didn't let go. "He might not have put it anywhere at all."

He could see the flick of her lashes, smell her anxiety. He kept his voice as even as hers. "I think he did."

"What makes you so sure?"

"Cable TV."

She just stared at him.

"I've taken to watching some of the new shows. As soon as you mentioned the tattooing equipment it clicked."

"It clicked?" *What clicked?*

Lint glowed like magic in the dark strands of her hair. He started at the crown, looking for a pattern to fluoresce on her scalp. "Hmm."

"What? Did you find it?"

"No, but there are some areas of drier scalp here."

Her hand snapped back. "Don't you dare tell me I have dandruff."

He let her hand connect with his chest. He'd never met a woman who needed to whale on something as much as Miri. She kept so much anger packed so deep, it was a wonder she didn't explode. "I wouldn't dream of it."

"Jace?"

"No, you don't have dandruff."

"That isn't what I was going to ask."

He tilted her head to the side. It wasn't easy, with her trying to look at him to assure herself he was telling the truth. She yanked her hand back, bumping his wrist. The light dropped. Jace grabbed for it and caught it. As he did his sleeve caught on her hair. She yelped and grabbed the strands. A flash of luminescence caught his eyes.

"Hold still."

She froze, not moving, not blinking, not even breathing, her anticipation a half beat behind his. For all his big words, he hadn't really been sure this was the answer, but he'd hoped. Harder than he'd let on, putting his faith in the logic of his deduction. And a clue from the cable TV show featuring tattoo artists and the safety of glow-in-the-dark tattoos. Not that he thought Miri's safety was of primary importance to anyone at the Sanctuary, but tattooing someone with glow-in-the-dark ink would make sense if one had limited time and resources and didn't want to leave a trace that could be tapped in her mind. He pressed Miri's right ear back and brought the lamp up and stared.

"Well, hell."

She slumped against the table. "It's not there?"

"It's there."

A house number and street, all neatly done in tiny letters on the back of her ear, close to her scalp. The miracle of it, the relief, shook him to his core. So much so, that he had to hold perfectly still or he'd start shaking like a child staring at a bucket of chocolate on Christmas morning.

"Oh, God." Miri's knees buckled. He caught her before she hit the floor, his reflexes slowed with the same realization that took the strength from her legs. The light fell unheeded to the floor. Glass shattered. "Our daughter's at 256 Maple Lane."

Her hands clawed up his chest and linked behind his neck as she shuddered. "Say it again."

He knew just how she felt. He dropped to his knees, cradling her in his arms, breathing her scent, trying to absorb the enormity of what that address meant. "Two fifty-six Maple Lane."

"Where is that?"

"I don't know, but I know how we can find out."

She followed his gaze through the door to the reception area. "The computer? But how will we keep them from knowing what we searched?"

"You know about computers?"

"Of course. Ian is adamant about all pack members keeping up with technology."

Were he and his brothers the only ones who'd been distrustful of technology? Well, with the exception of Slade. Slade had been in lust with every technological progression before it'd even been born into reality. "Well, I don't know how to keep them from knowing, but I know someone who does."

"We can't go back to my pack."

The light pause that invited denial didn't escape his notice. He wished he could give pack acceptance to her, but she'd lost that when she'd married him. Though it hadn't been his choice, it didn't change the end result. "No, we can't, but we can go to the Circle J."

Her hands lowered from his neck. "The McClarens are there."

"They won't hold to the code."

"You don't know weres. They won't tolerate a werewolf with a vampire let alone a werewolf turned to something in between."

"You don't know the McClarens."

She stepped back, some of the color draining from her face, leaving it pale with only the amber of her D'Nally eyes. "They'll kill you."

"I'm not arguing some will try, but their chances of success won't be good."

Miri bent and picked the light up off the floor, putting it on the table before squatting down and sweeping the shards with the side of her hand. "They'll kill me."

"They'll never touch you."

The scent of her fear covered his assurance. The taint of fresh blood alerted his senses. She'd cut herself. "Leave it, Miri."

A thin trail of blood spread across the floor in a black smear, broader at the start, thinning as it reached the end of her sweep. Glass tinkled in protest as it lumped together. "We don't want to leave any sign we were here."

"Bloodying the floor is a hell of a sign."

Only then did she seem to realize what she was doing. "Oh." She scooped up the glass. Tiny fragments shimmered amid the glistening blood like stars in a night sky. To an ordinary human, they wouldn't mean anything. To a Sanctuary hunter, they would be the key to the kingdom. She stood looking around. He pointed to the wastebasket. "Might as well dump it there."

He picked up the gloves off the floor, grabbed the antiseptic cleaner off the counter, and sprayed the floor, cleaning it until he couldn't detect a speck of blood. The whole time he worked, he could feel Miri watching him, feel a surfeit of emotion pouring off her. He just couldn't tell what that emotion was. He straightened. Miri didn't move, just stood there, her eyes shining, her hands clenched in fists in front of her. He grabbed another paper towel. "What?"

"Nothing." Plastic rustled as she took the bag out of the trash container. When he turned, she was right behind him.

"It's something."

She bit her lip and then gave him the smile that haunted his dreams, the one that banished all barriers, that lit up her face with the radiance inside. "Two fifty-six Maple Lane. We know where she is."

He didn't want to banish her hope, but she'd lost so much already. "It might just be a clue."

She shook her head and held out the bag. "It doesn't matter."

Since her smile didn't diminish, he supposed it didn't. He dropped the paper towel in, caught her hand in his, and sealed the cut on it with the stroke of his thumb and a kiss, holding her gaze throughout, not understanding the elation pouring off her along with complete exhaustion. He needed to get her back to the Circle J. Needed to get her safe. "Why?"

"This means it wasn't a trick. Faith is alive."

✺ 6 ✺

MIRI'S strength gave out three hours before he got to the Circle J. Stuck as he was on the back side of the mountain, he couldn't put in a call for transport. He'd had to carry her. To make matters worse, the conversion had resumed, her pain transmitting to him, torturing him with his inability to do anything about it. He didn't know if this was normal conversion or not. He didn't care. Whatever it was, it had to stop. Whatever was required to balance the change had to be given, because he would not let Miri continue to suffer. He put on another burst of speed, feeling the burn in his muscles. Goddamnit, Slade and that brilliant mind of his had better have an answer. He pushed doubt aside with the same ruthlessness with which he pushed himself. Slade would come up with an answer because Slade would take one look at Miri and make it his mission. Everyone had their passions. With Slade, it was little things and knowledge. He couldn't stop caring about the first and he couldn't stop seeking the second. Slade would find the answer.

Jace came up to the edge of Circle J land and sent a wave of energy ahead, alerting the guards at the pass that he was coming. The acknowledgment came back in a subtle brush of power. Jace stepped out of the shadows. Two McClaren sentries, Paul and Justin, nodded, looked at the woman over his shoulder, and then did a double take, their nostrils flaring as they caught Miri's scent. Their posture lost the relaxation of welcome. Their stance drew taller, legs widening, shoulders squaring. Wonderful. Even his local pack was adopting an attitude.

Ignoring the weres' rumbled displeasure, he raced on through the narrow cut in the mountain. Miri was his, and ancient feuds, prejudices, and other such protests were just going to have to fall to the wayside, because he wasn't letting her go. He approached the house. There were guards all around the perimeter of the large log home and tension hung thick in the air. Something was wrong. He slowed his pace. Approaching the stairs, he asked, "What's going on?"

Jonas, another McClaren, glanced at the upstairs window. "Allie's having the baby."

That explained the tension. "I thought Caleb had a bunker in the basement set up for the grand event."

"Allie feels it's important for the baby's first breath to be of fresh air."

"She was angling for a bower in the forest," Jonas's twin, Micah, added, folding his arms across his chest and leaning back against the log wall.

"But they compromised on the upstairs bedroom with the window open a crack."

"Caleb's negotiating skills must have improved." Jace eyed both young men, just realizing they were now fully mature weres with the muscles and confidence common to the McClarens. Damn, he was getting old, because he remembered when they were just pups annoying everyone in sight with their slingshots and their immature humor.

"It was more that he lucked out. Labor hit so fast Allie didn't have time to prepare the space."

"Ha, and Caleb said Lady Luck didn't cozy up to him."

"I haven't heard him say that since he met Allie," Jared said, coming out of the house, his dark brow lifting at the sight of Miri, draped unconscious, over Jace's shoulder. Of his three brothers, Jace was probably the closest to Jared, mainly because Jared understood the intensity of the emotions that often overtook him.

"True enough. She does remind him how to smile."

Allie had a way of making everyone smile, which just made the scream that ripped out of the second-story window that much more disturbing. Nothing could happen to Allie. Caleb wouldn't be able to take it. Hell, none of them would. Allie could light the darkest moment with her irreverent humor and her refusal to accept defeat. She'd made believers of all of them and even if Jace hadn't loved her for herself, he would have loved her for the joy she brought his often too serious older brother.

He glanced up, trying to see through the closed curtains. "Is there something wrong?"

Jared ran his fingers through his hair, the fingers on his other hand opening and closing as they always did when he was anxious. A habit left over from his gunslinger days, when limber fingers meant the difference between life and death. "They can't stop the bleeding."

"Shit." The men lined up on the porch took on new significance. Allie could only feed from Caleb, which meant he'd have to feed a lot more frequently. "She's draining him that fast?"

"Yeah, but she's getting too weak to drink."

Jace gave Miri a mental order to wake and he let her slide down his body. "Caleb must be in hell."

"He's not a happy camper," Jared said, nodding at Miri. "This her?"

"Yes."

Miri stood shakily. Jonas and Micah frowned as she swayed.

"She okay?"

"I don't know." He pulled her in to his side, not liking the way she almost collapsed against him. Another scream came from the house, muted by the wind, quickly smothered by something he couldn't see. "Slade's with Allie?"

"For all the good it's doing." Jared narrowed his gaze. Miri shuddered as his power touched her, then gasped. Her eyes opened. A growl came from the weres and a curse from Jared. His power lingered.

"You didn't tell us she was an Alpha D'Nally," Micah said, his gaze locked on Miri's face.

"What makes you think she's either?"

Jonas rolled his eyes. "If her scent didn't mark her as D'Nally, those golden eyes would. Only the D'Nally Alphas have them."

Micah glanced over at him. "Ian is going to kill you."

"Ian is going to have to get in line."

Jace focused on Jared and his frown. "What?"

"She's converted, yet not."

The McClarens growled, and the others picked up the rumble. Jace cut them all a glare. "Get over it, or get out."

He had no patience for were prejudice.

Jared motioned the twins back, stepping between them and Jace. "In case you've forgotten, the McClarens are our friends."

"And Miri is my wife." She took a step away, more of a stumble. Her energy was getting stronger. Jace kept his hand on her arm, letting her find her balance.

"Which is going to take time for everyone to absorb," Jared pointed out reasonably.

Jace didn't have time.

Another cry came through the window; this time it was abruptly cut short. In the next second, Allie's voice slid through the open window, strong yet hoarse with weariness. "I swear, Caleb, if you try to help me like that one more time, I'm kicking you in the face. I've got this."

Jace had to smile. "Doesn't sound like she's too weak."

"Caleb just gave her blood again."

"And a bit of his attitude as well, it seems."

Jared laughed. If Jace ignored the grim edge, it was like the good old days. "That came naturally, I think."

"Probably." Allie had a will of iron.

Miri swayed again. Micah reached out. Jace's reaction was immediate, instinctive, and as possessive as any were's. He snarled a warning and pulled her against him.

Micah stared at him, the challenge in his stance no less strong for the mildness of his expression. "You'd better get used to it. Many weres will try to take her from you. She's fertile and Alpha. There isn't a stronger aphrodisiac for a were."

Miri growled, responding instinctively to the tension. Jace ran his hand over her hair and down her back, keeping her close. "Then many weres are going to die."

"Who's going to die?" Miri asked groggily.

Miri would have to come fully conscious right then. Jace held Micah's gaze. "No one, yet."

She pushed the tangle of her hair away from her face. Her other hand dropped to her stomach as she looked around. She immediately stiffened as she spotted Micah and Jonas. "Yet?"

"Yet."

She looked past them to the other weres scattered across the porch, then back at Jace, and then again at the weres. Her shoulders squared. A growl hovered in her throat and she put all one hundred twenty pounds of herself in front of him. As if she could protect him from a fully mature male. Jace crossed his arm over her chest and tucked her back against him. "No need to get all wolfie on anyone, princess. You're among friends."

Jonas snorted. The look Miri cast him was inscrutable.

"I'm among wolves," she corrected.

"And family." Jared stepped forward, too close for Jace's vampire to tolerate. Another snarl rumbled in his chest. At his own brother, no less. Jared just smiled, amusement replacing worry.

"You've definitely got it bad." He inclined his head toward Miri. "Welcome to the Johnson clan."

"Thank you." Her hand connected with Jace's thigh as the last of his growl trailed off. Was she trying to calm him or slap him?

Another high-pitched cry came from the house.

Miri glanced at the door. "Who's hurt?"

"My sister-in-law is making me an uncle."

She looked around at the men standing on the porch, and then over her shoulder at Jace. "Your sister-in-law isn't vampire?"

"She's definitely vampire." It was Jared who answered.

"Vampires can't have children."

Jace rubbed her arms. "That's what everyone keeps telling us."

Miri went still, terror scenting the air around her. "Oh, my God, they can't know."

It didn't take a genius to figure out who "they" were.

"The Sanctuary already do."

Barely perceptible tremors started in her core. She grabbed his forearm, her talons sinking through his skin. The surrounding wolves took a step forward. This time, Jace's vampire didn't snarl back as strongly. No wolf could ignore a woman in distress. It went against their personal code of honor and their instincts.

"You have to protect her," Miri ordered, holding him, staring at Jared, the tremor in her body shaking her voice. "You can't ever let them get her."

"No one will touch Allie," Jared answered calmly. Jace felt the touch of his energy, the request for permission to enter Miri's mind. Jace shook his head. As much as Jared wanted to help, Miri would not see anyone else entering her mind as anything but another rape. Jace eased her closer and stroked a path of calm through the terror as Jared continued.

"And even if they ever get close to her, they'll find she's still one tough cookie."

Allie was a psychic vampire, able to rip a man's mind from him the way others ripped tinfoil from packages.

The only catch was that the act completely drained her and left her completely vulnerable in the aftermath, but during that burst of energy she was every vampire's living nightmare.

"No one's that tough," Miri whispered.

A memory flashed from her to him, Miri defiantly refusing to open her legs. A man's face, the agony that seared through her as he casually applied a Taser to the top of her thigh and held it there. The agony that exploded through her, the complete disruption of her brain function, the utter degradation of being unable to prevent them from touching her. The memory came clearly across the link.

Jace brushed his lips across her hair, channeling the rage that consumed him deep inside, where it could simmer until the moment came to unleash it, keeping his voice soft because the one thing Miri didn't need now was more violence. "No, sweet, no one's that tough."

"Which is why she'll be guarded as closely as you will be," Jared added, his normally even drawl almost a snarl. One look confirmed that Jared had still been linked to him as the memory had crossed over. Flames lit his brother's eyes, vivid against the almost green irises. The edges of his fangs were visible and his energy writhed about him in an invisible lash. The weres, reacting to the energy, picked up the snarl.

Miri shrank back against him.

Cut it out.

From one blink to the next, Jared had himself under control.

"Don't mind Jared. Without his wife around, he forgets his manners." In truth, Raisa was an anchor for Jared, emotionally and physically, a true mate for all the energy that surged within him, and just as deadly in her own way.

As calm spread, Miri looked down at his arm and gasped. "I'm so sorry."

She removed her claws from his flesh. The hot sting remained, a lingering whisper of pleasure.

"No harm done." Before she could protest, he let her see the desire simmering inside him at the erotic claiming.

Her shock made him smile.

Weres can't be that much different from vampires.

How would I know?

She wouldn't. He'd been her only lover.

You'll have to trust me.

Her snort of disbelief no sooner ended than Allie's angry voice surged. "Get the hell away from me with that, Slade."

"You need help, Allie."

"I told you, Caleb, I'm having this baby naturally."

"There's not a thing natural about this." Caleb's deep baritone rasped with impatience and worry.

"Well, you're not introducing anything *less* natural."

Jace looked at Jared. His brother just shrugged. "She's determined not to do anything that will traumatize the baby."

Allie's voice carried on the night's calm, tired but reflecting all the stubbornness he'd learned to associate with her. "Raisa, if Slade comes near me again with that oversized salad fork, geld him."

"Done."

Despite the gravity of the situation, Jace couldn't help but smile. That "Done" had contained a hefty dose of eagerness. "Raisa still holding a grudge over Slade's last experiment?"

Jared nodded. "Yup. She didn't appreciate being knocked on her ass by her own energy."

Miri pulled his hand away from her chest and turned to face him. She was very pale and didn't look any too steady. He cupped her shoulder in his hand. Moonlight touched her eyes, bringing out the gold in her irises. "Raisa's here?"

Jared was the one who answered. "Yes."

"I didn't think she'd make it. She was so weak."

"Yet you sent her out anyway?" There was a dangerous quality to the question.

Miri didn't flinch. "She was dead if she stayed."

The simplicity of the response stole the thunder from Jared's energy.

Through Raisa, they all knew what the Sanctuary did to women in the pursuit of science. Through Raisa, they knew what Miri had committed to endure so that Raisa could live.

"You ever want or need anything, all you've got to do is ask," Jared said to Miri with utter conviction.

"You don't owe me anything. Raisa and I worked together."

"But you stayed behind."

She shrugged. "There really wasn't any other choice."

Jace squeezed her arm. "Don't be so quick to let him off the hook. I kind of like the idea of Jared in my debt."

"He considers himself in my debt, not yours."

"Same difference."

He felt the brush of Jared's energy as he tapped Miri's mind.

No, it's not.

Hell, his own brother was ganging up against him.

Another yell came from upstairs, followed quickly by male swearing. Miri rubbed her arms and glanced at Jace. "I'd like to help."

"You're too weak."

"Not that weak." She pushed off his chest and propelled herself toward the porch stairs. Jonas and Micah stepped back. They inclined their heads as Miri climbed the steps to the porch. Miri stopped so suddenly at the customary deference, she almost overbalanced. Jared made a grab for her. She eyed both weres warily. They stared back impassively. Jared reached for her hand even as Jace placed his palm in the middle of her back. She ignored them both, climbing the steps, crossing the porch, moving away from him.

"She needs to feed," Jared said, frowning at her back as she entered the house.

"Probably."

"Why do I hear a 'but' in there?"

"She also probably plans on kicking up a fuss about it. She's into rituals and taboos."

"What's that got to do with the price of tea in China?"

"Were females don't drink from vampires," Jonas offered.

Jace glanced toward the twins. Nothing in their expressions implied anything. "Why would that be?"

"It's forbidden," Jonas answered.

"I gathered that." He glanced at Miri. She was almost to the door. "It'd be interesting to know why."

"A lot of things are going to get interesting around here soon," Micah murmured.

Which wasn't an answer to Jace's question, but raised the hairs on the back of his neck anyway.

This might have been a mistake. Miri stood unnoticed in the doorway and observed the chaos in the room. A woman with brown hair plastered to her skull with sweat was lying on the bed with her knees drawn up. A man with sable brown hair and broad shoulders sat on a stool at the foot of the bed. Another sat at the head of the bed. He looked up, noticing her. The family resemblance to Jace was strong—same square face, slashing cheekbones, and intense eyes—but this man's eyes were more green than gray, and his face less harshly defined than Jace's. Which made him no less handsome and no less intimidating than her mate. He had to be Caleb.

"Who are you?" he asked.

"Miri."

"Jace's Miri?" The woman on the bed struggled up onto her elbows. "Really?"

Caleb put his arm under her shoulders, supporting her. "The introductions can wait, Allie."

The man at the foot of the bed turned around. Again the similarity to Jace, the frown on his face also familiar.

"No, they can't." Allie swatted the big vampire as if he were a gnat, showing absolutely no fear of his power. She wasn't an attractive woman, especially with her face smeared in blood and sweat, but she had the prettiest blue eyes, and when she smiled, Miri knew why Caleb looked at her like she was his world. She was beautiful. "I'm so glad he found you."

"Thank you."

Allie clutched her stomach and doubled over. "Oh, crap. Hold on."

Caleb held her, blood appearing at his temples. Obviously he was trying to take the pain from her. "She doesn't need to hold on. I'm sure she'll get that this is a bad time and come back later."

"I came to help."

"Do you know anything about having babies?"

"She should," a woman said behind her. "She had one herself."

Miri would recognize that voice anywhere. Raisa.

She turned, facing a woman she almost didn't recognize. Gone was the drawn face, pale skin, pain-filled eyes. This woman bloomed with good health. "You look wonderful."

Raisa tossed her head. The thick mass of her hair spilled across her shoulders. Light gathered in the blond strands and rippled across their length. "So do you."

Miri wanted to hug her, share with her all the emotion churning inside, but she was frozen in the unreality of the moment, unsure the connection was still there without desperation to bind them. Afraid to touch for fear of falling apart. "I guess anything looks better than when we saw each other last."

"Amen to that."

"Did you bring those ice chips, Raisa?"

"Caleb!" Allie gasped. "You're interrupting their reunion."

He was totally unapologetic. "They can catch up later."

Miri blinked. Yes, they could. And that in itself was a novel concept.

"Have you met?" Raisa asked, crossing the room and handing Caleb a cup.

"We were just getting around to introductions," Allie said, popping an ice chip into her mouth.

"No, we weren't," Caleb growled. "And damn it, Allie, that piece is too big."

Allie rolled her eyes while Caleb watched her like a hawk.

"Ignore him," Allie panted. "He's just stressed out from too much coffee and the imminent arrival of his son."

Caleb was not a man Miri would ever ignore, even if she wasn't wolf and raised to defer to Alphas.

"If I'm stressed out from anything," Caleb snapped, "it's dealing with your unnatural beliefs about childbirth."

"I'm not introducing drugs and God knows what into his body." The last word ended on a squeal as another contraction hit. Caleb wrapped his arm around Allie and murmured soothingly into his wife's ear, his frustrated anger muted under his concern. But it would be back. Of that Miri had no doubt. Men like the Johnsons were more comfortable fighting something than just sitting back and letting it roll out as it would.

Allie groaned. Caleb rocked her gently. It was so different from the birth of Miri's child. The pain was clearly the same, but the emotions surrounding it were totally different. Desperation and terror did not make for an easy delivery. Even an artificial one.

Raisa looked at Miri. "Do something."

"What would you have me do?"

Raisa shrugged helplessly. "You're the one who had a child."

"They cut mine from my body."

All sound in the room ceased. Four pairs of eyes locked on her for the space of a heartbeat. Oh, God, she'd said that out loud.

The man at Allie's feet spoke. "And we'll make them pay for it, don't you worry."

He'd looked so sedate until he said that, a spot of calm amid the chaos of the room, drawing her notice with his very lack of activity, but then he looked at her and she saw the illusion for what it was. The man was a time bomb of emotion waiting to explode.

She did not want to be the one to set him off. She made her "Thank you" very calm.

He went back to frowning, staring at Allie. Though Miri couldn't see the energy coming off him, she could sense it. He was studying her from the inside out. Allie drew her knees up. The sheet fell down her shins.

"You damn well better not be looking, Slade."

Caleb sounded so much like Jace just then that Miri felt a spurt of liking for him.

"Kind of hard to deliver a baby without my vision."

Caleb swore. "As soon as this is over I'm wiping your memory clean."

"Thank God!"

"Well," Allie sniffed. "That was hardly flattering."

"Son of a bitch, you made her cry." Caleb wiped his thumb across his wife's cheek.

Slade looked appalled by the very idea. "I didn't mean anything, Allie, I'm just getting Caleb's goat."

"Well, get it when I'm not feeling so horrible."

"Will do."

"It might be easier if the men leave."

Miri might as well have dropped a bomb as make that suggestion. She was suddenly the center of attention. Allie looked hopeful, Raisa amused, Slade and Caleb belligerent.

Miri elaborated. "Among weres it's not customary for men to"—she bit back the word "invade" as the men frowned harder at her, and substituted—"frequent the birthing room."

Caleb didn't twitch a muscle; he just sat there on the bed like an immovable object and said, "I'm not a were."

She moved farther into the room. "But I'm thinking your wife is wishing you were right now."

Allie tossed her a grateful glance as Caleb glowered. "What in hell makes you say that?"

"Because you're focused on one thing, and she's trying to focus on something else."

"We're having a baby. What the hell else is there to focus on?"

Raisa came up beside her, not touching her, understanding her problem with people touching, maybe because she had it herself. Allie was the one who answered, "A lot."

Caleb didn't move. "I'm not leaving you."

Clearly someone had to take charge of this mess. Miri crossed to the bed, letting Jace control her pain, ignoring her weakness.

"How long have you been lying down?" Miri asked, nudging Slade aside.

"Hours."

That wasn't good. She motioned to the foot of the bed. "Do you mind if I take a look?"

Allie waved her hand. "Why not? Everyone else has."

Miri couldn't help her grin at the disgruntled proclamation.

Slade watched her carefully as she pulled the covers back.

Allie was dilated, but not anywhere near enough. And there was a lot of blood. More than she'd ever seen a were lose. She glanced up at Caleb. "You can replace all the blood she needs?"

His mouth set in a straight line, a gesture she'd seen Jace adopt more than a time or two. Apparently all the Johnson men were stubborn. "Yes."

"Good." She dropped the sheet. "How does standing up sound to you, Allie?"

"Like heaven. I've got a cramp in the base of my spine."

"You didn't tell me that," Caleb accused.

"There's a lot I don't tell you."

"And don't think we're not going to be discussing that when this is over," he growled, hands hovering at the ready as Allie shoved the sheet back.

"Is it safe?" Slade asked.

She had no idea, but from what she could see, the greatest danger Allie faced was blood loss. "It will probably speed up her labor."

At least it did for weres, and vampires couldn't be that different. They all had the same equipment.

"How do you know so much about this?" Raisa asked.

"The women of my line are midwives."

Slade's heavy brows came down. "Your line?"

She nodded her head. "D'Nally."

His gaze searched her face, lingering on the betraying color of her eyes. "Any relation to Ian?"

"His cousin."

"Damn, Jace is screwed, isn't he?"

She brought Allie's knees together and swung them to the side. "Not if I can help it."

"See," Allie said, tugging down her pale blue nightgown and kicking the cover off her legs. "Not everyone is doom and gloom." She stood carefully. "I can't wait to see your baby, Miri. Is it a girl or a boy?"

Pain, white-hot and sharp, ripped through Miri. If not for the discipline she'd learned at the Sanctuary's hands, she would have dropped to her knees. She held her hand out for Allie's. "I had a little girl."

"I bet she's just precious."

"Yes. She is."

"What's her name?"

"Faith."

Allie paused, whether from another contraction or the name, Miri couldn't tell. "That's a good name," she gasped.

"I thought so." The pain inside Miri grew to a yawning hole that threatened to swallow her completely. She changed the subject. "Have you settled on a name for yours?"

Caleb was in their way. If the Johnson brothers' reputation was anything to go by, there wasn't a sweet bone in them. Just cold, deadly skill and a tendency for revenge that even hard-edged weres respected and admired. Yet, watching Caleb with Ally was sweet. There was no doubt that they shared a soul bond: her pain was his, her hope was his. It went against everything she knew about vampires. She elbowed Caleb aside, ignoring the discontented rumble in his chest. Clearly he wanted to be the one supporting Allie, and if Miri didn't think he'd whisk her back to bed after the first step, she'd let him. But right now Allie had momentum and it needed to keep going. "Don't you need to . . . replenish before you can give her blood again?" she asked.

A wolf couldn't be more distressed, which meant Allie had to feel Caleb's anxiety as much as she did. Not good.

"Yes."

Miri adjusted her grip on Allie. "I believe there's a whole line of weres downstairs willing to supply it."

Another concept that took some getting used to. Weres who trusted vampires to the point of being their food supply. She'd call them trolls—wolves enslaved to the vampires—but there hadn't been anything subservient about Jonas or Micah. The only moment of deference they'd displayed had been when they'd acknowledged her status with a bow of their heads.

"Vampire takeout," Allie quipped. "Hurry and get yourself some, Caleb, before they get distracted and run off in pursuit of something."

Caleb laughed. Allie took a step and then groaned. "How can something so good"—she cut a glance toward her husband, forced a big smile, and, in a voice pitched slightly higher than normal, finished—"be so distinctly uncomfortable?"

"I know exactly how much pain you are in, Allie girl. No need to butter up the words." Caleb turned to Miri. "My wife's newly turned—could that affect things?"

Miri absorbed that. "Define 'newly.'"

"Within the last year."

Newly turned, wife to a vampire, and delivering a baby. She had Miri's total sympathy. "I don't think so."

Caleb hesitated in the doorway, his need for blood battling with his need to stay with his wife. "You going to be okay?"

"I'm having a baby, Caleb," Allie answered, "not taking a bullet."

His right brow arched up. Apparently all the brothers had that attribute. "And that means?"

"I'm okay. Go tank up." She glanced down. Blood marked her progress across the room in a bright crimson trail. "I'm going to need it."

With a curse, he vanished.

"Thank God he's gone." Then, just as fast, Allie whipped her head around and glared at Slade. "If you hurt his feelings by telling him I said that, I'll geld you."

Miri blinked, not only at Allie's words, but at the fact that Slade was still in the room. She'd forgotten about him.

"Wouldn't dream of it."

She looked at him again. The man had a way of blending into his environment that would have made a wolf proud, but now that she looked at him, she wasn't sure how he did it. If a person focused her attention on him he practically vibrated with energy. A genius, Ian had called him. A man of science. She ran her gaze over Slade from the top of his head to the toes of the scuffed boots he wore. She'd never seen a man of science look more like a predator waiting for a moment to pounce. "Why are you here?"

They had reached the end of the room. She turned with Allie, matching her pace to the shorter woman's.

An enigmatic smile touched the corner of Slade's mouth. "Playing doctor."

Allie pushed Miri aside. "If you don't mind," she gasped, panting through a contraction, slowly doubling over as the grinding pain tightened her muscles, "I'd like to try this on my own for a bit."

"Of course." Miri watched as she took a couple steps. Many women couldn't stand to be touched when in labor. Too much going on to take any more stimulus.

Raisa came up beside her as Allie took one step away, then two. Toward Slade. Miri didn't worry about her falling. The second she'd let go of Allie the man had snapped to attention. He'd catch her if she faltered.

"How are you really?" Raisa asked in a low voice.

The sympathy in the other woman's voice almost did Miri in.

Her physical pain had nothing on the mental agony she battled. She felt like she was teetering on the edge of a huge black chasm, and all she had to hold on to was a thread, and her dwindling strength. "I'll be fine when I get Faith back."

It was her mantra. The statement with which she refueled her strength.

Raisa's hand grazed the back of hers. "The brothers will get her back for you."

Allie faltered. Slade leapt to his feet in a move too fast to see, even with her wolf abilities. Miri took a breath, bracing herself. "I know."

She turned her head and met Raisa's warm brown gaze. The woman's health and energy struck her like a blow. So did the memories. Raisa's small face distorted in a scream, the pain in her eyes nothing compared to her determination not to give in. That vampire stubbornness of hers so much stronger than her body. Miri remembered watching the Sanctuary scientists make her bleed, suffer; holding the threat of more suffering for Raisa over Miri's head if she didn't cooperate. More than anything she remembered those cold eyes watching and waiting for one of them to break. Neither of them had. Not before Raisa had been sent from the Sanctuary and not in the month since. "I don't know how I thought you frail when I first saw you in that hellhole."

Raisa smiled, her pixie features blooming with a beauty that made Miri blink. "I didn't have the benefit of Jared's blood. It doesn't make me sick like everyone else's."

All it had taken was Jared's blood?

"Or it could be my size," Raisa continued jokingly. "Everyone thinks I must be a delicate flower."

"Uh-huh." Allie grunted, coming back toward them in shuffling steps, Slade hovering behind her. "Are you the same woman who had Jared coming back to the house to remove a spider last night?"

"Just because I don't like spiders doesn't make me helpless."

"You could have just squashed it," Slade offered in a deep voice that resonated along Miri's mind in a tendril of energy that felt so good she instinctively opened to it.

"That would have been gross."

Raisa's answer drifted through a cloud of comfort that seemed to increase the more Miri focused on it.

Raisa stiffened beside her and grabbed her arm. "Cut it out, Slade."

The tendril dropped off. Miri blinked, disoriented with the abruptness of the disconnect, her talons instinctively surging in reaction to the helplessness of the moment.

"I was just checking her health."

Allie stopped and spun around, holding her belly and gasping as she did. "What did you do?"

"Nothing."

"He was in my head." The horror of it lingered. Slade had been in her head, and she hadn't been able to prevent it any more than she'd been able to stop the Sanctuary from probing her mind. *Jace.* The cry was instinctive and from her heart. *Jace.*

The pointless call only served to further blur the line between past and present. He'd never heard her before. It didn't matter if he heard her now.

Right here, princess.

His life force poured into her consciousness in a steady stream, finding the cracks in her control and filling them with a surge of strength her soul embraced. She was wrong, Miri decided, as Jace bridged the gap in her reality and anchored her in the here and now. He mattered. Too damn much. Allie's eyes narrowed as she glared at Slade. Energy shimmered off her in waves that were reinforced by the equally bright rays of energy coming off Raisa.

"You are so out of here."

Slade didn't move. "I'm afraid not."

"Yes. You are." Allie pointed to the door. "Miri's helping. You're not."

Slade didn't move. "Miri has been a Sanctuary captive for a year and her mind is an open book to anyone who wants to manipulate it. She's not the sort of help you need."

Miri stared at him, pain lancing through her in a shocking wave, mentally stepping into the comfort Jace immediately offered. "I would never side with the Sanctuary."

"You'd do it and never even know you had."

Beside her, Raisa drew up as taut as a stone and hollered, "Jared!"

She didn't say anything more. She didn't need to. Three seconds later, Jared appeared in the door, Caleb on his heels, Jace to his right. "You bellowed?"

Raisa jerked her chin to the side. "Remove Slade."

Jared's brow went up and he glanced at Slade, the women, and then back at Slade. "What the hell did you do to get Raisa all imperious on you?"

Slade didn't flinch, just stood there staring them all down. "Pointed out the truth."

"Meaning what, precisely?" Jace, asked, his gaze on Miri's face. Miri had a feeling, despite her efforts, that her emotions were an open book to him.

Allie waved him away. "That doesn't matter; just remove him."

Caleb was back at her side as she began to straighten. Miri could tell from Allie's movements that the pains were coming faster now that she was vertical; stronger, too. It was good. "He's the closest thing to a doctor we've got."

"We've got Miri."

"She's Sanctuary," Slade cut in. "You can feel their touch all through her brain."

Raisa took a step toward him, her hair blowing back with the dark energy gathering around her. The hairs on the back of Miri's neck stood on end.

Danger.

"Remove him, Jared, or I'm going to practice my energy-sucking technique."

Slade stood. In the next second Jace was in front of Miri, blocking her view. He tipped her chin up. She kept her expression blank as she tried to keep her energy field hidden. "I promised Miri not only would she be safe here, but that she'd be welcome, Slade. You making a liar of me?"

"I'm not blinded by lust."

"No." Jace's thumb stroked over her lips in a soft caress that centered the splintering panic going off inside her. "You're just blind."

He didn't look away from her as he added his order to Raisa's. "Get him out of here."

Caleb was the only occupant of the room who looked torn. "Allie needs him."

Allie piped up. "Allie needs a midwife, which Miri is."

His "If Slade's right . . ." cut through Miri like a knife.

Allie dismissed Caleb's concern with a thoroughness Miri herself wasn't sure was warranted. "Miri's not Sanctuary."

Sanctuary taint or not, she did have some skills and they weren't dependent on psychic ability. "I *can* help."

"And pass it all on to the Sanctuary while you're at it?" Slade asked.

Miri gave him the truth. "Not consciously."

Caleb cut her a sharp look. Allie rolled her eyes. "You couldn't just say 'No'?"

"I don't want to lie."

"Hedging." Allie grunted, heading back toward the bed. "It's called hedging, Miri, and you'll find it saves us all a lot of arguing."

Jared leaned against the doorjamb, snagging Raisa's hand as he did, pulling her with him, away from Slade. His hand grazed up the small woman's arm and around her shoulder. Miri expected Raisa to fight, the way she'd seen her fight men before. Instead, Raisa flowed into his side, her cheek resting against Jared's torso, trust and acceptance defining the relaxation of her body. Jared kissed her tenderly before catching Miri's eye.

"If Miri can handle the medical," Jared said, straightening, "I'll handle any spillover of energy."

Caleb met Miri's gaze over Jace's shoulder as he asked, "Can you handle the medical?"

She wanted to flinch away from the challenge in his gaze. "Can Jared handle the other?"

"Easily."

Which only left the question of whether she could handle her end of things. Jace's energy smoothed along hers, gentling the wild surges, creating a break in the panic big enough for her to feel the confidence in her abilities. From the bed came a high-pitched wheeze of pain. Allie needed her. She'd been trained to meet that need. It didn't get more basic than that. "Yes."

Caleb motioned to the bed. "Then get to it."

⇻ 7 ⇺

MIRI never wanted to go through that again. The battle to keep Allie hydrated with blood while she struggled to give birth to her child had made her feel sometimes like she was in a race she couldn't win. Yet they had. Thank God.

Miri stumbled out of the room. Jace caught her. She didn't even have the strength left to lodge a protest. Truth was, his arms felt too good, the heat from his touch too welcome, the illusion that everything could be all right as long as they were together too tempting. He took her weight easily, guiding her down the hall.

"I'm an uncle?"

"Yes."

"The baby's well?"

"It was a very difficult birth. Everyone's tired."

At least she hoped that was all it was. The baby had been very quiet, weak.

"Including you," Jace murmured. She nodded, wrapping her arms around him because they felt so empty without her daughter, and she needed to hold something solid.

His lips brushed over her hair. "I'll get her back for you, Miri."

"I know you'll try."

"That was a promise."

But there was no guarantee he could keep it. "I know."

"Whatever it takes, I'll make sure she comes home to you."

"Thank you." It dawned on her that they'd reached the bottom of the stairs. The entryway was just ahead. Jace guided her to the door. "Where are we going?"

"To one of the cabins."

He leaned around her to open the door. A cool evening breeze blew across her face. Moonlight spilled onto the covered porch, too far away to touch her, beckoning her weary soul, lifting it. She stared across the open yard to the trees beyond. Her people had a special affinity with the moon. She wished she wasn't so tired. She would love to run in the moonlight, feel the wind blowing through her hair, enjoy the exhilaration of being part of a universe she understood.

"Feeling the urge to run?"

She stared into the woods beyond, the wide open wilderness that she could lose herself in. "Yes."

"What's keeping you here?"

Was he hoping she'd say him? She pushed her hair back. "Because I'd drop right there by the cars."

His fingers opened over her back. His energy probed. "That tired?"

"Yes." And it wasn't natural, but she didn't know what to do about it and didn't know who to ask about it.

Jace urged her out into the moonlight. It touched her skin with a subtle warmth, shimmered along her mind's eye in a memory of sweeter times.

"Then how about I carry you?"

Be held against him in the moonlit night, feel the illusion of freedom in the wind in her hair while safe in the protection of his arms? "It's too dangerous."

"Probably." He scooped her up. "But we can risk it."

She slipped her arms around his neck. The skirt she'd borrowed from Allie's closet fluttered up her calves. Her heart fluttered right along with it. She was female and were. She appreciated a strong man. And Jace was very strong, even for a vampire. He nodded to the weres lounging at the bottom of the steps. "Would you gentlemen care to go for a run?"

"Why not?" Jonah said, rolling to his feet. The glance he cut her was speculative, but not forward or critical. Her breathing eased.

They scooped up their rifles, fancy things she'd never seen the likes of, slung them over their shoulders, and flanked Jace, a solid mass of muscle. "Lead on."

"Where to, princess?"

She didn't know the lay of the land. "Over the meadow and through the woods . . ."

The smile started in his eyes, moved to the crease at the edge of his mouth, and then spread to his lips. "To Grandmother's house we go?"

She rested her cheek against his shoulder, the soft laugh feeling strange in her chest, as if the muscles had forgotten how to work that way. "To wherever you want. I just want to feel the wind in my hair, breathe the night, and pretend all is well."

"Then that's what we'll do."

With a smooth leap, Jace cleared the steps. She didn't feel his feet hit the ground, didn't feel the jar of his steps, but she did feel the wind tear at the long stands of her hair, feel the tempting call of the moon, the answering cry of her wolf, the heady scent of the forest, that breathless feeling of being a part of it all. They cleared the woods. Jace picked up the pace. The wolves kept position alongside, running with the same wild freedom. A glance up showed Jace smiling with the same wildness she felt inside. He loved this. Maybe that's why they got along so well, why she'd sensed such an immediate affinity with him. In many ways he was more wolf than vampire, more in tune with the elements, his emotions, everything. She met his gaze and answered the question in his eyes by pulling her hair free of his arm, letting it stream across his chest a second before flipping it back and, with a shake of her head, inviting the cool night air to play with the locks. Desire flared in Jace's eyes as strands wrapped around his back, brushed his thighs. Dark as the night, almost undetectable, a fragile bond weaving their life forces together. She tilted her head back, arching her neck. Above her, he growled. She could feel his gaze, imagined it focused on the vulnerability of her throat. Another laugh welled from inside as the temptation she presented to him flashed from his mind to hers. The rich glow of her skin, the feminine arch of her neck flowing to the curve of her breast, the beauty of her in his eyes. Grass caught at the ends of her hair, creating little tugs. Even the pain couldn't put an end to her joy. She was free. Free.

Jace slowed. She opened her eyes. His eyes were very dark, with flickers of vampire fire lighting the edges. Over his shoulder, she could see the weres watching from a discreet distance.

"Why are we stopping?"

He let her feet drop. Her hips slid down his body, grazing the thickness of his erection. "I need a kiss."

Bold, uncompromising, he laid his needs in front of her. She wanted to shy away. She didn't.

"Why?"

"Because I missed you."

If he'd have said something flowery and sweet, she could have resisted, but a bald statement of fact cut through her defenses like a hot knife through butter, and like butter, when his hands opened on her spine she melted against him. Her thighs tucked naturally against his, her breasts smoothing into the hard planes of his chest, her face raising, lips pursing, as hungry as he was, despite everything, because of everything.

The touch of his lips was like the night itself—a smooth caress of the familiar. Beloved, wanted, and the tingle of awareness that spread outward from their mouths covered the pain of their separation with a healing balm. His mouth opened.

"Jace."

His name escaped on an ache of longing, drifted from her to him in a throaty moan. A breathless entreaty she couldn't help. All it would have taken to crush her was for him to utter a single sound of amusement. She felt so vulnerable.

She waited for it, muscles taut, body hungry, dreading it. It never came. All that came at her was the heat of his desire and a groan as hungry as her whisper of his name. His kiss deepened.

Oh, God, yes! Her arms went around his neck, pulling herself closer as his mouth slanted over hers. *Yes. Just this, just now. Just right.*

He kissed her as if he'd been dying for it, as if he truly hadn't believed he'd ever see her again, as if he'd been as desperate as she; and it broke her like nothing ever had. The first tear dripped to her ear. The second to his shoulder. The third to the seal of their lips, salting the moment with the hunger of the past and the desperation of the moment.

Oh, Jace.

Right here.

Hold me.

Always.

And he did, pressing her to him as if he wanted to hold her inside him forever, which maybe he did. Jace was as possessive as any wolf, as domineering as any Alpha, and he could make her laugh so hard when he wanted to. She would love to laugh with him again.

Jace's grip eased. She clutched his neck.

"We've got company, sweet."

She blinked. He touched the corner of her mouth with his thumb. Another touchstone to the past she'd relived over and over in her mind during her captivity. It wiped out the last of her resistance. She couldn't hold on to the anger, the push and pull between love and hate that had given her the strength to go on when she'd been imprisoned. This was Jace. The man who'd given her the wind in her hair and the moonlight on her face just because she'd needed it. The man with whom she'd mated eighteen months ago. For better or worse. "I'm sorry."

Sorry for doubting him. Sorry for putting walls between them. Sorry for not being able to let go of the last of her defenses.

"I'm not." His smile was that gentle one he only used with her. "This is good, Miri."

Did he mean their kiss or what was between them?

"We've got to move," Jonas called out. "If we stay here much longer, any Sanctuary hanging about will locate us."

Jace glanced at the were and then back at her. "I'm going to have to cut our run short tonight."

"That's okay."

He hiked her up with one arm. "It's not, but I'll make it okay someday."

She wrapped her legs around his waist. "You don't need to."

"Stop forgiving me."

"I haven't."

"Then act like it."

"I can't."

"Why not?"

"You're my mate."

He reached behind and unlocked her right ankle from around his waist, drawing it to the side with a slide of his hand up her calf. "And that makes holding a grudge impossible?"

"Apparently."

"Well, shoot." He hitched her up in his arms, supporting her with an arm around her shoulders and the other under her knees. "Being married to you is going to be a breeze."

The weres snorted in disbelief. She tucked her chin under Jace's and listened to the steady beat of his heart as she whispered, "I'll try to make it so."

* * *

JACE didn't set Miri down until he got inside the door to the small cabin. She stood where he put her, watching him the way she had since that kiss in the meadow. Hungry, fearful, and oddly accepting of the conflict. It was a far cry from the open trust he was used to.

He held her hand as he locked the door and set the alarm, a restless part of him unable to believe that she was here with him. That any second he wouldn't wake up and find her gone. Just one more dream that wouldn't stick around.

"Do you really think an alarm is effective against the Sanctuary?"

"If it were an ordinary alarm, no, but Slade says this one'll give a hell of a notice."

She tugged at her hand. "I'm surprised he hasn't set it to warn against me."

"He wanted to, but I wouldn't let him."

Her eyes went big and she stopped breathing. "Really?"

Nothing had ever condemned him more than the badly hidden fright in that question. He should have known better than to tease now about something like this. He was not the man he should be. Never had been. And he certainly wasn't the man for her. He glanced down to where their fingers linked. At the way she gripped tightly, with faith that he would protect her. Against his brother. Damn, if that wasn't irony. "No. I was just pulling your leg."

She glanced out the window. "He doesn't like me."

"He's on edge in regard to anything Sanctuary."

They all were. That full lower lip slid between her teeth. Her fingers tightened to the point of pain on his. "Will it keep him from helping me find Faith?"

"Faith is a Johnson. Nothing will keep any of us from bringing *our* daughter home."

Her lip didn't come out from between her teeth. He gave her arm a tug. She tumbled against him. He tucked his hand, still holding hers, into the small of her back, arching her spine. Her head naturally fell into the hollow of his shoulder. He waited until her gaze met his. "Nothing."

"When?"

He couldn't blame her for the question. She didn't know Slade, didn't know his dedication to the family, to a cause. Didn't know that, when presented with the information that Faith was missing, he hadn't even stopped to feed, despite his obvious need. He'd just gone to work with the information presented. "Soon."

Jace frowned as he realized Slade had been doing a lot of meal skipping the last six months, to the point that Jace was getting worried about him. "Slade's working on the address now. Come tomorrow's nightfall, we'll know where to go."

"Nightfall." Her eyes closed slowly, dark lashes fanning against her cheeks. Startlingly dark. Highlighting her pallor and her exhaustion. "That's only fourteen hours away."

"Don't be wishing that time away. We need it."

She opened her eyes a crack, peeking at him through her lashes "For what?"

"To rest up and prepare."

"You prepare. I'm wishing."

"What you're going to be doing is sleeping."

He walked her backward in the direction of the kitchen, not changing their stance, keeping her off balance, a silent dance to music only he could hear. "Right after you eat."

She was shaking her head before they crossed the small living room to the kitchen. "I'm not taking your blood."

"You've really got a bee in your bonnet about that, haven't you?"

"Yes." At the kitchen threshold, she felt behind her with her foot.

"You realize, of course, that it's ridiculous to be fussing about something you've already done once."

"I've done a lot of things once. It doesn't make me good at them, or them good for me."

She stumbled on the next step.

"If you'd just follow my lead," he pointed out, "you wouldn't be having such problems."

Her quick glance up let him know she caught his double meaning. "I prefer to do things for myself."

"Then we're going to have some problems in this relationship."

Another two steps and he'd have her to the table.

"Why, because you can't stand a woman with an independent mind?"

"No, because, if you remember back, I like doing for you."

She stared up at him, a look of confusion on her face.

The back of her knees hit the chair. He gave a little push and she landed in the wooden seat. The legs rattled on the floor. "No need to look like a deer caught in headlights. That's a good thing."

He headed for the freezer.

"Where are you going?"

The panic in the question was much higher than the six feet between them warranted. "To get your dinner."

"Dinner?"

He glanced over his shoulder. Her lip was back between her teeth. "Yes. Dinner. As in steak."

The growl of her stomach interrupted the tense silence.

"I take it that's okay with you?"

"Yes."

He opened the door and pulled out a couple of rib-eyes. Wolves had a voracious appetite. He and his brothers kept the place well stocked just in case of visitors. When he turned around, Miri was right behind him, a broiling pan in her hand. He indicated the pan with an arch of his brow. "Did you miss the part where I was preparing you dinner?"

She cocked her head to the side. "Vampires don't eat, do they?"

With a twirl of his finger, he indicated she was to head back to the table. "Afraid I'm going to ruin your meal?"

She didn't budge. "Maybe."

Instinct told him her reasons went much deeper. He crowded her backward, hooked his foot on the leg of the chair, and pulled it to the left before pushing her into the seat. "I won't."

She didn't look any more relaxed when he took the steak out of the wrapping. He pretended to fumble the steak. She leapt to her feet.

He deftly tossed the meat onto the rack. "You have control issues, don't you?"

She narrowed her eyes at him. "What do you know about control issues?"

"Allie's been dragging all of us into the twenty-first century."

Her hand clenched into a fist. "All of you?"

He turned on the broiler, opened the oven door, and carefully slid the pan in. "Yes."

He turned to find her glaring at him, energy pouring off her in an angry wave. He leaned his hip against the counter and folded his arms across his chest. "Any particular reason you look ready to commit blue murder?"

A blink, and that fast, she had her expression under control. Her chin came up. "None at all."

"Uh-huh." He waved his hand. "You might as well spill whatever it is before you explode."

Her jaw set in a rigid line and her gaze avoided his. "I have no right."

"Seems like I just gave it to you."

"I mated you, knowing how it would be."

He wondered if the stab of satisfaction he got when she admitted to his claim would ever go away. He ran his fingers through his hair. "I'm tired. Paint a picture for me."

"I knew you were vampire."

She said that as if it explained everything. "And I knew you were wolf, but that's not clearing up the gray area."

"I knew you wouldn't be faithful."

It was his turn to blink. How had they gone from dinner to

cheating? The only woman mentioned had been Allie . . . The anger started slow, unable to get over the initial hurdle of incredulity.
She thought he'd slept with Allie? His brother's wife?

He stared at her face, taking in the mutinous lines, the hurt, the
forced acceptance. Emotion made the leap over shock, and right
along with it came disgust. "You think I slept with Allie?"

The answer to that was a shrug that wouldn't fool a two-year-
old. Son of a bitch, she did.

"And you're okay with that?"

"I knew what you were before I mated my life force to yours."

Not "who" but "what." "And you think I'm the type of bastard
who leaves his wife to whatever fate has in store for her, and while
she's suffering, amuses himself by fucking his brother's wife?"

Her expression paled. Her eyes widened and locked on his. Her
talons extended. The scent of fear covered the heavy scent of cook-
ing meat. She was finally catching on that he was pissed.

"Answer me this." He took a step forward. "Does my brother
know I'm screwing his wife? Or am I just slipping it to her on the
side?"

Another step. Her chin came up, but she couldn't hide the
tremble in her lower lip. "He would have to know."

He cupped her chin in his hand and asked her, "Then how is it
I'm still alive?"

Her gaze searched his. "You're vampire."

The fine trembling shaking her voice vibrated along his fingertips. "Meaning what? I heal fast or he doesn't care?"

"Vampires share their women."

She didn't look away as she said it. There was no higher pitch
in her voice, no hesitation, just a flat acceptance of what she saw as
the truth.

Goddamn. She honestly believed it. He placed his thumb over
her lower lip, stilling the shaking she didn't want him to see, focusing his attention on the small gesture, making sure to place the pad
dead center of the sweet dip he liked to stroke his tongue around.

Fury pounded reason, demanding an outlet. She had to scent it. Hell, she probably felt it. His energy was a wild thing clawing for release. It took everything he had to keep his drawl steady. "Tell me something: do vampires also beat their women?"

He noticed she wasn't so quick to toss out that answer. Smart woman.

She hedged. "Why do you ask?"

"Just seeing what permissions I have before exercising my options."

She tried to jerk her chin off his hand. She wasn't successful. Becoming vampire had given him incredible strength and stamina. More than one little misguided wolf could ever overcome.

"I won't let you beat me."

"That wasn't my question, though I don't see how you intend to stop me." He tapped her lip and tightened his grip on her chin, a silent order to give him what he wanted. She went still, accepting his physical dominance. The answer he was looking for came hissing out at him. "Yes."

"So, pretty much, in your opinion, vampires are disloyal, cheating, amoral wife-beating creatures with no staying power outside the sheets?"

"Everyone knows that."

"Everyone" being were. He'd run up against a lot of prejudice in his time, but this took the cake.

"We really didn't talk too much last time, did we?"

She didn't have to ask what he meant. "No."

He pulled her lip away from her teeth with a slight downward pressure. The points of her canines caught his eye. He remembered the scraping across his skin promising, but never delivering, the bite he craved. "You knocked me for a month of Sundays. I couldn't get enough of you. All I wanted to do was cherish you and make you smile every day."

She blinked again, this time faster. The glimmer of tears reflected the light of the overhead lamp, making her eyes gleam.

"And all that time you thought I was the scum of the earth."

Her "No" wrapped around his thumb.

"That's what you just said."

She shook her head. His thumb fell to the corner of her mouth. That soft skin he loved to caress.

"I didn't know what to believe. There was what I'd always known about vampires and then there was you. I was trying to sort it out."

"But you still believed I might turn ugly?"

She nodded, a flicker of shame crossing her features, followed just as quickly by anger. "A little. Before you left."

He wasn't going to argue the semantics of leaving again. Words weren't going to fix that particular injury. "Yet you still mated with me."

"Yes."

"Why?"

He'd been hoping she'd decided he was different after all; it would give him a little something to hold on to. She knocked his hand aside and looked at him as if he'd lost his mind. Her answer was short and to the point, devastating to his growing hope.

"Mating is not a choice."

⇥ 8 ⇤

MATING is not a choice.
      Fourteen hours later, on their way to the Maple Street address for their daughter, Jace still couldn't get the matter-of-fact way she'd said that out of his head. All these months, and he'd thought she'd chosen him, the same way he'd chosen her, regardless of convention or obstacles. He thought she'd fancied herself in love with him, had exploited that supposition to cement the bond between them before he had to leave so she'd be waiting for him when he returned. He'd never done that before. But, with Miri, Jace had wanted every bond locked down, every emotional tether forged. And now she was telling him it wasn't love but fate. Cold, unemotional, nonnegotiable fate.

      He glanced away from the road to where she sat beside him in the SUV, outwardly composed, her beautiful hair braided, the lustrous strands gleaming like satin in his night vision. His own lush little Madonna, who harbored on the inside a morass of emotion so strong he was having a hard time bearing the spillover without reaching over and holding her hand. But she didn't want that. Didn't see him that way. A husband held a wife's hand. A mate, apparently, just fucked and protected her and if there were children, guarded them also. Even after hours of lying on the couch staring at the ceiling, contemplating that little tidbit, or maybe because of it, he was still angry.

Metal came together in a soft clank behind them as the weres assigned to protect them in case the Sanctuary had beaten them to Faith's location shifted position in the backseat. Miri jumped. She'd been on edge since he'd sent her to her room alone. Clearly she'd expected him to jump her bones. Stake his claim. Not that he hadn't wanted to, but he'd be damned before he'd come to a woman's bed because she saw him as a duty to be fulfilled.

"We're getting close. Pull over here and let me drive."

Jace didn't look back at Tobias. "I've got it."

The SUVs in front and behind pulled into the rest stop. The back door opened. "That wasn't the plan."

It didn't take more than a glance to determine that Tobias wasn't going to back down. Jace shoved the door open. "You are one driven SOB, aren't you?"

That twitch of the lips might have been a smile. "I like things neat."

Around the other side of the car, Micah helped Miri out of the passenger seat. Despite the previous night's sleep and food, her pallor had not improved. Strain etched fine lines by her mouth and around her eyes. She needed to feed, but she refused, still clinging to her were beliefs and customs. She closed her eyes and stood there, gathering her strength, swaying with the night breeze. A pale ghost haunting the hope that this time, at the end of the night, her daughter would be in her arms.

His anger melted away as her anguish reached out. It didn't matter why she was with him, or what she believed. It only mattered that she needed someone to hold on to and he wanted to be that someone.

Miri opened the back door and slid inside. Tobias met Jace's gaze over the hood of the car.

"She needs to feed."

"Don't tell me, tell her."

"You're her mate. It's your responsibility to do what's right for her, regardless of her wishes."

"Force her?"

The big were didn't even blink. "If that's required."

"Is that what you do with your mate?"

"I'm not mated, but were my mate suffering, I would put an end to it."

Jace glanced into the car, took in the mutinous set of Miri's chin, and sighed. "Talk to me when you have a mate."

He ducked into the vehicle, swearing when his knees damn near bumped his chin. Miri glanced at him. "I'm not going to feed."

He reached for her. "That's the fourth time you've mentioned it. Do you think I'm hard of hearing?"

"No, but I get the impression you can be stubborn about accepting it."

He leaned against the door and stretched his legs out to the other side.

She kicked at his feet. "This is my side of the car."

He plucked her over so she leaned against his chest. "Not anymore."

A slight shift and her shoulder dropped beneath his. The heel of her hand dug into his ribs. "I'm not comfortable."

"Considering the list of crimes you've already stacked up against me, I'm not overly concerned."

He tipped his hat down over his eyes.

"You're going to sleep?" She sounded shocked.

"Yes."

"We're almost there!"

If she bothered to check his energy, she'd see that he was as on edge as she, but being were, she was probably checking with her senses. In the last fifty years, he'd learned to hide most of his emotions from that sort of detection. "We've got an hour."

"How can you sleep?"

"Preparation." He tipped his hat up. "Just in case whoever has Faith might have some objections to handing her over."

"You might want to prepare yourself by feeding," Tobias offered over his shoulder.

"You might want to mind your own business," Miri snapped.

"As I'm half D'Nally, you are my business."

Tobias was D'Nally? Shit. Jace hadn't known that. "She's Johnson now."

"Not according to pack law."

"Excuse me?" That was news to him.

"According to pack law, marrying Miri makes you a D'Nally now."

That he hadn't figured on. "That has got to be sticking mighty hard in some craws."

Tobias inclined his head, pulling the car out into traffic. "There are some who would like to remove the blight on the family name."

"Are you one of them?"

Beside him, Miri stiffened.

"I'm waiting to see how it plays out."

"You tell my cousin that I'm not going to tolerate any interference in my life," Miri growled, rising.

Jace tucked her back in and removed her hand from his ribs. "I assure you, Miri, for all my immoral, characterless ways, I can take care of myself."

"You'd do better to remind her of her place," Micah said from the passenger seat, disapproval heavy in his tone. "She is an Alpha female, not Alpha."

"The semantics of that escape me."

Miri continued to glare at Tobias. "Leave it that way."

"You know it can't be left unaddressed forever."

Jace pushed his hat back. "What exactly would *it* be?"

Miri pulled his hat down over his eyes. "Nothing."

"You want me to accept 'nothing'? Just when things are getting interesting?"

"You've mated with an Alpha female who holds the succession for the Tragallion pack should the current leader die. If that occurred, Miri and her mate—you—would go live with that pack and her mate—you—would be leader."

Now that was news. "I can't see that settling well."

"A vampire has never led a D'Nally pack," Micah added.

And that tradition would be broken when hell froze over. The message came through loud and clear. "Well, seems my wife has been keeping some pretty pertinent details of our marriage hidden."

"I never hid anything."

He cocked his eyebrow at her. "Just the fact that I could get the chance to lord it over a bunch of high-nose weres."

"It just wasn't important."

"Why not?"

"Because you wouldn't be interested."

"It doesn't matter if he's interested," Tobias injected, heading down the road. "There are plenty of weres looking to take the position from him."

"Absolutely. Now that you're back," Micah agreed, "he'll be challenged at every turn."

"We won't be living among weres."

She said that as if it settled everything. Jace tipped his hat back down. "That's not going to stop them from coming."

She propped herself on his chest. He could feel her staring at him.

"Of course it will. There'd be no point."

"You clearly have no understanding of men."

"I understand wolves."

"But you don't understand men and power," Tobias countered. "And killing Jace will buy someone a lot of power."

"Why?"

"Because if anything ever happens to your cousin Travis, Jace will be leader of the Tragallion weres."

The shock went through Miri in a sharp contraction of muscle.

She looked at the car ahead where her cousin rode. She frowned at the lead SUV and then back at Tobias. "Is that why Travis happens to be on this mission? So something can happen to him?"

"He rides with us because his family, your daughter, has been taken and it's his right to protect her."

Miri didn't look convinced. "You've never liked him."

Tobias glanced back. "He is not an easy were to like."

"Ian said you wanted to challenge Travis."

Tobias didn't look over his shoulder this time. "Ian has a big mouth."

The discussion was fast disintegrating into argument. Jace flattened his palm on Miri's spine under her coat and asked, "How many cousins do you have?"

"Just the two."

"I take it there are no male heirs on his side?"

"Succession is through the females."

"There's got to be someone in place to step in."

Micah cut him a glance over his shoulder. Light gleamed off the barrel of his specially designed pistol. "Yeah. You."

"He doesn't want the job," Miri argued.

"You're damn quick to pipe up with that."

"You don't like responsibility."

"What in hell gave you that idea?"

Her look said it all. No doubt more of her "you're a vampire" excuse that seemed to cover all eventualities.

"As long as you're alive," Micah continued, "you'll always be a threat to the leader in that you could challenge his authority."

"What if I just challenge him and then just lose?"

Miri shook her head. A tendril of hair fell across her cheek, dropping into the channel of the scar, filling it with darkness. She cut a glance toward Tobias. Her energy flickered. The big werewolf made her nervous When this was over he'd find out why. "A fight for Alpha is a fight to the death."

Wonderful. He pushed the hair back, tucking it behind her ear, lingering in the soft skin behind. "So, it doesn't matter if I want the job or not."

"Pretty much."

From under his hat brim Jace could see the tightening of Miri's fine lips. He wanted nothing more than to pull her down and kiss her. And when new lines of strain took up residence beside the old, he wanted to kick himself. He was angry because she didn't see him the way he wanted her to see him. Angry because she was scared. Angry, as if she didn't have a right to be scared and full of doubts after the last year. The car hit a bump in the road. He took advantage of the jostle to wedge her tighter.

"It's not a problem, Miri."

"It is if they come after you."

"That's not our main worry right now."

He could have shot himself as soon as the words were out of his mouth. Immediately her thoughts turned to Faith. The sadness, the agony of hope, the horrible loss leached the energy from him into the black hole of her despair. She needed her baby. He brought her head down to his shoulder. "Ah, sweet, we're going to get her back."

Her nails cut through his shirt, into his chest, tightening with slow precision as she struggled to maintain her composure in the face of her torment. So slowly he could hear the individual threads pop.

It was a losing battle. "What if she was sick?"

He pushed his hat back. "What makes you think she was sick?"

"Like Caleb and Allie's baby. What if she's sick? What if she needed me and I wasn't there? What if there's no need for us to be driving anywhere?"

"There's a need."

Her voice rose. "How do you know?"

He tried to hold her. "I know."

She shoved him back. "You can't."

He probed her mind. She cursed and swung at him. Her elbow

caught against his chest. Her arm jerked off target. All she succeeded in doing was knocking his hat askew as she whispered, "She could be dead."

The car swerved. Micah cursed. Jace grabbed her shoulders and held her above him, shaking her a little until she looked at him. Her braid slid over her shoulder, slapping against his chest.

"She's not dead."

"Words," she gritted out. "Those are just words."

"No, I know."

"You don't know anything."

"I know you. I know how hard you love, and there's no way in hell, as much as you love our daughter, that you wouldn't know she's dead."

The weres looked at him, then at each other. If he hadn't been preoccupied with Miri, Tobias's nod would have worried him.

Miri drew a shuddering breath. "That's just a myth."

"Until you can look me in the eye and tell me you know in your heart that Faith doesn't walk this Earth anymore, I'm going to keep looking."

Her eyes searched his. She could have been looking for a speck of doubt, an ounce of subterfuge. Whatever she searched for, she wasn't going to find it. His mother had always had a sense about her children, knowing when they were hurt, when they were safe. Miri was were, with more developed senses. No way was her daughter dead and she didn't have an inkling.

She braced her palms on his chest. Her lips thinned and then relaxed. "She doesn't walk at all. She's a baby."

He lowered her down until she supported herself. "You know what I mean."

"I know."

Another bump in the road. This one rocked her against him. He picked up the movement, stroking her hair as she whispered, "I'm sorry."

"What do you have to be sorry for?"

"The closer we get, the more difficulty I'm having believing."

"So am I."

"You're kidding."

"Nope."

She whipped his hat off and dropped it to the floor. "How come it doesn't show?"

Cupping the back of her head in his hand and stroking his thumb over her cheek, lingering on the scar, he said, "Because I've had a lot of practice facing down hopeless."

Her lids flinched.

"And, baby, this isn't hopeless."

"Then what is it?"

It was a plea for something to hold on to. He gave her his hand. "Complicated. Damn complicated."

"But you know she's not dead?"

"Yes."

"We're ten minutes out," Tobias interrupted.

Jace both felt and heard Miri's panic. A quick hug and then he set her aside. "When we get there, I want you to wait in the car."

"No."

He checked his pistol, making sure the safety was on. "That wasn't a suggestion."

She held out her hand for the gun. "That's my daughter in that house."

He didn't give it to her. "And one of my family at risk is enough."

"I'm coming with you."

The car turned a corner. The trees lining the street, broken up by evenly spaced driveways, highlighted the transition from highway to a residential neighborhood. He glanced out the window. "If you ignore the fact that everyone lives on top of each other, it's a nice neighborhood."

Miri didn't appear appeased. She reached over and grabbed his revolver. "Appearances can be deceiving."

She looked entirely too comfortable with that pistol in her hand.

"Who taught you to shoot?"

"What makes you think I can?"

"The way you're cuddling that gun like a lover."

"Maybe I just have a natural affinity for violence."

"Maybe." Except she'd never let him kill anything, not even bugs, claiming life was sacred. "What happened to your life philosophy?"

She placed the gun across her lap. "I've decided to suspend it for the Sanctuary bastards."

A laugh came from the front seat. As she glanced at Micah, Jace was treated to the clean line of her profile. The elegant, but arrogant, line of her nose; the slight thrust of her chin and her full pink lips; the big eyes with their dark lashes. The sheer elegant beauty of her. The softness in her features that was totally lacking from his. His gaze dropped to the gun in her lap and his gut twisted. "You shouldn't be within a hundred miles of this."

"I believe that was Slade's point," Miri pointed out.

"His reasons weren't valid."

That chin he liked so much—the one he loved to feel digging into his chest as she smiled up at him after they made love—lifted. "Neither are yours."

He took the gun out of her lap. The car slowed. "I'm not risking you."

"I'm nothing without my daughter."

He tucked the gun behind him and cupped her chin in his hand, raising her eyes to his. "That's where you're wrong. You're everything."

THEY parked the vehicles the next block over and cut through a vacant lot, approaching the house cautiously. There was no telling what traps the Sanctuary had laid if the Sanctuary had gotten here first. They were smart and had plenty of money accumulated through the legitimate businesses they invested in to finance their immoral projects. Jace couldn't begin to imagine what Slade could do with the same resources. Probably solve the problems of world hunger and the half-life of radioactive waste.

He blended his energy with that of the nearest tree, projecting the illusion, matching shimmer for shimmer, shadow for shadow, and listened. With his ears and his mind, he listened. The house was quiet. Dark. Not unusual for humans at two in the morning. Very unusual for Sanctuary strongholds. And his gut said this was Sanctuary.

"It's too quiet."

Even whispered through the transceiver, Jace could hear the worry in Tobias's tone.

"I can't sense anyone inside."

Neither could he. "They could be cloaked."

"Or there could be no one there."

There had to be someone there. His daughter had to be in there. He couldn't really picture her in his mind. Every time he tried, the image skittered away, as if even trying to picture her was tempting fate. He liked to think she had her mother's soft gold-brown eyes, though. A little girl who looked like Miri would be just about perfect. The glimmer of anticipation and hope was completely foreign to his normal pre-battle calm. He pushed it away. "Move in, but be careful."

They had the house surrounded. Sixteen badass weres and three Johnsons—himself, Jared, and Slade. If his daughter was in there, Miri would be holding her in a matter of minutes. *Steady, Jace.*

Jared. The man could sense the slightest break in attention.

I'm okay.

I'm sensing something.

For the benefit of the weres, Jace switched to voice. "Good or bad?" The half second it took for Jared to identify something stretched like a lifetime for Jace.

"The Sanctuary has been here."

"How long ago?" Tobias asked.

"Impossible to say."

"Not something I wanted to hear," Jace whispered back.

"Sorry."

Jace moved up to the window. Nothing disturbed the quiet. No false echoes of energy, no shadows denser than they should be, no echoes of faint heartbeats. Of all the above, the last was the most disturbing. With his back to the building wall, he peered inside. Through the partially closed blinds he could see something suspended on an object in the middle of the room. The myriad intricate shades of black and gray provided by his night vision indicated that it was probably brightly colored in normal light. The way children's toys were. "I've got signs of kids."

"Good. I'm anxious to meet my niece," Slade cut in.

Not nearly as anxious as he was to meet his daughter. "Better be prepared to lose your heart if she looks anything like her mother."

"Let's hope she looks like her mother."

"Focus, gentlemen. On the count of three. One . . . two . . ."

A disturbance in the air behind him whipped Jace around. His gun was up and his finger tightening on the trigger before he recognized the shadow slipping toward him.

"Three!"

Doors and windows opened on almost undetectable slides.

"Shit."

What is it?

Jace moved to the window, manipulating the lock, aware that he was behind the others now, creating a hole to the advantage of anyone waiting inside. *Miri.*

I thought you told her to wait in the car.

Jace motioned her flat against the wall with a cut of his hand. *I did.*

I heard you're some hotshot Alpha now.

Jace tracked Jared's energy through the house.

So I'm told.

And yet you can't get one little wolf to obey? Jace covered Miri's mouth with his hand when she would have spoken. *Some wolves are tougher than others.*

He pointed to the spot where she stood and made the motion to stay. She shook her head. With another jab of his finger he emphasized his point.

He slid through the window and dropped soundlessly to the floor. "I'm in."

"And Miri?"

He heard a footstep behind him. He was going to kill her. "Here, too."

A brief chorus of hard chuckles prefaced Jared's "Stay there."

He didn't have a choice. Jace grabbed Miri's arm and directed her to a corner, pushing her down, crowding her back, putting his body between her and the door.

Her nails raked his back. A warning. He ignored it and countered with an order.

Stay down.

Let me up.

"This doesn't look good" came clearly through his transceiver. Then Jared snapped, "Jace, get Miri out of here."

Jace spun, grabbed Miri by her waist, and leapt toward the window. He tossed her through, following so quickly he was over her before she could get to her feet. Voices spoke in his ear, breaking into static, but he couldn't hear them for the pounding in his ears. He wanted to be in there, part of the action. He rolled to his feet, scanning as he did, looking for a threat. Two McClarens came up beside him, guns ready. He reached down and pulled Miri to her feet. The weres grabbed Miri's arms and pulled her back.

His transceiver was dead.

"What's going on?" he asked, covering their retreat.

They only had to say one word. "Bomb."

Jace glanced back at the innocuous-looking house. His brothers were in there. His friends. Maybe his daughter. "I'm going in."

Both weres latched on to his arms. "Jared's orders are that you're to stay here."

"Like hell."

They'd have to kill him. A breeze disturbed the tension. He had a glimpse of dark hair and pale skin off to the side, running hell-bent for the house. They'd forgotten about Miri. Silent, deadly, determined, all wolf in her quickness, she was already halfway back to the building. Goddamn it.

He leapt across the distance. When he landed she was no longer there, desperation putting speed on her already quick wolf reflexes.

He brought her down on the next leap, instinct flaring faster than thought as he felt the change in energy. He dragged her beneath him, taking the slash of her claws, her curses as the world exploded around them. The repercussion of the blast pounded him like a sledgehammer, knocking the air from his lungs. He crawled a bit further over Miri's body, covering her as the reality fell around hotter and heavier than any debris. Faith. Faith. Oh, God, his little girl.

The scream wasn't just inside him, it was all around, guttural and shrill, the cadence rising and falling in an ungodly howl that mirrored the pain in his soul. Miri. Miri was screaming for their daughter. The sound stopped with an abruptness that was just as disturbing. Voices filled the void, deep male and thankfully recognizable. The transmitter was working again. Horror froze one section of his mind while another clicked along with practiced logic. Slade, Jared, Michael, Tobias. He listed the names, sighing, relief swallowing reality. They'd all survived.

"What in hell did you do?" Jace asked.

"Jace, is that you?"

It was a stupid question. Jared never asked stupid questions. "Yeah."

"Why the hell didn't you answer, then?"

"My transceiver was out."

"You never fucking rely on your own power."

That wasn't strictly true. He just trusted technology more.

Beneath him Miri stirred. "Did everyone get out all right?"

"We're still trying to locate Travis. And Jace?"

"What?"

"It was a trap."

"No shit."

"Faith wasn't here."

"Ever?" The whisper came from beneath him. He was pressed so tightly to Miri that her sensitive ears were picking up the conversation. Aided, of course, by the way Jared was yelling.

"Are you aware you're yelling?"

"Yes."

Jace would bet a hundred dollars that was a lie. Jared was always very much in control. "Well, cut it out and answer the question." He didn't want Miri overhearing news that would upset her. "Was Faith ever in there?"

"I'm not sure."

Shit.

"What did he say?" Miri asked.

"Faith wasn't in there." Jace refused to believe otherwise. Refused to tell her otherwise.

"Are you all right?" he asked Tobias as he and Micah came up to them.

"My ears are ringing, but I'm good," Tobias answered.

Jace glanced at Micah, who nodded. "You heard?"

"Yeah."

"They'll find Travis."

"I know." In an easy motion, Tobias stood and held out his hand.

"What about Faith?" Miri asked from beneath him.

As he rolled to the side and sat up, Jace said, "All we know is that she's not there."

"But you said there were signs of kids."

"They don't have to be Faith."

They couldn't be Faith. He stood. Before he could lend a hand she was on her feet, staring at the building as if debating running into the fire. She leaned forward. The weres lunged for her. Jace grabbed her hand and pulled her back.

"The fire can't tell you anything, baby."

"All the clues are in there."

"And I'm sure the team collected them before the building blew."

He wasn't sure of anything, but if treating a likelihood as a truth gave her some peace, he'd run with it.

The eyes she turned on him ripped his soul from his body. So much pain. "You can't know that."

"You can't know otherwise."

Tension hummed under her skin in a fine trembling. Flames from the fire reflected in her eyes. He didn't let go of her arm. He really didn't trust that look in her eyes, and, judging from the way Micah and Tobias were watching her, neither did they.

The receiver crackled. "We found Travis."

"And?"

"He didn't make it."

Damn. "My condolences to your pack. You lost a strong Alpha."

Miri spun around and glared at him. "Why wasn't I given one of those things? What happened?"

Because he had a need to spare her from the blunt reality delivered in this kind of situation. He held her arm tighter, pulling her back as the heat of the fire grew. "Travis didn't make it. They found his body."

Her lips compressed.

Is that why he happens to be on this mission?

What she'd said in the car came back to him. Shit! Now he was wondering.

Packs were tight. He was talking about her cousin. She merely gave a jerk of her head and staved off his hug with a cold "He'll be missed."

Tobias frowned.

Micah motioned to the gathering crowd. "Unless you can cloak our presence along with your energy, we've got to get out of here before someone bumps into us and discovers their nightmares are real."

"I hear you."

At the same time, Jared grunted into the transceiver, "Pull back."

Weres faded back along the perimeter, Jared among them, his energy visible only to Jace. They needed to fall back, too. The crackle of the fire sounded like Sanctuary laughter in his ears. He stared at the wall of flame, the ache of loss growing. His daughter might have been in there. Might have spent the last five months playing within those walls, learning about the world, making smiles and tears without her parents. Son of a bitch, the people who had her had better have made sure there were more smiles than tears in her life.

A touch on his shoulder brought his head around. Tobias jerked his thumb over his shoulder. "Let's go."

He didn't have to tug Miri; she went on her own, back the way they'd come, through the vacant lot, a slender shadow fading into the darkness after Micah.

"She's not taking this well," Tobias murmured, dropping in beside him.

"There's no reason she should." After a few moments, he said, "A shame about Travis."

Tobias's "Yes" was noncommittal.

"You don't sound overly grieved."

"His death saved me some effort."

"You were going to kill him?"

"I'm an Enforcer. Alphas who betray the pack answer to me."

"How did he betray the pack?"

Tobias cut him a glare. "That's pack business."

Jace eyed him carefully. No emotion colored the flat statement. The man was one cold son of a bitch. "Well, just as long as you don't expect me to step into the breach."

"That's not my call."

"Nor mine."

The corner of Tobias's lips twitched. "That decision will likely be made for you."

"Ian can't make me do anything."

Tobias motioned to where Miri strode ahead, head up, shoulders back, spine straight. "The pack kept Miri alive after her parents died. If you think her roots aren't deep, you don't know your mate."

He was right. Jace knew that. He'd felt the aching hole within her every time their minds touched. "The D'Nallys won't accept me."

And no way in hell was he letting her go.

"Not as you are, no."

"What in hell does that mean?"

Tobias didn't answer.

They stepped out of the trees. The groups stood beside the cars, hugging the shadows rather than invisibility. Jace checked his brothers first. Jared had some burn holes in his coat but appeared all right. While Slade . . . He sucked in a hard breath when he saw his brother suspended between two weres.

"What in hell did you do?"

Slade's back was a mess, flesh torn away from bone, bloody gashes gaping between the shreds of material. Even with the proof of Slade's energy touching his, Jace couldn't believe he was alive.

"Had a little discussion with a bomb" came the typical Slade response, understatement covering emotion.

"He threw himself on it when Travis and Bob tripped it."

"Then how'd he get his back torn up?"

"You don't think I'd let a Sanctuary bomb take us out, do you?"

Quite frankly, Jace didn't know how Slade'd intended to prevent it.

"Damn fool threw himself over it and messed with the energy and spiraled the blast."

"Shit."

"I had something stronger to say," Tobias said.

"It fucking worked, didn't it," Slade grunted.

"By the grace of God."

"By the grace of logic," Slade countered.

Jace shook his head. "One of these days logic is going to be the death of you."

Slade shrugged off the supporting weres. "Lack of logic is what's going to do that."

❧ 9 ❧

JACE entered the kitchen. Caleb and Tobias sat at the scarred table with cups of coffee in front of them. Both looked weary.

Caleb glanced up. "How's Miri?"

"As good as can be expected. I made her sleep."

Caleb nodded. "Good idea."

"Made?" Tobias asked, eyebrows raised. "As in hypnotized?"

Jace didn't appreciate the question or the were's interest in how he cared for his wife. His lip lifted in a snarl. "As in, encouraged her to give in to her natural need to sleep."

Tobias's reaction was an uncaring slouch and a small smile that revealed his canines. Both reactions were interesting in that they were the reactions of an Alpha confident in his power, yet Tobias had no claim to Alpha status.

"You're a nosy son of a bitch," Jace told him, not for the first time.

Tobias took a sip of coffee. "It comes in handy at times."

Jace just bet. No one seemed to know much about Tobias, just that Ian put a stack of faith in his abilities and used him for special jobs. Jace was pretty sure those jobs had more to do with violence and not much to do with questions.

Enforcer. It took on a whole new meaning after what he'd learned tonight. Jace glanced over at Caleb. "How's my nephew?"

The shadow on Caleb's face darkened. "Better since Slade got back."

"Better" didn't imply thriving. "Shit."

"Allie's frantic with worry, which isn't helping."

"She's doing okay, though?"

He threaded his finger through the handle of his coffee cup. "The bleeding's slowing." He took a drink.

That would explain the pale, drawn look. Jace motioned to the cup. "That can't be helping you."

Caleb loved his coffee but it didn't agree with his vamp digestive track. Too much and he puked. Caleb took another sip. "Leave my coffee the hell out of your bad mood."

"Does Slade have any idea what's wrong with Joseph?"

"No, but he's in the lab working on an idea."

Slade hadn't even had time to recover from the battle and his wounds, and already he was back in the lab. "We can't keep letting him do this to himself."

"We don't have any choice. He's all we've got."

"But he *can't be* all there is."

"Shit." Caleb dropped his forehead to his hand. "It's not like I haven't thought of that, but where the hell are we supposed to find brilliant vampires we can trust?"

"It might help if you associated more with your own kind," Tobias offered.

"We tend to rub them the wrong way."

"I can see why."

Caleb glared at him. "What in hell does that mean?"

"It means you think more like a wolf than a vampire."

"Christ, we're not going back to those stereotypes, are we?"

Jace was sick and tired of being judged by myth rather than fact.

"They're not stereotypes. Whether you want to believe it or not," Tobias said, "there's a reason most vampires fall in line with the Sanctuary, and most weres fall in line with the Renegades."

"Might be because the majority of Sanctuary are preying on were females."

Tobias took a long pull. "That could be, but it also could be because most vampires are made, not born, and suddenly becoming immortal, and more powerful than you've ever dreamed, has a way of corrupting people."

"Can't argue with that."

"There's also the fact that they lack pack cohesiveness."

"You mean community?" Jace asked.

"Yeah."

"Interesting theory," Caleb mused.

Jace knew that tone. "Don't go thinking you can convert Sanctuary, Caleb."

The door opened and Jared came in, bringing the scent of early morning and deep satisfaction with him. His eyes were a clear hazel, something that only happened when he was at peace. He'd been with his wife. The jealousy that fact brought Jace cut like a razor.

Don't look at me. You want your wife to love you up, sweet-talk her.

Mind your own fucking business.

Jared merely smiled and grabbed a chair. "So, who's thinking of converting Sanctuary?"

"Caleb."

Caleb cocked his eyebrow. "I didn't say a thing."

"You have that look."

"Gotta admit," Tobias said, "there was a look about you."

Caleb leaned back in the chair. His shirt strained across his chest.

"I was just thinking, like Raisa, there may be a few folks hooked up with the Sanctuary who don't quite follow the principle, but are unsure of an alternative."

"I've been thinking for a while that only a vampire could have sneaked Faith out after she was born," Jared mused.

"And, sure enough, someone has a path to Allie's mind," Caleb cut in.

"Thought you said it didn't feel vampire."

"Doesn't mean it wasn't," Caleb replied. "Just means that I didn't recognize it."

"Raisa didn't mention any sympathetic vampires at the Sanctuary?" Jace asked Jared.

"Maybe she didn't know. If they can alter their energy, it wouldn't be a tag she'd know." Jace turned to Jared. "Did Raisa mention running into any vampires?"

"No, and she's good with energy. She would have recognized one."

"Only if she was looking." Miri stood in the doorway, her hands wrapped around her arms. "And we weren't looking."

Jace stood. She motioned him back. He ignored her. "I thought I told you to sleep."

"I thought I told you to stop giving me orders."

She stepped into the room, her face so pale from exhaustion her scars all but disappeared. She needed to feed. She needed care. She needed her child.

"Neither Raisa nor I had the time and energy to do much."

She looked around the kitchen, seemed to just notice Tobias, blinked. Jace caught her before she could step back.

"It was different there." She rubbed her arms, not stopping when he drew her against him, just shifting her efforts to the right side. "We weren't strong."

"Doesn't appear to me you're all that strong now," Tobias said before taking a long pull on his coffee.

She licked her lips. It was beginning to dawn on Jace that the big were made her nervous. "Trust me, I'm a lot stronger now."

"Looks to me like a puff of wind would knock you over."

Tobias didn't move but Miri's scent spiked with fear. She leaned back, looking up at him. Shadows haunted her eyes as aggression tightened her muscles. "Why is he still here? His job is done."

"Ian sent him."

Caleb's chair came down on four legs with a distinct tap. "Is there a reason he shouldn't be here?"

Miri exchanged a long look with the were. Her hand settled on the tabletop beside a sharp knife.

"No."

"Before you go believing that, you might want to ask her what kind of were business this is," Jared interjected.

Miri's start was palpable.

"Jared's very good with reading minds," Jace murmured.

"My ears work fine, too."

"So what kind of were business is Tobias here for?" Caleb asked.

"He's sitting right there," Miri countered, her fingers inching the knife into her grip. "Why don't you ask him yourself?"

Jace didn't think Miri caught the dip of Caleb's eyes to her hand, but he did.

"Because I have a feeling he'd lie."

"He'd never lie."

Jace believed her. The question was: what made her so sure?

"How do you know that?"

She licked her lips. "That's were business."

Her fingers wrapped around the knife handle. Was she planning on using it on Caleb or Tobias?

Tobias reached across the table. "I'll get that out of your way."

With a very smooth move, the knife was removed from her grip. Miri's respiration increased, and from the tilt of her head, she was watching every move the were made.

Enforcer.

The word screamed through his head, leaping from Miri to

him, fear riding double with respect. Jace shoved Miri behind him and dropped into a crouch as Tobias palmed the knife.

"Who in hell are you?"

"Tobias D'Nally." His gaze went past Jace to Miri.

She gasped and touched his back, the trembling in her fingers vibrating up his spine. "Good grief, don't upset him, Jace!"

"Hell, sweet, if he doesn't stop scaring you, in about two seconds I'm going to pop his head off his shoulders."

Chairs clattered as Jared and Caleb stood. "What's going on?"

Tobias took another drink of his coffee. Jared kept his eye on him and Jace moved Miri back.

"I don't know yet."

Miri tried to come up to his side. He pushed her back again, keeping himself firmly between her and the were. "But I think our friend here just wore out his welcome."

"You can't hurt him," Miri said.

"Watch me."

Miri made a sound between the hiss of a cat and a choke. "No, I mean you *can't* hurt him."

He didn't take his eyes off the were. "Explain."

"He's an Enforcer."

"The picture's not getting any clearer."

Jared cleared the table in one leap, landing beside Tobias. "According to legend, in exchange for their promise to uphold the laws of their people, they were given superior strength, superior skills, and some abilities more rumor than fact, as no one's ever seen them in action and lived to tell about it."

Tobias put his coffee cup down. "You're well informed."

"Jared's always been a sucker for fairy tales."

The corner of Tobias's mouth lifted. "A smart man always hears the truth in the legend."

"Why are you here?" Caleb asked, that same deadly quiet radiating from him that radiated from the were.

"For me," Miri whispered.

"Technically, no." He pushed the cup toward Jared. "Top that off, would you?"

Jared didn't move.

He sighed. "Technically, I'm here for Faith."

"You can't have her." Carefully enunciated, cold, the words flowed into the silence. Miri stepped around Jace and advanced on Tobias.

"She's pack," Miri snarled.

Jace reached for her. She evaded his grip and took another step toward the powerful were. The scent of blood mingled with the scents of coffee and rage.

"She's pack," Miri repeated as she cleared the table in a blinding flash of speed, "and she's mine." Miri shoved her face into Tobias's, her claws pressing into the hollow of his throat. "You try to touch one hair on her head, and I'll make one aspect of myth a lie."

Jace lunged forward. Caleb grabbed his arm, holding him back when he would have yanked her back.

Unbelievably, Tobias smiled as if blood wasn't welling from the four points where Miri's claws pressed. "You're a pretty little thing."

"Fuck you."

His fingertips touched her cheek. "Whenever you want."

"Get your goddamn hands off her," Jace swore as an invisible energy surrounded him, immobilizing him. He felt his brothers' shock. The same energy that surrounded him imprisoned them.

Tobias glanced over. "She doesn't appear too happy with you."

"What makes you think that?"

"You don't bear her mark." He stroked his finger down the corner of Miri's mouth. "Pretty little weres happy with their mates can't resist marking them."

That was news to him.

On a *Got it* from Jared, the energy around them lifted. With a snarl, Jace leapt for Miri, his brothers for Tobias.

Jace wrapped his arm around Miri's waist, yanking her away

from the were. Tobias didn't resist when Jared and Caleb grabbed him by the arms. "I've heard about you. A vampire with Enforcer powers." The statement was directed at Jared as Tobias stood quietly in their arms.

"So you came to check me out?"

"Yes."

"And take my niece."

Tobias shrugged.

"Interesting time to lose the power of speech," Caleb noted.

"He can't lie," Miri said.

"Literally?" Jace asked, holding her tighter into his side, the horror of having been trapped while she put herself in danger too strong to allow him to release her just yet.

"Yes."

"Which would mean you're not here just to take Faith. You're here to make a decision about her."

No answer from Tobias.

"He's here to kill her," Miri said too calmly.

That hit Jace wrong. "No, he's not."

Miri's claws raked the backs of his hands. "He's an Enforcer. He has to."

Jace looked at the man. Sure, he had the cold eyes of a man used to doing what needed to be done, and he had enough gall for seven men, but there was a sense of honor about him. A clear purpose that came from a clear conscience. "Killing a baby isn't an easy thing, Miri."

"Everything's easy for an Enforcer. They have no conscience."

Jace had met his share of conscienceless men in his day and the man studying Miri and ignoring the two vamps holding his arms wasn't one of them. His eyes lingered on the scars on her cheeks and pity touched the edges of his gaze before disappearing behind the mask of his blank expression.

"You get your information on Enforcers from the same place you got your information on vampires?" Jace asked.

"Yes." She yanked at her arms. "What are you waiting for? Kill him."

"I'm considering the source."

The flicker of a smile over Tobias's face was another surprise. Miri's hiss of anger was not.

"Did Ian send you?" Caleb asked.

"Yes."

"Why?"

"To protect his interests."

Ian's interests were pack interests, which meant Miri and Faith. Ian had sent the most powerful were he knew to protect them.

"Are you here to kill me?" Jace asked.

"If necessary."

That was honest. Over Miri's snarl, Jace asked, "What would make it necessary?"

"I'll let you know when I find out."

"Fair enough." Jace nodded at Caleb and Jared. "Let him go."

As soon as he was free, Tobias grabbed his coffee cup and strolled over to the pot as if the room wasn't seething with tension.

"Are you crazy?" Miri gasped, staring at Tobias.

He was a lot of things, but not that. "No."

"He'll kill Faith."

"Whatever rumors you've heard, I'm looking at a man, princess, and killing an infant isn't something a man does easily."

"Well, he wouldn't find it hard to kill you."

"I don't go down easy, Miri. And any man whose personal code forbids him to lie would have pretty tight rules about when he could kill."

"Pack law says he has to kill you if he doesn't want control of the pack to go to a vampire."

"Pack law says he can kill Jace, not that he should," Caleb interjected, watching Tobias in the way he had of doing when he was working on a puzzle.

"What difference does that make?" she asked, pushing against his side.

"About as much difference between a mate being marked and not marked," Tobias answered, leaning back against the counter.

Miri shifted uncomfortably and glared harder at the were. "That's none of your business."

Tobias shrugged. "It is if I decide it's so."

Another if. The man talked a lot in ifs. And every one seemed to pluck at Miri's nerves. Enough so, that Jace was beginning to wonder if he was doing it on purpose.

Caleb sighed and ran his hand through his hair. "Hell. What do you want to do?"

"Sit down," Tobias said.

Jared nodded. "I can go for that." He cocked an eyebrow at Tobias. "What about you?"

"I didn't want to get up in the first place."

Jace shook his head, his sense of humor tickled despite his weariness. "True enough."

It took about a minute for everyone to calm down enough to resume their seats and when they did, Miri was at the far end of the table on Jace's lap with a wall of Johnsons between her and Tobias. The were's only reaction was another twitch of his lips.

Damn, but Jace found himself liking the guy.

Miri turned her head so fast their noses bumped. "I can't believe you thought that. He's planning to kill you!"

"That hasn't been established." And then he realized what she'd done. "You read my thoughts?"

"Not on purpose."

Jared laughed. "Jace has always been contrary. Liking a man who wants to kill him is right on course."

"How did you know—" She cut herself off, acceptance in her sigh. "You're very good with energy."

"Yup."

She glanced at Caleb. "What are you good at?"

"A lot of things."

"And you?" She glanced at Tobias.

"Upholding the letter of the law."

Her chin came up. "Just keep the letter of your law off my mate."

Tobias took a sip of his coffee. "You're claiming him?"

Miri's answer was a flash of her canines.

Pretty little weres happy with their mates can't resist marking them. The Enforcer's words came back to him. She was protecting him with every snarl she had, yet Miri hadn't marked him. And marking was significant. Son of a bitch.

Jace pulled her tighter against him, the tension in her body transferring to him. Where did wolves leave their mark? On the shoulder, the neck? He pictured Miri beneath him as he loved her, her face beautiful with her passion. Projected where her mouth would land. His right pectoral burned. He wanted her mark there.

Jared cleared his throat and Tobias laughed. One glance at their faces and he knew he'd been projecting.

"Just shut up."

Miri frowned. "What?"

Hell, if he had to project, why hadn't it been to her? "Nothing."

Caleb leaned back in his chair. "If we're done playing king of the hill, can someone tell me what the hell happened tonight?"

"We walked into a trap."

"Faith wasn't there?"

"Someone has been there, but we don't know if it was Faith."

"Why the hell not?"

"We tripped a booby trap before we could get Miri in to confirm the scent."

"It was Faith."

There was no doubting the conviction in Tobias's voice. Miri certainly didn't.

"She's alive." It wasn't a question. "She was there until about four hours before we arrived."

"How could you tell?" Jared asked.

Tobias shrugged. "Part of my special powers."

"Do your special powers have the ability to tell me who has my niece now?" Caleb asked, almost conversationally, though anyone who knew him could tell he was coiled tighter than a rattler ready to strike.

"No, but the overwhelming scent there was vampire."

The only vampires Jace knew outside of themselves were Sanctuary. The small expulsion of air Miri made was almost indistinct, yet every eye turned to her. Hell, she didn't need to hear this. Jace pulled Miri close, as if through the tightness of his grip he could keep her from understanding what that meant. It was impossible.

"You're saying they have her."

"I'm saying a vampire has her."

"It's the same thing."

"Maybe not," Caleb offered. "We're pretty sure it was a vampire who got her out of the Sanctuary stronghold."

"He said he was were."

"A were wouldn't have had the powers to get a baby out of the Sanctuary."

Jace held Miri tighter, looking at Tobias again, suspicion licking hot along his control. "But an Enforcer would."

"Don't look at me," Tobias countered. "If I were the one who had Faith, she'd be tucked away safe among the D'Nallys."

"But not with her mother," Jared murmured.

Tobias shrugged. "I didn't know where she was and my first priority would be the safety of the baby."

"But not the safety of her mother?"

"Had anyone known Miri was alive, her safety would have been a priority. We only became aware of her situation recently."

"Has my wife been telling tales again?" Jared asked.

Tobias didn't say a word. He didn't need to. Jace was beginning to think the man's silences were more important than his words. Apparently, so did Jared.

"I can see my Raisa is a bit overdue to have her butt paddled."

Miri's rage slammed into him like a hammer as her snarl ripped into the room. "Don't you touch her!" Jace caught the back of her shirt just in case she intended to go for the man. She didn't, but tension was in every line of her body. Her elbow connected with his side. "Let me go!"

Jared merely cocked a brow at Jace. "Hell of a temper your wife has there."

"She's passionate about everything she cares about," he muttered, reeling her in with an arm around her waist.

Miri dug her claws into Jace's arm, adding new cuts to the old. "Tell her you're not going to touch Raisa, before she turns me into a pincushion."

Jared, of course, chose that moment to become uncooperative. "What I do with my wife is my business."

The claws cut deeper. "Let me go!"

"No." Miri's snarls rolled from her throat, punctuated with tiny, high-pitched gasps as she struggled to get free.

"Miri, sweet, settle." Instead of settling, she struggled harder. Her claw caught on his cheekbone, just under his eye, nicking the skin. He didn't think she noticed as her attention was all on Jared. "No," she snarled as her muscles gathered to fight, her gaze fixed on Jared. "I won't let it happen again."

It was the first clue Jace had to the mystery of what she locked so deep. Witnesses or not, he wasn't losing it. "Not let what happen, Miri?"

Sweat poured off her, bitter with fear and stress. Images flashed through his mind: Raisa screaming, agony in her eyes, her pretty face distorted by whatever was happening; another woman, another face, this time blood; men's bodies surrounding the woman as they held her down. Faces whirling through guilt. So much guilt for surviving, for not being able to give them what they needed so no one else would be hurt. It was as if Raisa's and the other woman's screams had gouged permanent holes in her soul. Wounds that would never heal. Aching wounds she hoarded for the time when she could find a way to forget.

A rumbling joined the screams. A chair scraped back. Jace looked up and found the same snarl on his brothers' lips that was on his own. Not surprisingly, he'd been projecting, but that low rumble was coming from Tobias.

"Not again what, Miri?" Jace repeated.

"He's not going to hurt her because of me."

"Son of a bitch."

Jared came around the table, squatted down in front of Miri, and lifted her chin.

He waited a second, studying Miri's face, his eyes lit with flames, before he continued. "Nothing will ever hurt Raisa again. I promise you."

None of the tension left Miri. "You're vampire."

Jared cocked his brow at Jace in silent question.

"Just rank yourself around the level of a cow turd. It saves time."

"If we're so despicable, why'd you pick one as your mate?"

Without a pause the words came tripping off her tongue. "Mating is not a choice."

Jace was getting damn sick and tired of hearing that.

"Well, I'm not pack, and for me it is a choice. I waited a long time for Raisa to come into my life, so you can rest easy on one score—it's my life's work to keep her happy and smiling."

"He's pretty good at it, too," Caleb offered. "Think it's been a whole week since she set him on his ass."

Miri just blinked. Drops of blood dripped onto her shirt, sinking into the pale pink of her blouse. She tugged at her hand. He released it. She reached up, touching the spot. When she stared uncomprehendingly at the red on her fingers, he turned her in his lap, resting his cheek on her hair. "It's not the Johnson way to hurt a woman."

"Actually, it's rumored they spoil their women," Tobias offered.

He didn't say that with approval.

Miri just lay against him, unconvinced. "Jared would die rather than harm a hair on Raisa's head, Miri."

"Then why did she put him on his butt?"

Jace brushed his lips against her hair. Hair that usually smelled like a clean breath of spring, but which now harbored the scents of panic and fear and stress.

"Because he likes to tease her and because they've only been together a few weeks, he can be dense as to when enough is enough."

"True enough." Jared smiled. The sternness of his features softened as he pushed to his feet. "And the fact that she feels a need to make it up to me afterward is darn attractive."

"Figures sex would be in there somewhere."

"Like it doesn't with wolves."

Tobias shrugged. "I wouldn't know. I'm not mated."

Miri slowly straightened. Her gaze locked on the were as if a puzzle piece had fallen into place.

"That's why you're here, isn't it?" Miri asked. "You're looking for an outlaw. You think he's here."

Tobias neither denied it nor confirmed it.

"That's a pretty damning silence," Jared offered.

"And here I thought it was just silence."

"You've got an outlaw Enforcer on the loose?" Caleb asked.

"We're not sure he's Renegade."

"How can you not know?"

"Because he's not one of us," Tobias answered, an edge to his voice.

"What in hell does that mean? If it walks like a duck and quacks like duck, it's a duck," Jared snapped.

"Unless there's no record of the duck's existence. Then it can be about any damn thing it wants."

"Son of a bitch. Things didn't used to be so complicated back in the day. We had the occasional cattle rustler, rabid fox, Indian raid, but at least we knew who in hell was the bad guy."

"Feeling nostalgic?" Jared asked.

Caleb finished off the last of his coffee. "Things are changing too fast."

"Vampire, Enforcer, what does it matter?" Miri whispered. She turned her face into his chest. "How are we going to get Faith back if we don't know who has her?"

The soft whisper slid into the silence, putting all their fears into the open.

Jace cupped her head in his hand, holding her close, taking her pain into his own, doing his best to shelter her from both. "By not giving up until we find her."

❧ 10 ❧

LOST. Miri moaned, holding her stomach against the pain. Her little girl was lost. She'd sent her out into the world because she'd wanted to do what was best, and now her baby was lost in the hands of a monster.

"Don't go believing the worst, Miri."

She shook her head, denying the hysterical bubble of laughter that burst against the hard muscle of Jace's chest. "Why would I have to do that? Imagining the best is bad enough."

"I hate to be the one to point it out," Jace said, his drawl low and confident, "but your optimism is slipping."

"You just noticed?"

"I can be slow on the uptake."

He'd never been slow on anything, but he was trying to spare her by providing a distraction. She could feel him probing her mind, siphoning off emotion in gentle sips, fighting for her sanity harder than *she* ever could. She licked her lips and took the lifeline he offered. "Why am I in charge of optimism, anyway?"

"Because I'm in charge of kicking ass. Jared's in charge of search and destroy. Caleb is in charge of planning, and Slade is in charge of survival. That just leaves optimism for you."

She pushed her hair off her face, but she didn't push away. Jace was solid. Strong. And he was holding her lifeline. The hope that someday she'd get her baby back, her faith back, her trust back.

"We just might be in trouble."

"No. We're not." He eased her a step away. She resented the cool air that filled the gap between them. She resented the time between them. Resented more than anything that their lives weren't normal, that their daughter wasn't here. He bent. She reached. In the next second she was in his arms. "Where are we going?"

"To bed. You need to rest and recover."

From the abortion or her conversion?

The answer slipped into her mind with the delicacy of a kiss. *Both.*

I can't talk about that with you.

She didn't have to explain what she meant. He knew.

You will.

She closed her eyes and buried her face in his neck. *No.*

Even as she thought it, she knew she would.

Jace nodded to the others. "We'll catch you all later tonight."

She looked over his shoulder. Tobias was watching her. As she'd known he would be. "Don't go anywhere," he told her.

"Wasn't planning on it."

The reminder made her uncomfortable. She spread her fingers wide, covering as much of Jace's neck as she could. If she didn't need him so much, she would have ordered the brothers to get rid of the were, but she did need him. She needed everything she could throw at her daughter's rescue. And an Enforcer was a very big something.

"You don't need to shield me, Miri," Jace said. "Tobias isn't the type to stab me in the back."

A hitch of her arm between them and she could see Jace's face. "How do you know?"

"He's an honorable man."

"He's an Enforcer. They're capable of anything."

"Capable is not a bad thing, sweet. And if you'd stop wiggling, I'd take you back to our cabin and prove it to you."

Sex. He was talking about sex. "Do you think of anything else?"

JACE opened the kitchen door, breathing deeply of the early morning air. Dawn was cracking the shell of the night, pale beams of light filtering through cracks in the darkness and filling them with light.

"After a year of doing without, not hardly."

The soft puffs of her breath ceased, retracted, started again.

"You don't have to lie to me, Jace."

The comment hit him harder than it should. His response was dry. "Let me guess. Fidelity isn't something vampires are capable of."

"That isn't what I said."

The cabin was next door to the house. Too short a walk in which to get rid of his anger, long enough for him to feel the burn of her disbelief. He skipped the stairs and leapt to the porch.

"You know, with all those negative thoughts you have about me, it's a wonder you took up with me at all."

She had the gall to look surprised. "I don't think badly of you."

He let her slide down his body as he reached for the door. "Well, if that's the case, you might want to start communicating something positive before my ego takes any more of a beating."

She stood there, arms wrapped around her torso as the breeze toyed with her hair, blowing strands across her face in tentacles of darkness. She didn't push them away. "Your ego seems healthy enough."

He cleared the hair from her face, enjoying the slide of silky softness against the back of his fingers as he tucked it behind her ears. "That's because you're only looking at the surface."

She blinked. He felt the brush of her mind. It was easy to deflect the probe. Just as easy to understand the source of her frown. If she wanted answers, she could just ask him. If she wasn't going to believe those answers, then she could just stop wasting time by asking.

Reaching around her, he opened the door. It swung inward on a soft creak. Just inside, the alarm panel flashed. The two steps it took for him to get close enough to push the buttons seemed to put a mile between them. In the old days, her energy would have trailed him, reaching out in subtle tendrils, caressing him, connecting them. But now when he stepped away, he left her behind on the other side of a deep chasm. On the surface that gap looked too wide to bridge. He sent out a whisper of energy; immediately her energy wrapped around it. On the surface. He turned back. Miri was standing just inside the door, smothering a yawn.

"As soon as we get you fed, you can hit the bed."

She dropped her hand from her mouth. "I'd rather just go straight to bed."

That wasn't going to happen. She was too thin, too weak, and too determined to be part of everything going on to stay disabled. "You'll eat first."

"I'm not hungry."

"Whether you feel hungry or not, your body needs food." He grabbed her hand. Her fingers felt very small in his. Her bones seemed very fragile, and her were skin was too cold. "And you need to feed."

"I do not want to feed from you."

"I have it on good authority that in cases like this, I get to tell you, 'Tough.'"

She knew exactly who he was talking about. "No one goes to an Enforcer for social advice."

"Why not?" He tugged. She planted her feet. "As keepers of the law, I'd think they'd be the perfect ones to ask. Besides, he offered, I didn't ask."

"I just bet." She grabbed at his fingers and pried.

He didn't actually have to drag her into the kitchen, but he wouldn't say she went willingly. "I'm only going to feed you. There's no need for the drama."

"What drama? I'm following along like a lamb to the slaughter."

He pulled out a chair. "Seems to me, for a wolfie, you've got your predators mixed up with your prey."

She stood by the chair. "I don't feel much like a wolf these days."

"I got that impression." He motioned. "Sit."

She did, slowly, as if she was worried about falling. Eyes narrowed, he looked beyond the lines of strain to the life force beneath. "Just how weak are you feeling?"

"What makes you think I'm weak?"

"What makes you think you can hide it from me?"

"What makes you think I can't?"

"What makes you think I'll keep playing this game?"

She blinked rapidly and opened her eyes angelically wide. "Wishful thinking?"

He couldn't help it; he cupped her head in his palm and kissed her hard, laughter and exasperation spicing the moment. He rested his forehead against hers, taking her anxious breaths as his. "You might be a bit down and out, but you sure haven't lost any of your sass."

"Did you want me to?"

He rested his forehead against hers. "I never wanted you to lose a damn thing."

Her lashes lowered, covering, but not hiding, the way her eyes darkened until her irises blended into the black of her pupils and only the D'Nally gold rimmed the outside. Her lips tightened into a full line. She blinked, fighting tears. He hated himself again for not understanding what she'd needed from him back then. For the arrogance that assumed love would be enough. For ignoring her culture and how that would affect her needs. For not putting her first in a way she understood.

"I might have been an arrogant ass a year ago, too full of myself, too confident of you to look beyond my own needs, but there hasn't been a minute since I met you, that I didn't love you."

Her tongue came out and moistened the curve of her lower lip. It wasn't a sexual gesture, but his starved body reacted as if it were. His cock stretched and engorged, his pulse picked up, his breath quickened. Being were and his mate she had to scent his interest. The tear that had been hovering in her eye dripped down her cheek. He caught it on his thumb; it pooled for a minute before giving up the fight with gravity and sliding down his finger.

"This is not supposed to make you cry."

"It's too late for us."

"Why do you say that?"

"Because it just doesn't matter anymore. I'm not the same woman you knew. I can't be who you want, see things the way I used to." She shrugged. "It's just too late."

She really believed what she was saying. His defection, as she saw it, the torture she'd endured the last year, her fight for her baby, then the loss of the last, they had all taken a toll on her optimism. He knelt down so his face was level with hers. He cupped her cheeks in his palms, placing his thumbs over the scars he knew shamed her. "It's not all about loss, princess."

"Right now it is. My pack, my mate, my daughter . . ."

He stroked his thumbs over her cheekbones. "You never lost me."

"I know that, now." Her fingers wrapped around his wrists, a fragile connection. "It was just the illusion of who I thought you were."

A stable, steady were. He got that. "That doesn't have to be a bad thing. A little difference keeps a relationship interesting."

She licked her lips. "I know when we got together, I gave you the impression I was looking for excitement, and maybe I was, but I've learned that I'm not really that kind of person. I'm a were to my bones. I need a mate I can depend on. One who doesn't leave me guessing if he's coming home."

The words struck him like a hard rain of body blows. They emphasized more than anything else how much damage had been done to their relationship. The worst part was, he couldn't blame her. He had let her down. It didn't matter that it had been unintentional. The results were the same. "I won't leave you again, baby."

The sadness of the world was in her eyes as she looked up at him. "It doesn't matter anymore if you do."

"You said mating wasn't a choice."

"I did."

"I'm not getting your point."

"This is not the time for this."

"It is if I say it is."

"I don't love you anymore, Jace."

The hell she didn't. He wanted to shove that fact down her throat, force her to face what he knew had to be in her heart, but he couldn't. Not when she was looking at him like that. Not when she was so weak her hands trembled. He was her husband. Her mate. And no matter how much he'd fucked up in the past, from here on out he was going to be the man she thought he was. "You're tired."

The look she shot him let him know she knew what he was doing. "That doesn't change the truth." Her gaze did not flinch from his. "Beyond the mating pull, there's no connection between us anymore."

He paused, his thumbs centered on the sharp ledge of her cheekbones beneath those wolf eyes that saw so much. "Then I guess it's going to be up to me to reconnect us."

Her lower lip quivered. That vibration shivered into his palm, lodging in the nerve endings there, opening a pathway from her to him. He took full advantage of it, lowering his head, bringing his mouth to within a hairbreadth of hers. She didn't move, didn't breathe, just sat there frozen so the only thing joining them was the expectation of his kiss. He waited to see if she would be the one to bridge the distance between them, if she could take that first step.

It didn't happen. It didn't matter. He wasn't afraid to take the leap. She might think that mating wasn't a choice, but it was for him. From the moment he'd seen her sitting on that rock surrounded by trees and wildflowers he'd known this was his woman.

Every time they'd been together, every time their energy touched, it had just reinforced that reality for him. He'd thought it was the same for her. And it had been, but her need had more levels. He hadn't realized that then, but now that he knew what she needed, he could give it to her. No holds barred. Every way she wanted. Every way she needed.

He closed the gap between them. The firmness of his lips touched the softness of hers, absorbed that softness, reflected it back, every beat of his heart, every bit of his emotion in the incredibly tender kiss he tried to give her. Communicating with his body, reaching with his mind, looking for the connection, he found her caution instead . . . and didn't care. After all these months of worry, he had her mouth back under his, her breath mingling with his, her body in his arms, her breasts pressed against his chest. His world was righting itself and that was all that mattered for both of them.

With a shudder, Miri collapsed against him. The scent of her desire perfumed the air around them. It mingled with his, lighter, feminine, perfect. An aphrodisiac unto itself. Jace trusted their need to keep her put, sliding his hands down over her shoulders to just below her shoulder blades. His fingers spanned her ribs as he pulled her down off the chair onto his lap, turning her sideways, resting her thighs across his. Her neck slid into the crook of his shoulder as if it'd been created for just that spot. Which he firmly believed it had. He threaded his fingers through that long glorious hair he loved to feel sliding over his skin. Her head tipped back. His doing or hers? He didn't know, didn't care. He was just enjoying the beauty of her face and the surety that she was his as it settled deep into his bones.

She watched him, eyes clouded with desire, darkened with indecision while those full lips parted as if anticipating his kiss. His lips ached with the same expectancy. His head tilted, lowered. Electricity sizzled between them. Miri shivered. Sparks danced over his skin, vibrant electrical impulses shimmering in readiness, as if every bit of desire he had suppressed from the last year had waited for this moment to come back to life, surging forward as the moment culminated in the most delicate of connections.

He took her gasp, demanded her compliance as his mouth opened over hers, easing his tongue between her lips, expecting to have to search for her response, but instead finding it waiting. Her hands crept up over his shoulders and her fingers laced around his neck, the nails nipping his skin in an erotic invitation to take more.

He did, demanding the response that had always been his, getting it with a sigh of relief. No matter how she wanted to deny the emotional connection, it was there behind the fear, behind the desperation. It was there. And all he had to do was reach with his mind to find it. He did, locking her to him. Her moan, as she surrendered, was as betraying as any he'd ever heard.

"Ah, princess, I've missed you."

The sadness that flowed over the energy between them told him of her fear that this was just physical. He drew her closer, sharing his heat and conviction with her.

"I didn't just miss you for this, sweet Miri, though this is good. Very good. I missed your smile and your laughter, the way you get all feisty when I tease you, the way you smile when you're happy." He kissed her nose. "I just missed you."

"I didn't miss you." There was more belligerence than truth in that statement.

"I just bet you didn't. You were probably too angry at me to have charitable thoughts." Her small start was another betrayal. She'd never been raised to hide her feelings. She'd been pampered and indulged. And if he had his way, she'd have gone to her grave with only a pampered, adored knowledge of life. However, nothing had gone his way. "I know about being angry, Miri."

The break in her breathing was as telling as the quick dart of her tongue over her lips. "Who have you been angry with?"

"My brother."

There was a lot of desperation in her "Why?" and a loss of substance. She was about played out.

He stood, easing off the intensity, but not letting go completely of the emotional link. "After you eat, I'll tell you."

"I'm not hungry."

"Yes, you are."

"How you know?"

"Your stomach's gurgling."

Her hands slid to his shoulders. "What does it know? It's just a stomach."

He smiled. "Apparently, it has the good sense to know when it needs to be fed."

"It also knows when it's going to throw up whatever goes into it."

Jace frowned. "You're feeling nauseated?"

He placed his palm over her stomach, probing within. Her outer muscles were smooth, lacking tension, but when he probed beneath, he could feel the contraction of her stomach. The protest against being denied. The need for blood. His blood. "You need to feed."

"What difference will it make if all I swallow comes right back up?"

"Not eat . . . feed."

She blinked and stubbornness replaced tiredness in the faint lines etched around her eyes. "I'm fine."

"You're not fine. You're married to a vampire. As much as you want to deny it, your life is bonded to mine. A blood exchange is necessary."

"I won't bite you."

"Why the hell not?"

"Because that *is* my choice."

And she hadn't decided to choose him. Jace brushed the back of his fingers down her cheek. A smile tugged the corner of his mouth. "Is that a challenge?"

A flare of panic, then she bit her lip before shaking her head. "No."

No doubt she remembered how much he enjoyed a challenge. "I think it is." He slid her to the side, steadying her with his arm around her shoulders before getting to his feet. "What's more, I think I'm going to take you up on it."

She took his hand. "Doesn't what I want count for anything?"

He pulled her up. "What you want pretty much counts for everything." He tapped her chin with his finger until she met his gaze. "But until you can look me in the eye, open your mind, and tell me to stay out of your life, I'm sticking around."

It was a brutal thirty seconds while Jace waited to see if she'd send him packing. Seconds ticked by, but while Miri didn't look away, she also didn't say a word.

"This is your chance, princess. This is a chance to get me out of your life once and forever. All you have to do is open those pretty little lips and tell me to get lost."

Her fists clenched. Her mouth worked, but she didn't say a word. In some ways he wished she would. He wished she'd just light into him and tell him how angry she was, tell him what he had to do to fix it. He wished she'd let it out instead of keeping that pain buried so deep it was like a cancer, eating her from the inside out.

After a full minute had passed, he pulled her back into his arms. Her cheek pressed against his chest, the top of her head snuggling beneath his chin. Just like it always had. Again, the sense of rightness poured over him. He rested his cheek on the top of her head.

Her arms came around his waist slowly, hesitantly. There was a change in her energy. A break in her defenses punctuated by a broken sob. His name came out a faint whisper. "Jace?"

"What?"

"Stick around. Please."

She didn't have to beg. "You prepared to give me a chance?"

"I want to."

"Then it's going to take a crowbar to get me out of your life."

HE managed to get her to eat a peanut butter sandwich. Even got her to drink some milk, though she swore she hated the stuff. He took the empty milk glass from her hand and placed it on the counter.

When he turned around, she was staring at him again. "What?"

She pushed her chair back and got up. "I'll do the dishes."

He took the plate from her hand halfway to the sink. "I think I can handle a milk glass, plate, and knife."

"But you prepared it."

"And you're stalling."

"I prefer to think of it as avoiding a fight."

"Because you think you can out-stubborn me?"

"Because I know I can."

He didn't want to fight with her, either. "Maybe you should just distract me instead."

She cocked her head to the side. Her hair fell over her shoulder. "And how would you suggest I do that?"

He motioned with the plate and gave her his best smile. "You could slip that shirt off your shoulder. You have very pretty shoulders."

She snorted, a very ladylike snort that got her point across. He put the dishes in the sink, not taking his gaze from hers. "No striptease, huh?"

"You've seen all there is to see."

"Doesn't mean I'll ever get tired of looking at it."

"I'm were, remember. I expect my mate to desire me. This is not impressing me."

"Well, hell. You know what that means, don't you?"

"No, what?"

"Some of my best lines are as good as dead and buried."

A very wan smile touched her lips. "I guess so."

Although her smile was wan, it was strong compared to her energy. Jace left the dishes and came to her side. He took her hand and brought her within scooping distance. She didn't struggle when he picked her up. Just lay against him with a weary acceptance that worried him.

She patted his chest. "You did promise me a story."

"How about I make it a bedtime story?"

Her hair spilled across his arm as she shook her head. "I want a shower first."

"I can probably arrange that."

"It's a simple procedure that doesn't require much arranging."

He shook his head at her blindness. "In case you haven't noticed, I'm trying to pamper you."

"Is that what you're doing?"

"Yup." He set her down on the big bed. "What did you think I was doing?"

She leaned back. Her breasts thrust against her shirt. "I thought you were keeping tabs on me."

Damn, she had pretty breasts. "Do I need to?"

She shrugged. "You're pretty safe, at least until we find Faith."

"You've put that much stock in me?"

Again, the shrug. "You're all I've got. First mating isn't a choice, and then there's no other option."

He leaned in, following her down as she fell back, catching his weight on his elbows, imprisoning her against the mattress with his body. "You don't leave a man much confidence."

She placed her palms against his chest. As barriers went, it wasn't much. Especially when he took into account the way they rubbed in subtle enticement.

"I was going to take a shower."

He settled his hips between hers. "I know."

"What are you doing, then?"

He lowered his torso, and the softness of her breasts cushioned the last inch of his descent. "Stealing a kiss from my wife."

"What if I don't want to give you a kiss?"

The catch in her breath betrayed her interest. He didn't answer until his lips were a shiver of a "Yes" from hers. "That's why it's called stealing."

She grabbed his shirt, a fierce expression tightening the skin at the corners of her eyes. The tips of her canines flashed between her parted lips. "No one's taking anything from me, ever again."

He didn't move, just let her aggression surge over him, tracing it back to its origin, funneling it off. "Then why don't you give it to me instead?"

Those fangs sank into her lower lip. Her head canted the slightest bit to the side, lifted . . . The hardest thing he'd ever done was to not bend his neck and take what they both wanted. "You're killing me, Miri."

Her "How?" whispered over his cheek.

"You know."

"You're hungry."

"Starving."

"For a kiss?"

"Your kiss."

Her eyes closed for a poignant moment. "Oh, God, I'm so afraid to do this again."

He couldn't do anything but let her torment flow over him. Some things she had a right to decide for herself. "Do what?"

"Give myself to you again."

He slid his hand between her and the mattress. "I never let you go."

"But you wanted to."

"Never."

Her fingers fluttered over his cheek. "I thought you did."

"I'm sorry for that."

Tears gathered in her eyes and pooled at the corners "Why the tears?"

"Because I believe you."

He brushed a tear away before it could fall. "And that hurts?"

"It all hurts."

"Share it with me, Miri. All of it. Let it go, baby."

She shook her head. "I can't."

"I can take it."

"I can't."

"Then kiss me instead."

She did. A kiss salted with tears, flooded with heartache. A kiss that twisted his heart in his chest. Her lips parted, and he accepted the invitation, letting her into his soul, his mind, allowing her to keep herself apart, understanding why she felt she had to.

Her arms came around his neck, pulling him down. He went, giving her a bit more of his weight, groaning as her legs wrapped around his hips, pulling his groin to hers, wiggling a bit in a sensual greeting.

He caught her hip in his hand. "Easy."

She kissed the corner of his mouth. "Why?"

"Because you're tired and hurting, and you've just lost a baby."

Fear tainted the beauty of arousal. "It wasn't something I wanted."

He knew damn well she didn't think of that lost baby as an "it." The fact that she kept using that term when talking to him was telling. "But that baby was part of you."

She blinked rapidly. "I didn't want to betray you."

"You didn't."

"They thought they'd found someone I would be compatible with. They implanted the fertilized egg, gave me drugs to keep it alive—"

He cut her off. "You don't have anything to apologize for. I'm not were, I'm vampire, and even before that I used to be known as a fair-minded son of a bitch."

Her neutrality slipped. "I didn't want him at first."

"It was a boy?"

She swallowed and nodded. "I didn't want him, but he was alive, part of me. Before they aborted it, I felt his presence."

"Jesus Christ."

"I couldn't hate him. I tried to shield him, but I couldn't."

She buried her face in his shoulder, her tears soaking his shirt, not making a sound, just crying tears that spoke of a pain too deep for words. He held her, giving her the only support he could, trying to imagine how that would have felt. To have a pregnancy forced upon her, to have felt the life, knowing a were husband wouldn't tolerate another's offspring, not knowing how he would have reacted, to have bonded with that first faint stirring and have it ripped away. He couldn't, but he could give her one small bit of peace.

"I would have welcomed the child, Miri."

"It doesn't matter."

He tugged her head back and wiped the moisture from her cheek with the heel of his hand. "It matters to me. He would have been part of you. That alone would have made me love him."

She sniffed. "Thank you."

"You believe me?"

"Yes."

At least she knew that much about him. "Thank you."

His thumb wasn't doing such a good job of cleaning up her face. "Hold on a sec."

He unlocked her ankles from behind him and got up. When he came back she was almost asleep. He wiped her face with the warm washcloth, plucked a couple tissues off the bed stand, and handed them to her. When she finished blowing her nose, he held the small trash can for their disposal. She could barely keep her eyes open.

"How about we hold off on that shower until morning?"

"You were going to tell me a story."

"I'll tell you while you get ready for bed."

She turned on her side and tucked her hand under her cheek. "I'm ready."

Tenderness suffused him. "Then close your eyes."

She was out before he brushed the hair off her face. He undressed her down to her underwear, pausing to take in the sharp edges of her ribs, the knifelike points of her shoulder blades. He pulled back the covers before laying her up on the pillows. He stripped down and slid in beside her, spooning his much bigger body around hers, wrapping his arm around her waist, pulling her into his heat. She murmured something. Maybe approval. He kissed her hair. "Sleep, princess. Things will be better tomorrow."

➤ 11 ➤

THINGS were not getting better. The conversion pain in Miri's stomach was intensifying, the despair in her soul increasing as past and present warred with wrong and right. Everything in her wanted only one thing: the one thing she was afraid to accept. Jace. He lay in the big bed beside her, his hand cupping her thigh in his sleep, his warmth encompassing her in a persistent hug, but in some ways there might as well be miles between them. Miri turned on her side in the big bed, into the sleep-warmed heat of Jace's embrace. The broad expanse of his chest filled her vision. Large bones padded with beautifully sculpted muscle. Totally masculine. Totally tempting. She placed her finger in the muscle cut just under his shoulder joint, where her mark would go if she decided to complete their union, before following the well-defined groove down over his side. Power and passion, that was Jace. The light dusting of dark hair on his chest tickled the back of her knuckles as she admired the visual proof of his strength. No wonder he made her feel both distinctly feminine and distinctly vulnerable at the same time. If he were the violent type, he could probably break her back with just a single blow.

She drew her fingers away until only the sensitive tips were bathed in the warmth of his skin. One of her greatest pleasures pre-Sanctuary had been to lay her cheek on his chest and listen to the steady beat of his heart, feel her own slow its beat, hear his increase until they were in total synch. It made her feel safe, secure, part of a much greater whole. The way belonging to the pack did. That sense of total rightness was what had made the devastating decision to turn her back on her pack possible.

She understood now that it had been too easy. She was a female were brought up in security, her gender and lineage promising a life of pampering and adoration. If she had been thinking along with feeling she would have experienced at least a qualm at the prospect of leaving all she knew. Yet one look at Jace and the wildness he wore so easily, and she'd thrown herself into his arms, embroiled herself in his life because it called to the wildness in her that would never be let out as the cherished, protected mate of an Alpha were.

She did not want to make that mistake again.

She scooted up on the pillows, being careful not to jostle the bed and wake Jace. He got so little sleep. Aligning her face with his, she placed her hand on his chest, dead center between the slabs of his pectorals. Against the side of her thumb she could feel his heartbeat. Slow and steady and dependable, not the least erratic. Like the man himself.

I would have welcomed the child, Miri.

She believed him, which raised all sorts of havoc with her convictions again. A year and a half ago, she'd declared Jace all wolf. After her imprisonment, she'd declared him all vampire. Now she had to pick one extreme or the other or settle on a third option. That maybe he was a man she didn't know as well as she should. The last was scary because it meant she had to look at him in a new light, evaluate him again with an open heart. Expose herself to hurt again.

She shifted on the bed, studying his expression, wishing the answers she sought were written on his face as clearly as was his confidence. She loved Jace's face. Loved the way the wildness of his nature was etched in every harsh plane. The way the slash of his cheekbones proclaimed the predator within, the way the jut of his chin declared his determination. And right now, he was determined to complete the union between them. Moving slowly, she eased her cheek onto his shoulder. The pain in her stomach bit deeply. She didn't know how much longer she was going to last against it. Jace's vampire was definitely outmaneuvering her wolf when it came to pressure to complete the conversion. But she could hold out a little longer, give herself time to make the right decision. As if he heard her thoughts, Jace's lashes flickered, and he frowned. The sheets whispered a warning as his hand moved, whispering again when his fingers opened across her lower back and pressed. She felt the touch of his power. The nausea abated and so did the pain, dropping out of her consciousness to beat harmlessly against an invisible buffer. The frown on Jace's face smoothed out. He grunted in satisfaction.

Watching his expression for a couple of minutes, she assured herself he was still asleep before sighing and snuggling a little deeper into his embrace. She'd made a mistake a year and a half ago in judging him by were standards. Probably because a lot of things about his personality made her think of pack—his absolute loyalty to family, the honor that made his word his bond, his self-control, and his care for things that were weaker than him. Those were all very familiar Alpha traits, and what she'd clung to when making the decision to mate outside pack. She hadn't wanted to see all of him. Just the part that was familiar, because that she could understand, and she'd needed the comfort of a husband she understood. In many ways, she was beginning to understand that the problems between them were her fault. Jace had never asked her to be more than she was, but she'd wanted him to change, to the point that she'd dismissed any part of him that hadn't been wolf-like. Not a comfortable realization, but one she could no longer ignore. *I would have welcomed the child, Miri.*

Again the calm statement, spoken with absolute assurance, replayed through her mind. It was no small gift Jace had offered her. Complete acceptance of her and all important to her, no questions asked. It would have been harder for a were to give that acceptance; their culture adored children, but male weres were defined by their ability to protect. A stolen mate returning with a child not his own would be hard for a were male to accept easily because of what it represented: failure in the two things he'd been reared to do, protect his mate and guard his pack. Jace, however, had a more open view. He was as aggressive as any wolf in guarding what was his, but in his world, "shit happened." And when it did, people adjusted and moved on. It was a less absolute view of the world, and one she could appreciate, standing on this side of hell.

Ever so lightly, Miri touched the stubble on Jace's cheek. The difference in her skin color from his was just another mark of the difference between them. Her coffee and cream fairness looked pale against his deep tan. Being vampire, he should be pale. He would blend better with other vampires if he was pale, but Jace wasn't interested in blending. He wore his past of outlaw and gunslinger like all the Johnsons reportedly did—as a banner and a challenge. She smiled and touched her nose to his. Her outlaw. His eyes cracked open. A sleepy smile tipped his lips. "Morning."

It was silly to feel shy, but she did. She scooted back. "Good morning, yourself."

The mattress dipped as he shifted his weight more onto his side. "How are you feeling this morning?"

Achy. Depressed. Optimistic. "Better than last night."

"Why do I get the feeling that you're hedging?"

She let her palm come to rest against his cheek. "Maybe because I am."

He reached up, his fingertips grazing her back, her shoulder, and her forearm before covering hers, holding them against his face. "Want to tell me why?"

Surprisingly, she did. "I never got to know the real you, did I?"

"That was my impression."

Nothing in his inflection gave her any idea, plus or minus, how he felt about that. "I think I was afraid if I did, I'd have to let you go."

His eyebrow kicked up. "You act like I wouldn't have had a say in the matter."

It seemed so natural to lie there his arms, drowsy from a full day's sleep and talk about the past as the night settled like a soft dream around them. "In the pack, women do the choosing."

Turning his head, Jace pressed a hot kiss to the center of her palm. Tiny lines fanned out from the corners of his eyes, betraying the smile still working its way fully to his lips. "And it's the man who does the persuading." Another kiss, a deeper smile, and the butterfly touch of his tongue. "And it would be a real pleasure to persuade you all over again."

With a shimmer of sensation, his energy slipped over hers, increasing the illusion that it was just them in this room, in this house, in this time. It had been so long since she'd had that feeling of safety, that special peace, and she didn't want to lose it by being afraid to take what was offered. "Maybe you should."

Everything in him went still. "Should what?"

Now he had to go all obtuse. "For one thing, not question an invite once you get it."

"Uh-huh." He shifted over her. "I don't want any more misunderstandings between us."

She could accept that, but she couldn't accept this distance between them. "Kiss me, Jace."

He propped himself up on his elbow. His shadow fell over her. "Why?"

The roughness of his beard pricked her skin as she touched the pad of her thumb to the softness of his lower lip. This was hard, scary, and liberating all in one. "I need you to remind me of how it was."

"I'm afraid I can't do that." He skimmed his hand up her arm, over her shoulder, until his fingers threaded through her hair at the nape of her neck. "The past is gone."

The pain of his admission stabbed deep until his thumb tucked into the corner of her mouth and he whispered, "But I can show you how it's going to be from here on out."

Yes. Something to hold on to. To believe in. That was what she needed. What they both needed. Her whisper was just as soft. "Show me."

The flex of his muscles was the only indication that she'd surprised him. "What are you asking, princess?"

"I want you to make love to me, Jace. Not like a man seducing an innocent were with too many stars in her eyes. Not like a man who has something to make up for, but just as . . . you."

His gaze narrowed. Invisible sparks arced between them in a sizzling perk of awareness.

"I'm not sure what you mean."

"Men have used my body for a lot of reasons."

"I never used you."

She touched his frown, understanding coming to her. "Yes, you did. In the nicest possible way, but in the short time we were together, part of the reason you made love to me was to persuade me to bond with you."

Annoyance flashed from him to her. "I made love to you because it was damn pleasurable."

"Yes, it was, but what was between us never got to grow into anything more. We ran out of time."

His brow cocked. "But you want it to grow tonight?"

The skepticism in his "tonight" wasn't lost on her. Neither was the hope in the word "want." She pressed her thumb against his mouth in a parody of a kiss. "With everything in me, I want tonight with you."

He adjusted his sexy, powerful body so it loomed fully over her, blocking the remnants of light that fed her night vision, plunging her into darkness where there was just the heat of his body, the scent of his skin, and the touch of his energy. "You sure you want me to make love to you?"

"Yes."

"Do you know what you're asking?"

The barest hint of a growl textured his drawl. "I'm asking for you to show me who you are."

"I can be wild."

She smiled, knowing he could see it and the anticipation flowing through her. "I know."

"I might scare you."

There were a lot of things she could imagine Jace doing to her, but scare her? That way wasn't one of them. "No, you won't."

He paused, head canting to the side, allowing a bit of light between them. His thumb stroked her cheek. "I know you were raped, Miri."

The ugly truth lay between them. She had been raped in the beginning, as a punishment and a form of persuasion, but as it hadn't worked and had set back their experiments for two days, the Sanctuary vamps had moved their focus to other tactics. Tactics that had been so much worse. Methods that took her humanity away and made her into nothing more than a vessel for their goals. Until she'd felt like Miri had disappeared and number seven-eight-three-four was all that remained.

That rape of her individuality had been so much worse than the rape of her body. She turned her face away from the past and looked into Jace's eyes, holding on to the emotion there, the caring, the way he saw her—as a person. His princess. She blinked back the sting of tears. "It doesn't matter."

He wouldn't let it go, his gaze homing in with that internal radar of his to the turbulence churning in her mind. "It's going to matter if I do something that triggers a memory."

"There's nothing you could do to trigger those memories." *Except ask about them.* "And even if you do, I'll control it."

He was shaking his head before she finished the sentence. "I don't want you to control it. I want you to trust me with what happened, let me help you through it."

"I'll be fine." Miri scooted her hips closer to his. The kiss of his erection was a soothing balm to her worries. Even though there had been others, he still wanted her. Taking his hand in hers, she placed it on her breast.

As his fingers shaped to the curve, a sense of familiarity flowed with her indrawn breath. After so much wrong, this was so right. The sheer pleasure of it pulled her lids down.

"Tell me what you're thinking."

His drawl was a deep husk, the human equivalent to a satisfied growl. She didn't hesitate. "How right your touch feels."

His thumb stroked over her nipple, the calluses dragging against her sensitive flesh. "Compared to what?"

She frowned, not wanting to analyze the feeling, preferring to just enjoy it. "Compared to nothing. It's just . . . right."

She opened her eyes. He was watching her, his eyes lit with vampire heat, his expression fiercely tender and passionate.

"Yes, it is."

This time his thumb lingered and pressed. A curl of heat spread from her nipple inward, stretching straight to her core. She lifted herself that fraction of an inch required to connect their bodies.

The sheets rustled. The mattress sank as Jace countered her move with one of his own. Not completing the connection, just holding it, reminding her he'd always been one for prolonging the moment, building the anticipation.

"This time it's just going to be you and me," she breathed.

"And a hundred memories that you can't hope to forget."

Miri didn't want to think about that. She didn't want to believe that the past she was working so hard to bury and forget could intrude upon this time between them. "I just want it new between us, Jace."

"There can't be new without old, princess. I know that and you know that. That's why you're fighting so hard against thinking."

She raked her nails down his chest the way he liked, leaving a trail of red streaks, transient marks, not the permanent one she would give him if she believed this could last. But her mark all the same. His groan encouraged her soft whisper, "You know you want to make love to me."

He thwarted her efforts to finish the joining with a hand on her hip. "Not like this, Miri. Not now, with the biggest pretense in your life wedged between us."

Yes, now. She needed this now, before she disappeared, before she lost the courage. "It's not your place to deny me."

"Is that a were rule?"

"Yes."

"Well, it's one we won't be following. When we make love, it will be because both of us feel it's right."

The rage ballooned within, searing her fingers, her mouth, her soul with the endless pain she'd always smothered but found she now wanted to release at him—a scream that had no point anymore. She gritted her teeth and held it in through sheer force of will. "We're mated."

His hand brushed her cheek before drifting down to her throat as if they had all the time in the world, resting on the pulse beneath. She didn't have a prayer of hiding how fast it was beating.

"And you're hurting." There was no budge in the steel underlying the carefully drawled statement. No break in the caress of his touch, the softness of his energy that held her even as he delivered the killing blow to her plans. "That gets fixed before the other gets indulged."

Damn you! The thought roared through her mind, hovered on her tongue. It took everything in her not to set the curse free. And through the violent but brief struggle, Jace watched her, probably learning more than she wanted in the few seconds it took her to regain control.

A knock at the front door erupted into the tense silence. Jace was out of the bed in a flash. Miri clutched the blankets to her chest. Knowing he could read the energy she could only sense, she asked. "Who is it?"

"Jared and some others."

The pounding came harder, more urgent. "Jace!"

"Wait here." Jace didn't bother with clothes, just strode out of the room, unself-conscious in his nakedness, the flex of his taut buttocks as he moved a potent definition of male grace and beauty. Miri swung her legs out of the bed, clutching her stomach against the surge of nausea. Grabbing the sheet, she wrapped it around her, tugging it free of the bed as she scooted to the edge of the mattress. The front door opened with a disjointed creak. Straining her ears, she caught one word out of the murmur of voices. "Baby."

She didn't need to hear any more. She ran to the front of the house, yanking on the sheet as it caught on a chair leg, almost falling, ending up tripping her way to everyone's attention. Jace caught her with a deceptively casual reach, his fingers wrapping around her arm.

Tobias and Micah stared at her, disapproval in their dark gazes, whether in regard to her state of undress or her barging into a male conversation, she didn't know or care. Jace's reaction was just as easy to read, seeing as his gaze was focused on her chest. She glanced down. Her breasts were all but bare.

"I thought I told you to wait in the bedroom."

She hitched up her sheet to a more modest level. "Someone mentioned a baby."

He sighed, pulling her to him. "Yes."

As if he knew how devastating the wrong word could be to

the fragile thread of her sanity, Jace spoke very carefully. "Word is there were some Sanctuary vamps spotted with a baby thirty miles south of here."

Miri's breath stuttered to a stop, swelling against the constriction of her throat, burning with hope. *Faith. Oh, my God. They might have found Faith.*

She reached up and grabbed Jace's hand where it rested on her shoulder. "Faith."

"Don't get your hopes up, Miri," Jared cautioned. "We're just checking every lead. It might not be her."

"How many were babies could there be running around without their mother?" she managed to rasp out.

Jace turned her in to his side, hugging her tightly. Beneath his skin, she could feel the same electric charge of disbelief colliding with hope.

"It doesn't seem likely that there would be a lot of them. But we can't know for sure until we get there."

"It could also be a trap," Tobias interjected in that cool, measured tone of his.

Miri looked from him to Micah, hating them for the sympathy and pity in their eyes. Sympathy that tried to stifle the hope she wouldn't give up.

"But that's not going to stop you from looking, is it?"

Her heart trip-hammered in her chest. Adrenaline flowed through her system, driving the pain and nausea in her stomach higher. It couldn't stop them.

She felt the brush of Jace's energy, then her heartbeat slowed and her anxiety lowered. He tipped her chin up. "Nothing is going to stop us from looking."

It was a promise. She breathed it in along with his scent. No. Jace wouldn't let them stop looking.

Almost silent footsteps sounded behind her. "The plan is to search while taking as many precautions as we can."

She snapped her head around. Jared emerged from the shadows. She pinned him with her glare. "Take risks."

"We are."

"We're just not risking you," Jace clarified.

Which explained the disapproval from Tobias and Micah. They'd thought to keep this from her, their naturally protective instincts demanding she be spared the stress of "maybes." They needed to understand that wasn't an option. "Even me."

Jace tipped her face up. "You're never on the table."

Tobias checked his watch. "We need to move."

Miri ducked out from under Jace's arm. "I'll be ready in ten."

Tobias looked at her with those cold amber eyes of his. "You're not coming."

"You can't stop me."

"I'm forbidding it."

"I'm not pack anymore."

"Once pack, always pack."

She blinked. That was a very radical thing for an Enforcer to say. They were more known for upholding tradition than breaking them. And her mating to Jace put her outside the pack because a vampire would not be allowed to lead, no matter what tradition said about her husband. "I'm going."

"No."

She met his gaze and held it, not feeling one bit of discomfort at so blatantly challenging an Alpha male. After the last year, he was going to have to do a lot better than a glare to scare her into submission. She held his gaze for another second and then the enormity of what Jace had said rolled over her. A baby. The thought wouldn't leave her head. They'd found a baby without a mother. A were baby caught up with vampires. The breath caught in her lungs. Her eyes closed, blocking Tobias's expression from view. Blocking out everything except the hope. It had to be Faith. Had to be.

Jace's energy touch the edges of hers. "Breathe, Miri."

She didn't think she'd ever breathe again. She spun on her heel, heading for the bedroom and her clothes. Jace caught her shoulder. She glanced back at him, only catching a glimpse of his face. It was enough to let her know he agreed with Tobias. She turned the rest of the way, her hand coming up, her lip curling in a snarl. "Don't say it."

"It's too dangerous."

"You're going."

"I'm a vampire at full strength with lots of experience kicking ass."

Frustration boiled over. "What you really mean is you're a man."

"Being male does give me a lot more muscle."

She yanked on her arm. "I don't care."

"I do."

His energy surrounded her, tested her determination. She didn't block him. She wanted him to see the truth. If he left her here, she'd just follow.

His hands moved over her shoulders to the sides of her neck, searching, probing. His gorgeous eyes glowed with a beauty from which she couldn't look away. His energy tugged at hers. Regret touched his expression.

"I'm sorry."

A push of his energy, a sudden pressure from his fingers, and then everything went black.

JACE caught Miri as she fell, supporting her head with his hand.

"She's going to be pissed as hell when she wakes up," Slade said, coming into the house.

Jace glanced over at him as he scooped Miri into his arms. "Facing her temper is better than having her get caught up in trouble."

"She's definitely had more than her fair share of that," Tobias agreed, following Slade inside.

"And she's had all she's going to have." Miri wasn't rational when it came to finding Faith. She was too desperate, too willing to sacrifice herself. He couldn't allow that. "She needs to be protected."

"I get that, but I'm not so sure Miri's going to."

"Well, I'll deal with that when the time comes."

In the meantime, she'd be safe. That was all that mattered. He hitched her up as he turned sideways through the bedroom door. Keeping Miri safe and getting his daughter back—he blew out a breath—God willing, tonight he'd accomplish both.

He stopped just inside the door. The rumpled bed, the lingering scent of their passion dominated his senses.

Make love to me.

Her hair brushed his calf, sliding over his skin in the memory of a caress. One of these days she'd be back in his bed. All of her, not just the parts she thought he could understand. After she got over the anger of what he was about to do, that is.

He laid her on the bed, placed his hand over her forehead, and sent a command deep into her mind.

He felt a presence. He didn't look up, giving the order first.

Sleep.

"That'll hold her for about two seconds."

He glanced at Jared, lounging in the doorway.

He smoothed his fingers over the pleat between her brows. "I need her to sleep for a hell of a lot longer than that."

Jared crossed the distance to the bed, his power surging before him like a living entity. People called Jace wild because he didn't hide who he was, but in his book, his brothers were the ones to watch out for. Caleb with his exceptional abilities cloaked by that ruthless control. Jared with his power that no one ever saw coming unless he allowed it. Slade with his intelligence that overlay an outlaw's disregard for rules. Hell, they were all much more dangerous than he.

Jared brushed his fingers over Miri's brow, the tips grazing Jace's knuckles. "You have to do it like this if you want it to override her maternal instincts."

Jace followed Jared's energy into Miri's mind, studied how he attached the command like a lock on the door of her subconscious, trapping her in her own mind.

The analogy made him uncomfortable.

"Do you want her following us as soon as we leave?" Jared asked.

"No." He couldn't allow Miri to put herself in danger. He left the mind block there and glanced at Jared. "Thank you."

A smile kicked up the corner of Jared's mouth. "I'm not so sure you should be thanking me. She's not going to like this."

"So you already said."

"So I did."

Jared studied Miri. "She has a lot of weird ideas about vampires, doesn't she?"

"I guess myth can override reason in immortals as well as mortals."

"Maybe."

"You don't sound convinced."

"Miri strikes me as a very rational woman."

Jace waited, knowing there was more coming.

"Whose sanity is hanging by a very thin thread," Jared finished.

Jace blinked. "It's that obvious?"

Jared shrugged. "Her mind is an open book with very few natural defenses."

Pain in his hands and the scent of blood alerted him to the fact that his talons were cutting into his palms. "The Sanctuary would have taken advantage of that."

Jared nodded. "Slade was right. Their touch is all over her mind."

Jace asked the one question he was afraid to find out the answer to. "Are they controlling her?"

"No, but they didn't leave her a hell of a lot to rebuild on." He studied Miri, his power centering. "She needs something to anchor her."

"I'm trying."

Jared frowned, his energy intensified. Miri moaned. Jace controlled the primitive urge to lash out at his brother, to drive him from his mate's mind. He needed answers more than he needed a testosterone moment, as Allie would call it.

"She relies on your strength, but she needs more."

"What?"

Jared shrugged. "I don't know."

Great. Just what he needed. A directive with no guidelines.

With a jerk of his chin, Jace motioned to the door. "As soon as I get her settled here, I'll catch up with you."

Jared nodded, turned, and then hesitated in the doorway. "I'm glad you found her, Jace."

"Thanks. I am, too."

Another hesitation and then he turned back, his gaze following Jace's. "You probably already know this, but she's a hell of a fighter."

"I know." He traced the line of her jaw, the tip of her chin. Jared still didn't leave. Jace looked up. "What?"

"I think with the right incentive, the old Miri will come out swinging."

It would help if someone could tell him what she needed, what incentive would work. "I'll keep that in mind."

He felt more than heard Jared's departure.

Jace slid Miri down on the bed, unwrapping her from the sheet, shaking it out over her. He touched her pale cheek. She was still beautiful, in spite of the scars and the loss of that vibrant life that used to surround her. As he pulled the comforter over her, he whispered, "We've just got to find the key, princess, and it'll all fall into place."

Jace joined the others on the porch. Slade tossed him a gun. He caught it with his free hand, leaning his rifle against the wall. He checked it over. "Anything new on this one?"

"The sunlight replicator is a hell of a lot stronger."

Jace sighted down the barrel. "That'll come in handy." He brought the gun down and told Slade, "You look like hell."

"Thanks." Slade ran his hand through his hair, the too-long bangs falling over his forehead, giving him an untamed look more suited to the outlaw side of his past than his current life as a scientist. The dark circles under his eyes and the bearded shadow on his face added a disreputable look to the overall package. "Joseph isn't doing so well."

Damn. "Any idea why?"

"I'm running tests, but from the information I have . . ." He slung his rifle over his shoulder. "I don't have a clue."

Slade looked to the main house and the lights burning there. The door opened. A man came out. Only one man carried himself like that, walked like that. Caleb.

"Shit, I told him to stay here."

Even from this distance, Jace could feel the worry coming off Caleb. When Caleb reached them, Jace said, "As much as I appreciate this, you need to stay here with your wife and son."

Caleb's gaze met his, the green of his eyes intense, the set of his mouth resolute. He held out his hand. Slade passed him a rifle. "If it is Faith, you'll need me."

"But if it's not—"

"We don't know that it's not." He glanced at Slade. "You look like hell."

Slade settled his hat on his head. "So I'm told. When I get around to cloning myself, I'll make a note to give him rosy cheeks."

Tobias pushed off the railing and came into the circle.

Caleb slung his rifle over his shoulder and accepted a pack of ammunition from Tobias. "We need to find you some help."

Slade shrugged. "Good luck finding someone bright enough, who we know for sure isn't Sanctuary."

And that was the hell of it, Jace knew. Slade was the only one with a scientific bent to his mind who was a hundred percent Johnson. They had too much to lose to risk trusting outsiders. "Thanks for coming." He looked over at Caleb. "But I think you should stay here. Your wife and son need you."

"My wife is the one who pushed me out the door."

"Uh-huh." He didn't believe that for a minute. No new mother with a sick child wanted her husband going into battle.

"For your information, Allie said she'd have my head on a platter if I didn't go with you."

"What about Joseph?"

A shadow crossed Caleb's face; worry darkened his gaze. He blew out a breath. "Right now he's stable. The concoction Slade created seems to be keeping his food down."

The men looked at each other. It wasn't hard to tell what the weres were thinking. If little Faith had the same problems that Allie's baby was having, she might not be alive to come home.

As much as he wanted his brother's help, Jace couldn't accept it. "Your responsibilities are here."

"I'm not denying it, but there's no telling how long it will take us to get the baby out of there, and I'm the only one you can trust to get her home if the sun comes up."

"We can handle it," Tobias offered.

The offer came a bit too fast for Jace's comfort.

He exchanged a glance with Caleb.

Miri doesn't trust him, Jared reminded them both.

There was a chance Miri wasn't thinking straight. There was also a chance she was.

And Tobias wasn't family.

Caleb gave an imperceptible nod and turned to Tobias. "Are you stronger than me?"

Tobias didn't flinch at the straightforward question. "Can you walk in sunlight?"

Caleb hitched up his rifle. "Yes."

Tobias's shock was reflected in the ripple of murmur that went

through the other weres. Vampires walking in sunlight was un-
heard of.

Tobias recovered quickly. He shook his head. "You Johnsons
are a contrary bunch, aren't you?"

"I believe the politically correct term is 'immortally maximized,'"
Slade interjected.

Caleb snatched up a gun. "Well . . . me and my immortally maximized self are going with you. Looking at the three of you, little
Faith is going to wonder if she's landed in a family of disreputables."

"Oh, yeah," Jared growled. "And looking at your face is going
to put those fears to rest?"

"A hell of a lot faster than looking at yours will."

Jace looked between his brothers and the weres as the bickering
picked up momentum. The sacrifices they were all making were
tremendous, yet they didn't hesitate. His daughter needed help. They
were there. It was that simple. There didn't seem to be anything
else to say except thank you, and that just didn't say enough. He
grabbed the energy shield and tossed it to Tobias. "Let's get a
move on."

❧ 12 ❧

AFTER the long, tense ride getting close to the area, followed by a cold hike across the snow-covered ground to the remote cabin, the actual battle was going to be anticlimactic. Jace looked through the window. There were only a few Sanctuary vamps guarding the place, and they clearly weren't expecting company. Inside, two vamps sat at a table playing cards. Through the whisper of his transceiver, Jace heard the weres checking in.

"Target one down."

"Target two down."

They were an efficient lot.

Jace slipped through a window. Across the way, Caleb mirrored Jace's movements—approaching his target at the same speed, cloaking his presence with illusion and masking his energy with the overtones of common threads already existing, visible only to each other through their mental path.

The two Sanctuary vamps snarled over a bet, clearly bored. That didn't mean they were harmless. They stank of Sanctuary perversion and enhancement. Their amplified aggression practically seethed with the need for an outlet. Jace was more than happy to give it to them.

Aligned behind his target, Caleb nodded.

Remember, neat and clean.

I hear you.

There was just going to be a slight change in the plan.

In the blink of an eye, Jace dropped illusion, nodding at the shocked vamp across the table. Caleb swore as the table flew across the room. Both vamps sprang to their feet and leapt for the enemy they could see. Jace.

Big, powerful, they wanted his blood. Jace wanted the fight. He smiled.

"Son of a bitch, Jace."

Caleb didn't have time to grab his vamp. Jace did. With a grim smile and the superior speed granted him at his conversion, he stepped into the attack, sliding sideways under the outstretched claws. With smooth efficiency, he slit the first's throat, tossing him back toward his brother, the spray of his tainted blood feeding the primal rage welling inside. They had his daughter. They might even be the ones who had hurt Miri. He needed to kill them with his bare hands.

Caleb caught the injured vamp and tossed him to the ground. Brilliant light flashed as the sunlight replicator seared through his chest.

"This is supposed to be clean, Jace," he growled.

"Uh-huh."

The second vamp grabbed Jace from behind, confident in his strength. Jace broke his hold and spun fast enough to catch the shock in his expression. He smiled, punching his hand through the other vampire's chest, closing his fingers around his heart. "Where's the baby?"

The vamp held perfectly still. "You're Jace Johnson."

Jace squeezed, enjoying the other man's grimace. "That wasn't an answer."

Cunning joined the desperation on the vamp's face. "You've got a pretty mate."

Jace lifted him off his feet, holding on to his control with a thread, enjoying the vampire's spastic jerk as his heartbeat was aborted. "Where's the baby?"

"Jace . . ." Caleb warned. "We need him."

The vamp's eyes glowed red; blood dripped from the corner of his mouth. Jace set him on his feet and relaxed his grip on his heart for the few seconds it took for the man to get his breath and for his heart to resume beating.

Hate warped the vamp's expression.

"I'm not going to tell you a thing," he snarled at Caleb. He spit blood and met Jace's glare. "But you, I'll tell a little secret. Your mate has the tightest, juiciest little—"

Another blinding flash of light, and a burning heat seared Jace's cheek. Before him, the vamp's head exploded. Bone, blood, and brain blew backward, splattering the wall. Jace dropped the body and stepped back. He glanced over as Caleb stepped forward. "Weren't you the one who warned me we needed him?"

Caleb stood over the body, his expression cold as ice as he burned out the heart. "We don't need him that badly."

"It was my right to kill him."

"You were taking too long."

"Uh-huh."

Jace cast his energy through the tiny three-room cabin. There was a lingering scent that could be the infant, but nothing fresh and nothing concrete. Tobias appeared in the doorway. He took in the blood and gore. His eyebrow went up.

"Having fun?"

"Not as much as I'd like," Jace growled, the rage still prowling through him. The bastard had touched Miri. He wanted to take him apart, bone by bone, layer by layer, one nerve ending at a time.

Stay with us, Jace, Caleb cautioned.

Jace shook his head and buried his rage. "Any sign of the baby?" he asked the Enforcer.

"No. The rooms are clean."

Not what he wanted to hear. He looked around. "They were guarding something."

"Yup."

"She might have been moved," Tobias offered, entering the room.

"Maybe." But Jace didn't think so. There was a nebulous something nibbling at the edges of his subconscious.

Jared came into the room. "The perimeter is secure." He looked around. "From the gore, I'm guessing it's secure in here, too."

Caleb grunted and asked Jared, "Can you feel any stray energy here?"

"Hell, it's going to take an hour for this violence to subside enough to read anything."

"Damn."

Jace moved farther into the room. The nebulous something didn't get stronger, but it didn't go away, either. A man came up beside him. Tobias.

"What do your senses tell you?"

"I don't know."

Energy, distinctly male and powerful, slid over his and then withdrew. Jace should have been surprised that the Enforcer was telepathic. He wasn't.

"You're an empath," Tobias said.

"Not that I've noticed."

"It's enough that *I* have."

Jace walked around the room, but all he could smell was vampire tainted with the perversions the Sanctuary gave its members. "Keep it to yourself."

"I got bottles in the fridge," Slade called.

The baby had been here. The certainty sank deep. Jace spun on his heel and almost ran Caleb over. "It doesn't seem likely that they would have moved her already."

"Not and leave the bottles behind." Tobias dropped his rifle butt to the floor and then frowned. "All the guards are vampires, right?"

"Yes."

Tobias looked around. "It's a damn sunny cabin for a vampire to hang out in."

Jared cocked his head to the side. "Yes, it is."

Jared strode to the back door and opened it. "There's no cave entrance and no obvious hillside."

The back door closed. Jared came back into the room. Slade stomped on the floor in the middle of the living room. The sound was different than when Tobias had tapped it with his rifle butt. "This place have a basement?"

Jared extended his talons and slid them into the crevice between the wood slats that composed the floor and pried upward. "Let's find out."

Nails screamed and wood cracked. He tossed the board aside.

Jace looked into the dirt basement beneath. Unease spread over his skin. "From the looks of things, not much of one."

They didn't bother looking for the door. Tobias ripped up another board, Jace another. Damp, musty air rose out of the room below. Jace set his rifle on the floor and braced himself on the edge of the opening. "Cover me."

Slade grabbed his arm. "Give us a minute and we might be able to—"

Jace wasn't waiting for anything. His little girl might be down there. He dropped into the hole and landed softly on the hard-packed dirt floor. The place was dark, no light of any kind. A dank, merciless grave.

The baby's energy was clearer down here, not strong enough to identify whether it was Faith or not, but near enough to identify were and vampire attributes. Jace followed it, tracking it to a room on the far side. He cast about with his energy. There was nothing. No guards, nothing, just the weak thread of energy belonging to a tiny life.

A sick feeling welled in Jace's gut. Faith's captors knew the brothers would come looking for her. She'd be heavily guarded.

Whoever this baby was, it probably wasn't his daughter. Still, hope wouldn't die. He did not want to go back to Miri again empty-handed.

The baby's energy got stronger as he got to the end of the short tunnel. There was nothing familiar in the pattern. Nothing familiar in the scent that trickled to him. The only thing he did know was that she was female, and were, with a strange resonance of vampire. It could be Faith.

"Jace?" Jared called.

"All clear," he belatedly called back.

He entered the room. It was tiny, little more than a closet. A box was sitting on top of a rickety table against the wall. IV bags hung off pegs driven into the wall above. Lord only knew what liquid was dripping down the tubes that disappeared into the interior of the box. The place smelled of mold and decay. The way he imagined a tomb would smell. And there was a baby in there. The knowledge soured in his gut.

A faint sound, like a kitten crying, came to him. The baby. He couldn't make himself move forward. He heard footsteps behind him. He looked over his shoulder. The grim horror he felt inside was reflected in the tight expressions on Jared's, Caleb's, and Slade's faces. Tobias, in contrast, wore no expression at all. Caleb came up beside him.

"Afraid of what you're going to find?"

"Yes."

"You want me to go?"

Jace shook his head. If that was his daughter in there, he wanted the first friendly face she saw to be his. "No."

He sensed energy ahead of him, little tendrils of light that searched randomly for a connection. He mentally touched one. The light retreated, a terrified cry in his mind. Another little hiccup of sound disturbed the quiet, so faint it might have been a figment of his imagination. Except it wasn't.

He took one step and then another. The next brought him

close enough to see the box and smell the stench of urine and fe-
ces. At first he thought it was a lump of rags, that the baby was
gone and the IVs and tubes were the discarded remnants of occu-
pation, but then the rags twitched. With his finger he reached into
the box and moved a flap of dirty material aside. His bile rose.

The tiniest of babes lay there. Scrawny, pale, almost blue with
cold. IVs pierced her legs and her arms, and another entered her
chest. Liquid dripped in a steady stream into her body. Everything
in him demanded he pick her up, warm her. He didn't dare touch
her for fear she'd fall apart. "Slade."

"Right here."

"Is it her?" Jared asked.

"No." There was nothing of him or Miri in the infant's energy
or scent. She was were, strangely mixed with vampire, but she wasn't
his daughter. But still, he'd never seen anything more in need of
saving. Her big brown eyes watched him with a mixture of terror
and resigned acceptance.

Jared looked over his shoulder. "We killed them too fast."

Slade grunted and skimmed his hands over the fragile body.

"Yeah." Jace couldn't wait any longer. He slid his hands under
the chilled baby until she rested on the cushion of his palms,
feeling the flat hardness of the box beneath. They hadn't even padded it.

Jared pointed to two bite marks on her forearm. "Looks like
they tried to convert her."

That explained the vampire energy. Jace carefully lifted her up.
The tubes trailed behind her, foul tentacles connecting her to her
prison. Jace wanted to rip them out. He set his jaw and forced
himself to speak calmly.

"Does she need to be hooked up to this?" Jace asked his
brother.

"Hell," Slade retorted just as quietly, examining the unmarked
bags. He poked his talon through one and sampled the contents. "I
don't even know what this stuff is."

"Are any of natural substance?" Caleb asked.

Slade tapped one bag filled with clear fluid. "This is saline."

"Leave that one, then," Jace said, every drop of the unknown fluids that seeped into the infant's body making him sick. "Remove the rest."

It seemed to take forever for Slade to disconnect the ugly tubes from her torso.

The baby kicked her feet. The rags heaved.

"Whoa!" Slade turned his head for a moment, blinking against the released fumes, keeping pressure on an insertion point to keep the blood from flowing. "She needs a bath."

It was likely a trick of timing. Jace knew she had to be too young to understand language, but when her lower lip trembled and her face crumpled, he wanted to hit Slade. Tears dripped from her eyes and flowed down into the wells of her sunken temples. "Watch what you say, Slade."

It came out sharper than he intended. Slade snapped his head back, took one look at the little girl's face, and swore. "Oh, hell."

"What'd you do?" Caleb asked, checking the hall before coming into the room.

"He made her cry."

Caleb took one look at the baby's face and added his own curses to the mix. "Poor tiny mite." He glanced up at Jace when more tears seeped from her eyes. When she sucked in a ragged breath, he snapped. "Don't just stand there, fix her."

"What do you propose I do?" Jace asked.

"Something."

Slade slowly pulled out the needle in her chest. The baby screamed a high-pitched warble.

"Hurry up, damn it!"

Sweat beaded on Slade's temple. "I'm going as fast as I can. It's in the heart. I've got to heal as I go or she'll bleed out."

The infant shuddered from head to toe. The needle was almost out. "Jesus, how long is the thing?"

Another shudder and Jace couldn't stand it. He wrapped the baby in his energy, drawing off her pain and stress, striving to impart comfort and caring. It wasn't easy. Not only was the baby's mind less developed and therefore less focused, it was obvious that she'd never known a kind touch. Any connection at all terrified her.

He found an opening and slipped within. Her scream stopped as abruptly as it had started. She stared up at him, not blinking, not moving, just staring as if she didn't dare believe. It reminded him so much of the look Miri got in her eyes when she thought he couldn't see.

"I've got you," he promised her, his voice hoarse with the in-humanity of it. Of the deprivation this tiny little mite had endured.

Slade slipped the needle out.

A fragile beam of energy reached out to Jace. A quivering, hesi-tant query. He lifted the baby carefully and pressed her tiny body to his chest. Her head bobbed. He cradled it in the palm of his hand, supporting her, ignoring her stench, focusing on the emo-tion pouring from her to him, the fear, the hope, the wonder of contact. His hands shook as he laid his cheek on her tiny head. Dear God. "I've got you, peanut."

"She's cold," Caleb said.

Jace covered as much of her back as he could with his hands.

"Let me get these other needles out, and we can wrap her up." Slade's drawl wasn't any steadier than Jace's hands. And no wonder. There were some things too ugly to take stoically.

"The sons of bitches," Caleb snarled, shrugging out of his coat before stripping off his shirt.

"You're the one who was in an all-fired hurry and started blow-ing off heads," Jace retorted.

"Next time I'll know better." Caleb draped the soft cotton shirt over Jace's arm. "You can use this for the first layer."

"Thanks."

"She's probably too young and definitely too weak to monitor her body temperature," Slade said, slipping the last needle free.

"I'll keep her inside my coat."

"That'll work."

Jace looked up. Tobias stood guard, his rifle braced on his hip, watching them with a strange expression on his face. It could almost be called satisfaction. "Do you have a problem?"

"Just the opposite."

"What in hell does that mean?"

Tobias didn't answer, just came into the room, staring at the baby. The baby's heartbeat accelerated with the were's approach. Her arms flailed and her feet kicked. She was scared. Jace's vampire rose. His lips drew back from his fangs. Tobias either didn't notice or didn't care.

"That's close enough," Jace warned.

The words were slightly slurred as his bones morphed.

Tobias stopped, his eyebrows raising. The baby kicked again. His gaze dropped. He frowned. "At least we know how they got her."

"How?" Slade asked.

"I'd say she's from a fundamentalist pack."

"You have fundamentalist packs?"

Tobias nodded, taking another step forward, touching the wisps of hair on the baby's head. "Not many, thankfully, but they hold to the old ways and old superstitions."

"Boggles the mind what an immortal could consider the old ways," Jared commented dryly.

The baby stilled under Tobias's touch. Jace stayed on guard, but then the were did something, and the chaos in the baby's mind cleared. Connected as he was, Jace felt her weariness and her happiness at being held. The uniqueness of the experience for her. Her contentment at the stroke of Tobias's fingers down her back, the tickle as his fingers touched her foot. He glanced down. Her clubfoot.

"Were babies are rarely deformed," Tobias explained. "In the fundamentalist packs, any that are tend to be regarded as bad omens and left out in the woods to be reclaimed by nature."

"That's a pretty way of saying left to die," Slade drawled.

Tobias glanced up, his hand never leaving the baby. Jace didn't protest because something about the hard-eyed Enforcer softened when he was touching the child. Peanut's eyes drifted closed. Her lips pursed and made odd little rhythmic kissing sounds as if she sucked on an invisible pacifier.

"They regard it as letting nature right a mistake."

"They can regard it any way they want, it's still murder."

"Or worse," Jared growled darkly, glancing around the room before taking the shirt draped over Jace's arm and holding it up.

"How old do you think she is?" Jace asked Slade as he held the baby away so Jared could wrap the shirt around her.

"Two months. Maybe."

He unzipped his coat while Caleb shrugged back into his. "Young."

The baby's eyes opened as he drew her back against his chest. When he resettled her cheek against his throat, a shudder shook her little body. He pulled the lapel away as he zippered it back up, making sure the zipper didn't catch her hair. "I know somebody who would love to meet you, little girl."

His words ruffled the wisps on the top of her head.

"You plan on bringing her home?" Caleb asked.

He looked at his brother. "Do you have a better idea?"

Caleb shook his head. "Just wondering."

Tobias pulled the lapel back to look at her face. "Miri won't thank you for this."

"Why not?"

Miri had arms that were aching for a baby and a need to be needed. Peanut needed a mother.

"Miri's hurting."

She needs something to anchor her.

Four hours ago, Jace hadn't had anything to offer Miri that would give her purpose, but now he did. Jace kissed the soft spot on the top of the baby's little head, felt the silkiness of the hair there. "So is Peanut."

It was his ace in the hole.

MIRI was waiting for him on the porch when he got home. In the predawn light, it was easy to make out the hope lighting her face and the nervousness that had her clenching her hands in front of her. He didn't need to read her energy to know how anxious she was. Her grip on her hands was white-knuckled and her shoulders were hunched while her head was thrown up and back, almost like she was expecting a blow.

Damn, he'd been hoping she would be inside.

He glared at Jared. "You said she'd stay asleep."

"Must be she's stronger than I thought."

Miri's gaze dropped to the bulge in Jace's coat, his hands, the way he was cradling that bulge. He felt her hope flare, the breathless excitement. She watched him with unwavering intensity as he approached. Jace didn't want to keep her in suspense, but he didn't want to tell her the bad news before he was close enough to catch her when the bitter disappointment hit. His facial muscles ached with the effort it took not to show how much he hurt for her.

The closer he got, the less hope there was in her expression. When he reached the bottom of the steps, her lower lip was between her teeth and anguish was in her eyes.

"You found a baby."

"Yes."

She waited painful seconds. He couldn't bring himself to elaborate.

"It's not Faith, is it?" The question drifted on an insubstantial cloud of breath.

He climbed the four steps, cupped his hand behind her head,

and leaned in. She ducked away. The rejection went straight to his center. "I'm sorry, Miri."

She crossed her arms over her stomach and rubbed her hands up and down her upper arms as if to ward off a chill. "Whose baby is she?"

"I don't know."

"Her mother must be going crazy."

"Tobias doesn't seem to think so."

"That's insane."

He reached for the zipper of his coat. Miri took a step back. Her tongue flicked over her lips. "No. I don't want to see her."

"I've promised to take care of her."

"Promised who?"

"Peanut."

Surprise flared in her gaze at the endearment. "You call her Peanut?"

"I've got to call her something. I don't know her name."

She took another step back. "I guess."

"Slade's going to be over in a bit with bottles and some formula."

Miri's nostrils flared, instinctively searching for the child's scent. Her frown deepened, no doubt exacerbated by the child's unique makeup. Were and vampire. Like their daughter. "Can she eat that?"

He opened the front door. "I don't know. I guess we'll find out. One thing's for sure, she needs to eat something."

She waved her hand in front of her nose as he passed by. "She stinks."

He could feel her resentment that he had brought this child to her instead of her own. He could even understand it. It didn't make a difference, though. "Tell me about it."

Miri followed him into the house, maintaining her four-foot safety zone. "We don't have a crib."

"We'll make do."

"We don't know the first thing about babies."

"We'll learn."

"We might screw things up."

"We can't do any worse than the Sanctuary."

"We—"

He turned and cut her off. "Miri?"

"What?"

"I understand you want Faith and this baby isn't her. I understand you're resentful and anxious, but while you don't have to have a thing to do with her, I can't turn my back."

She didn't say a word, just stared at him with those golden-brown eyes that revealed the ache in her soul. He headed for the kitchen. On the way he turned up the thermostat. The furnace kicked in when he was halfway to the sink. The baby jumped. He lifted the lapel and looked down. She was still asleep, her tiny mouth sucking on a fold of his shirt.

He felt Miri's presence behind him. He didn't turn around, just turned on the hot water and waited.

"Why?"

"Why what?"

"Why can't you give her to someone else?"

Because she'd already been thrown away once, and it wasn't in him to do it to her again. Because if someone found Faith in the same circumstances he would want them to take her in, give her love. Because someone had to make up for what the Sanctuary had done. But he couldn't tell Miri any of that without explaining the conditions in which they'd found Peanut. He would never put Miri through that, never give her that reality on which to base her worries for Faith.

"You'll just have to take my word for it."

The water was hot. He added cold and tested the temperature until it was perfect. He needed to take Peanut out of his coat.

"How are Allie and Joseph doing?"

"Allie's bleeding has stopped, but Joseph threw up his last bottle."

That meant the enzyme mixture wasn't working.

"Damn." He'd been hoping for good news on that front at least. "Could you get me a couple bath towels, a facecloth, and some soap?"

Miri jumped on the excuse to leave the room like a bird on a beetle. "Of course." Her relief lingered in her wake.

Jace waited until he was sure she was gone before shrugging out of his coat. He tossed it across a chair, which rocked under the weight, the legs clattering on the floor. The infant's arms and legs shot straight out to the sides as she jumped.

"Easy there. Didn't mean to startle you."

He heard the hall closet door close. When Miri didn't immediately come back, he sighed. "This might be a little more difficult than I planned, Peanut."

Peanut didn't move, and the death grip her energy had on his didn't weaken. He unwrapped her from the shirt. Her eyes opened as the cool air touched her skin. They were brown with no trace of gold. At least they knew she wasn't D'Nally Alpha.

Peanut sucked in a deep breath. Her ribs pushed against his hand. If she'd been stronger he was pretty sure she'd have busted his eardrums with the protest she let out.

Miri came running back into the room. "What are you doing to her?"

He stared in dismay at the dramatic change in the infant. "I'm not doing anything."

"She's crying!"

"Hell, I think the entire mountain can tell that."

"She's scared."

"How can you tell?"

"Babies only cry like that when they're scared."

"You know what that sounds like?"

"Everyone knows what that sounds like."

To him, all the baby's cries sounded the same. He rocked Peanut back and forth. "Could you put one of the towels in the sink?"

Miri cut him a funny look. "Sure."

He turned so she couldn't see Peanut while she did as he asked. "Thanks, I'll take it from here."

"You will?" There was a world of doubt in that agreement. She put the soap and shampoo on the counter.

She stepped back but didn't leave. Jace eased Peanut away. Her cries grew louder. "Shh, you'll feel better when we get you cleaned up. I have it on good authority that a bath puts all women in a good mood."

"Are you by any chance misquoting me?" Miri asked.

He glanced over his shoulder. "I thought you were leaving."

"I was just curious."

"About what?"

A long pause and then she said, "How is the sink going to drain with a towel in it?"

He hadn't thought that far ahead. It was already filling up. He'd have to stop it before it got too deep. Or else clean Peanut really fast. "It won't."

"Oh."

After testing the water again and adjusting the flow, he laid Peanut down on the towel. "That's better than a cold hard sink bottom, huh?"

Peanut didn't seem impressed. She just kept howling. He lathered up the facecloth and bathed her carefully. No matter how careful he was, he couldn't keep the soap from burning the chafed skin of her bottom. Her energy reached for his. He responded immediately, holding her tightly mentally, drawing off the pain. And still she cried.

"If you're not careful," he warned her, "I'm going to pull out my last resort. And trust me, no one wants to hear me sing a lullaby."

A hand touched the hollow of his spine, softly, hesitantly. "I'd like to hear that."

Jace couldn't move for fear of scaring her off. Peanut needed her. Hell, so did he. He kept his "No, you wouldn't" light.

He counted three breaths before Miri slipped one hand and then the other around his waist. Her forehead pressed into his back. "I don't want to be like this," she said in a despair-laden voice.

She was talking about her reluctance to accept Peanut.

"I'm not holding it against you."

"Maybe I'm holding it against myself."

"Why are you saying this when I can't hug you?"

"Punishment?"

Ah, hell, neither of them needed any more suffering. "I think we've both been punished enough. Heaping more on top of what we already have is overkill."

She rubbed her head back and forth. Her hair rustled against his shirt. "Tell me how you found her."

"We had a tip." He cupped his hand and dribbled water over the baby's puny body. The care with which he did it didn't seem to get through. She just kept crying, mouth so wide he swore he could see her tonsils.

Miri raised her voice to be heard over the cries. "I meant *how* you found her."

"I knew what you meant."

"But you're not going to tell me?"

"No."

The last of the soap was gone. He turned off the water, lifted Peanut up, and placed her on the dry towel. Behind him, Miri shifted. He blocked her with his elbow and a mental command. *No.*

Miri ducked beneath both. "Why not?"

"Damn it!"

It was too late. She saw it all—the frail little body, the bruises from the IVs, the sunken eyes, the clubfoot.

He put one hand on Peanut's chest and the other around Miri's shoulders, caught in the middle, the common link connecting their separate anguish. He couldn't manage either.

"Oh, my God!" Miri gasped. Her claws sank into his skin. "They threw her away."

✻ 13 ✻

JACE had a thing for throwaways, Miri decided. First her, and now this poor, pathetic baby who needed a mother and was stuck with her. The woman whose throat closed up and extremities went numb when she tried to touch her. The infant who was supposed to stay asleep the whole time Jace was gone to meet with his brothers. The infant who naturally woke up ten minutes after he left. The infant who was now lying in the padded drawer that was functioning as her crib, screaming her head off. The infant she couldn't touch because . . . "Hush," she whispered. Peanut did no such thing. She was probably hungry or dirty. She probably needed care.

If Jace were here he'd know immediately what the problem was, but he wasn't here. He was over at the main house meeting with Caleb. Miri glanced out the window. There was no sign of movement in the yard. No stray passerby she could impress into duty. There was just her. And, unlike last night, when she'd hid her problem by spending the night ostensibly helping Allie, it was all up to her.

The baby cried louder. The sad sound scratched over her nerve endings like the roughest sandpaper. Her chest tightened in the same adverse reaction she'd had since the first time she'd tried to pick Peanut up. It should be so easy to pick her up and fix whatever was wrong. A simple stretch and then flex of muscle. She rubbed her sweaty palms down her thighs. A simple stretch and flex that eluded her no matter how desperately she tried. No matter how much she wanted to, she couldn't touch that baby, couldn't close the door on the hope that Faith would come back. It was irrational. It was neurotic. It was illogical. She knew all that, but still, nothing she told herself shook the belief that if she picked up Peanut, all hope of Faith coming home was lost.

She was a terrible person.

Miri?

Oh, God. It wasn't bad enough that she knew she was a terrible person. Now she'd alerted Jace that she was a terrible person.

He mentally called again. She ignored him and took a step closer to the baby. Her heartbeat accelerated. Peanut screamed louder. She couldn't get her foot to move closer. She paused and inhaled slowly through her nose and carefully exhaled out her mouth, as Allie had taught her last night. Searching for calm, she did it again. It wasn't helping. The tension increased. The edges of her vision blurred.

She moved her foot forward. It dragged across the wood floor. In the end she wasn't even sure how big a step she'd managed, but she tried another. And another. By the time she reached the crib, she was so light-headed she didn't dare bend over and pick the baby up. Assuming she could get herself past the mind block that said to do so was to kill Faith.

This was ridiculous. She'd had no problem picking up Joseph. Allie had said that was because Joseph didn't depend on her, so she felt safe. She'd said Miri was afraid of being needed and failing. Miri tried to take a breath. All she got was a squeak of air. Allie had said a lot of things as they'd walked the floors with poor Joseph last night. None of them were helping her right now.

Peanut continued to cry. She continued to stand there, trapped in the hell of her self-induced torment. No air entering her lungs, none of the dictates of her brain reaching her muscles. The front door lock rattled. The door swung open. Jace stepped through. She couldn't even turn her head to look at him. Anxiety had her completely paralyzed.

Jace closed the door and locked it behind him. Barely glancing at the alarm, he keyed in the code. She watched from the corner of her eye as he approached. He looked at her and then at Peanut. His frowned deepened. "How long has she been fussing like this?"

Nothing could have made her feel more of a failure than that one question. "About five minutes."

He bent over and picked Peanut up, settling her against his shoulder, rubbing her back. He did it so easily. She felt so useless.

There was no more escaping his question than there was escaping his gaze. "How long have you been standing like that?"

"I'm not sure."

A couple of jostles and the infant began to settle. On a last snuffle that Miri could have sworn ended on an accusatory glare at her, Peanut stopped crying.

"You were just lonely, weren't you, Peanut?" Jace crooned to the baby, who soaked up the affection like a sponge, her little head bobbing and her feet kicking with happiness at the sound of Jace's voice.

"I tried . . ." Miri let her defense trail off. It didn't matter what she'd tried. She hadn't succeeded.

Jace's arm came around her shoulder—heavy, warm, and familiar as he tucked her in to his side. "I can see that. I can also see that you're tired and you've worked yourself into almost as much of a tizzy as Peanut."

His understanding annoyed her. It wasn't okay. She wasn't okay. She pushed against him. He didn't let her go. The urge to throw a total tantrum built. She stood still in his embrace and warned, "You might want to reconsider holding me here."

"I might?" He cocked his eyebrow at her.

"I'm about to launch into a major whine."

"Why?"

It was so natural to rest her forehead against him. "I don't want to be like this, Jace."

"Peanut understands."

Peanut couldn't understand anything. "Peanut needs a real mother." She glanced over at the little girl who was already looking better after a day of Jace's care. "And a real name."

"When you're ready, we'll name her."

"You can't wait for me."

"Why not? I've got forever."

She rolled her eyes. "Because there's a distinct possibility she'll be standing at her mating ceremony in her beautiful claiming dress, and her Alpha will stand up and be forced to call across the pack hall, 'I claim Peanut.'" She shook her head, letting her hair fall over her face. "Trust me, it will completely ruin the moment."

As if that were nothing, he laughed. "I'll take my chances."

She threw up her hands. "How can you laugh and say that like it doesn't matter? I'm making such a mess of this! It's not like I don't want to help her, I just . . . can't."

"Allie says it's a panic attack, and it's not forever."

"Allie is an optimist."

"She's also rarely wrong." Jace rubbed his hand up and down her arm. "You'll get through it."

"What makes you so sure?"

His head bent, and she felt the brush of his lips on the top of her head. "Because of who you are and who Peanut is."

"What's Peanut got to do with it?"

"Peanut wants you as her mother."

His heartbeat was a soothing throb under her ear. "Peanut doesn't know I'm alive."

"Peanut cries so much to get your attention. She likes your energy."

"How do you know?"

"She tells me."

"She's telepathic?"

He had the grace to look ashamed as she pushed back from him. His arm reluctantly fell away. Hands on her hips, she demanded, "She talks to you?"

"Sort of."

"How long has this been going on?"

"Since this morning."

"And you let me believe all night that you were some kind of super father who just instinctively knew what she needed?"

A smile crinkled the corners of his eyes. "Got to admit, I was kind of enjoying those worshipful looks you've been sending my way."

"You rat!" The corner of her mouth itched to tilt into a smile. She *had* been rather impressed.

"Vampire," he corrected, as if that was a good thing.

"That just makes you a flying, blood-sucking rat," she pointed out.

The smile spread to his lips. He was an incredibly handsome man when he smiled. "Or a vampire who knows his wife."

"So this all isn't coming to you instinctively." She waved her hand. "She's guiding you?"

"It's very random right now, but she definitely has her preferences."

She stared at the tiny infant. "And she wants me?"

"Yes."

Peanut gummed her knuckle. Miri shook her head.

"She's probably going to grow up to have lousy taste in men, too."

"She's were." He shifted Peanut up and chucked her under her chin. "She won't have a choice, remember?"

"She'll have a choice." She wished the words back as soon as she spoke them.

Jace got that predatory stillness about him that didn't bode well for hedging. "You don't."

Miri ducked out from under his arm. "She'll get to choose where she loves."

He frowned. "I don't get it."

"I know." She backed up before he could grab her. She grabbed her coat and bolted out the door before he could demand she explain.

It would have been the perfect exit if she hadn't forgotten about the alarm. It went off with a screech that echoed around the compound. Doors opened; men with guns spilled into the interior courtyard. Behind her, she heard Jace yell, "All clear." She turned. He was watching her, naturally. A woman didn't get to drop a bombshell like that and just run away.

She covered her ears and mouthed, *I'm sorry*.

He nodded and leaned back. She couldn't see his hand, but she assumed he was punching in the code. The alarm shut off as abruptly as it had started.

The men shook their heads and dispersed. All except Tobias and Jace. They both watched her as if she was going to do something crazy at any minute.

"I just forgot to deactivate the alarm."

Peanut started crying again. Miri remembered what Jace had said about this infant wanting her to be her mother. She took a step back.

"I'm sorry." She didn't know if she was saying it to the baby, to Jace, or to all the people she'd scared, she just knew she was sorry. Jace motioned her over. No doubt to hug her again and make her feel better. To take care of her. She shook her head. She didn't want to be taken care of anymore. She was long overdue in learning to take care of herself. She took another step back, and he frowned. Her heel slipped off the porch step. She would have fallen backward if strong hands hadn't caught her.

"Careful."

Caleb. Jace's brother. The one he looked up to. She expected Caleb to push her back up onto the porch. Instead, he swung her around and set her on the ground beside him. Ice cracked under her feet in a brittle accompaniment to how she felt inside as she looked into his face.

There was a world of understanding in his green eyes as he said, "Why don't you go up to the house and spend some time with Allie and Raisa?"

Miri glanced in Jace's direction. She rubbed her arms against the cold. Caleb gave her a little push in the direction of the big house. "Go, before you freeze to death."

"I . . ." She couldn't look away from Jace's gaze.

"Will it help you make a decision if I tell you I'm here because Allie asked me to come get you?"

Yes, it did. She gave him a grateful look. "Thanks."

Caleb touched her shoulder, the hesitation in the gesture just one more indication of how much she'd changed. People didn't used to fear to touch her, didn't used to gentle their voices when they spoke to her. People didn't used to think she was crazy.

"Jace will wait, Miri. For as long as it takes."

It hurt deep down inside that he would, too. She wished Jace would condemn her, but the understanding in those gray eyes of his never wavered. Neither did his belief that he'd have the mate back that he remembered. She wasn't that woman anymore, but she also wasn't this woman—the emotional wreck who couldn't function. She had to find her feet. She nodded to Caleb. "Thank you."

She headed toward the big house, slipping into the darkness, moving into the welcoming light pouring from the door. Her footsteps sounded unnaturally loud on the porch, and the eyes of the weres guarding the compound settled on her in a heavy stare. Did they condemn her for mating with Jace?

Tobias stood on the porch. For all the nonchalance of his stance, his amber eyes watched her closely.

"I told Jace you wouldn't accept the baby."

Asshole. She lifted her chin and met his gaze, not flinching, though everything in her wanted to cringe at the power there. "Now you're a fortune-teller as well as an Enforcer?"

"No, just a werewolf like you."

"I'm not pack anymore. I'm vampire."

His strange eyes narrowed a fraction. She felt a tingle down her spine.

"Right now, I think you're hurting too much to be much of anything, but that will change."

"Any helpful hints on when?"

He smiled. "My powers only go so far."

Exasperation, anger, and even amusement rushed forward. "Your powers come and go pretty conveniently. "

He didn't look one whit apologetic. "They do, don't they? Must be the mountain air."

"It's something, all right." She shouldered past him into the house. The bright cheeriness of the decor immediately flowed over her in welcome.

"Hello, anybody home?"

Footsteps on the landing preceded Raisa's appearance. "Hey, Miri," she called, her light Russian accent giving her words a pleasant depth. "Did you bring the baby?"

She shook her head. "Jace is taking care of her."

It was only a slight misrepresentation of what had happened. Raisa sighed. "Still can't touch her, huh?"

"No."

"Well, come on up. Allie is with Joseph."

"How's she doing?"

"She's fine." Raisa looked over her shoulder and came halfway down the stairs. "I'm really worried about Joseph, though. And if the expression on Slade's face when he thinks nobody is looking is any indication, so is he."

"What does he think is the problem?"

"It's like whatever he eats doesn't really feed him."

"Allie must be frantic."

Raisa waited for her to catch up. "So you would think."

"She's not?"

Raisa shook her head and bit her lip before whispering, "I think she's in denial."

"She's not accepting it?"

Granted Miri didn't know Allie that well, but she didn't seem the type to deny reality. She seemed more the type to grab it by the throat and make it do what she wanted.

"She says she knows in her gut Slade will come up with a solution."

Poor Slade. It seemed everyone relied on him. "What did Slade say?"

"He muttered something about it probably just being indigestion and then went back to the lab to make some more of that enzyme mixture."

They crossed the short landing. From the bedroom to the left, Miri could hear the sounds of a woman speaking in soft tones. More a murmur than actual words, the sounds and rhythm were clearly meant to soothe. Miri peeked into the room. Allie was sitting in the chair with Joseph on her lap. He was wrapped in a bright blue baby blanket, his head tucked into the crook of her elbow.

She knocked. Allie looked up. Her smile was as soft as the baby's skin looked as she motioned them forward with a flick of her fingers. "He's almost asleep."

Miri tiptoed over to her side and about melted when she saw his face, his lashes fanned across his cheeks, his little mouth parted slightly. "Aw, he looks like an angel."

"He looks like Caleb."

He did. Even though the baby was too thin and his perfect skin paler than it should be, Miri could see Caleb in his chin and the shape of his eyes, and Allie in his forehead and his cheekbones. There was no doubt who his parents were and, looking at him curled in Allie's arms, no doubt that he was loved.

Allie looked up at her from under the thick fringe of her bangs, her eyes looking very blue. "How's your little one doing?"

"Good. Jace says she's telepathic."

"How cool! Can you hear her?"

"Not yet." Probably because they weren't bonded.

Allie smiled serenely. "Don't worry, you will."

Miri flipped her hair behind her shoulder. "Can I quote you on that?"

"Absolutely." She glanced down at little Joseph. "Are you going to be able to do that someday, urchin?"

Joseph made a little smacking noise with his lips.

"Urchin?"

Allie shrugged. "After the way he's been keeping me up, I didn't want to give him too cute a nickname. He can't think both his parents are pushovers."

"I'm guessing the pushover would be Caleb?" As hard as that was to believe.

"Beyond a goner." Allie shook her head, kissing Joseph lightly on his slightly furrowed brow. "He actually worries ahead of time, if you can believe it." She rolled her eyes. "Having him around is like trying to sleep in a hospital. Every time Joseph starts to drift off, Caleb wakes him up to check something."

"That's kind of self-defeating, isn't it?"

Allie snorted. It wasn't a ladylike sound. "Totally. I sent him off to fetch you so Joseph could go to sleep."

"I was wondering why you sent for me."

"I needed saving."

"Glad I could help."

"You could always just threaten to withhold Caleb's bear paws pastries to keep him in line," Raisa suggested.

"I'm hoping to avoid going to extremes."

Allie gave the chair a little rock, cradling Joseph in her arms, looking so contented and at peace it hurt Miri just to look at her. She wanted that, with her baby. With Peanut.

"Miri?" Raisa asked.

Miri blinked. She must have been projecting emotion. The tears she'd been fighting ever since Peanut came into the house burned her eyes.

She motioned to Allie. "I just wish I could be like that."

"With Peanut?"

Allie glanced up. "Seriously, you need to give her a better name."

"I need to do a lot of things, starting with being able to hold her."

"Still having the panic attacks?" Allie asked.

"I did make it to the side of her bed."

"That's improvement."

"But not enough."

"You've got to walk before you can run," Allie offered.

"I'm sick and tired of being damaged." She ran her fingers through her hair. They caught on snarls. It was the absolute last straw. She yanked them through, accomplishing nothing more than pain in her scalp and creating a mat. "Damn it!"

Raisa grabbed her hand and put an end to her yanking, drawing her hand down and untangling the strands from her fingers. Her gaze met Miri's. "You've got to give yourself time to heal."

The only thing that kept Miri from lashing out was the fact that Raisa had been there, too, knew what she was going through, because she must have gone through some part of it herself. "I don't want to be like this," she whispered. "I want to be strong again."

"You're one of the strongest women I know."

She bit her lip. "Not inside, not where it counts."

"Inside, outside, and everywhere else."

Raisa gave her a hug. The first they'd ever been able to share. Miri just stood there as Raisa's arms came around her, paralyzed by the past, a desperate voice in her mind screaming a warning, *Don't let them see. Don't let them see.*

Raisa's voice.

"Fuck them," Raisa whispered, picking up the chant in her head and bringing it into the light. "Let them see. They couldn't touch us then, and they sure as heck can't touch us now."

Miri brought her hands up, shaking inside and out, emotion pouring out of her on a harsh sob. Feeling like the ground was disappearing beneath her feet, she hugged Raisa back, for a moment suspended over nothingness, trapped with no hope. And then, something shifted inside her, came forward from the hiding place where she'd buried it. Something she'd hidden so well she'd lost track of it. As it snapped into place, she could breathe. She dragged air into her lungs, hugged Raisa as hard as she'd wanted to hug her when they'd been imprisoned together. "Definitely, fuck them."

Energy brushed along the edges of her mind.

Miri?

She stepped back and wiped the tears from her cheeks with the heels of her hands.

Jace?

You okay?

Miri looked at Raisa and Allie, who were crying right along with her, then looked inside herself for the missing piece that had come back. A fragile piece of herself. She took a breath and grabbed hold of Jace's energy, concentrating, following it back.

I think I really am.

She felt his surprise that she'd answered and then his hope at the emotion behind the words. His energy came at her harder, stronger, wrapping her in warmth.

Damn it. Come home so I can hug you.

Miri walked over to the window and pulled the lace curtain back, looking at the cabin they shared across the way. Home.

She wasn't trapped and alone anymore in that place where any caring led to suffering, where any weakness was exploited. This wasn't an illusion. She was free of the Sanctuary. She had a future. Jace had given it back to her. And he wanted her home so he could hug her. She wanted that hug, but she needed a little more time to herself before she could share it with him.

I'll be home soon.

An hour later, Allie's cell phone rang. As she listened, her smile slipped until it became a full-out frown. She snapped the phone closed. "That was Tobias."

"Tobias has your cell phone number?" Raisa asked, sitting forward in the wingback chair. "Does Caleb know?"

"Caleb doesn't need to know everything."

"What'd he want?" Miri asked, a queasy feeling starting in her stomach.

Allie tossed the phone on the couch beside her. "Apparently the McClarens have had a meeting, the results of which they wish to discuss with Jace."

Raisa uncurled her feet from beneath her. "In regard to what?"

"They want to discuss Peanut's situation."

"She doesn't have a situation."

The sick feeling in Miri's stomach grew. Pack law was absolute. Parents had a right to handle the deformed child any way they wanted. They could accept it, love it, or give it back to Mother Nature. In the absence of a parent, a pack taking in a child had the option of following the parents' original choice or making a new one.

Miri took a breath, held it until she knew her voice would be steady, and then released it. "Yes, she does. The pack can decide that the parents' original wishes should be followed."

"Derek would never let that happen," Allie protested.

"Derek isn't here," Raisa pointed out.

"What happens then?"

Allie and Raisa both stared at her while they waited for her to answer. They weren't going to like what she had to say. "In that case, the pack could require the council to make the decision, and that's a majority rules verdict."

A council decision could go badly for Peanut. There was no doubt that the little girl Jace loved so much had been abandoned. No doubt the Sanctuary had taken advantage of that, and experimented on her, changing her from what she had been—fully were. It wasn't Peanut's fault they'd altered her chemistry, but the fact that she wasn't fully were anymore would be enough for some members to want to enforce the parents' original choice.

"Jace won't allow anything to happen to Peanut."

"I'll take this moment to point out that this compound is full of weres," Allie interjected. "The Johnsons are outnumbered."

"That won't stop the brothers from protecting Peanut if it comes to that," Raisa said, her talons extending.

Allie didn't look any less fierce. "And warring among ourselves will accomplish, what? We need a plan, not a pointless fight. So"— she glanced at both women—"what are we going to do?"

This was all her fault. "We aren't going to do anything." Miri walked over to the window. "What I should have done in the first place."

"And what would that be?"

Only a sliver of moonlight lit the courtyard. It was enough for her were vision to see quite clearly. Jace and Caleb were standing on the porch of the cabin. A group of weres approached. Even from here she could see the tension in Jace's shoulders, see the way his hands were laid protectively across the baby's back. He'd die for Peanut and not regret it for a moment. A ripple went through the weres. It increased as Caleb came to stand beside him, feet braced shoulder width apart. One thing the pack understood and respected was a fight to the death for family. And from the way Jace was holding Peanut, it was clear she was family. Unfortunately for Jace, without a female were to speak for the child, his claim was void. "I need to set a misunderstanding right."

Allie came up to the window as Caleb invited the men inside. "And what would that misunderstanding be?"

Miri headed for the door. "That Jace is in this alone."

Raisa grabbed her coat. Allie scooped up Joseph and smiled. "Now you're talking like a Johnson."

ALL sound stopped when the women walked into the living room of the small cabin. Everywhere Miri looked, male weres stood with shoulders squared in a way that said they had an opinion and they wanted it heard. Caleb, Jace, Jared, and Slade stood with the same determination. She hadn't known the last two would be here, but it figured. What touched one Johnson brother touched them all. They were amazingly pack-like in their behavior. It was always comforting to realize that.

Tobias stepped forward, blocking their path, a slight smile on his face. "This is a council meeting."

Allie breezed past him, striding through the group like a queen walking to her throne, undeterred by the frowning weres around her. She even went so far as to wiggle five fingers at an elder were and give him a saucy grin.

"Allie . . ." Caleb warned, his face a bit too serious, probably to counter the smile ghosting the corner of his mouth.

"What?" She looked innocent. "Just because it's a council meeting doesn't mean I can't say hi to the people I know and like."

Caleb caught her hand as she got close, pulling her in to his side and dropping a kiss on the top of her head. "Hate to break it to you, but pretty much, it does."

"I'm sure kissing your wife at council meetings isn't considered appropriate, either."

This time it was Tobias who answered. "Pretty much."

Raisa walked through the men with the same confidence in her step as Allie had showed, her gaze holding her husband's as love radiated between them in an arc of energy so pure Miri could almost see it. "You-all really have to modernize your meetings," she informed the weres in general.

"We kind of like things just as they are," someone called from the back.

Allie gave the man a dismissive glance as she leaned back against her husband's chest, little Joseph snug in his sling. "People always say that when it's time to change."

It was an intriguing idea, that the highest resistance occurred right before change. Miri looked over at Jace standing there between his brothers, prepared to fight for what he wanted. Had he truly always wanted her?

Yes.

The mental answer didn't spark that familiar dart of fear and knee-jerk denial inside her. That was a good sign. Maybe she was healing. Maybe she could do this.

A murmur of displeasure went through the crowd, flicking over her upbringing. As if echoing the disapproval, pain flared in her abdomen. Across the room, Jace's gaze met hers. Not with passion, but with a question. She didn't know the answer. She didn't know if she had any backbone left. Peanut fussed. With a rub of his big hand on her tiny back, Jace soothed her before handing the baby to Raisa. All the while he watched Miri, the question still in his eyes.

She pushed away from the doorjamb. If there was one thing she'd learned in the last year, it was that one couldn't walk away from one's heritage. The reality was that she was an Alpha were female. She had responsibilities to her pack, to the other wolves around her, to Jace, and to the baby he held in his arms. The baby who needed her now as much as her own baby needed somebody to be holding her. Miri stepped into the crowd. She would find the backbone to do what needed to be done.

The men immediately closed in around her, pressing close. She wasn't surprised. Instinct alone would have them blocking her access to a vampire, but that reflex was totally out of place in this instance. Jace was her mate. Pack law gave none of them the right to come between him and her.

She growled low in her throat. A warning. On the other side of the crowd, she heard a "Jesus" and then Caleb's caution to someone: "Stay back." Even she knew that wasn't going to happen. Jace wouldn't let anything come between him and her, and the weres were obligated to put up at least a token fight. If for no other reason than to make a customary display, to prove her worth to them. From the snarling, to sounds of fists meeting flesh, Jace didn't care much for custom. Two seconds later, several male weres were tossed to the side and Jace was beside her. His face was half morphed and his fangs were exposed, and when he reached for her, his talons glowed dully in the lamplight. He was a very scary vampire. The were nearest her snarled a warning. But he was also her Jace. She placed her hand in his.

Immediately he yanked her behind him, crowding her backward until they reached the fireplace and his brothers.

Weres poured into the path, closing it off. There was no retreat now. It was us against them. "Us" being the weres. "Them" being the vampires. Placing her palm in the middle of Jace's back, she felt Jace gather himself for the kill, his instincts in overdrive.

"You can't do this, Jace."

Tobias laughed.

She glared at him. "This is not a laughing matter."

"I guess that would depend on which side of the argument you're standing on."

"Back off, Enforcer."

Jace placed himself between her and Tobias, every muscle tensed for a fight, his energy flaring out into the crowd, snapping back to stroke over her before flaring out again. "What are you doing, princess?"

She stepped out from behind him. "I'm fixing things."

"It appears to me you're starting things," Caleb inserted.

"Fiddlesticks," Allie snapped. "You men have had too much say in this already."

"This is a council matter," one of the elders said.

"It's a family matter," Miri countered, feeling her former confidence flow over her, feeling the rightness of standing here beside Jace expand outward from her center.

She took a cautious breath and let the feeling spread. When it filled every cold, empty corner inside, she bit her lip and raised her hand. Silence crashed through the room. It was now or never. Pulse pounding in her temples, she reached toward Peanut, where she was cuddled in Raisa's arms. Her fingers met air. She was too far away. The room blurred out of focus. Closing her eyes, she took the next step on faith, hoping against hope she wouldn't freeze up. Her hand connected with a petal-soft blanket. She was touching her. Touching Peanut.

Please, don't make this either/or. Don't let saving Peanut cost me Faith.

Jace's "You did it, princess" came to her on a thread of pride. She shook her head. Not yet, she hadn't.

Another breath, another prayer.

Please, please, please.

The desperate prayer still playing through her mind, she opened her eyes, seeing Jace's concern and pride, feeling his support. Not looking anywhere but into his eyes. Holding Faith's image tightly in her mind, she announced:

"I'm Miri D'Nally. Alpha female of the Tragallion weres. And this is my daughter." She couldn't bring herself to officially name her Peanut by calling her that in a claiming.

She looked around before holding out her hand, palm up, to Jace. Without hesitation, Jace put his in it. She brought it to her lips, trapping his gaze with hers, noting how his eyes burned blue fire as she said, "This is my mate, Jace Johnson." The flickers leapt to flames as he realized what she was doing. His energy swirled around her, rich and hot. She kissed the back of his fingers in a gesture of submission and acceptance all weres would recognize. Still holding his gaze, she finished the ritual. "All who wish to challenge my choice may step forward."

Out of the corner of her eye, Miri saw Jared push away from the wall and stand at the ready for a fight.

"Shit. I don't like the sound of that."

Jace switched his grip to the back of her neck. His fingers pressed delicately, tipping her head back. He lowered his head, his shadow blocking the light but not his satisfaction as he said, right before their lips met, "I do."

❧ 14 ❧

"**F**OR a were who prides herself on her control, you sure do have a temper."

Not that Jace was complaining. He liked it when Miri got her dander up. Jace watched as Miri grabbed ice from the dispenser and dumped it into the towel. Residual anger reverberated in the way she banged it on the counter to break up the chips.

"They had no right to attack you."

"It was a challenge. You invited them to."

"All they had to do was put up a token fight and tradition would have been honored."

"Princess, you're not a woman to inspire token anything."

She brought the towel over. Jace wanted to kiss her for the frown on her face as she pressed it to his bruised cheek.

"Even if they beat you, it wouldn't have won them anything."

"It would have won them you."

"No, it wouldn't." She touched the cut under his eye. "Tobias didn't need to hit you so hard."

He cupped his hand over hers, pressing the pack to his cheek. "Is that why you went all Alpha on their butts?"

The way she went still against him made Jace wonder if she thought he thought that was a bad thing.

"I wasn't raised to be meek."

He nodded. "Just obedient. Interesting dichotomy."

She very gently eased the ice pack down to his jaw. "It's my job to balance pack law."

"And that slash you gave Tobias? That created balance?"

"Yes."

No one had been more surprised than he when she'd waded into the pile of weres on top of him. Snarling and slashing, driving them back with the force of her fury.

With the tips of his fingers he brushed the hair off her brow. "You could have gotten hurt."

Her eyes glowed. "They were hurting you!"

"I was holding my own." In truth if she hadn't jumped in right then, making it impossible for him to throw the were off, he would have done some serious ass kicking. "Not that I'm not appreciative, but jumping in when you did put a crimp on my moment to shine."

"You're shining just fine," she said, moving the ice pack to his blackening eye.

He caught her hand and took it from her and set it down.

"Ice doesn't work nearly as well as kisses," he explained when she gave him a questioning look.

"You want me to kiss it better?"

He tugged her down on his lap. "Yup."

Her arms went around his neck. "This is some sort of secret vampire healing process?"

He shifted her legs over a bit to give her a better angle. "Very secret, known only to me."

The anger left her eyes to be replaced by a spark of humor. The touch of her lips to the underside of his chin was a benediction of hope.

"So anytime I find a wounded vampire I should employ kisses to heal him?"

Despite the fact he knew she was teasing, his vampire snarled. He felt her inner joy at the possessive surge. She was were. She welcomed such displays. "It's only effective on me."

Those softer-than-soft lips grazed the line of his jaw. "Ah."

He tilted his head to give her better access to his neck. "What does 'ah' mean?"

"It means I understand." The sharp edges of her canines found the cord of his neck and traveled downward. His heart stuttered and then took off in a race of optimism. His skin sensitized, the nerve endings beneath aching in anticipation of her bite. Her mark.

From the other room, Peanut let out a wail.

Shit!

Miri leaned against him. Her shoulders shook. Her breath hit his skin in amused puffs. "She's just lonely."

"She's got lousy timing."

"She wants her daddy."

He tipped her face. "Her daddy wants her mommy."

Her eyes dilated at the blunt declaration. The pound of her pulse increased. He stroked his thumb across her lower lip. She still had a way to go until she reached his level of desire, but he'd take panting.

"I do not pant."

He smiled. "Caught that, did you?"

"Yes." She pushed off his lap. Peanut wailed louder. "It was not appreciated."

"I'll work on my aspirations." He tucked his feet under him in preparation of getting up. Miri placed a hand in the middle of his chest, keeping him put. Her fingers slipped between the buttons, sliding across his skin in a brush of fire. "I'll get her."

"You sure?" Beyond that light touch at the impromptu council meeting, she hadn't touched Peanut. Whatever had happened earlier had brought back more of the woman he remembered. Jeopardizing that recovery was not an option. "Positive."

For all the confidence of the statement, there was just the barest of hesitations as she reached the archway leading to the second bedroom.

"You don't have anything to prove to me, Miri."

She looked over her shoulder. "But I have a lot to prove to myself."

He didn't know what to say to that.

Mentally racking her progress through the rooms, he felt as well as heard her stop before she reached the baby's makeshift crib. "Hey, Peanut."

Peanut wailed louder. She didn't move forward. Her dread was as palpable as her hope. He rolled to his feet. The three seconds it took to get to her didn't see any resolution to her dilemma. As he came up beside her she said, "I'm afraid to try."

He wrapped his arm around her waist. "I know." He looked over the crib to the red-faced baby. "Hey, Peanut. Anyone ever tell you that you have lousy timing?"

He'd be damned if Peanut didn't give him a watery smile.

"Did you see that?"

Miri's chuckle was as weak as Peanut's smile. "I did."

"The imp is scamming us."

She made no move forward. "I think she's just very happy to be a Johnson."

The statement opened a door he'd been longing to peek through. "And what about you? Are you happy to be a Johnson?"

Her hands came over his, pressing them into her stomach. He could feel the nausea building and the pain threatening right behind. It drove him crazy that she made herself suffer rather than take his blood.

"Giving up my pack was the hardest thing I ever did."

"I know that."

"But I'm beginning to understand that I didn't give up a pack when I mated with you. I just moved to a new one."

He sent energy inward, masking her discomfort while pretending outrage to distract her from what he was doing. "Are you call-ing me a werewolf, woman?"

Her fingers slid through his, tucking down his palms, squeezing lightly. "You and your brothers think so much like pack that I some-times forgot you're not."

He made a face at Peanut, who stared at the strange contortion, fascinated. It kept her from crying, which was the goal. "I think I've been insulted."

"You know you haven't, so don't try to distract me with false outrage."

"Damn, you're too quick for me."

"And don't you forget it." She took a step toward the baby. His instinct was to snatch her back. He forced himself to let her go.

She stood there a second, heartbeat racing. His raced right along-side. He wanted this so badly for her. She bent. Reached out. Stopped breathing.

So did he. *Don't cry now, Peanut.*

Peanut stared up at Miri, but didn't twitch or fuss as Miri slid her hands under her tiny body and lifted her up.

Miri just stood there, holding Peanut halfway to a cuddle, her ribs heaving with the stress of what she was doing. "Quick, tell me this doesn't mean I'll never get Faith back, that I'm not condemn-ing her to death."

Ah, hell, was that what she thought? He wrapped his arms around her torso and dropped his cheek against her tear-dampened one. His beard-roughened skin slid on her smooth cheek. "You're not killing Faith, princess. Faith will come home. Letting yourself give Peanut what she needs is just throwing good karma out there for Faith to catch."

"Karma?"

"Hey, I haven't been a total recluse the last couple centuries."

She still didn't move. He could feel the discomfort in her mus-cles, in her mind. Peanut, bored with the position, started to pout.

The plea came in the barest of whispers. "Help me, Jace."

He'd give her his soul if she needed it. Comparatively, putting his hands under hers and providing the muscle power to cuddle Peanut against her chest was a piece of cake.

As soon as the baby leaned against her chest, her breath released on a soft "Oh."

"What?"

She shook her head. She cradled Peanut's head in her palm and pressed her against her throat. She turned to face him. Tears were pouring down her cheeks, and the most poignant of smiles filled her expression. "It just feels so good."

Emotion poured from her to him, waves of it, so many intertwined it was hard to sort them out, but when he did, the predominate ones were love and elation.

His heart twisted in his chest. "Yeah, it does."

AN hour later, with the dawn creeping through the window and Peanut hopefully down for a good sleep, Jace sat on the edge of the bed and listened to Miri fuss in the bathroom. Moist air from her shower flowed out from under the door, redolent with the scents of wildflowers and rosemary. He loved the way she smelled. He leaned back against the headboard and enjoyed the intimacy of the moment and the satisfaction of knowing that the woman in the other room was his wife, that when he woke come nightfall, more than a memory would be beside him.

He closed his eyes. At last.

The water turned off. Jace imagined Miri standing on the other side of the door, hesitating, nervously licking her lips. The way she had their first time. He cracked his lids. He wasn't going to make the same mistake this time that he'd made the last, though. Left too much to her own thinking, Miri could work herself up into a self-defeating lather.

The doorknob turned. Apparently Miri had learned some things, too.

He opened his eyes all the way. The door slowly opened, spilling yellow light into the shadows. He sat up, desire throbbing with the heavy beat of his heart. She stood, hands stroking down over the sheer material that barely covered her thighs. "Hi."

"Hi, yourself."

She didn't move.

"Is there a problem?"

She licked her lips. "No."

"I hear a 'but.'" He swung his legs off the bed. She jumped. "You've been thinking, Miri."

"Just a little."

"Any angle in particular you've been playing?" When he got close enough, he held out his hand, palm up. She placed hers in it. So much smaller than his. So much more fragile—he rubbed his thumb across the back—yet possessing so much strength. He drew her to him with a slow motion, giving her time to resist. She didn't. She just flowed into his embrace, waiting until he had her tightly in his arms before confessing.

"What if it's not the same?"

He wrapped his hands in her damp hair, tugging her head back. "Baby, every time I'm with you is unique."

Her gaze ducked his. "I'm no longer beautiful."

He kissed the scar on her right cheek. "You really did have a long think."

"It was a long shower."

"It wasn't that long." He turned his attention to the scar on her left cheek, giving it the same special care.

"There has never been, nor ever will be, anything more beautiful in the world to me than this face." He kissed her mouth, feeling it tremble. "Nothing that could sound more perfect than the sound of your voice." He turned her around and toppled her onto the bed, coming down over her, catching his weight on his elbows. "And nothing that could feel better than this body against mine."

Her arms came around his neck. "Are you sure?"

"Never been surer. And to prove it, I'm accepting your claim."

"What claim?"

"The one you made downstairs."

She blinked. "I was getting you out of trouble!"

"Uh-uh. You claimed me." He slid his fingers up her arm, teasing her sensitive skin with his nails, not stopping until he reached her hands so he could weave his fingers between hers. "Maybe not according to pack policy and maybe not in any way that the pack could formalize, but you claimed me, and now you're stuck with me."

"I'm sorry. That wasn't fair to you."

"Do you hear me complaining?"

"You should be. I'm still such a mess inside, Jace."

She said it like it was a secret. He brought her right hand up around his neck. "But you're my mess."

He brought the left hand up next, pausing with his fingers on her wrist, and she said, "You should reject me."

"Now, why would I want to do that? When you fit me so well?"

He pushed her hair off her face, stroking the back of his fingers over her cheek, marveling in the softness of her skin, feeling the ridge of the scar. Her lower lip slid between her teeth. He felt the brush of her energy and, just as immediately, its retreat. "Talk to me, Miri."

"About what?"

"About the real worry you're chewing on."

"What if I'm not ready to talk?"

"You have to anyway. If you can't find the words, then I'll help you. And if you're not ready, then you'll tell me and we'll work around it. What you can't do is keep it all inside and hide, because this isn't something from which either of us can walk away."

She stared at him, the shadows in her eyes multiplying, all but obscuring the glimmer of hope that peeked between the swirling edges. Her fingers curled into fists beside her head. He placed his hands over hers, prying her fingers open one by one. The scent from the shampoo she'd used on her hair teased his senses—wildflowers and Miri. A combination indelibly etched in his mind. Miri naked and lying in the white moonlight, reaching for him with her mind and body, offering him the home he'd always sought, without fear.

"Remember our first time, princess?"

"Yes."

"You didn't even hesitate. You opened yourself to me so sweetly."

He kissed her cheek, her nose, her lashes, smiling when they fluttered shut.

"You lay down amid the daisies and dandelions, accepted me flaws and all."

"You have no flaws."

"If you weren't immortal, you'd have to worry about going to hell for that whopper. I'm far from perfect."

"You were perfect for me."

"You sure thought so, but the truth is, you had a lot more to fear from me then than you do now. Then, I was an unknown vampire lusting after your nubile young body." The corner of her lips twitched. "I was intent on having my wicked way with you."

"I remember."

He unbuttoned the shimmery concoction that kept her breasts from him. "I intended for you to be fully debauched come morning."

Her eyes opened. Her smile bloomed. That gorgeous smile that stole his soul the first time he saw it. "I was."

He spread the material, exposing the sweet curves of her chest. "When I claimed you then, it was a forever thing for me."

He slipped his hand beneath, watching her expression for fear. There wasn't any.

She arched her breast into his palm, filling his hand with the promise she'd given him that first night. "I know."

"No, you didn't. You thought 'forever' for me was as long as I desired you, but I was willing to work with that, sweet-talk you around to believing in me."

"But then you had to leave."

"Temporarily. But to you that meant it was over. You thought I'd left. I'm sorry I didn't understand that." A brush of his lips over the ledge of her cheekbones. "Very sorry."

"I'm sorry, too."

"Good."

"Jace?"

"What?"

"What's different about now?"

"Ah, now." He plumped her breast in his hand, admiring the generous soft mound it made beneath the silky nightgown, the way the darker tip made the smallest of tentings. It would take very little effort to dip his head and take that soft peak in his mouth, lave it with his tongue, nip it to that delicate hardness in the way that always made her moan in bliss.

He had to focus on what he wanted to say to get the words out. "Now you know there was never any danger at all. Now you know what kind of man I am, what kind of lover I am. You know I'm the sticking kind. And I'm safe."

She blinked. "Safe?"

Her skepticism did wonders for his ego.

"Absolutely."

She shifted and the gown pulled taut.

"Where'd you get this sexy little gown?"

"Allie." She twisted under him, watching as his thumb passed over the tip. He'd forgotten how she liked to watch. The gap in his memory bothered him. What else had he forgotten? The neckline slid to the side, exposing her breast with its peach-colored tip. The nipple was semi hard, demanding his attention.

He leaned in. "I'll have to thank her."

Her head snapped up so fast, she almost cracked his jaw. "Don't you dare!"

He chuckled as she flopped back onto the mattress. "I'm pretty sure she knew what would happen when you wore it."

"I don't care. Promise me you won't say anything."

Since he didn't want her distracted by the worry, he promised.

Another twist exposed more buttery-smooth skin. Her breast shimmied; he accepted the invitation, bending his head, taking that sweet tip into his mouth. Her taste spread across his tongue. Soap and Miri. He closed his eyes, imprinting it anew into his senses, letting it sink to his center in a long-awaited flow of re-membered pleasure. He'd been so long without her. Needed her so badly. "I love the way you taste."

She arched her energy, weaving through his in an erotic temp-tation.

Jace.

Only Miri said his name like that, as if heaven was in his hands and she only waited for him to give it to her. He shifted up to see her face. Her eyes were filled with tears. "Hey, sweet talk isn't sup-posed to make you cry."

She swiped at the tears with the back of her hand and sniffed. "I think you're out of luck."

He stood, bringing her with him. Her legs went instinctively around his waist. He turned, sitting on the mattress. Letting her support herself with her arms around his neck while he stroked the damp trails on her cheeks. "Because that was too corny?"

She shook her head. Her hair swished across his thighs. He took a handful and draped it over his shoulders, binding them to-gether, following the path back until he could curl his fingers around her nape.

"Because I blinked and you didn't go away. You're real."

He felt the same way. The joy that she was here, the lingering panic that it was just another dream he'd wake up from, her name an echo of desperate hope in his head. He tilted her face to the side with a press of his thumb, skimming his lips over her cheek to the sweet spot behind her ear, the one that if he kissed it just right would send goose bumps up and down her arms. "Very real. Want me to show you how much?"

She canted her head away, providing him with easier access. "Yes."

He was happy to oblige. Following the desire that moved hot and rich through his blood, he touched the spot with his tongue, her pleasure his as she shivered. He smiled against her skin. "It's nice to know some things don't change."

Her hands cupped his head, holding him to her, offering herself to him. "Yes, it is."

The passion he'd been fighting roared forward, ripping apart his control, wrecking havoc with his good intentions. He took a steadying breath. "Princess, saying things like that to me right now is hell on my control."

Her tongue touched the corner of his mouth. Lightning bolts of sensation arced outward, shooting down his spine before gathering at the base in a hot aching urgency. "So who wants you controlled?"

"You do, because I want you too much to play games," he rasped out.

"Who's asking you to play games?"

"I've been a long time hungry and a long time hurting."

He turned his head so the softness of her lips matched the firmness of his, so her breath blended with his, so her energy melded with his. "And the one thing I won't ever be is the next thing that hurts you."

"You can't. Not you."

She stroked her tongue over his. He shuddered, unable to control his response. He wanted that hot little tongue lapping all over his body. "I could lose my head, take you too roughly."

She placed her hands on his shoulders, scooting up on her knees before pushing backward. "There's only one way to find out."

He took her weight gladly, thrusting up when she pressed down, anchoring her with his hands on her hips. "I was thinking along the lines of talking about it."

"You said, if I wasn't ready, we'd work around it."

"I did say that. Do we need a work-around?"

She stretched her torso along his, took his earlobe between her teeth, and nipped. "Yes."

His grip spasmed on her hips. She laughed at the loss of control, the soft expulsions fanning the fire racing across his skin.

"What do you suggest?" he asked when he could find his voice.

"I was hoping you'd make love to me."

He rolled them so she was beneath him. A bit too quickly, if her momentary disorientation was anything to go by.

He smiled down at her. "Were you, now?"

Her palms flattened on his chest, her thumbs going to his nipples.

"I was thinking on it."

Her gaze held his as she flicked them with her nails. His breath hissed in as his cock jerked in his pants. He studied her as she lay beneath him, the fine arch of her brows above the warm golden-brown of her eyes, the elegant line of her nose above the lush perfection of her lips, and that stubborn chin. He traced the lines of her cheekbones, enjoying the smoothness of her skin, so enhanced by the peaches and cream of her complexion. For him, there was nothing more perfect than the way her features came together in a boldly feminine way that combined incredible strength with incredible vulnerability. She was so damn beautiful.

He grabbed her hand and brought it to his lips, pressing a kiss into her palm. He met her gaze. "Hold that thought."

Her tongue ran over her lips. "What if I don't want to?"

"You don't have a choice." He could feel the pain building inside her again, could feel the weakness in her caused by the imbalance of a mating not completed. "There is something we need to do first."

"What's that?"

He sliced his nail across his chest. Blood flowed, the scent rising between them. Her nostrils flared. So did her hunger. "You need to feed."

She shook her head. "I'm fine."

She was far from fine. He captured a drop of blood on his fingertip and smeared it across her lips. "I can't watch you suffer anymore, princess." It was the closest he could come to an apology. Her pupils flared as the taste crept between the seal of her lips. "Besides, we have a long night ahead of us." His gaze wandered to her breasts, with their hard nipples and creamy softness. "And you're going to need to be at full strength if you plan on keeping up."

A long night.

Identical words she'd heard in the past. The scary, dark memories buried within the syllables clawed their way out, battering at her control. She took a breath, held it for the count of three, and then let it out. This was Jace above her—strong, indomitable Jace with the laughing eyes, the quick temper, and the incredible touch. Jace, who inspired the hunger in her. A natural hunger, not the perverted imitation the Sanctuary had tried to manufacture in the hope it would help her to conceive.

His hand behind her head brought her face to his chest. "You have to feed, Miri. You need to be strong."

She took a breath, letting his scent sink deep. She wouldn't let the memories rob her of him. Meeting his gaze, she gave him the smile—the one from so long ago, the one she'd practiced in the mirror when she would dream about a suitor who would one day bond with her. The smile she'd perfected to the point that it was sultry, hot, and biting. Guaranteed to blow his socks off.

Her reward was a blink of his gorgeous eyes, and then a slow smile.

"You have a snack, baby, and I'll take you up on that invitation."

The tightening of his hold coincided with the lowering of his head. She couldn't look away from his eyes. They were hazel, then blue, and then lit with fires that danced in patterns that intrigued. The brush of his lips was petal soft, the parting an open invitation to the passion beyond. She wanted that passion, wanted the secrets she read in his eyes, that she felt inside herself. She took his kiss, as he took her control, in slow increments, letting the surprise of it unravel in a slow, lazy persuasion. The familiar subtle adjustment of his fingers directed her mouth downward, over the column of his throat, across the ridge of his collarbone, and over the smooth flex of his muscle, replacing the taste of his kiss with the potent spice of his blood. Enthralled, she followed the mental lure, succumbing to the urge to drink, moaning aloud as her cells exploded with bliss as the life-giving fluid slid over her tongue.

Jace's fingers stroked down her breast, readying her for his touch, making her wait for it until the anticipation had her moaning, his laugh breezing by her ear as she opened to him, mind, body, and soul, taking his passion as hers, giving her passion to him, weaving them together with desire. His name echoed in her mind, tumbled from her lips. "Jace."

"Right here."

"I need you," she whispered against his chest, her blood hunger abating to be replaced by another. His fingers encompassed her breast, plumping it to his touch. His thumb flicked over the tip in a tiny culmination. She gasped against his chest, hot, breathless energy surging within her, searching for an outlet. "I need you."

Jace pulled her up into the power of his kiss. "You're not ready."

"I don't care." Miri watched helplessly as he sealed the wound on his chest. She licked her lips where his taste lingered. "I just want you."

"You'll have me. Every inch of me." He milked more pleasure from her breast, more burn to her flesh, more need to her core. "But I'm going to explore you first, reacquaint myself with all the touches in all the places that make you cry out."

She wrapped her legs around his waist and with her free hand tugged at his jeans while pressing herself up. His erection dropped against her sensitive flesh. "No."

He pulled back, his eyes lit with flames more blue than hazel locked on her. His fangs flashed white. Her neck tingled. She wanted to feel his bite.

"No?"

She could feel him shaking, feel the film of sweat on his skin. He needed her. "This time speed," she breathed. "Next time explorations."

"Don't tempt me."

She arched her breasts up to his chest "Why not?"

He didn't have a ready answer. She nibbled on his upper lip, raking her nails down his chest in a meandering pattern that had him arching like a jungle cat into her touch.

His answer, when it came, was couched in a growl. "Because this is you."

She cupped his cheeks in her hands, loving the flames at the edges of the irises in his beautiful eyes, loving knowing that they burned for her, just for her. She loved that he was worried about her.

"In the last year, Jace, people have used my body in all kinds of ways, for all kinds of things, none of which I wanted."

He kissed the inside of her wrist, heartbreak in his eyes. "Goddamn, baby."

She didn't want him sad.

"I don't think I can last another minute with those memories in my head. Not now, when I could have the real thing. Please, can't you forget, just for tonight, and make love to me the way you would if you'd come back as you'd planned, and I'd been there waiting?"

"Miri—"

She didn't want him cautious, either.

"I always imagined it'd be quick because we'd be so hungry for each other, like a thunder and lightning storm rushing in. Wild, crazy."

"Miri?"

"What?"

His forehead dropped to hers. Laughter shook his shoulders. "You win."

He reached between them. There was the sound of a zipper sliding and two seconds later she felt his cock against her—hard, hot, big, and ready. "Oh, God."

"Hold on."

She did, grabbing his shoulders, her nails sinking into the thick muscle with the same steady pressure with which he merged their bodies. Her sheath stretched, flowered.

He paused, giving her a minute to adjust, while his eyes burned down at her, challenging her.

Did he think she wasn't up to it?

She held his gaze, digging her heels into the mattress, pushing up, taking him in a smooth glide, gasping as the burning pleasure detonated into something more.

Jace. At last, Jace.

She kept her eyes open, locking her mind to his as desire exploded through her, crying out as the bliss took over, reaching out, reflecting back, her pleasure becoming his, his pleasure hers, binding them together in a maelstrom of satisfaction that screamed only one thing.

Mate!

✦ 15 ✦

THE McClarens had been challenging Jace for four days and she'd about had enough of it. Miri stood in the kitchen waiting for Peanut's bottle to heat and glared at Tobias, who lounged in the doorway. "When are they going to accept that he's not going away?"

"Probably about the time he stops winning," Tobias answered, pushing away from the doorjamb.

"That doesn't make sense."

He shrugged. "They're weres, and they've got a point to make. They don't have to make sense."

She wanted to whack him on the head with a pan. "You're an Enforcer. You can make anyone do anything."

"That's what they say."

She rolled her eyes. The edginess rose. "Just my luck, an Enforcer with no muscle."

All the insult did was jar loose a laugh. "As your husband pointed out, there are rules."

"You don't look the type to worry about rules." She took the bottle to test it. Peanut reached for the pan. She pulled her back, dropping the bottle and splashing hot water on her arm.

"Darn!"

Tobias turned her arm over and smoothed his thumb over the small burn. The sting disappeared. "And you can relax." His gaze met hers. "Eventually they'll realize this is not progressing and that they have to come up with another solution."

"Meanwhile they beat up on Jace. That's so comforting."

"Have you seen the McClarens?" The flick of his eyebrows and the twitch of his lips conveyed his amusement. "I think he's holding his own."

She didn't have anything to say to that. Jace *was* holding his own. She was just darned tired of seeing him with bruises. Miri expected Tobias to remind her that she could put an end to this with one special little bite. He didn't. He merely chucked Peanut under her small chin and said, "I heard you named her."

She was grateful for the diplomacy. She didn't think she could explain the panic mixed with longing that the thought of marking Jace inspired. "Yes. Penny."

"Trying to stick close to Peanut, eh?"

Not that she wanted to admit. "I think the name suits her."

Penny fussed. Miri jostled her, distracting her from her hunger with the excitement of movement. She wished it was as easy to distract herself. She'd been restless all day, her blood seeming to run hotter, her temper closer to the edge, and the love bites Jace had sprinkled over her body last night tingled with an excitement she couldn't rub away. Feeding from Jace had not only made her stronger, it had changed her. She just wasn't sure how.

"Well, they can't challenge him now. So if you're bringing one, just turn around and take it back out the door. He hasn't had a chance to heal from the last time."

Tobias held out his hands for the baby. "I don't think that's your call."

"I'm making it mine."

Miri handed Penny over and watched the miracle of the deadly Enforcer turning to mush right in front of her eyes. It happened every time he held the little girl, and every time, it was like watching a mini miracle. This time was no different. As he swung her above his head, the harsh lines of Tobias's face melted into a gentle smile.

"Penny's a good name for you, little one." He gave her a little wiggle. "You're certainly just as bright and shiny as a brand-new one."

He brought the baby down and tucked her against his side. Penny rooted around and then latched onto the collar of his leather coat. Tobias didn't pull the material away from her, just patted her on the back as he raised an eyebrow at Miri's stare.

"Enforcers are human, you know."

She hadn't realized she was so obvious. "You can read minds?"

The right side of his mouth kicked up. "No need to work that hard when what you're thinking is so clear on your face."

Which wasn't exactly a denial of an ability to read minds.

She sighed. "Jace says the same thing."

"It's not a bad thing."

"It's not a good thing, either."

Especially when people were trying to get information out of her. Which it seemed everyone had been trying to do the last few days—from Allie just trying to be sure she was okay to Tobias trying to see . . . She glared at the were. She didn't know what he wanted to know, but he was looking for something.

She turned the gas off under the pan of water, a sense of inadequacy coming at her out of nowhere. The flame went out with a little puff that echoed her annoyance. The only one who seemed to think she hadn't done her best while she'd been imprisoned by the Sanctuary was her. While everyone else praised her for hanging on, she couldn't shake a sense of failure. That somehow she should have been stronger, found a way to get away, a better solution to the problem of how to save Faith. That it was her fault Faith wasn't here now, being spoiled by her father and all the other men around. She was an Alpha female. She should have been able to do something other than what she had. Miri stared at the half-full bottle. She should have been able to do something.

"Is the bottle ready?" Tobias asked.

On a last blink, Miri shook off the pall of inadequacy and turned. The were was attempting to pry little Penny's mouth from the collar of his leather coat. She wasn't happy with the attempt. The more he worked, the harder she sucked.

"I'm sorry. Here, I'll take her."

Tobias didn't hand Penny over. "No problem. I'm just thinking this probably isn't the cleanest thing for her to chew on."

He looked so domesticated she had to blink again. Enforcers were all-powerful in were culture, a blend of legend and reality. They were the ultimate law, the ultimate decider of fate. They were the bogeymen mothers used to modify children's behavior. They were not potential fathers, yet one was standing in her kitchen fussing over a baby, letting it suck on his collar while worrying about germs. He couldn't have looked more fatherly. To the point that, if any female saw him like this, he'd leap to the top of the potential mate scale. Except she'd never heard of an Enforcer taking a mate. A mate would be a weakness, a vulnerability. Enforcers weren't allowed to be weak.

Miri tested the formula on her wrist. It was lukewarm. Close enough. "I'll take her now."

As soon as Tobias tried to move her away from his body, Penny's little face went into a pout.

"Come now," he coaxed, holding her face level with his. "You don't want to cry your way out of a good bottle, do you?"

Penny, didn't lose her pucker, but she didn't scream, either, as Miri took her. Which was a relief. Penny's lungs had gained considerable strength over the last week.

Tobias smiled when Penny didn't stop frowning at him even as Miri got her settled. "She's got opinions, that one."

Miri tucked her into the crook of her elbow. "She does that."

The instant the nipple touched her lips, Penny latched on, sucking hard.

Tobias watched her closely before asking, "She's not having trouble with the food?"

Miri shook her head. "She seems to be thriving."

"That's good."

Yes, it was. It gave her hope for her own baby. That maybe she was doing just as well and not struggling like Joseph.

"Yes, it is."

Tobias studied the baby a few seconds more and then asked, "Is Jace around?"

The hairs on the back of her neck rose. Her upper lip jerked with the urge to snarl. "Not if you're bringing another challenge around."

"No need to jump down my throat. I'm just the messenger."

She highly doubted that. Tobias had the look of a man who was behind a hell of a lot of things, and in control of everything. She put the bottle on the counter. Penny always drank too fast and the nipple on this bottle was cut too big. She rested her against her shoulder and started patting her back. "So, are you?"

Tobias snagged the dish towel off the front of the stove and tucked it under the baby's chin. "I'm not sure."

"Not sure about what?"

Jace strolled into the room, his power seeming to fill it as his energy reached out to surround Penny and her. Her pulse accelerated in welcome and remembrance. The memory of the night before was in his eyes. He'd come to her wild. She'd welcomed him just as wildly. A second tendril stroked over her in an intimate caress. The restlessness inside her quieted, focused, centered. Her breasts ached and swelled.

The knowing smile on Jace's lips touched her anger as much as the cuts on his cheek and jaw enraged her soul. The McClarens had no right to keep doing this to him. Penny gave a tiny little burp and started rooting around on her shoulder.

"I think Penny is ready for her bottle again."

She shook her head. She'd been fooled too many times before not to know this was premature. "Not just yet."

Just then Penny belched way too loud for something her size.

Both men laughed, as if it was a good thing for a little girl to belch like a grown man at a burping contest.

"That's hardly a ladylike sound, little one," she told Penny, trying to keep her focus there rather than on Jace. Her desire rising, her longing for his touch was almost palpable and would be easily detectable for an Enforcer of Tobias's caliber. Which would be embarrassing.

Her hopes to stay neutral were dashed when Jace crossed immediately to her side and tucked her, baby and all, under his shoulder. Tingles went up her arm into her chest, catching on her heartbeat, accelerating it, before surging outward in a vital awareness. She battled the small rebellion into submission with several deep breaths. That lasted until he started running his fingers up and down her arm. A quick glance up showed the faint smile lines at the corners of his eyes indicating he knew exactly what he was doing to her. And how much he was enjoying it. If she hadn't had the baby in her arms, if Tobias wasn't standing four feet away watching them with that same kind of smile on his mouth, she would have kicked him in the shins.

"Leave her be, Miri. A healthy appetite is nothing to shake a stick at," Jace said.

She immediately thought of Joseph. No, it wasn't. She kissed the top of Penny's head as Jace asked, "So what brings you here, Tobias?"

"I have a message from the D'Nally."

"Does he want to challenge me, too?"

Jace's energy hummed with an inner tension. The spot on her neck where he had bitten her this morning during their lovemaking burned. She rubbed her cheek on his arm, trying to soothe him while doing a mental probe for the cause of his upset. She was clumsy at the mental thing. Her efforts were thwarted with the softest of rebuffs. She sighed. Jace gave her a quick squeeze. An apology or a warning?

"No. It would be the Tragallion pack that would challenge your right to be their leader."

"What does he want, then?"

"Apparently, to talk."

"About what?"

Tobias shrugged. "He wouldn't say."

Miri frowned. Try as she might she couldn't scent or feel any underlying clue to the were's emotions. Was he lying? Was it a trap? "Well, until they do, nobody's meeting with anybody."

Tobias could look amazingly arrogant when he wanted to. "That's not your call."

She didn't care. "I'm making it mine."

Penny bobbed on her shoulder, her face crumpling in the warning pout that always prefaced a scream. She shifted the infant's position, trying to keep her eye on both men and the baby as she did.

Jace placed a kiss on her hair and dropped his hand from her shoulders. "Why don't we take this discussion outside so we don't disturb the baby?" he said to Tobias as Penny started to cry.

Miri brushed the corner of the baby's mouth with the bottle, eyeing Jace knowingly. "You wouldn't be trying to exclude me from this conversation, would you?"

"Not at all. Just figured I'd get some fresh air."

Who did he think he was kidding? "It's ten degrees outside. About the only thing you'll get out there is an ice cube."

He shrugged his shoulders as he grabbed his coat off the hook by the door. "I'm a vampire, Miri, love. If I want ten degrees to feel tropical, it will."

She rolled her eyes. "Please, you're just going outside because I can't take the baby out there."

Tobias laughed, opening the door. "She's on to you."

Jace grabbed his Stetson off the peg on the wall and settled it on his head. "So it would appear."

"*She's* getting annoyed being spoken about like she's not here."

Tobias smiled, his long brown hair blowing back over his shoulders as he stepped onto the porch. "It's good to see she's got her spirit back."

Jace laughed. "She gets much more back, and I'll be fighting as much at home as I have been outside of it lately."

He didn't sound at all upset at the idea. "You wouldn't have to fight so much," Miri countered, as she teased the corner of Penny's mouth with the nipple, "if you'd just turn one down now and then."

Jace angled the hat down over his brow, his eyes glittering from underneath while his energy flowed over her in a touch of pure sin. "And deprive the McClarens of their fun?" He shook his head. "They'd never forgive me."

THE night air was a balm upon his skin. Jace slowly closed the door behind him and tugged his coat on.

Tobias motioned over to the right, toward the practice field. "Do you want to talk over there?"

Jace looked over his shoulder to the kitchen window where he could see Miri staring out, watching them. They didn't need to be in earshot of the house for this conversation. "Works for me."

Particles of ice crunched under their feet, setting an easy rhythm to the pace as they passed the two houses between them and the field. Beside him, the Enforcer walked head up, shoulders back, an easy confidence in every step, looking completely at ease.

Tobias glanced over. "How's Miri really doing?"

Jace, however, was not at ease with the other man's preoccupation with his wife. Tobias was here for a reason. Jace didn't like the sense he was getting that it had to do with Miri. "What business is it of yours?"

"She's a D'Nally."

"She's my mate."

"One doesn't negate the other."

He cocked his eyebrow at him. "Funny, I had the impression that it did."

There was the barest interruption in the were's energy. "Yeah, I could see why you'd get that impression."

Tobias stopped at the edge of the trees that delineated the rectangular field. There was a shift in his energy, a honing of focus.

"Does this mean the guessing game as to why you're here is finally coming to an end?"

Tobias smiled. "Have we been playing a game?"

"I think so. Caleb agrees, but he's letting you stay because he says you're an honorable man for all that you're a dangerous one."

And he wanted to know what the game was.

Tobias smiled. "I'll take that 'dangerous' as a compliment, seeing as Caleb has a reputation in that department, too."

"And every bit of it deserved."

Tobias leaned back against the tree, folding his arms across his chest. "So do you. I got the impression that reputation is what the D'Nally wants to talk to you about."

Jace glanced over. "I was under the distinct impression the only thing the D'Nally wanted to talk about with me was my impending death."

"They were unhappy about how you used and abandoned Miri."

Jace narrowed his eyes. "I did not abandon her. I finished a mission."

"To a wolf, there's not much difference."

"So I'm told, but I'm finding it hard to believe that no wolf has ever left his mate, especially in the middle of this war."

"Ah, you figured out there's a catch."

Jace shrugged his shoulders. "There has to be."

"Did you know there's more than one level of were mating?"

"No. Either a body's married or it's not."

Tobias hooked his thumbs in the front pockets of his jeans. "That's because you're looking at it from a human perspective. Where anything to do with another is a choice."

"Miri straight-out said mating is not a choice."

"She's not feeding you a line of bull. There's just more than one level of were mating."

Another level of commitment would explain the sense he had that Miri was holding back. "I figured there had to be a catch."

"Many mated weres are not in love. There's usually friendship, understanding, and certainly passion, but there's not always love."

That was an eye-opener. And a potential explanation about the aggressive possessiveness of were males. A twinge of it was going through him right now. "What happens if they are mated and fall in love elsewhere?"

"They do their duty and work something out, a compromise, but only if neither is marked."

There was that reference to marking again. "What the hell kind of compromise can somebody reach in that situation?"

"Mating at its most basic is for procreation, as only mated pairs can conceive. That being the case, some couples only come together for that purpose."

"And?" He had a feeling where Tobias was going, but he couldn't wrap his mind around it. Especially when it came to the very Alpha, very possessive weres he knew.

"An unmarked mated couple are free to form emotional attachments elsewhere."

Like hell. Jace would kill any were who even thought of approaching Miri for any purpose. Just the thought of it had his lip curling and his talons extending. "I would think the potential to be killed would be a deterrent for compromise."

"It's not as difficult as you would think. Weres are very open when it comes to children, and if neither is marked, they can usually work around the relationship."

Not in his book. "What does marking have to do with it?"

"Weres don't have a choice with whom they mate, but they have complete choice whom they mark." Tobias gave him a pointed look. "Miri hasn't marked you."

Jace smiled a cold smile that felt as stiff as the muscles in his face. "I sure as hell put my mark all over her."

He'd been wild last night, unable to control himself, leaving love bites all over her, subtle little marks that anybody would be able to see. Marks that stated she was his and no other's.

"I don't think there's any doubt that you want her."

Implying there was doubt that Miri wanted him? "Would that happen to be the reason the McClarens feel compelled to fight me every time I turn around?"

"Yes. It's part of the mating process."

"Killing the mate?" He shook his head. "Hell of a process."

"They're giving you a way to prove yourself to Miri."

"At least that explains why they've been holding back."

"I wondered if you'd sensed that."

"I'm not a fool. If they'd really been trying, with the numbers they've been coming at me, I'd be dead."

"Could you be that understanding in regard to the D'Nallys?"

The D'Nallys were the most rigid bunch of weres he'd ever met. Fierce fighters, intensely loyal, but once they had a notion in their heads it was hard to knock it out, and right now they had the notion that he was better off dead. "It would depend on what the D'Nallys want."

"They want to talk."

That would be the day. He cocked an eyebrow at Tobias. "Just talk or talk with challenge?"

"Just talk."

"For now."

The were nodded. "For now."

"Why?"

"The baby."

"Faith?"

Tobias shook his head. "No, the little imp you brought back from the hellhole."

"Penny?"

"Yup."

"How do they know about her?"

"Word travels."

"With you being the conduit?"

Tobias didn't deny it. Jace got an uneasy feeling in his gut. Was Ian thinking of claiming Penny? That would kill Miri. "In that case, you can pass on another message." He bared his fangs. "Tell Ian that Penny's a Johnson."

"If Ian wants her, he'll take her."

"He can give it his best shot."

Tobias cocked his head to the side. Jace felt the touch of his power. He pushed it back. The probe immediately died. Too easy. That had been too easy. Jace's unease built as the sense of something going on grew.

"Do you think you can defeat him?"

"Yes."

Tobias merely appeared curious. "Because you're vampire?"

Jace's talons stretched into his palms. He could feel the bones in his face begin the change. Penny would not be taken. "Because she's mine."

Tobias nodded as if satisfied. "Ian will be glad to hear that."

What the hell did that mean? "Ian is a perverse son of a bitch."

"And you're a possessive one. You two should get along fine."

"I'm not interested in getting along with him."

"Seeing as he's your cousin now, it'll make things awkward at family get-togethers if you don't."

"Uh-huh. I'll work my way up to giving a shit about that." Jace leaned his shoulder against a tree, forcing calm through the suspicion eating at him. "So what about Penny has Ian asking questions about me?"

"The fact that you insisted on saving her and then brought her home as your own."

"I'm not following."

"A vampire would have left her when he discovered the child wasn't his."

"I disagree."

"He's wondering if you're truly vampire."

Jace bared his teeth again. "I even have the fangs to prove it."

"When you meet with the D'Nallys"—Tobias jerked his chin, indicating his display—"I'd play that down."

"Who says I'm meeting with them?"

Tobias raised his eyebrow, looking as imperious as any Alpha. "You're going to turn down a request from the D'Nallys?"

Jace didn't say word. He really didn't need to. They both knew that wasn't going to happen. Jace couldn't endanger the alliance just because he wanted to kick Ian's ass.

With a twitch of his lips Tobias acknowledged the "No" couched in silence. "I didn't think so."

"So when does Ian want this meeting?"

"Immediately. And he wants Miri to come, too."

"Not too pushy, is he?"

"He has his reasons."

"Just as I have mine for saying no to Miri coming."

"They're cousins, Jace. He's worried about her."

"She's my wife. I'm worried about her, too. As in, what guarantee do I have that this isn't a trap just to get me there and get Miri back into the D'Nally stronghold?"

Tobias straightened. "My word."

Hell. How was he supposed to argue with that? According to the McClarens, the word of an Enforcer was law.

He studied Tobias's energy and body language as he asked, "Is Ian aware you're giving it?"

Not by a flicker of anything did the other man indicate deception. Just nodded and said, "I put conditions on the delivery of the message."

"That must have gone over well."

"It had its moments."

"Yet Ian agreed?"

"Yes."

He hadn't really meant it as a question. "Ian must be softening in his old age."

"Times are changing, and Ian's changing with them."

"Hell, I'd pay to see that."

Tobias smiled a smile that said he knew he'd won. "Yet it won't cost you a thing."

Just maybe Miri. Loneliness for her pack was a constant ache inside her. Once she got back among them, she could decide to stay. The selfish part of him wanted to say no, to keep her away from temptation. The part that loved her understood the loss of family and how much she suffered for it. Shit! "Tell Ian I'll be there."

"With Miri?"

Inside, his vampire snarled a protest. His honor prodded. Damn. He needed more selfishness and less honor. Jace nodded. "Yes."

"**ARE** you sure this is safe?"

It was about the third time Miri had asked that question in the last five minutes. About the thirtieth time since they'd left the SUV four hours back to head in on foot. The hell of it was, she wasn't worried about Sanctuary. She was in fear of her own pack. Even with Tobias with them, or maybe because of it. Jace shook his head.

"Ian's your cousin, Miri."

"He's also pack Alpha."

"Princess"—he held a branch back so she could duck under— "Ian grew up with you. You grew up D'Nally. All the laws in the land are not going to make it easy for them to kill you."

She didn't look convinced. Her lower lip slipped between her teeth. Her gaze bounced off his. "Not to mention you'll be there."

"Not to mention that."

A breeze ruffled her hair against the deep blue of her parka as she ducked under the branch, the long strands catching bands of moonlight and reflecting it back in pale sheens of white on onyx.

She stopped and turned. "Ian can be very rigid."

"Tobias said he's changing, adapting with the times."

"You're sure he's talking about Ian?"

"He seemed convinced of it. Either way, in a few minutes, we'll get to find out for ourselves."

Miri glanced quickly at him. "We're that close?"

He pointed ahead. "See that big rock leaning into the mountain there?"

She squinted. "Yes."

"That's not really a rock."

She stopped dead and frowned at him. "It's an illusion?"

"Yes."

It was impossible to read the expression on her face. "Does Ian know you have a back entrance into the D'Nally compound?"

"Yes."

Her frown deepened. Pretty soon it was going to occur to her to question why vampires might have access to a secret back entrance to a were stronghold. Pretty soon turned out to be a couple seconds. Miri patted Penny's back in a staccato display of tension.

"You created this before you formed the alliance, didn't you?"

"Yes." He didn't have to read her mind to know what she was thinking. "Ian was a pain in the butt for a while."

The emotions that came off her were clear and predictable. First instinctive alarm and then a forced sense of calm. "Do all vampires know about this secret entrance?" she asked carefully.

She might claim she was no longer pack, but every instinct she had said otherwise. Vampires having this knowledge was a threat to her pack and she was reacting accordingly. "No."

She licked her lips and shifted the baby to her other hip. Her nylon parka whispered a protest. "Just the Johnsons?"

"Yes."

She looked at him, her eyes nearly black in the moonlight.

"Ian must have a lot of faith in you."

"He used to."

She sighed. "Until me."

He shook his head. "Until he ran up against the need to change. Ian's not a big fan of change."

No, but apparently, he's working on it."

"I'm taking it as an encouraging sign."

"And that's why you're not worried about this meeting?"

He let the branch go. It snapped back into place. He watched her walk away, admiring the sway of her cute butt. A smile touched his lips. He'd put a mark there, too. "That and the fact that Ian is an honorable man, and honorable men do not set traps for friends or invited guests."

The look she cast over her shoulder was pitying. "You so do not understand weres."

Jace patted that cute fanny, letting his fingers linger on the spot where his mark rested. "And you so don't understand men."

She scooted away, casting him a reproving glance, her cheeks flushing pink. "Huh!"

He supposed it was a good thing that she didn't say anything more on the subject. Truth was he was uneasy about this meeting. Miri was were. She wasn't committed to him, and based on his discussion with Tobias the night before, there might just be a loophole to exploit when it came to his marriage.

The hairs on the back of his neck raised as a strange tingle of energy teased his awareness. Vamp, but not vamp, about a hundred yards to the right side of the open field ahead of them. He raised a finger. Tobias nodded.

Jace halted Miri with a tug of his hand. He backed her up and leaned her against a big pine tree, putting his finger over her mouth when she would have spoken.

Quiet.

He masked her presence and the baby's with a second layer of energy that matched that of the surrounding trees, making her invisible to any probe. *Stay here. I'm going to check the lay of the land.*

She nodded, her eyes huge, her fingers spreading protectively over Penny's back. He motioned for Tobias to head left. He headed right, sliding into the shadows at the edge of the clearing. The energy moved, working the edge in the opposite direction from him, back toward Miri. Jace backtracked swiftly, cataloging the energy as he went, implanting its nuances into his memory for future reference. Slade would want to know about this.

As fast as he was, the energy was faster. It got within twenty feet of Miri before he reached her. Coming up beside her, he slipped his hand over her mouth, covering her start. She pressed Penny's face into her parka as she jumped. Vibrantly aware of the invisible source of energy off to the right, searching, Jace rested his cheek against hers, calming her with a stroke of his energy.

Don't move unless I tell you to, but if I tell you to, run like hell back to that rock.

He gave her the key to the illusion, mentally imprinting the combination in her mind, ignoring her fear and the clinging of her hands.

The D'Nally compound is two miles through that tunnel.

She shook her head, her lips firming, eyes narrowing. *Not without you.*

If she had to run, he'd be going down and he wasn't going down without knowing she was safe. *Obey me in this.*

The energy was coming closer. His talons extended; he could feel the fire burning in his eyes as the vampire came to the fore, ready to do battle. *Promise me.*

She finally nodded. Looking into her eyes, seeing her terror and the determination overlying it all, he cursed the decision not to bring a bigger escort, but a big party was hard to mask. Which just meant it was a good thing that he'd been gifted with incredible power and speed. It might be put to the test tonight. Especially if the Sanctuary had come up with a new enhancement with which to pervert their members.

He tested the energy again. There was still something off about it. Something he couldn't quite put his finger on. A subtle flux in the link.

He looked for Tobias. He wasn't anywhere in sight. Jace couldn't risk calling to him for fear the vampire would trace the source. Damn.

He moved away from Miri, The energy didn't move, just stayed were it was, hovering. Had the movement toward Miri just been a coincidence? When he was a safe distance away from Miri and the baby, he leaked a trace of energy. Still no movement.

He crept closer, almost close enough to make contact. The energy winked out. A movement across the field. Six weres stepped out from behind the illusion. Their dark hair and skin proclaimed them D'Nallys. As if he'd needed that to identify the taller of the two in front. The arrogance with which that one walked marked him as surely as a name tag. Creed D'Nally. Ian's second in command. In his hand he held a box, and on it were a lot of switches. There was a slight movement and the energy flashed to his left; he spun around. Just as fast it flashed on his right. Creed smiled across the distance separating them. Jace's warning died in his throat. The energy winked out. The weres kept coming. The energy didn't reappear.

Jace straightened. What the hell was going on? Creed inclined his head when he got close enough. "Vampire."

"Wolf."

A smile lingered at the corners of Creed's mouth. Jace knew damn well the man wasn't happy to see him, which meant something else was amusing him. "Looking for something?"

Jace glanced at the control and then back at Creed's smile. The pieces fit into place. Creed was controlling the energy.

"I was." He motioned to the box in the other man's hand. "I didn't realize weres had anyone working on an energy replicator."

"Ian feels we need to keep up."

"It's more of a mirror," the other were supplied. He was a younger version of Creed.

"A relative?" Jace asked Creed, indicating the young man with a jerk of his thumb.

"My nephew, Bain."

"As in 'bane of your existence'?"

The younger were smiled. "I try."

Creed cut him a look that was more affection than disgruntlement. "And succeed more often than not."

"Then my job here is done."

Jace shook his head, removed the shield from Miri.

Come here.

She did, hurrying across the space between them, a tremulous smile on her lips, her gaze locked on Creed.

"Hello, Creed, Bain." She nodded to the others, her smile shaking at the edges.

"Hello, Miri."

There's more than one level of were mating.

Tobias's words echoed in Jace's head at the warmth coloring Creed's greeting. Jace pulled Miri in to his side, away from the werewolves who circled around. Penny whimpered, sensing the tension. Miri's attention diverted to quieting her.

"So what did you think of our new toy?" Bain asked.

"Clever, but it needs refinement."

Creed smiled, displaying his canines. He was an arrogant son of a bitch. "It got you going."

"The energy is not quite right. I would have figured it out with more time."

"Shit. We were worried about that," Bain muttered. "I'll need you to give me feedback on that while you're here. Vampires sense energy differently than weres."

It wasn't phrased as a request. Arrogant pup. "No problem. As long as you're planning on sharing the technology."

"Of course he'll share," Miri interrupted, her cheek rubbing the side of his chest as her energy slid along the edges of his in an unconscious soothing. She didn't want him fighting with her kin.

That was going to be damn hard to accommodate, considering how the men watched the gesture, the younger with a hint of flames in his eyes. Jace took a step toward him. "If your nephew wants to live to see another minute, he'd better get his eyes back in his head and off my mate."

Bain's taunting smile marked him even more as Creed's kin. "You wear her mark?"

Jace gritted his teeth. "You value that pretty-boy smile?"

Miri grabbed his arm. The pup squared his shoulders. Tobias materialized out of the shadows. "We don't have time for this."

Jace waved at the wall of men. "Tell your friends that."

Tobias ignored the comment and held out his hands for Penny. "Hello, bright eyes." She smiled and went to him easily. He swung her up. "Did you miss me?"

"Hell, no," Jace retorted as Penny made a liar out of him with her happy squeal. "She's got better taste than that."

"I think she disagrees," Creed noted.

Tobias chucked the infant under the chin. She gave him another big drooling smile. "C'mon, little one. Let's get your mommy and daddy to the stronghold before your daddy embarrasses himself by committing needless mayhem."

Jace flashed his fangs at one of the bigger weres in an aggressive parody of a smile. One whose eyes had lingered a bit too long on Miri's thighs. "Who says it would be needless?"

Miri's claws nipped his palm as she tugged him forward. "I do."

✻ 16 ✺

IF one more male were stepped out of the traditional homage of D'Nallys lining the path leading up to the Alpha's house and came up to Miri to welcome her back with a lingering handshake and a double-edged grin, Jace was going to knock the hell out of his smile. Along with a few teeth.

A tall were ahead of them tensed in anticipation of Miri's approach. Jace cut Creed a glare. "If these boys don't back off, the D'Nallys are going to be missing a few of their prime males."

"They're just checking on Miri," Creed said, no small amount of amusement in his voice as he eyed the weres fascinated with Miri and Penny.

"And pigs fly."

Jace recognized men on the prowl when he saw them, and the D'Nally males flanking either side of them were definitely prowling.

"They'd better back off a good twenty feet." The words were almost incomprehensible due to the snarl beneath them. The skin over his talons itched with the need to release them. His fangs ached.

"Jace!"

Miri's caution only made the situation worse. He was jealous, plain and simple. He wasn't used to jealousy, but the emotion was consuming him now, spurred by the way Miri's energy flickered and flared in an ever-changing pattern, waffling between excitement and fear as they walked the path up to the main house. He could sense her thrill at seeing the old friends standing in the welcoming line on either side of the path, feel the pack's reserved welcome, feel how it hurt her that the reserve was there at all. But most of all, he felt her longing for her home. She was pack, and even this stroll along the perimeter of acceptance fed something in her that he could never provide. A part of her he didn't understand. He didn't like it.

Her hand touched his; her gaze met his. "Please."

Hell, she knew what it did to him when she looked at him like that. Jace sighed and cupped Miri's elbow, forcing back his bad humor. Maybe later there would be repercussions for Miri when the pack got past the fact that she was alive and moved on to the issue that she was mated to a vampire, but right now, she was happy because she was home. He wouldn't take that from her.

The path curved up a steep hill. The pack line thinned here to a few well-spaced males—hard-eyed men with more suspicion than greeting in their gazes. Guards. Cabins dotted either side of the hill. The door to one opened as they drew alongside.

A familiar silhouette stood framed by the light. Derek.

Jace walked to the bottom of the porch. "You look like hell."

He did, too. His muscular frame had to be down twenty pounds, his face drawn to the point that the angles were almost brutally cut. Scratches marred his chest. A bruise darkened his cheek. Derek grunted. "I can't leave Kim long."

"Is she all right?" Miri asked, studying his face.

The smile on Derek's face was grim. "We're working out an understanding."

Miri snarled. "If you hurt her, McClaren—"

Catching her arm, Jace pulled her back.

Surprisingly, Derek smiled. It was a weary stretch of the lips, but a smile nonetheless. "In case you haven't noticed, I'm the one wearing the scars."

Shit, that wasn't encouraging. Miri tugged her arm free. Jace kept an eye on her. The last thing they needed was a civil war between packs. "Need help?" he asked Derek.

"I've got it." Derek glanced up the hill to the cabin at the top. "Besides, you're going to have your hands full enough soon."

"Know what Ian wants?"

"That's D'Nally business," Creed cut in.

Jace turned on him. "Who the hell asked you?"

Ian's second in command just stared at him coldly.

Derek nodded. "He's right. It's the D'Nally's place to make his plans known."

From the interior of the cabin came a moan and a harsh gasp.

"Your almost mate requires your attention, McClaren," Creed growled.

For a second Derek looked torn between his loyalties.

"Almost mate?" Jace asked with a quirk of his brow.

Derek's teeth came together with a snap. "She is a very opinionated woman."

"You've been known to have an opinion or two of your own."

"A were woman would not carry her defiance to this level."

"But you didn't mate were," Miri interrupted softly.

"I know." Derek's lips flattened to a straight line. "She doesn't understand any of this, fights all of it."

"She's been through a lot. You can't know what it was like for her—"

Derek's eyes flashed with were fury as he cut her off. "I know enough."

Distress came off Miri in acrid waves. Penny fussed. Jared put his arm around them both. "Derek would never hurt a woman."

Least, he hoped the hell not. The McClaren was stretched taut with inner tension. Another moan came from the cabin, followed quickly by a curse. Jace motioned with his gun to the door. "Take care of your mate. I'll handle the D'Nally."

"Call if you need me."

"I will."

"Tell Kim I'm thinking of her," Miri whispered.

Studying her for a second, Derek nodded. "I will."

He turned and entered the cabin. The door shut with a harsh click.

"The D'Nally does not get handled," Creed snapped, motioning toward the big cabin at the top of the hill. Lamplight poured from the windows, spilling down the steep hill in a golden glow. That was their destination. Stars sparkled in the deep black sky behind. It was an amazingly picturesque scene for what could be a very volatile encounter.

"The D'Nally will get whatever I give him."

Jace glanced over at Miri. Her cheeks weren't as flushed as they had been and he could make out the beginnings of circles under her eyes. Her energy was waning. Carrying a baby, even one as light as Penny, up that incline would drain her. She was going to need all her strength for the confrontation to come. "Pass Peanut over here. I'll carry her for a while."

"I can carry her."

"No need when I'm here." She looked pointedly at the males around them. It took him a second to make the connection. She was worried about his image upon meeting Ian. He tweaked Peanut's nose. She made a face and scrunched up her eyes. "If Tobias's ego can handle being seen carrying a baby, I think mine can take the hit."

"Men don't carry babies during formal occasions."

He took the infant from her arms, passing Peanut up high, the way she liked, getting a smile as the weres waited and watched. "That would be were thinking again, but Miri, I'm not—"

"Were," she finished for him. Nothing in her eyes told him

how she felt about that now that she was home among her pack. His jealousy grew stronger. "You could at least try to fit in," she groused.

He put his free arm around her waist as they started to climb the hill. "You can't make a silk purse out of a sow's ear."

He expected a protest, but instead she gave him a little more of her weight than normal. "Are you all right?"

She nodded. But he wasn't convinced. Did she need to feed again?

Creed, overhearing, turned around. His breath frosted the air between them. "She's tiring?"

Jace glanced over. "She's had a rough week."

"From what I heard, it's been a rough year."

"I'm fine."

Jace drew them both to a halt, shielding her from the view of the crowd behind. "It's no skin off my nose if you want to rest."

She shook her head.

Creed said, "No one will think less of you."

So that was it. He should have known. Miri was worried about her pack seeing her as weak. Alpha females were never weak. Under the guise of stealing a kiss, he whispered in her ear, "You lean on me, and I'll get you up the hill, pride intact."

"How?"

He stroked his hand down her arm in a seductive trail, knowing how it looked to the watching crowd. He nipped her ear, turning her slightly in to him. "By playing the jealous mate."

She shivered delicately. "Playing?"

He smiled against her cheek. "Got to admit, it won't be much of a stretch."

There was a long pause and then she leaned against him. "Thank you."

Over Miri's head, Jace caught a strange expression on Creed's face. Approval? A growl rumbled out of the crowd.

"You might want to save the public displays for private," the other man suggested.

"Where would the fun be in that?"

Creed shifted his rifle to the crook of his arm. "If you think provoking them is harmless, you don't know weres."

Jace looked into the eyes of the men around him, knowing they wanted what he had, knowing they would never have her, because he wouldn't give her up, mark or no. Law or no. He flashed them an easy smile and dropped a kiss on the top of Miri's head. "So everyone keeps telling me."

THE door opened as soon as they approached the porch. Even if Jace hadn't known Ian was Alpha, his posture would have proclaimed it. Shoulders squared, he stood waiting for the small group to reach him. Ian had the D'Nally coloring, complete with amber eyes that seemed to glow as he studied Miri and the baby. Jace wouldn't say he looked happy, but he also wouldn't say he looked angry. "Torn" might be the right word. The question would be, about what? As they reached the bottom step, Ian nodded. "Welcome home, Miri."

His long black hair blew about his face as he came down a step, each footfall sounding loud in the crisp night air. His golden eyes held a faint glow as he studied Miri. Standing behind Miri as he was, Jace couldn't help but feel her start and apprehension as he reached the ground.

Miri inclined her head. "Thank you."

Ian's gaze lingered on the scars on Miri's cheeks. He tipped her chin up, raising her face to the porch light. A growl rumbled in his chest.

He touched one with his thumb.

Against Jace, Miri quivered, her heart aching. Behind them, the pack watched. Jace slid under Miri's mental guard, touching her mind, searching for fear, finding only a soul-deep longing for a hug from the man she thought of as a brother. A sign that it was okay. That he still saw her as he always had. She wanted it with every fiber of her being.

The least you owe her is a hug.

Not by a twitch did Ian indicate he heard the message, but an answering thought came to Jace, loud and clear.

Do not interfere in were business.

Jace didn't give a shit about were business. All he cared about was Miri's pain as the silence stretched her out on a rack of dread. Opening a channel from Miri to Ian, Jace let Ian experience the emotion tearing Miri apart. There was a flinch at the corners of Ian's eyes. Snow crunched as his weight shifted. He reached out slowly. Miri stopped breathing as his hands closed over her shoulders. She went when he pulled, taking a small step toward him, then hesitating. Jace couldn't see her face, but he could guess at her expression. Hope clashing with fear beneath that brave front she wore. Jace wanted to snatch her back, shelter her. Take the pain away, buffer her from possible rejection.

Too low to carry far, Ian whispered, "Shit."

Then, very carefully, as if he worried she'd shatter with too much pressure, Ian hugged her. Hell. Maybe he wouldn't kill the big were after all.

Miri's chest jerked on a soundless sob, so painful to watch. Her hands came up, her fingers made fists in Ian's coat, her shoulders shuddered. Ian rested his cheek on her head, pulling her closer, holding her tighter as she sobbed. His eyes closed. "We missed you."

Miri's joy and relief flooded Jace in a staggering rush of emotion. Ian just held her harder, sheltering her, siphoning off her anxiety so deftly that Jace wasn't sure Miri even recognized the touch, but *he* did, and now he was going to owe the D'Nally. As if it was the signal they'd all been waiting for, the pack converged on Miri. Men and women welcomed her home, reaching out to touch her hair, her clothes, hundreds of touches that reinforced the connection between them. Every touch took her away from him, back into pack. Jace heard Miri give a harsh sob, had a glimpse of her tear-ravaged face before someone came between them, cutting him off. He held Peanut and forced himself to stay back. Miri needed this reunion the same way flowers needed the sun. As long as he could stand it, he would let her have it.

Tobias came up beside him. "Nice move."

He pretended innocence. "What?"

"Forcing Ian's hand."

"He was taking too long."

Tobias crossed his arms over his chest and watched the reunion. "You don't give a shit about tradition, do you?"

"Not if it hurts Miri."

"He would have hugged her eventually."

Jace noted that not only had Tobias known what he'd done, he'd known the reason behind it. "Miri was hurting then."

Tobias shrugged and cut him an assessing glance. "If I didn't know better I would say that was Ian talking."

"Stop comparing me to that bastard."

"Can't help it, when you're so much alike."

The weres stepped back, leaving a path through the center. "Looks like it's your turn and Peanut's."

Ian and Miri came toward him. Miri's face was red from crying, wet with tears, but her eyes were beaming. Beside her, Ian walked, holding her hand. Jace snarled. Ian laughed out loud. "Relax, vamp. She's my cousin." Ian's gaze dropped to Penny, where she slouched against Jace's chest, sucking her fist. There was something in the focus of his energy that raised the hair on the back of Jace's neck. "You have no claim on Penny."

Ian didn't spare him a glance. "Actually, I do."

Jace handed Penny to Miri. "Then we have a problem."

Miri growled and snatched Penny out of Ian's reach.

For an instant surprise flashed in Ian's eyes, then his expression closed up, but not before Jace caught a glimmer of hurt. Against his will, Jace found himself feeling sorry for the man. Clearly Miri no longer trusted her Alpha. That had to pain. "Don't mess with my family, Ian," Miri warned.

"You're calling a vampire and an altered were child family, Miri?"

Ian made it sound impossible. Maybe in his opinion it was. Miri's chin jerked up. Fire flashed in her eyes. For all that the last year had messed with Miri's confidence, she was still a hundred percent were and no one messed with a were's family. "You do anything to hurt either of them, and I'll kill you."

This time Ian's flinch was visible. Jace felt his pain and inwardly cursed. Damn! Some days it didn't pay to get out of bed. He wrapped his arm across Miri's chest as she backed toward him. Ian might be a son of a bitch, but Jace didn't believe for a minute he'd hurt Penny or Miri. "Thanks to the Sanctuary's influence, Miri has all kinds of worries, like that you're going kill me because I'm vampire, and the baby because she has a clubfoot." He pinned Ian with his gaze. "You know, silly things like that."

Ian's eyes narrowed. "In the old days we would have done just that."

"In the old days? You mean last year?" Miri, asked, sarcasm lacing her voice.

"Didn't Allie tell you?" Ian asked with a quirk of his brow. "The D'Nallys have evolved."

Jace looked over at the group of men who stood around him. Hard-eyed men with muscles developed through constant training. Given a choice between a gun and an iPod he could see this crew going for the gun every time. "Yeah, I can see that."

This time Ian's gaze was assessing. "I'll bet." He stood back and motioned them up the stairs. "Come on in and we'll discuss it."

"Said the spider to the fly," Tobias murmured.

"Do me a favor, stop helping." Jace steadied Miri with a hand on her elbow as she climbed the first step.

"Not a problem."

Miri glanced over her shoulder. "You're not coming in?"

Tobias shook his head. "I think you can handle it from here."

"Are you coming?" Ian asked.

"Just as soon as you tell my wife that no harm is going to come to her or Penny."

An elbow jabbed his side. Miri frowned up at him. "Or you."

"No sense pushing the man into promises he can't keep, princess."

Miri planted her feet. "I'm not going anywhere if he won't promise."

Again that flicker of something went over Ian's face—hurt?

"The D'Nallys will not harm you or yours. As Alpha I give you this promise."

Miri still didn't look convinced. Jace touched the edges of the were's mind. Ian meant what he said. With steady pressure on her back, Jace guided Miri up the stairs. "This is your cousin, Miri, the boy you grew up with. The man you trusted. The past year might have been hell and changed some things, but it hasn't changed everything."

She stopped at the top step. Her gaze locked on Ian. "He's also Alpha."

Ian's gaze focused on the scars on Miri's cheeks. There was no mistaking the emotion ripping through him now. Rage. White-hot flames lit the edges of Ian's irises. "Your Alpha, Miri Tragallion." Miri didn't back down. "The one who will be avenging the harm done you."

Like hell. "That privilege is mine." Jace wanted no misunderstanding there. Miri was his. Revenge would also be his.

The slow nod of Ian's head was the first acknowledgment that Jace had that the Alpha might just accept this mating.

"But you'd better be making it fast," Ian warned, his gaze still locked on Miri's scars, his fingers curling into a fist.

Or Ian would take over. Jace could respect that.

"I have a few things to settle first."

"Does that include the rescue of your child?"

Miri's chin came up another notch on that wording, a distinct resemblance to Ian's arrogance in the look she cast down her nose as she stepped past him into the cabin. "Our *daughter*."

Ian blinked in shock. Jace made a mental note. Ian hadn't known Miri's child was a girl. Interesting. He followed Miri into the house.

The first thing Jace recognized upon entering the cabin was that there was someone else present. Were, judging from his energy. Upset, if his scent was anything to go by. He knew the second Miri caught the scent. She went stiff as a board. "Who's here?"

"We need to talk about that."

Ian wasn't a man for hedging. This wasn't going to be good.

A man appeared in the doorway at the end of the hall. His hair was brown, his eyes haunted, and his hands clenched into fists.

"Shit." And Ian wasn't happy to see him.

"Is this them?" the man asked. Before Ian could answer, Creed stepped through the front door and headed down the hall. "I'll handle this."

Four rapid strides and he was at the doorway. With a hand on the man's chest, he pushed him back into the room, an office apparently, for bookcases were visible in the opening. The door closed. There was the sound of a scuffle, muted voices arguing. A crash . . .

Jace raised a brow at Ian. "Trouble in paradise?"

"You might say that." Ian ran his hands through his hair, pushing it back with a ruthless shove. "You Johnsons never do anything the easy way."

"Seems easy enough to us."

"You don't even know what I'm talking about."

"I'm still sure it was easy enough."

"I bet." Ian dropped his hands to his sides. All was quiet in the room for the space of three breaths. "It wasn't enough you took up with a were woman, you had to go and claim a were baby."

"I didn't see anybody else stepping forward to take care of her."

"Yeah, that complicates it."

"Complicates what?" Miri asked.

Ian didn't answer immediately. He did, however, glance toward that too-quiet room.

Penny woke up, blinking twice. Her stomach woke up a split second later. Her face crumpled into a pre-wail pout. Miri tried in vain to distract her while Ian just looked relieved at not having to answer the question.

Jace was not getting a warm fuzzy in his chest. "Miri, why don't you take Peanut into the kitchen?"

"But . . ." She cast a worried glance at him and then a suspicious one at Ian.

"It'll be all right."

She didn't move. When he looked down, she was looking up at him, waiting for something.

"What?"

"Bend down, please." He didn't understand what she wanted until her hand came up behind his neck—small, feminine, and strong. He leaned a little closer as her fingers played with the hair at his nape. Her head canted to the side. She came up on her toes. He slid his hand around her waist, supporting her as her lips parted against his, as her tongue slipped between in a hot caress—a tease really, just enough to get his blood perking—and then she dropped back to her heels and turned to Ian. "I meant what I said earlier. You touch him, and I'll kill you."

Ian's head snapped back. "You forget yourself."

Jace had to agree. Cousin or not, Miri had just crossed a line. Women didn't challenge Alpha males. She didn't seem to care.

"I haven't forgotten a thing. As a matter of fact, I've even learned a few new ones. Including that someone in my own pack handed me over to the Sanctuary."

"It wasn't me."

"How do I know that? How do I know you won't turn Jace over even if you weren't the one?"

"Enough, Miri." Jace put his hand on her shoulder, pushing her forward and to the left, past Ian, toward the kitchen. Her muscles were as tight as a drum. Penny, sensitive to emotion, kicked her wails up a notch.

"But—"

"You're making me look bad in front of the kid."

She planted her feet just inside the kitchen, glancing over her shoulder to where Ian waited. "You'll be careful?"

"He's your cousin, Miri."

"You don't know weres."

"I'm beginning to think I know them a heck of a lot better than you know them."

"What does that mean?" she asked over Penny's impatient scream.

He didn't have the heart to tell her she'd lost her faith. "I'm losing my bonding opportunity with Ian."

"I'm not sure I want you bonding with Ian over the need to shelter me."

He handed her the pack with the bottles in it. "Tough."

She took it, but gave him and Ian a suspicious look before saying, "Just don't bond too hard."

"I'll try to resist."

Behind him, Ian snorted. When Jace was sure Miri was occupied caring for Penny, he rejoined Ian.

"It's good to know they didn't break her," Ian said, a faint smile on his lips as he motioned Jace into a den.

"They came damn close," Jace said, the knowledge of that aching on his conscience. "There are days when she's particularly fragile, while on others she kicks ass."

"You're not mated." Ian took a whiskey bottle from the cabinet on the other side of the room. "Why is that?"

"Probably one of those were reasons she's always telling me about."

Ian's brows raised and he paused in pouring a glass. "Were reasons?"

"Every time I do something she doesn't approve of, she tells me I don't understand weres." He accepted the glass from Ian. "Seems to think that makes her point and settles the argument."

"So what you're saying is, you're committed to her, but she's dragging her feet."

Jace leaned back against the soft cushions and took a sip of whiskey. The smooth burn spread down his throat. Caleb swore the D'Nallys had the best whiskey. Jace had to agree. "Pretty much, but make no mistake about it. She's mine."

"You say that with the vehemence of a were."

"I'm saying that with the vehemence of a Johnson."

Ian took a sip of his whiskey, looking at Jace over the rim of the glass. "Some days, there doesn't seem to be a whole lot of difference between the two."

Jace lowered his glass. "I'm not were."

Ian shrugged. "But you'd pass for one."

And that seemed to be important for some reason. "What's up, Ian?"

"Maybe I just want to see my cousin settled."

"That's what drove the grand command for me to appear?"

"As perverse as you are, I couldn't just send an invite."

"I'm here. What do you want?"

"How much does Miri mean to you?"

"Enough." He'd be damned before he discussed his feelings with Ian. "Enough for you to live pack?"

He set his glass carefully on the tabletop. "What the hell are you talking about?"

"Miri is the female heir to the Tragallion. The pack is in trouble."

"Travis wasn't an ideal leader?"

"No." Ian sighed. "He drove the pack into the ground. Unfortunately, he got himself killed before things could be straightened out."

"Meaning what?"

"Meaning either I appoint you their leader through the right of tradition, or I kill you and start a mate hunt for Miri."

"With those options, I'm a little surprised to be sitting here chatting with you."

"Amazingly enough, I find myself reluctant to kill you."

"And why is that?"

"You might be a pain in the ass, without the proper respect for tradition, but you're the only pain in the ass Miri will have."

"You got that, eh?"

"Let's just say I believe her when she says her response to any attempt against you will be vengeance."

"And that scares you?"

Ian smiled that aggravating smile of his. "You have a lot to learn about weres, but one of the first things you should get is, while a D'Nally male will beat your ass, it's the females you have to watch out for."

"You want me to believe you've selected me to head up a bunch of weres because you're afraid of my wife?"

"Would that work?"

"Hell, no."

"Then how about the fact that you're honest and straightforward and can be trusted. Hard commodities to come by these days."

He had to be kidding. Except there was no look of amusement on the were's face. "It'll never work."

"With an ordinary vampire I'd say it wouldn't, but you're more were than vampire, and that might work for us."

"Us?" He raised his eyebrow. "From what I can see, the only one being asked to set himself up to get his ass kicked every day of the week is me."

Ian shrugged. "You've never run from a fight."

"You make it sound so damn attractive."

"It isn't attractive, but it's necessary. And there's also the fact that you're not going to go away."

Jace bared his fangs. "So clever of you to understand that."

"Just another were quality that will make you fit right in with the Tragallions."

"And what would that be?"

He reached for his whiskey.

"That aggressive defense of what you feel is right."

Jace took a pull on the drink. The smoky liquor burned its way down to his stomach. Ian had to be pretty damn desperate to suggest this. "There's nobody else to do the job?"

"No."

"And you think this is going to work?"

"Yup. Because not only have you and Miri given birth to a little girl, you saved another. Once you get the Tragallions past the minor inconvenience of your being vampire, you'll be a goddamn hero."

" 'Minor inconvenience'?"

Ian took another sip of his whiskey. "Call it whatever you want, but marrying Miri made you a D'Nally, and D'Nallys have responsibilities."

"Whether I want them or not, apparently."

"You want Miri to be happy, right?"

"You already know the answer to that."

"Pack makes Miri happy."

He knew that, too. "So what does it take to make this happen?"

"It's already done."

"Just like that?"

"One of the perks of being Alpha. My word is law." Ian polished off his whiskey. The glass clicked on the wood as he set it down. "And now we have to discuss something else—"

He never got to finish the sentence. A crash came from the office. A door slammed against a wall. Seconds later a scream erupted from the kitchen, followed by snarls. Miri!

Jace was out of his chair, reaching for her with his mind before he cleared the doorway. Ian was right on his heels. He felt her panic and anger. Peanut's scream put wings on his feet. Down the hall, Creed stumbled out of the office, blood dripping from his torn face and his arm wrapped around his torso.

"What the hell happened?" Ian growled.

"He scented the baby. I couldn't hold him."

"Shit!"

Jace burst into the kitchen. The strange were had backed Miri into a recessed area. Penny lay on a counter, crying. Miri's claws were extended and her lips drawn back, fangs exposed. The male were didn't look any more stable. And he had some damn impressive claws.

Edging around the perimeter, Jace kept his voice calm as he worked his way between Miri and the unknown were. "Miri, sweet, you have a real propensity for finding trouble."

She watched the were carefully. "I didn't find anything. It found me."

"Marc, stand down," Ian snapped.

"Go to hell, Ian," the man snapped right back.

Ian went right, Jace went left, and Creed brought up the middle.

"Nice to see you've got your pack under control, Ian."

"He's not mine, he's yours."

The man was bulky with muscle, enough to make Tobias look small, and he radiated a desperate aggression. And he was a Tragallion? "Figures."

"Neither of you are helping," Miri snapped.

"I'm working on it, princess." Jace moved in another foot, angling himself to the best position to attack if necessary. "I want you to pick up Peanut now and very carefully walk toward me."

She lifted her lip but didn't move.

"Nice to know you've got your mate under control, Johnson," Ian commented, inching steadily up on the right.

Jace flipped him the bird.

"I want my daughter," Marc growled.

Shit! "And who are you to be wanting anything?"

"Marc Tragallion." He motioned to Penny. "And that's my daughter."

Not good. Not good at all. A wolf would fight to the death for family.

"Assuming she is—" Jace began.

"She's not," Miri snarled.

Not taking his eyes off Marc, Jace tried again. "Assuming she is, why in hell would I give her back to a man who couldn't protect her?"

"Because I'll kill you if you don't."

"Seems to me, for someone in no position to do anything, you're making a whole lot of threats."

The man took another step forward. Jace went with him. Miri turned and grabbed Penny, pulling her in to her chest with enough force to set her screaming harder. The sudden move had the wolf jerking. His scent came to Jace along with Miri's and Penny's. There was no doubt the wolf was related to Penny; their scents were very similar. Something Miri had to recognize.

Jace looked over at Ian. "I'm betting were law's got something to cover this."

And as were law was pretty archaic, based on might making right, Jace was betting the old "finders keepers" rule applied.

Ian nodded, his eyes never leaving Marc. "All lost children belong to the finder if they claim them."

"She was claimed in front of the McClaren council," Miri said quickly.

Jace looked at her sharply. She'd thrown that out quick and fast like she'd been expecting this moment and had prepared for it.

Marc's "She's mine" rumbled low and deadly from his chest.

Jace had heard that line often enough from enough weres to know they were in one sticky situation. Marc's hands flexed, flashing claws long enough to slice Miri in half with one swipe. And he was within arm's reach and hanging on to control by a thread. Not good.

"You heard the lady."

"I challenge you for her."

"Good enough."

Creed came up to them, wiping the blood from his cheek. "This kind of challenge is to the death, vamp."

Jace's fangs strained and his face began to morph. "No problem."

Miri clutched Penny to her chest and backed up until she leaned against the counter, holding the were's attention. "You failed her once. I won't give her back so you can fail her again."

That was his Miri, going for the jugular. Marc stiffened. "I didn't fail her."

"Do you know how we found her? What they were doing to her? How they deprived her?"

There was only one description for the twisting of the man's features—anguish; pure, unadulterated anguish. "No."

Tears spilled over onto Miri's cheeks. Her face began to morph. Jace had never seen her inner wolf so close to the surface. Marc turned toward him. Jace had also never seen so much torment in a man's eyes, nor so much determination. He slid his mind along the were's, testing his emotions. Pain. Endless pain, guilt, and love. The love of a father for his child. So much, he wasn't sure how the man kept from screaming. Ah, shit, why were these things never easy?

"You killed them, vampire?"

Jace smiled. "Gutted them while they could still enjoy the experience."

Marc stared at him, face expressionless, and then he nodded. "Thank you."

"You should know that I missed one."

Marc's head snapped up. "He's mine."

"Only if you can get to him first."

"Were law—"

The rage Jace had been holding back flared. He took a step toward Marc. "I don't give a shit about were law. I was there; I felt her terror at a touch while everything inside her craved it. I had to pick her up out of the filth she lay in, in that glorified grave, had to hold her while Slade pulled the IVs from her heart. I held her energy and her terror and there isn't a goddamned law in this fucking land that'll keep me from making them pay."

Marc lunged at him and grabbed him by the shirt, the power of the move hurtling them both up against the cabinets. Jace let him, wanting the fight away from Miri. Wood splintered; dishes rattled. Over Marc's shoulder Jace could see Ian grab Miri as she lunged after him.

"Make a picture for me, vamp," Marc ordered in a guttural snarl. "In my head, show me what you found."

Jace was tempted. Very tempted. The man's anguish came at him again. Pity tempered his impulse. He shook his head. "You don't want to go there. Trust me."

Marc shook him, making the dishes rattle again. He stared at little Penny as she screamed in terror while Miri fought with Ian. Jace could have killed him right then. It would have been kinder than what the man was insisting he do. He didn't. Marc's energy coiled to a lethal tension, his snarl hoarsened as he turned back and met Jace's gaze. "If it happened to my daughter, it should happen to me, so make me a picture, vamp."

Jace did, sending the images so fast they were a blur. Marc's grip shifted to his neck. "Slowly."

Shit.

"They hurt her because you cared more about your image than you cared about your daughter," Miri called from behind, lashing the man with guilt as Jace fed memories into his mind.

Marc let Jace go as the last memory landed. He staggered back, face pale, hands shaking.

Ian released Miri. She raced to Jace's side. He pulled her in, accepting the snap of her energy as she turned on Marc. "They hurt her because you didn't care, you bastard!"

The one thing Jace knew absolutely was that this man cared. "Miri—mine."

She spun in his arms, pressing Penny's face to her throat. "Don't even say it, Jace. They tortured her, and he let them."

Ian and Creed flanked Jace, their warning snarls joining his when Marc reached out toward his little girl. Miri twisted away, her desperate need to hold on to Penny nearly as strong as Marc's to simply hold her.

Jace only knew one thing. No way had this man left his little girl anywhere.

Marc glanced up. "I don't want to hurt your mate, but I'm taking my daughter home with me." He reached out.

Fast as lightning Miri slashed his arm open. The scent of blood filled the room as drops splashed to the floor. "Don't touch her."

Strangely, Miri's attack didn't anger the were. Instead, it seemed to center him. He took a breath, his gaze on Miri and the protective way she held his daughter, and a little of the aggression left the set of his shoulders.

"My mate's pack followed the old ways. I left her to get food. She went into labor before I got home, and when the baby was born imperfect, she returned her to nature. When I returned, I made her tell me where she'd left the baby, but she lied, and by the time I figured that out, my daughter wasn't there anymore."

"Penny," Miri growled. "Her name is Penny."

Marc went on as if she hadn't interrupted. "I've been following sign for two months, looking for her."

Marc caught Miri's eyes. "I've heard you know the pain of knowing your child is somewhere out in the world needing you, hearing her cry at night in your dreams, but having no way, in the waking hours, to reach her."

Miri gasped and the agony, never far from the surface, flared. Jace pulled her in to his side.

"Another low blow like that and I'll gut you."

"Hell, I'll do it for you, right now," Creed snapped.

Marc lifted his chin. "There's nothing that will keep me from my child."

"You're a guest in my home, Marc, but you're beginning to wear out your welcome," Ian said.

Marc looked at Ian. "Then I'll take my daughter and leave."

"No." Miri's response wasn't as vehement now. Jace notched his mind to hers. Anguish, anguish, and more anguish. She couldn't let go of Penny, couldn't lose another child. Couldn't take a man's child from him. She was desperate for a solution to an impossible situation.

Jace glanced over her head at Marc. "You're a Tragallion were?" He nodded.

"How much do you want your daughter? Badly enough to bargain for her?"

His eyes narrowed, but he nodded.

"What about your wife?"

"My mate is no longer in the picture."

"Did you kill her?"

"No."

A vague impression came to him. But someone had. Jace couldn't make himself give a crap.

Miri turned her cheek in to his chest. *Don't do this to me.*

Awkward and clumsy, the mental plea broke into his mind. *I'm not doing anything, baby.*

Aloud he said, "My wife can't lose another baby."

"I can't lose my daughter."

"She'll need protection. The Sanctuary will hunt for her."

"The pack will help."

"Your pack doesn't have a leader."

"Travis is dead?"

There was absolutely no inflection in the question. "He died fighting Sanctuary."

There was a flicker of relief in Marc's eyes. "A good death."

For a not-so-good man? Jace wondered.

Miri's hand opened on his chest. *Don't, Jace.*

You can't keep a man from his daughter, baby. Not unless you're willing to lose your daughter the same way.

I know. Her tears soaked through his shirt. *But I can't say the words that will let her go.*

Neither could he. Not completely. He met Marc's gaze.

"Could you support a vampire for a leader?"

Miri jerked, disturbing Penny, who'd been about to fall asleep. She rubbed her back.

Marc also seemed to stop breathing. His gaze grew more wary. "Would you be that vampire?"

Jace couldn't blame him. Ian's solution was a radical one. "Yup. Ian seems to think I'd be good at the job."

Marc turned to Ian. "You support this."

"The Tragallions need a strong leader. The Johnsons are strong and Jace is mated to the Alpha female of your line."

"Appointing a vampire will tear them apart."

"Or bring them together," Ian countered.

Marc jerked his chin toward Jace. "Over his dead body."

Miri gasped. "No."

"Shh." Jace stroked his hand down her back, calming her.

Ian shrugged. "He's willing to chance it."

Marc's glance encompassed the way Miri was tucked against Jace, his hand stroking down her back. Understanding softened his frown. He motioned at Miri. "For her?"

The question was obviously directed at Jace. He didn't see any sense in hiding the truth. "Yes."

He'd do a lot of things to make Miri happy. Wading through a few head knockings to give her the pack she wanted was the least of it.

"Then I will not protest the appointment."

Which wasn't the same as supporting it. "You might want to hold off until you hear my condition."

"Spit it out."

"You declare Miri and Ian Penny's guardians by right of claim."

He was proposing a permanent alliance between the Alpha D'Nally and Marc's immediate family. It was a huge honor for any family and rarely given, as it meant the Alpha and his pack could be summoned to aid and they couldn't refuse.

Marc didn't take his eyes off Miri. "Will your mate be living with you at the Tragallion compound?"

"What does that have to do with anything?"

"I have no female relatives. My daughter needs a mother."

Jesus Christ! Was another were going to try to steal his mate?

Miri's hand on his arm cut off the possessive rage. "He doesn't mean what you think, Jace. Substitute mothers are common among weres and children often have more than one home."

Marc looked surprised and then amused as he realized Jace's concern. "I have no desire for your mate."

Before Jace could answer, Miri cut in, "And to answer your question—yes, I'll be traveling with my mate."

"I hadn't decided that yet, Miri."

She smiled sweetly at him. "I saved you the trouble."

Marc smiled. Ian and Creed chuckled.

The woman was hell on his image. "That was thoughtful of you."

"So, Marc," Ian asked, "what's it going to be?"

"I accept the bargain." Marc held out his hands. "May I hold my daughter now?"

Jace steadied Miri mentally as she eased Penny away from her body. "She doesn't always go easily to strangers . . ."

"I am not a stranger, I'm her father." His hands slid under hers.

"I just don't want—"

Miri never finished the sentence. With a look of wonder on her face, Penny went quietly into her father's arms.

And in Jace's arms, Miri's heart just as quietly broke.

❧ 17 ❧

THE Tragallion pack wasn't exactly welcoming them with open arms. Jace stood with Miri on the edge of the Tragallion compound and surveyed the array of weres fanning out in the traditional gauntlet of welcome. Most of the stares were downright hostile. Some curious. Some cautious. But no one was smiling. All in all they were an angry, weary-looking group. Jace tucked Miri a little closer in to his side. "Remind me to deck Ian next time I set eyes on him."

She glanced up. "If you hold him, I'll do it for you."

He laughed and dropped a kiss on her head, feeling the ripple of unease spread through the crowd as he did. "Nah, I want to do some damage."

Marc looked over his shoulder. "There's no need to put on a show. I can pretty much guarantee that the only thing anyone believes about you being here is that you're here for the power."

"I'm here for Miri."

"Well, that part will take some convincing."

One male were stepped away from the crowd. He carried himself with the confidence of a seasoned warrior. His hair was long

and brown, his eyes golden. A D'Nally Alpha. But apparently, not
next in line to lead. Jace let him get within ten feet before holding
up his hand. "That's close enough."

The man's eyebrows rose, but he stopped.

Jace looked down at Miri. "Stay here."

"I have just as much right as—"

He cut her off. "Until I know it's safe, you're not getting within
grabbing distance."

"The Tragallion weres are honorable," the unknown D'Nally
said, a frown on his face.

"You'll pardon me if I don't take your word for it where my
mate is concerned."

The man nodded. Vamp or were, the need to protect a mate
above all else was a universal instinct.

Marc stepped up and made the introductions. "Jace Tragallion-
D'Nally, this is Brac Tragallion. Second in command to the Alpha."

Jace eyed the man and did a quick check of his energy. It was
calm, which might mean he had nothing to hide, but then again
he'd been second in command to Travis, whom Ian clearly hadn't
trusted. That calm could just mean he was very good at masking
his duplicity, but Jace doubted it. There was strength in this man.
The kind of strength that came from a strong moral code. "I'm
sorry about Travis."

Brac nodded. "Thank you."

Yet another implication, through silence, that Travis hadn't been
a good man.

Miri smothered a yawn. Jace frowned. She was tiring more easily than he'd expected. "Is there a place we can clean up?"

"The leader's house has been readied." Brac motioned his hand
toward a house in the center of the compound. Large, with a well-
cared-for exterior, it had a prosperity lacking in the other homes.
"Follow me."

"Follow me" meant taking Miri through a line of weres that
stretched for a good fifty feet on either side of the road. A prickle

of unease went down Jace's spine. Miri came up beside him and slipped her hand into his.

"If we're going to do this," she whispered, "then we really do need to start as we mean to go on."

He eyed the motley collection of weres. "Hell of a time to be throwing my words back in my face."

She shrugged. "We have to trust someone, sometime. They're who we have."

She had a point. They'd come this far, and coming this far meant they were solidly in D'Nally territory. If the plan was to kill him and assign a new mate for Miri, they were way past the point of no return. "If they kill us, it's on your shoulders."

Her smile was shaky, but game. "Good thing my shoulders are broad."

He touched the shoulders in question. Feminine and delicate, inspiring the obvious retort, but the confidence in her smile stifled it. It'd been a long time since he'd seen that surety in Miri. Too long. Another sign she was finding her feet again. Agreeing to take over the Tragallion pack had been the right thing to do. In reality, up until the moment he'd made the announcement that he would take the position of Tragallion Alpha, and felt the joy surge through her, he'd never appreciated how much being pack meant to Miri. Pack to her was a lot like being a Johnson was to him. It was part of the definition of who she was. And returning to the culture she knew, even under these circumstances, had put the bounce back in her step.

Marc grunted and handed Penny to Miri to carry. "Your shoulders couldn't carry a gnat."

He took up a position on the other side of her and unslung his rifle from his shoulder.

Jace cocked an eyebrow at him. "For someone who's not expecting any trouble, you look damn prepared to meet some."

"I made a promise. It'll be kept."

Even if he had to kill someone to do it. Jace shook his head. In some ways, dealing with the Tragallions was like stepping back in time to his mortal days, when a man lived by the strength of his arm and his word. Which might explain why he found himself liking them so much despite their irritable ways. Something Tobias had hinted at before he'd headed off a few miles back to "take care of something."

Miri patted Marc's arm. The were, as always, frowned at the familiarity. Miri, as always, ignored his displeasure. "Thank you, Marc, but the gun's not going to be necessary."

"Uh-huh."

"Miri, if you don't stop touching the man, I'm going to have to seriously start considering him a rival."

"Fiddlesticks."

"Fiddlesticks? What in hell kind of word is that?"

Marc's lips might have twitched. Hard to tell. He went out of his way not to smile. Especially around Miri, who went out of her way to try to get him to. She said it was important for Penny. Jace had a feeling it was because she thought it was important for Marc.

Miri tugged the quilt away from the baby's face. "A perfectly good one, according to Raisa."

"That woman has a grudge against a good swearword," Jace groused, nodding to the patiently waiting Brac that they were ready.

"She's old-fashioned."

"She can be anything she wants as long as she keeps Jared smiling the way she does."

"He is smitten with her, isn't he?"

"No need to mince words. The man's a goner and everyone knows it."

She frowned. "Does it still bother you?"

He eased in front of her as they approached the crowd. "Because she was the one who turned Caleb?"

"Yes."

"No."

As they started up the road, moving through the sea of unfriendly faces, waves of displeasure came at him, blowing harder than the wind charging up the valley. Underneath, in a softer whisper, like a hint of spring, was a desperate sense of hope. He looked around again. The Tragallions had to be pretty damn desperate to pin their hopes for deliverance on a vampire.

Jace touched his mind to Miri's. It took a second for her to respond, but not as long as it used to. She was getting better at the mental communication.

I'm thinking Travis wasn't much of a leader.

MIRI thought Jace was right. There were certain things that spoke of prosperity and these people didn't have them. Yards and houses were barren of ornamentation. Clothing was of a uniform color and style, as if it had been purchased in bulk. Children's pants were too short, the knees patched. The compound itself had a general atmosphere of neglect, as if the very air was weighed down by sadness, with none of the laughter that came from the security of a well-run pack.

No wonder there wasn't a smile of welcome. If Travis's style of leadership was to keep all the best for himself, then the people were probably asking themselves how much more a vampire would take. Miri smiled at the woman to her right. The woman didn't smile back.

You're right. They don't look prosperous.

Movement flashed in the periphery of her vision. Even as she acknowledged it, Jace pulled her behind him. One look at the threat revealed it to be a little girl, maybe all of five years old. Her deep brown hair, pulled to either side of her head in neat pigtails, was the same deep brown of her eyes. Eyes that went wide in shock at the big vampire suddenly standing in front of her. In the same blink of an eye, Tragallion weres surged forward, Brac at the lead. Miri put her hand in the center of his chest, stopping him in his tracks. The shock of the contact reverberated up her arm. "Wait."

Brac looked at her hand and then back at her face, the arrogance not lost on her. She didn't care. They were starting as they
meant to go on, and she did not mean to go on as a squashed Alpha female, run over by the prejudices and fears of others. Marc
came up beside her, adding his muscle to her stance. His warning
growl rumbled in his throat.

A gasp drew her attention to the little girl, whose hands were
clasped in front of her, something clearly in their grasp. She looked
at Jace and her face crumpled, her eyes filled with tears as terror
replaced the determination with which she'd stepped out of the
crowd. Jace squatted down. Brac shifted. Miri didn't remove her
hand from his chest. "Jace would die before he'd hurt a child."

Brac didn't look convinced, but he didn't push her aside. Which
was good, because if he had they probably would have had a whole
new issue to deal with. Jace wouldn't have stood for that.

The violent aura around Jace softened. "Hello."

The little girl's lip quivered. Miri could imagine how that affected Jace. All Peanut had to do was think about crying and he
was mush.

"Is your mother here?"

The child nodded and motioned to a pretty young woman pushing through the crowd. The woman caught sight of Jace kneeling
in front of her daughter and cried out, "Brenda Lynn!"

The little girl's eye rounded more. "Uh-oh."

From where she stood, Miri could see Jace's amusement and
the twitch at the corner of his mouth. He raised his hand. The
woman stopped. Her fingers curled into fists. Miri gave her an encouraging smile. It was ignored.

"I guess you weren't supposed to say hi to me, huh?" Jace asked
in that deep, warm drawl that invited trust. Brenda Lynn wasn't
any more immune to it than any other female. Her lip paused in
mid-quiver, and her expression relaxed.

"I didn't want to say hi to you. You're a vampire."

"Brenda Lynn!" her mother gasped.

"It's all right," Jace told the mother. Miri could hear the laughter in his voice, though she doubted it was evident to anyone else. He turned back to Brenda Lynn. "Who were you looking to say hi to?"

She stared at him, the wobble in her chin firming before she glanced at Miri and pointed with her cupped hands. "Her."

"Why?"

Brenda Lynn opened her hands and carefully parted her fingers to reveal her treasure—a very tiny frog. "I've brought it for her."

"That's a mighty nice frog."

"She's special."

"I see."

Her lips circled into a pout and she frowned. "I want her to kiss it."

It was a sickly looking frog, with lots of bumps. Miri grimaced. There were limits to what Miri would do for a child. Beside her, Marc coughed. Or laughed.

"Do you think it's a prince?" Jace asked, maintaining a straight face with obvious difficulty.

Brenda Lynn gave him a look that clearly questioned his intelligence. "It's sick."

"And you think Miri's kiss can fix it?"

The little girl nodded so hard her pigtails bounced.

"What makes you think that?"

"My mommy said so."

Brenda Lynn's mother groaned.

"She did?"

No doubt the woman had said something not meant to be overheard and probably not too flattering. Definitely something she didn't want repeated, to judge from the worry in her expression.

"What did she say?"

"She said the female Alpha is either a saint or a devil . . ."

Miri could hear the punch line coming in the carefully recited quote.

"Because if she thinks she can make a no-good vampire into an Alpha, she has to be backed by either heaven or hell."

There was suddenly a flurry of coughing and face rubbing in those near enough to hear, which, with the acuity of wolf hearing, involved quite a few.

"Your momma is right. It takes someone special to do that."

I am not kissing a toad.

It's actually a frog, so you're good.

Frog, toad, she wasn't kissing it, and it was time to step in before Jace promised she would. Miri dropped her hand from Brac's chest. She handed Penny to Marc, who took her awkwardly, juggling the gun and the infant before he had to accept the inevitable and toss the gun to Brac.

Jace's energy reached out to her as she approached, circling her as she braced her hand between his shoulders. The thickness of his coat prevented her from feeling the shift of his muscles as he looked back at her. Nothing could prevent her from feeling his hug of comfort and his amusement. "This is Brenda Lynn. She has a problem."

"So I heard. Hello, Brenda Lynn."

All she got back was a determined look.

Leaning over, she studied the sad little amphibian. "I don't think he needs a kiss," she told the little girl, who reeked of lilac perfume. "I think he's just very thirsty."

The little girl didn't look convinced but she brought the frog up to nose level and stared it in the eyes and asked, "Are you thirsty?"

The frog didn't move, but Brenda Lynn's eyes crossed. She was beyond precious, and Miri couldn't help wondering if Faith would be that precocious at her age. And whether she'd get to see it. She took a slow breath to balance the agony before answering, "I don't think I can cure him with a kiss, but would you like me to take him up to the house and see if I can make him better?"

Brenda Lynn frowned. "It's a she. Her name is Wilhelmina."

"That's a pretty name."

"Pretty enough to kiss," Jace offered.

Miri slapped his back. "Hush."

Brenda Lynn went absolutely white, staring at Jace in horror. She didn't even blink as she stepped back. Around them, growls rose. Men moved in. Brenda Lynn's mother pulled her back. No one was looking at Miri. Everyone was looking at Jace.

In the same easy way he did everything else, Jace reached up, caught Miri's hand—the one that had slapped him—and brought it over his shoulder. The kiss he placed on her palm was neither discreet nor innocent. Flames licked up her arm, seared her chest, and suspended her breathing. By the time he was done, her knees were weak and her cheeks red.

"Pay no attention to him," Miri, struggling for normalcy, told Brenda Lynn as Jace stood, his arm coming around her shoulders. "He's always joking."

"He's awfully big."

Miri patted Jace's chest. "He's no bigger than Marc."

"He's big different."

Because he was Alpha. Because he could do whatever he wanted and, technically, no one could stop him. He could even bully little girls and their mothers and it would be his right.

Miri forced her smile to stay soft and her anger to stay buried. "That's so he can protect you. You know that's why he came, don't you? He knows Tragallions don't like vampires, but the D'Nally told him there was a little girl here who needed a special protector, someone to keep her safe. She needed someone big and strong who isn't afraid of bad guys." She shrugged as if the choice had been obvious. "He sent Jace." Brenda Lynn blinked, and her jaw dropped just a little. Part of her fear turned to awe. "The D'Nally sent him for me?"

The implication of that breathless query landed hard. Someone had dared hurt this precious little girl? "Yes."

"Will he protect my mommy, too?"

The question dropped into the silence like a stone pitched into a pond, the ripples spreading outward among the watching weres. Brenda's mother covered her daughter's mouth with her hand. She licked her lips and said in a voice as helpless as her glance around, "I'm so sorry."

Over the edge of her mother's fingers, Brenda Lynn's gaze shifted to Jace. She was clearly waiting for an answer. The same anger Miri felt inside was reflected in his energy, but not in his voice as he asked gently, "What's your mother's name?"

Brenda Lynn twisted free of her mother's grip. "Marjorie."

"That's a pretty name, and yes, I came to protect you both. No one threatens either of you without answering to me. And sweetheart, I'm one mean vampire when I want to be."

The statement was pitched to carry. A promise for everyone to hear. Another murmur rumbled through the crowd. Marjorie paled further and there was no disguising the panic in her expression.

Miri could have kissed Jace for having the understanding to say in a much lower voice, "There's no string on that protection, by the way."

"You don't like strings?" Brenda Lynn asked.

Marjorie covered the little girl's mouth again and apologized in a faint voice, "She . . . she just never knows when to be quiet."

Jace shrugged, still looking completely male, completely in control as he smiled indulgently. "Never knew a kid who could, and my promise still stands. If you know of anyone else who needs protection from anyone, outsiders or family, you have them send me a message. I'll handle it."

"You can't come between a male and his females," Brac protested.

Jace hitched his rifle up, looking more Alpha in that moment than she'd ever seen, standing shoulders back, feet slightly apart. Pride poured through her as he smiled that "I dare you to do something about it" smile and lazily drawled, "I can do whatever the he—heck I want."

The modified curse was obviously for Brenda Lynn's benefit.
"The males won't like it."

"The males will have to get used to change. I'm Alpha and a vampire. It's a guaranteed shake-'em-up combination."

"You left off that you are one of the Johnson brothers," Marc interjected, pulling the corner of the quilt out of Penny's mouth and replacing it with the pacifier. "Which is probably your most irritating characteristic."

"More irritating than being vampire?" Miri asked.

"Heck yes. Everyone knows once one of the Johnsons gets an idea in his head it's all but impossible to knock it free."

And Jace had decided to lead the Tragallions. Miri didn't know whether to take Marc's words as a warning or a threat.

Brac cleared his throat. He wanted to get moving. So did she. The pain was starting in her stomach and the knowledge of how damaged this pack was wasn't helping with the stress it added. "How about I take Wilhelmina up to the house and you have your mother bring you up in an hour and check on her?" she asked Brenda Lynn.

The child didn't hand over the frog. "I can't tell time yet."

Marjorie didn't step in with an offer to do it for her. Miri forced the woman's hand, relying on pack order to get the agreement she needed. As Alpha female, she had to start somewhere. This little frog was it. "Your mother can."

The woman said something under her breath Miri couldn't catch, then: "I'll bring her up in an hour."

She sounded like she'd rather face a firing squad.

Miri didn't care. With great reluctance, Brenda Lynn placed the frog in Miri's palms. With great reluctance Miri took it. The frog just sat listlessly in her hands. Not even trying to get away. She wanted to drop it. Instead she forced a smile and passed it to Brac. "I'll see you in an hour, then."

Marjorie placed her hand on her daughter's head. There was both exasperation and love in the gesture. "Thank you."

Miri knew just how she felt as Marc handed Penny to her, and the baby immediately began fussing. There wasn't a lot convenient about being a mother.

"Be careful," Brenda Lynn warned Brac, rubbing at her eyes. "You can break her."

His expression was properly solemn as he responded, "I won't break her."

That was good, Miri thought, because from the looks of things, enough was broken here already. The child was still rubbing her eyes. "Is there something wrong with your eyes?"

"No. They just get itchy."

Jace gave the frog a wary glance before putting his arm around her shoulders. "If I get warts I know who to blame."

Miri looked at him. "Warts are the least of our problems."

"What makes you say that?"

"Saving Wilhelmina here is our first official leadership job. If we fail, we're never going to be able to redeem ourselves in that little girl's eyes."

Jace eyed the little frog. "Then we'd better not fail."

THEIR new home was spacious, with big rooms and windows that let in a lot of light, which would be a good thing if Jace wasn't a vampire. A glance up revealed skylights blacked out by something.

Brac's gaze followed hers. "The pack didn't have much in the way of warning. We covered them securely, though."

Jace nodded as he looked around. "I appreciate it."

Miri didn't like the feel of the house. It was too open. She moved a step closer to Jace. "No light will get in when the shades are drawn?"

Brac's lips thinned at the implication. "I checked the shades myself."

Which didn't tell her anything. She didn't know how trustworthy he was. Jace put his arm around her shoulders and gave her a hug, and when he let go, somehow she was behind him again. She frowned up at him. How did he keep doing that?

His fingers grazed down her arm. "I'll be fine, Miri."

She had a sick feeling in her stomach that none of this was going to be fine. The pack was hostile, and Jace too exposed. And while this was just dawning on her, none of it was surprising to Jace. Which meant he'd known all along what he was risking for her, and he'd done it anyway. Because he was her husband, and because it mattered to her.

She didn't have a hand free, but she pressed herself against his back and kissed his shoulder blade through his coat. She'd thought the caress too light to feel through all the material, but when he glanced over his shoulder, flames flickered in his eyes. Along with questions. All she had to offer in the way of answers right then was a smile conflicted with the mix of emotions inside. Penny fussed again.

"Sounds to me like someone's getting hungry." Marc moved past her. "I'll get her bottle ready."

Brac looked at her, the frog in his hand. "Wilhelmina needs care, too."

He clearly was itching to get rid of the frog. She was very glad she still had Penny to hold. She hitched her up on her hip. "Why is all this suddenly my responsibility?"

"You're the female Alpha."

Of course he'd pull out that answer. "That's not working out to be nearly as glamorous as I was led to believe." The frog blinked. Being a little girl's princess in disguise apparently wasn't working for her, either. She sighed as Penny sucked on her shoulder, making wet smacking sounds. "We might as well head into the kitchen."

Her stomach was cramping, but not with the need for food. She needed blood. Specifically, Jace's. Her appetite seemed to split between blood and real food. Feeding on one over the other just caused an apparent imbalance that twisted her insides. Ignoring either had an equally painful result. "Miri?"

Rats. Jace had sensed the discomfort. She gave him a smile. He hooked his hand behind her neck and pulled her face in to his throat, letting her know he felt her pain. He lowered his lips to her ear. "You need to feed."

"Later."

His hand opened over the small of her back, massaging lightly. "Not much later."

It was an order. She immediately felt the conflicting needs to obey and to resist. Because neither was reasonable, she turned her mouth to his and kissed him. "All right."

His lips brushed her forehead before he let her step away. "Thank you."

Across the room Brac watched, his face expressionless. She lifted her chin and ignored her blush. She had nothing to be embarrassed about.

"It's all right," she told the man. "We're married. We get to take all sorts of liberties with one another."

The corner of the mean-looking were's mouth twitched. No other indication gave her an idea of whether he was annoyed or amused, whereas the cock of Jace's brow clearly indicated his amusement.

"Staking your claim, princess?"

"Maybe."

Jace's energy touched her with the intensity of a shock. A shiver ran down her spine as the heat of his query slid along her nerve endings. She didn't look around. She might not be running from their mating, but she wasn't making public knowledge how he could strip her down to defenseless and panting with just a look.

A sedate escape to the bedroom off to the right of the living room was called for. "Penny needs changing."

Jace watched Miri's retreat, everything Alpha in him demanding he follow up on the surrender in her words, her scent. Everything human in him understanding what a mistake it would be to embarrass her that way when she so clearly felt vulnerable. He listened as she spoke to the baby, heard the little fuss Penny made as Miri laid her down, heard the zipper slide as she opened the diaper bag.

In the kitchen, he heard Marc opening the refrigerator. Somewhere in the back, a generator hummed. He made his way through the hodgepodge of beautifully crafted furniture and lamps, frowning at the lack of uniformity in the pieces, except their value. They were obviously expensive. In his experience with the D'Nallys and the McClarens, the Alpha, while entitled to the best, served himself last. Judging from the poverty without and the wealth within, Travis hadn't subscribed to that philosophy.

Marc looked up from unpacking the bottles from the insulated bag when he entered. His gaze went past him, searching for Miri. Or maybe Brac? When he found neither, that blankness all the Tragallions seemed to muster at will replaced caution. Jace knew the look. Knew what it meant. This pack had secrets—bad ones, if he wasn't mistaken.

"Don't take this wrong, Marc, but I'm getting the impression that the Tragallion pack has fallen on hard times."

A little of that blankness slipped as Marc's mouth tightened. "We don't have the prime location of the D'Nallys. It's hard for us to build commerce in the things that we can do. We're too far out to have any real technology."

The oil lamp in the corner took on new meaning. "Do you have electricity?"

"Not all the houses."

Jace raked his fingers through his hair. That was going to play hell with Slade's devices. "Great."

Marc cut him a glance. "Anytime you want, you can turn around and go back home."

And steal from Miri the bubbling happiness she'd done her best to contain since he had announced he'd try his hand at being pack? Not likely. "You might as well get used to the idea. I'm here for the duration."

"I don't have to get used to anything."

The creak of the floorboard in the hall alerted Jace to Miri's return. Her scent flowed before her, her energy not far behind. Jace looked over his shoulder and then met the wolf's gaze. "Yes, you do, because I'm not going anywhere."

Marc raised his brows. "Because of her?"

"Because of a lot of things, not the least of which being that I made a promise to the D'Nally."

The wolf's expression didn't relax. "Just how specific a promise?"

"Specific enough that you might as well give up trying to scare me off."

Marc jerked his chin in the direction of Miri as she reentered the kitchen. "You think she's worth getting killed over?"

"Could be I just enjoy a challenge."

Miri's energy slid along his. If he wasn't mistaken there was a snarl in her voice as she asked, "Who's challenging you?"

Jace motioned to the stove. "That monstrosity."

He put his arm around her as she came to his side, tickling Penny's cheek with his fingertips in the way that always made her smile.

Miri stared at the cast-iron relic. "What is that?"

"A stove."

"From what century?"

Jace couldn't help a smile at the irony. "Mine."

Penny's smile at his touch dissolved to a pout and she made the grunting noise that signaled the onset of her displeasure. "Then you know how to operate it?"

"As a matter of fact, I do."

"Good, then could you heat up Penny's bottle?"

"No problem."

Another grunt, this one a bit higher-pitched, indicated Penny's growing discontent. "How long will that take?"

There was minimal heat coming off the surface. "About a half hour."

"Ugh, patience is not one of Penny's virtues."

"I'll see if I can make it twenty minutes."

Penny whimpered. "Then I'll show Penny our new home while you do."

Jace squatted down and opened the wood chamber. There were only embers left and no wood stacked beside the stove. "You do that."

He shut the door as Miri started up a lullaby and waltzed Penny out of the room.

"She does realize Penny is not going to be staying here?" Marc asked.

Jace nodded. "She just needs to do for her so that she can feel comfortable letting her go."

"Ah." Marc paused. "Thank you again for saving her."

"No need for thanks. There's not a man worth his salt who would have left that little girl there."

"My mate would have."

What was he supposed to say to that? He went for the obvious. "Why?"

"She was very much a fundamentalist."

"And you're not."

"No."

"Then why did you mate with her?"

"Matings are not a choice. When it became obvious we were compatible to breed we did our duty."

"It'll be a cold morning in hell before I see Miri as a duty."

"But you're here."

"I told you, I like a challenge."

"And your mate is pack." Marc opened the refrigerator door.

Jace shrugged. "That makes it work out all around."

"She loves my daughter."

"Yeah, she does."

"Even though she's deformed and not of her blood."

"Miri doesn't see the world in terms of perfect."

Marc nodded, putting one bottle in the fridge and keeping one in his hand. He closed the refrigerator. "I noticed that. She's going to be good for the people."

"Even if I'm part of the package deal?"

"I haven't decided about you yet."

That was at least honest. Jace dusted off his hands. "Is there a supply of wood for Bertha here?" He indicated the stove. "Or do I have to split it?"

"There's probably loads. Travis didn't like to be cold and made sure plenty was always delivered."

Jace cocked a brow at him. "He didn't cut his own?"

Marc's lips flattened back into that straight line that said so much. "Travis thought being leader gave him a lot of rights."

Jace settled his hat on his head. "I take that to mean he didn't split his own wood."

"Pretty much. He had pack for that."

Travis had used the pack for a lot of things. Jace opened the back door and stopped. There had to be at least ten cords of wood there. The place was big, but it wasn't that big, and this being the end of winter, the stack should have been on the opposite end of the scale from huge. He tried to remember seeing this much wood behind the other houses. He actually couldn't remember seeing any. He walked over to the nearest pile and grabbed an armful. When he turned, Marc was watching him.

"This the community woodpile?"

"No."

He hadn't thought so. Jace brushed past him, placed the wood on the floor beside the stove, and stirred the embers with the poker. "I haven't been around here long enough to know what's what, but if there's anyone in need of wood, bring some men up here and divide this pile up among those who need it."

The floorboard squeaked again. He glanced up. Brac stood in

the doorway, a clear bowl filled with what looked like colored rocks and water in his hands. "What makes you think anybody's in need?" he asked as he leaned his shoulder against the doorjamb.

Movement in the bowl indicated where the frog had ended up. Jace stacked kindling in a small pyramid. "That's a hell of a lot of wood to be still sitting at the end of winter. And my guess is a lot of somebodies went lean to keep it that way."

He could feel Brac looking at him.

"Do you think distributing some wood is going to get you in the pack's good graces?"

Jace twisted paper tightly and slipped it under his pile of kindling. "I don't intend for it to do anything but keep people warm."

Brac didn't look convinced. Jace didn't give a shit.

"Did you come for something or were you just feeling nosy?"

"I thought you'd like to know the women will be up shortly. And this frog still needs a home."

He blew on the embers. "Why?"

"Because I'm getting sick of babysitting it."

"Looks like you're doing a good enough job at it."

Brac held up the bowl. "I robbed a couple of those vases in the living room for some stones."

"Wilhelmina probably never had it so good." Jace glanced over. "Why are the women coming?"

"To see if there's anything Miri would like that she doesn't have."

"That's nice of them."

"I wouldn't call it nice. It's pack law."

Flames ate at the edge of the paper. "You're going to have to explain that one."

"It's Miri's right as female Alpha to take whatever she wants," Marc explained carefully.

Jace frowned. "We're good."

"Good for what?" Miri asked, coming back into the room. She stopped just in front of him, putting herself between him and Brac in that protective way she had. As if he'd ever use her as a shield.

"Good for all we need."

He caught her hand and tugged her back three steps to a point behind him. Brac watched the gesture with raised brows.

Jace ignored the exasperated glance Miri shot him. She kissed the baby's head. "I don't understand."

"It appears the Tragallions have a quaint old-fashioned custom in which they want to include us. One where we ransack their belongings for whatever we want. I've turned them down."

"Why?" Marc asked as Miri passed Penny to him.

"I provide for my wife."

"Travis supported it," Brac interjected.

"Travis is dead," Jace growled, walking over to the refrigerator and opening the door. Steak, steak, and more steak covered the shelves. There was enough food in that one refrigerator to feed an army. If Travis were still alive, Jace would have kicked his ass. "Did Travis have a big family?"

Marc's upper lip curled. "He never remated after his wife died."

"Ah." He looked over his shoulder. "Steak okay with you, Miri?"

She came over and caught the door before he could shut it. Her breath sucked in.

"Brac?" Miri called.

The were pushed away from the doorjamb. "Yes?"

"How close were you to Travis?"

"I was his second in command."

"That wasn't what I asked you."

"Princess," Jace warned as the were's scent changed.

She spun around, her elbow colliding with Jace's stomach. "What?"

"Treading on a man's pride can be dangerous business."

"I'm not treading on anything. I'm asking a question."

"A damn insulting question," Brac snarled, setting the frog on the counter.

Miri pushed Jace back, matching Brac glare for glare. "Who's your loyalty to, Brac?"

"My loyalty is to my pack."

"Not your Alpha?" Jace asked.

"The Alpha is an extension of the pack," Miri supplied, back to staring at the contents of the fridge, a strange tension humming off her.

"And if the Alpha is a skunk?"

"Steps are taken," Marc said, holding Penny in one arm while running a pot under the faucet.

"By whom?"

"Someone in the chain of command."

"Did you call the Enforcer, Brac?"

He folded his arms across his chest. "What if I did?"

Miri reached into the refrigerator and grabbed a packet of steak and slapped it on top of the lace tablecloth. "Then you waited too damn long."

She turned and grabbed another and then another, tossing them on top of the wood table, pitching steaks out of the refrigerator faster than Jace could catch them.

"Miri?"

Brac moved forward. Marc took a step in. Miri snarled and started throwing packs out two at a time. Penny started to cry. "Pack went hungry while that bastard sat up here hoarding food, didn't they?"

Jace shook his head before Marc could answer. A six-pack of beer hit the pile of steak and took a dangerous slide toward the edge. Jace grabbed it, setting it carefully on the floor.

"Brenda Lynn probably knows what hunger is, doesn't she?" Miri asked.

Jace didn't have to warn the others to say nothing on that. A fool could see Miri was winding up. He took a step in. Three packets of meat drove him back.

"And her mother hates this place for a reason, doesn't she? She doesn't want to come here because of the memories, right?"

She kicked the door open when it began to close, her arms loaded with packs of meat, condiments, and milk. "Right?" she demanded again when Brac didn't answer immediately. The were caught the door when it whipped back. Jars rattled.

"She might have some reason."

Miri dumped the food on the table. Marc made a dive for the milk, but because of Penny, he missed. The container hit the floor and popped open. The contents bled across the wood surface.

Miri just stood and stared as the puddle grew. "Shoot."

Jace bent down and picked up the carton, popped the cap back on, and put it back into the fridge. Miri immediately grabbed it back out. There was still a half carton left. "That's for Brenda Lynn."

She was back in motion. She scooped up a corner of the tablecloth and threw it over the pile with almost frenetic energy. Three steps and she was around the table, repeating the gesture until she had all the food bundled into the expensive tablecloth. When she would have pulled it off the table, Marc stopped her.

"That cloth is too fine to use for that."

"Melinda will be upset if you tear her grandmother's linen," Brac agreed.

"Who's Melinda?"

"Marjorie's aunt."

Miri groaned as if the information was more than she could bear. "Even the tablecloth is stolen?"

Jace opened his arms. Miri turned in to them. He caught a glimpse of the tears on her cheeks before she buried her face against his chest. "It wasn't supposed to be like this, Jace."

No matter how tightly he held her he couldn't keep her illusions from shattering.

"It's not supposed to be like this among my own kind."

"I know. But we'll fix it, baby."

Her fingers wrapped in his shirt. "Determination can't fix everything."

But it could fix this. Of that he was convinced. He tipped her chin up. Light caught on the tears in her eyes, turning the irises a lighter shade of gold. "Isn't that just like a woman to marry up with a man and then immediately try to change his way of thinking."

Brac motioned to the food. Jace nodded. The other man grabbed some paper bags out of the cupboard and started loading them up. Marc took the bottle off the stove and took Penny from the room.

"I'm not trying to change you," Miri whispered.

"You're trying to get me to believe in hopeless." He wiped the tears from her cheeks with his thumb. "And baby, hopeless isn't something I do. Especially not with you."

"I don't know how much more I can take."

"Then don't. Let me handle it for you." He needed her to let him handle this for her. "Just for a little while."

He held his breath while she debated. Her nod was the sweetest gift he'd ever received. Jace swung her up in his arms. Her arms went around his neck. Across the room, Brac stared, his eyes narrowed, his thoughts unreadable.

Miri tapped Jace on the shoulder. "Just a minute."

She leaned back so she could see Brac. "Tell the women to come for their belongings in a half hour."

"Excuse me?"

She waved a hand toward the parlor. "I want them to come get their belongings. I don't want them."

"That could leave you with nothing."

Jace took in Miri's pallor and her tear-splotched face. She needed to feed. "Tell them to be here in an hour."

✺ 18 ✺

IT was going to be easier to cure the frog.

Miri watched as, one after another, women came into her home to retrieve their furniture. The tiny hope she had that maybe at least one of them would welcome her died as two women struggled with the mattress for the bed. No one took the mattress from the bed unless they seriously wanted you gone.

She kept her voice as calm as possible as she said, "After you're done, could you all come back here, please?"

A few of the women gave her nervous glances. A couple of the looks were outright sullen. Most of the women didn't look at her at all. Miri sighed. Why couldn't something, for once, go easily?

The front door opened. Brenda Lynn came bouncing into the room behind her mother, bringing the stench of lilac perfume and the coolness of the night air with her.

"How's Wilhelmina?"

"I think she's a little better."

The little girl beamed. Her mother eyed Miri warily as she headed for the beautifully carved side table against the wall. Miri sighed again. No ally there.

"Brenda Lynn, come help me with this table," Marjorie called.

Brenda Lynn shook her head. "I want to see my frog."

"The table first, then the frog."

The little girl stomped over to her mother. Miri watched, humor mixing with the ache of loss as she did. Everything about Brenda Lynn made her wonder about Faith, projected her into the future, wondered if she would be the same at that age. God, she wanted her baby. Wanted her to have a future more than anything else in the world.

A touch of warmth surrounded her pain. Jace. She quickly shut off the emotion, not wanting to worry him. He had enough pain and guilt about their daughter. When he wasn't specifically guarding his emotions from her, she could slip under his shields and feel the agony he was trying to keep hidden. Part of her wished he'd share that pain. The more selfish side wanted him to keep it firmly locked up. She didn't feel strong enough to handle his and hers.

Brenda Lynn moved the lamp off the table. Miri frowned. The child's pants were too short and her shirt was faded. Earlier she'd thought that was because she'd been wearing play clothes, but no woman brought her child to the Alpha's house, even for a sign of nonsupport, in anything less than their best. The familiar feeling of anger and helplessness rolled over Miri, culminating in a sort of hopeless panic. One of the less favorable things she'd learned at the Sanctuary.

Hopeless isn't something I do.

Jace's words came back to her, along with the feel of his hand on her chin, the rush of his personality along with his utter belief that he could fix everything—her, their daughter, this pack.

She licked her lips. Jace believed in the impossible, the way other people believed in simply breathing. Where she'd been brought up with a sense of duty, but within an environment of ease, he'd been brought up fighting. She was used to warriors. Weres were warriors to the core, but Jace's edge was more honed. As a result, situations that left her doubting her ability just brought out his determination. She brought her fingers up and touched her lips. Touched her tongue to the surface, tasting the remnants of his kiss. She looked at all the women ransacking her house in their enthusiasm to reclaim bits and pieces of themselves. It was the same for her every time she connected to Jace. Bits and pieces of herself she'd thought lost just seemed to reappear, stronger than she remembered, as if nourishing the bond between them nourished other parts of her as well. Parts she'd missed, such as her self-confidence, her faith, her belief. Which was a good thing, because she was going to need them.

She winced as the heavy dining room table was dragged across the polished wood floor in a harsh scream of protest. The women froze and glanced at her, their expressions a mixture of horror and defiance.

She smiled. "I'm sure we can sand it out."

The women holding the table, the similarity of their features showing them to be obviously related, stared a second longer and then nodded. Albeit doubtfully.

Miri knew exactly how they felt. She wasn't sure of anything, either, other than the certainty that this pack had been abused. So had she. That gave them more in common than not. Learning how to grow out of the mess their lives had become was something they'd do together. She licked her lips again. With Jace's help. Even though she was married to him, she still found it hard to believe he'd agreed to become pack.

"What was wrong with Wilhelmina?" Brenda Lynn asked over her shoulder as she trailed her mother to the door, a small drawer from the table in her hands.

"I think she just had too much of the wrong kind of change."

The methodical stripping of the house paused, the break of silence in the commotion telling. Miri pretended not to notice. Brenda Lynn came back into the room, the drawer swinging at her side. "That doesn't make sense."

No, it probably didn't to a five-year-old. She tried a new tactic. "Wilhelmina is a very special kind of frog."

Instantly, the little girl was all attention. "Wilhelmina is special?"

Miri nodded. "Very special. She can sleep whenever she wants to so she can avoid whatever she wants to. She has the ability to take long naps when it's cold."

"Brenda Lynn," her mother called.

The child ignored the summons and frowned, rubbing at her eye with the back of her hand. "I know. I keep having to wake her up."

"Well, I think waking her up is making her sick. She needs to sleep."

The child cocked her head to the side and considered that. Marjorie came back into the house, saw where her daughter was, and frowned. Brenda Lynn ignored her mother's next call. "I don't feel good when I'm tired."

"And neither does she. And she needs to sleep in winter, right on through the cold until everything warms up."

"So if I let her sleep she'll like me again?"

"Oh honey, she never stopped liking you." Miri knelt down, putting herself at eye level with the little girl, and caught her hands. "But not being able to sleep when she wants makes her unhappy."

"So if I let her sleep she'll like it here?"

"Yes." Miri fully intended to talk the child into letting the frog go come warm weather, but for now, letting her hibernate would be good. Assuming she could hibernate in a house. "I think that change will do her good."

Brenda Lynn was quiet for a moment. She looked at her mother and then back at Miri, her hands clutched on the edge of the drawer. The muscles in her forearms shifted as her small hands gripped tightly.

"And maybe if you change things here, my mom will want to stay here, too?"

"Brenda Lynn!"

Miri wasn't surprised to hear Marjorie was planning to leave. The other woman had a tired, hopeless, trapped look about her. Miri might not know what inspired it, but she knew how that felt.

"I hope so." She waved Brenda Lynn in the direction of the kitchen, wincing at the overpowering scent of lilac. "Wilhelmina is in the kitchen. Do you know where that is?"

"Of course." She wrinkled her nose. "I used to live here."

Miri blinked in the aftermath of that revelation. Brenda Lynn skipped off.

She turned to her mother. "You and Brenda Lynn used to live here?"

Marjorie pulled herself up straight. "Yes."

"I was told Travis wasn't mated."

Marjorie lifted her chin. "He wasn't."

Miri blinked. "You're related?"

Someone snorted. Marjorie's chin went higher. "No."

No self-respecting pack woman lived with a male unmated. "You agreed to the arrangement?"

That chin came down in a short jerk. "I accepted the choice."

Which left a lot of room for interpretation. Proud and defiant, her attitude was almost a dare. Knowing what she did of Travis and of pack custom, Miri was willing to bet some sort of coercion had been involved and, despite the other woman's hostility, couldn't suppress the well of empathy. "We all do what we have to."

Marjorie's lids flickered. "Excuse me?"

From what she could see, Travis was the one who needed to be excused, but there was no way to address that and not smear Marjorie's pride in the dust.

Help came in the form of Brenda Lynn. She came out of the kitchen, the familiar energetic bounce to her step, the glass bowl

containing Wilhelmina in her hands. Water and stone sloshed around
as the frog clung where and how it could.

"Slow down, sweetheart," Marjorie called, the love for her child
clear in her voice. "Wilhelmina is going to get sick."

Brenda Lynn immediately sat down, asking the frog as she did,
"Are you feeling sick, Willy?"

Her face, as she anticipated the little frog's answer, was precious. The child was precious. Marjorie had tears in her eyes.

Miri touched her arm. "I'm going to make it better for her."

Marjorie's expression snapped closed. "Talk is easy."

"So is giving up," Miri shot back.

Marjorie bristled. "Word is, you gave up a long time ago."

Miri folded her arms across her chest. "In what way?"

Marjorie squared off against her. "You mated with a vampire."

"I mated with your Alpha, and I'm willing to bet he's a better
man than you've seen in a long time."

"You haven't marked him," one of the women near the door offered.

No, she hadn't, and she was beginning to see how ridiculous
that was. "That's between Jace and me."

"If you don't trust him, why should we?"

Good question. "It's not that I don't trust him."

"Yeah, right."

She ran her hand through her hair, tugging it through the snarls.
How much to tell? She looked around at the mixture of hope and
suspicion reflected back at her. This was her pack. These women
would follow her lead. Secrets weren't going to help any of them.

"I was a Sanctuary captive for a year." She licked her lips as
shame rose within her. Immediately there came a soothing touch
of calm. This time she didn't shut herself off. The women were
right. If she didn't let herself trust Jace, why should they? "It left
me with some issues."

"You should let your mate handle them," a cute blonde, whose
name she didn't know, piped up.

"It's not that easy."

"Do you fear he won't want you if he knows everything?"

She ran her hand through her hair and shook her head. "Jace is an incredibly loyal man."

"Then you should stop being foolish and mark him," Marjorie retorted.

"As soon as you're done here, I'll get right on it."

Now, that I am looking forward to.

"They say you saved Marc's daughter," the blonde continued, ignoring her sarcasm the way Miri was ignoring Jace.

"That business wasn't done well," Miri heard another woman mutter.

"On that we're in agreement, and I wasn't the one who saved her or claimed her—that was Jace."

"She has a deformed foot."

Murmurs rippled through the room in expanding waves, as if a clubfoot was the end all and be all of what made a good person.

The anger inside rose, catching in Miri's throat in a suppressed growl. "She also has a beautiful smile and the sweetest little nature. Of the three, I'm thinking the last two are more important."

"She'll bring bad luck," a woman with very old energy interjected.

Marjorie spun around. "It's worse luck when a pack abandons innocent children to outdated superstition."

Another murmur went through the women. The woman with the old energy stayed back, but the other women moved forward, just a little.

"Much worse. I was raised to believe pack supports pack unconditionally, without qualification." Miri glanced at Marjorie. "And not just when it comes to children."

An "Easy for you to say" drifted out of the slowly tightening group of women.

"Yes, it is." Miri folded her arms across her chest. "Which brings me to something else."

"Change your mind about giving back our belongings already?"

She should, considering they were taking everything right down to the soap sponge in the sink. "No. It's my husband's job to provide for me, so I'll let him."

Thanks.

Miri ignored the dry interruption. "But from here on out, no more families are going hungry, and no more children are going to be left in the woods. We're Tragallion weres, members of the D'Nally clan, and that stands for something."

"Yeah, neglect," the older woman muttered.

Miri had had about enough out of her. "Anyone unhappy with the way things are going to be run is free to leave."

"You can't kick me out. Only the Alpha can."

"I think it's safe to say I can pretty much get him to do whatever I want."

The woman shut up.

True. For the right incentive you could get me to do just about anything.

Images of her naked body covering his, her hair sliding over the hollow of his abdomen in a seductive blanket, flooded her mind.

Perv.

Not interested?

I didn't say that.

That's what I thought.

Hush, now.

You're very sexy when you go all queenly.

Hold that thought.

I'd rather hold something else.

There was no mistaking the smile tucked into the declaration. She had to suppress her own smile. Jace was absolutely outrageous. And every day she was remembering more and more how much she enjoyed it.

Let me do my job.

Will you make it up to me later?

She carried his image a step further, felt his gasp in her head, the heat that surged through his body. And cradled a thrill of satisfaction that she could do to him what he did so easily to her.

Absolutely.

She refocused on the women, who were eyeing her oddly. And no wonder. It probably looked like she'd spaced out there for a moment. "Do you want to leave or stay?"

There was a tense pause. Miri held her breath. She couldn't afford to lose anyone, least of all an elder of the pack. A vote of no confidence at that level would take years to overcome. The woman's gaze dropped just short of a direct challenge "Stay."

Miri let out the breath she'd been holding. "Good, because it's going to take a lot of work to get us to where we need to be and it's going to take everyone's cooperation to get there."

"Where is there?"

"I don't know, as I haven't been here long enough to know where we need to go, but I do know, from here on out the Tragallion-D'Nallys are focusing on results."

"What kind of results can we expect, when your mate is a vampire?"

"What *is* your name?" she snapped at the older woman.

"Helen."

"Well, Helen, if my mate being vampire doesn't bother the D'Nally, I fail to see why it should concern you."

"The D'Nally doesn't have to live with him."

Miri smiled sweetly at the attractive brunette. "Neither do you. I can have Brac escort you off Tragallion land tomorrow morning."

A knock at the door punctuated the collective gasp at that announcement. The door opened soundlessly. Jace strode in. The women stared, and not because he was vampire. Jace walked into every room like he owned it, and that confidence and strength, combined with his charisma, would be attractive to any were. Her mate, to put it bluntly, was a very handsome man in face, manner, and presence.

He could have his pick of any woman in any room. A spurt of inse-
curity fluctuated within.

I've got the one I want.

She blinked back the sting of tears at the softness of the emotion that flowed from him to her. He was such a strong man. He
deserved a strong woman.

Why me?

He reached her side. His hand slid behind her neck. With a
brush of his thumb, he tipped her face up. Flames flickered in his
eyes. A tiny smile creased the corners of his mouth. His head lowered. She couldn't look away, just stared, as enraptured as every
other woman by the intensity he projected. His breath eased over
her lips. She inhaled, bringing the caress inside, holding it close.

Just before his lips touched hers, he whispered mentally, *Because
I love you.*

She'd expected him to say it with the arrogance of a vampire,
could accept the dominance of a were, but he said it the way he
said everything—with the unbending certainty of his human heart.
And it shattered her. Way down deep where she'd sworn she'd
never break again. She just stood there stunned as he claimed her
mouth, her soul. He wasn't with her because of destiny or duty. He
loved her. He really did love her. The way she'd always dreamed
her true mate would.

The tears she'd been trying to suppress spilled to her cheeks,
flavoring the intimacy of the kiss as she brought her hands up to
his face and pulled him closer. If she could have, she'd have crawled
inside his skin. Awareness dropped away. There was only hunger
and need and Jace.

Someone cleared their throat. An audience. The realization made
a feeble stab through the haze of passion. They had an audience.

This isn't the time for this.

I think it's the perfect time. Kiss me back.

I am.

His hand slid around her back, settling into the hollow of her spine, lifting her up onto her toes, tucking her legs between his, her hips against his.

Harder.

She did, giving him all she had, uncaring that they had witnesses, or maybe giving it to him because there were witnesses. She was wolf. This was her mate. It was as natural as breathing to stake her claim.

She eased her lips from his, reveled in the rasp of beard against the softness of her lips, following his jawline to his ear. Lowering herself to flat-footed, she nipped his lobe, hearing his groan, feeling the stares, her canines itching with the desire to mark him, to irrevocably declare him as hers. She followed the taut cord of his neck downward, scraping the skin with the points of her teeth. Jace's fingertips dug into her back and neck, holding her to him for a brief second before he wrapped her hair in his fist and pulled her head back.

"No."

She fought the pressure, his dominance, the pings of protest from her hair spiking her passion even more. "Yes."

He brushed his lips across her forehead. "I've got some pretty specific plans for when you mark me," he murmured.

So he had known what she was doing. "The mark is my gift."

"And I can't wait to receive it, but—"

The creak of a floorboard was faint. One second she was staring into Jace's beautiful eyes, and the next she was falling backward, the breadth of his shoulders filling her vision as he spun to meet the threat. She stumbled. Someone caught her. She glanced over her shoulder and met Marjorie's gaze. For once it wasn't hostile.

"Thank you."

The woman nodded, her expression strange as she looked at Jace, but when she turned back to Miri, she was dead serious. "If you don't mark him soon, someone else will. An Alpha like him won't be neglected here."

A look around proved the truth of that. Lust and hunger were on many women's faces. Miri took a step closer to Jace and glared at Helen in particular. Her gaze looked to be the most lustful.

Surprisingly, Helen laughed, launching a string of titters and smiles around the room. Miri noticed, however, that humor didn't diminish the hunger in the other women. Her lip curled in a warning snarl.

"You're easily distracted, vampire," Brac said.

"By my wife, while among friends? Absolutely." Jace's weight settled onto the balls of his feet. For all the easiness of his tone, he was ready to fight. "Did you want something?"

"The men are here to distribute the wood among the pack."

"Good." He arched that brow in that deliberately goading way. "The wood's out back."

"The men want permission to enter the property."

Jace nodded. "Granted."

"We're getting wood?" Brenda Lynn asked with absolutely no regard for the undercurrents flowing through the room or the appropriateness of the question. Jace knelt down in front of her, resting his forearm across his knee. Marjorie immediately came to her daughter's side, not looking one bit reassured by Jace's smile.

"All you need."

The child's immediate withdrawal was aborted as she looked into Jace's eyes.

"Enough to warm even my bedroom?"

Miri felt the flick of Jace's energy that was his anger, but all the child saw was his nod. "Enough to make your house so toasty, you'll have to bring in sand so Wilhelmina and your friends can have a beach party."

"A party? I can have a party with other kids and everything?"

His drawl deeper than normal, Jace nodded and told her, "I definitely think you should have a party."

Marjorie tried to pull Brenda Lynn back. "That's really not necessary."

The child tugged her hand free of her mother's restraint. Her little shoulders squared as she frowned at Jace. "If my friends come out to play, do you promise not to suck their blood and feast on their bones?"

Jace didn't even blink at the gruesome image. "I promise."

Marjorie made another grab for Brenda Lynn. She missed. The child opened her mouth. Marjorie's "Oh, God" was a low moan of resignation.

"Even if my friends are boys?"

There was another stutter in Jace's energy. "Yes."

"Why?"

"Because I think that friends are as important as pack and little boys are as special as little girls."

"Really?"

"Cross my heart and hope to die, stick a thousand needles in my eye."

Brenda Lynn frowned. "You didn't do it right. It doesn't count if you don't do it right."

"I agree," Brac interjected with an utter seriousness that was belied by the amusement settling into the creases fanning out from the corners of his eyes. "Promises like that have to be done right."

Jace cut him a glare. "What's right?"

"You have to do this." Brenda Lynn made an energetic crossing motion over her chest and then spit into her palm before making a fist.

Jace arched a brow at her. "Seriously?"

Miri couldn't blame him for the question. It was a rather gross image to associate with such an angelic-looking child.

She nodded emphatically, pigtails bobbing. "It doesn't count otherwise."

"Well, I certainly want it to count." Jace made the appropriate sign and then spat into his palm. "I promise."

Brenda Lynn watched as his fingers curled around the last syllable. She reached up and caught her mother's hand, her eyes round. There was a rapt two-second pause before she looked up at her mom and whispered, "You don't have to cry anymore, Mommy. He really did send someone for me. Just like you prayed."

Marjorie half gasped and half sobbed as she grabbed her daughter to her. Brenda Lynn didn't fight. With a big smile, she turned and wrapped her hands around her mother's waist. "And I'm going to have a party."

❖ 19 ❖

TWENTY minutes later, the women trailed out. Marjorie, Brenda Lynn, and her frog were the first out the door. Helen, the last, and she didn't leave without casting a lingering look over her shoulder at Jace. Or maybe Brac. They left the mattress and box spring. Miri chose to think of it as a peace offering.

"Looks like a friendly group," Jace observed in his deep drawl, putting his arm around her shoulder.

She leaned her cheek onto the back of his hand before kissing the base of his thumb. "Don't get any ideas."

His hug was quick and hard, as was the kiss he dropped on the top of her head.

"The only woman who gives me ideas is you."

"I'd better be."

Brac snorted. "He's vampire. Don't hold your breath."

That level of disrespect could not be tolerated. Her hair whipped across her face. "He's your Alpha."

Brac shrugged. "He's still a vampire."

"He's *my* vampire."

Brac didn't straighten or otherwise look upset. "Not that anyone could notice."

They were back to the fact that she hadn't marked Jace.

"Don't you have something to do?"

"I'm doing it."

"Here?"

"Yes. I'm your security."

"I don't need security in the middle of my own pack." Miri turned to Jace. "Do I?"

"Not everyone is welcoming us with open arms." It was a flat statement of fact, but beneath each syllable lurked emotion she might have missed before. Guilt. His guilt that the pack she got wasn't the pack she wanted. Guilt that he'd committed them to this. They didn't need any more misplaced guilt flowing between them in an ever-expanding river. She pushed her hair out of her eyes. In the past, she would have waited for him to build a bridge across the pain. If she waited, he'd no doubt be the one to do so again. She wasn't waiting. She put her arms around his lean waist and hugged him. "We'll win them over."

She felt his start, and then his pleasure. Had she really been that cold to him, that such a small gesture affected him so much?

"Until we do, you'll need security."

The slight roughness to his drawl gave her that answer. Yes.

"I don't want security."

There was a wild flare in Jace's energy, a vague impression of their daughter's face and an agony and fear she never would have sensed if she hadn't learned to open her mind as his leapt the barriers he'd put in place. "You'll learn to accept it."

She nodded against his chest as his pain overwhelmed her. Pain he would rather have died than share. Not because he was proud, but because he thought she couldn't handle it. Because she'd convinced him she was that fragile. That he had to carry both their burdens. And that he had to do it in silence. She'd never been more ashamed.

"Okay."

He pulled back. "Just okay? No arguments?"

"Yup. Just okay." She was the Alpha female, and Jace's mate. It was about time she started acting like both.

He stared, then blinked, and then pushed her hair off her cheek the way he did when he wanted to know what was going on inside her. She felt the touch of his mind, so much lighter than the brush of his fingers. So much more intimate.

She answered his unspoken question. "I really am fine."

"Good."

She pressed her cheek against his chest, looking at Brac as she listened to the steady beat of Jace's heart. "How did this pack get so out of whack? Why didn't someone do something?"

"There wasn't anyone here to do anything. Travis volunteered the warriors to the D'Nally. When we got back, the damage was done."

"And someone had to undo it," she finished.

Brac nodded. "Steps were taken immediately to mitigate what had happened while the proper procedures were followed."

It was as close to an admittance that things had gotten so bad that Brac had been the one to call in the Enforcer.

The were's golden gaze lingered on the way Jace held her. He pushed away from the table he'd been half sitting on. "And now the process that was begun is in your hands to finish."

Another undone thread of her life to be rewoven into her future. So many. Jace, her daughter, Penny, the pack. It should be terrifying. "Yes, it is."

Jace cocked an eyebrow at her. "You don't sound upset."

She looked around. Her voice echoed in the nearly empty room. "I've got a lot to live for."

And after the year of hopelessly creating pointless challenges to try to keep herself sane, having so many real ones just waiting to be picked up was exciting.

He crooked his elbow, tipping her head back. "So do I."

Desire flowed between them in a peaking arc. Every muscle in her body softened with anticipation while the flames in his eyes leapt.

"Shit, an unmated male should not have to endure this," Brac grumbled, opening the front door. "I'm going to oversee the wood. Try not to get yourself killed by anything in the interim."

The flames in Jace's eyes leapt higher as he drew Miri up into the descent of his mouth. His laughter was a sultry burn against her hot cheeks as she perched on tiptoe, straining for the connection he withheld. "I'll try to find something better to do."

"Uh-huh."

The door clicked closed.

Miri didn't look away, just let her happiness in this moment flow out at him, seeing it catch in the lines that deepened beside his eyes, feeling it reflected back at her tenfold. Feeling how right it was that their energy connected.

He cocked his eyebrow. "They left us the bed."

She wrapped her fingers in his coat. "So I noticed."

He leaned in, tipping her off balance. She didn't even gasp.

His head canted slightly to the side. "Used to be, you'd panic when I did that."

"Used to be, I thought I'd fall." She reached up and took his hat off, removing the last shadow from his eyes. She tossed it across the room, where it hit the floor with a soft plop.

His fingers stretched down, pressing into the cheeks of her rear. He shook his head. "You were a very foolish girl to think I'd be responsible for one bruise on this sweet body."

"Yes, I was." She ruffled the hair at his nape with her fingers before sliding them into the cool strands, giving him full responsibility for holding her up as, with her other hand, she went to work slipping shirt buttons from their holes. "But I'm a very sensible woman now."

Arousal spiced the air between them. His energy tugged at hers in little pulses of invitation. A silent *come play with me* she eagerly accepted.

"How sensible?"

The question was gruff. Her response was throaty. "Sensible enough to know we're not going to make it to the bedroom."

He laughed and spun them in a slow circle, his lips nibbling at hers as he waltzed her back in gliding steps. "Have I ever mentioned how much I enjoy a sensible woman?"

"No, but feel free to elaborate." She tugged his shirt free of his pants. His pectoral muscles flexed, and on the next step, thick slabs of resilient power bunched with every move. She pressed her fingernail against one, absorbing the heat from his skin with her touch. Her canines ached as she watched her nail sink the tiniest bit into the hard muscle, marking the tan flesh with a white rim. His whole body jerked.

"Shit."

She looked up. Jake's gaze was locked on her mouth with an intensity that sent a shiver down her spine. The skin was tight over his cheekbones and, against her stomach, his cock throbbed with the same rhythm pounding in the hollow of his throat.

She glanced up from beneath her lashes, the filter softening the harshness of his expression. "You want me."

"'Til the day I die."

"You're immortal."

"Which means good things for you."

Her heels bumped the mattress. "Oh, yeah? Like what?"

His smile would have done the devil proud, it was so full of hot temptation. She couldn't look away from the heat in his gaze, the intensity of his emotion. Three tugs on her clothing and cool air hit her abdomen. The razor-sharp edge of the talons that had just done away with the impediment of her shirt skimmed up her belly. With a flick of his finger he sliced through the front of her bra. "Like how much time I'm going to have to learn what pleases this hot little body."

"Hot?"

The rougher flesh of his palm grazed the underside of her breast.

She didn't even try to hide the devastating purity of the pleasure that shot through her at the tantalizing touch. She wanted to share everything with him. She needed him to share everything with her.

"Definitely hot." A knowing edge lifted the right corner of his mouth at her gasp as he rubbed her nipple. "Undo my belt."

Oh, God! She closed her eyes as a hot rush flowed through her at the order. He did know how to make her feel good. She worked her hand between them, teasing him a bit with the scrape of her nails, his harshly indrawn breath as seductive as his touch. The belt buckle opened, she moved on to his pants. The button gave immediately. The zipper slid slowly, the quiet rasp a staccato beat of anticipation, falling into the rhythm of their heartbeats. When it reached the bottom of its slide Jace stopped breathing altogether, and she took things a step further. Reaching inside, she found his heat and hardness waiting for her. She squeezed. He groaned. His forehead braced against hers as his hips pressed his cock deeper into her grip. "Tease."

"I learned from the best."

"So you did." Satisfaction flared in his gaze. He liked being reminded that she'd given herself to him first.

"No one makes me feel the way you do," she whispered against the hollow of his throat.

"And how's that?"

A shift of his weight and they were falling backward. She grabbed for his neck, caught his shoulders instead. They sank slowly to the mattress, rotating as they went, until he was lying flat on his back and she was straddling him.

His grip shifted to her hips. "You were saying?"

"Like the world is made of the hottest fire." She groaned as his hips pressed up into hers, sending passion soaring through her. "And we're the center of it."

In the next second the constriction of her pants was no more. As the thick material slid down her thighs, she licked her lips and mentioned, "I don't have much of a wardrobe."

"It's not a problem." His hand came behind her neck as he urged her face down. "I like you naked."

In the middle of a firestorm he created the haven of laughter.

I love you.

The thought stuck in her head, her lips closed helplessly on the silent syllables. Her muscles stiffened with effort to get the words out. His fingers stroked down her nape. "Princess?"

She loved how he said that. Soft, with just the slightest emphasis on the first syllable, as if everything special for him was reflected in the endearment.

She shook her head and levered his cock free. Tears burned her eyes anew as it sprang into her palm, hot and potent. He deserved so much from her. She stroked him softly, trying to tell him through touch what she couldn't with words.

"Look at me."

She didn't have a choice.

"What's wrong?"

"Nothing."

"The sight of a man's appreciation always sets you to crying?"

Appreciation. That was such an old-fashioned way of phrasing it. The smile she forced wobbled at the corners. "No, just yours."

"Not exactly the reaction a man hopes to inspire."

"I know."

She traced the vein on the underside of his shaft with her thumb. He jerked and moaned. If only everything was as easy to control as the passion between them. "I want to explain something to you."

His gaze dropped to where she was caressing him. "Does it have to be now?"

She could see his point. She couldn't take her hands from his flesh, nor could she hold the words back, so she shrugged her apology. "Apparently."

Out of the corner of her eye she saw his hands ball into fists.

"Then explain away."

"While I was with the Sanctuary, I did a lot of things to keep

my sanity." She could tell she had his full attention from the way
his mind snapped to a fine focus. "I'd make challenges for myself,
impossible goals to keep from screaming in boredom."

The brush of his fingertips along her nape was more potent
than a kiss. Except she wanted a kiss. She bent over, letting her hair
fall in a curtain around them, and fit her mouth to his, kissing him
with all the tenderness locked up inside. She expected him to take
over, to turn it into more. Instead he closed his eyes and held her
to him, drinking the moment in, letting her feed her emotions into
him the only way she could. When she would have pulled away, he
kept her there, murmuring against her lips, "It doesn't matter, Miri,
if you can't say the words yet. This is enough."

Yet. Such a liberating word. Freeing in the expectation that what
hindered her was temporary. "Your patience is amazing," she sighed
into his mouth.

His lips twitched against hers in a prelude to a smile. "I keep
telling you I'm an amazing man."

The statement flowed into her, mentally, physically binding them
with their shared breath.

"Yes, you are."

He was amazing in his ability to keep moving forward without
faltering, in his ability to hold on to his faith, for her and her
daughter. Amazing in his ability to share that faith without making
it a burden.

She pulled back. "I just made Faith a promise."

"What kind of promise?"

The kind she couldn't break in her heart. The kind that held
her together at the memory of the Renegade were putting his big
hand over her daughter's mouth, silencing her cries at being separated from her mother. She relived her daughter's terror, felt her
cries for help, experienced again the devastating guilt at watching
little Faith's cries being smothered and doing nothing to stop it.
Because it had been the only way to get her to safety. The only way.

Wrapping her arms around her waist, she squeezed hard, trapping the pain of the memory inside. Oh, God, she needed her daughter in her arms.

Jace caught her face in his hands, tilting it to his. His breath warmed her cheeks. "You'll get her back, princess. I promise you."

Had she been telegraphing her thoughts? Please let the answer be no. She didn't want to burden Jace with that. One of them having to deal with those memories was enough. "I promised Faith, Jace. When he was taking her away, I promised her that I wouldn't say those words again until—" Her breath broke on a sob. "I didn't realize how unfair it was going to be to you when I promised. You have every right to expect—"

His thumb covered her lips, pressing inward, cutting off the frantic flow of words. His eyes were very dark as they met hers, vampire fire glowing at the edges.

"You keep your promise to our daughter, Miri. You keep it until I put her in your arms and then you can tell us both what you need to." The pressure on her lips eased. His thumb stroked in a soft feathering from one side of her mouth to the other. "This is enough for me."

This was his mouth melding with hers. This was the thrust of his tongue that demanded the parting of her lips. This was the claiming of her mouth that commanded her obedience. The fire returned, burning through her tears, her resistance, finding her confidence, launching it forward.

Yes, for now this was enough, but soon they'd have more. Soon they'd have their daughter and their love. Miri braced her hands on Jace's chest and levered herself a hairbreadth away. "I will give you more someday."

The flames in his eyes leapt higher; his energy seethed. "How about you just give me what I want right now?"

She snuggled her chest to his. He was all hard angles and planes that complimented her curves perfectly. "What's that?"

His hands cruised over her shoulder blades, traced their way down the hollow of her spine and then back up over the swell of her hips before gripping hard. "Your mark. Mark me as I take you, princess, and I guarantee I'll be a happy man."

He was willing to settle for so little.

Guess that all depends on your perspective.

He'd caught her thought. Emotions foreign and strong, distinctly masculine, swirled over hers in a heavy wave, leaving her floundering until out of the midst came a hunger that threaded them in one powerful projection. Her leaning above him, her body appearing incredibly lush and feminine as it curved over his, the silken caress of her hair brushing his skin as the molten heat of her sheath teased the tip of his cock with the same deliberateness with which her teeth teased his skin. Pleasure surged; anticipation heightened.

"You want my bite," she whispered, feminine power skipping along her nerve endings in a thrill of delight at the realization of how much he wanted her.

He brought her down to whisper in her ear. "I want your mark."

"Here?" she asked, skimming her hand along the strong column of his neck.

His growl drew a grin and more of that feminine power from deep within. "You know where."

She traced his collarbone. "Here?"

He centered his shaft with a shift of his hips and it was her turn to gasp. He was deliciously thick and her muscles tightened. His grin was knowing. "It's not nice to tease the vampire."

She drew little circles on his chest, working her way down to his flat nipples. "It might not be nice . . ." She gave one a little pinch. "But it definitely is fun."

With a half laugh, half growl, he flipped her over, coming down over her in a big dark threat, realigning himself against her with a smooth efficiency that brought everything female in her to fevered attention.

"I'll show you fun," he snarled in a voice that should have terrified her, but instead brought out her wild side. His fangs nipped at her jaw, her earlobe. She arched into the shivery sensations until they became too much. And then she tried to curl away, but there wasn't any place to go. The mattress was at her back and the rest of her was surrounded by vampire. Her very intense, very passionate, incredibly loving vampire.

Jace.

He kissed the pulse in her throat, his fangs delicately scraping the tender skin over her jugular. She arched her head back, wanting to give him everything. Needing to.

Her canines throbbed with the rhythm of desire. His scent enfolded her, beckoned her. Her muscles parted as he pressed down, entering her that first bit. She closed her eyes and struggled with the differences between them, as always her first instinct to brace herself.

"No, baby, just relax. You know I won't hurt you. Just go all soft and sweet for me, and let me make you feel good."

Good. The word sank through the haze of erotic enchantment. This had started with her wanting to do something to make him feel good. His arm brushed her cheek. His cock pressed deeper. She moaned as she remembered. A tremor shook her from head to toe with the sheer pleasure of it. He wanted her to mark him. Locking her gaze to his, she curved her fingers into his shoulder, pulling him down.

His energy flared. His lips set in a straight line. "No. You're not ready."

She'd passed ready ten minutes ago. "Don't be such a baby."

It was probably the shock of being called a baby that dropped him down that crucial inch that enabled her to hook her hand around his neck. After that, it was just a matter of taking advantage of his nature. As soon as she tugged, he pulled back, giving her the resistance she needed to draw herself up. Her lips brushed the hair-roughened skin above his pectoral. He froze. She touched the salty expanse with her tongue, preparing him. His breath hissed in, between his teeth, as his muscles tensed. His hips jerked, piercing her a tiny bit more. His big hand cupped her skull, pulling her in even as he gave her one last chance. "Miri . . ."

"Just relax, Jace. You're going to like this."

The irises of his eyes were totally consumed with vampire fire. The same fire she wanted licking over her flesh, burning into the center of her being, joining them.

"Too much, that's the problem."

"It can never be too much."

She kissed the spot once, twice, feeling the glands in her mouth swelling in readiness. He cradled her head, supporting her as she lavished upon him the only gift she had to give: herself.

On the third kiss she lingered. He groaned. She bit, tasting the spice of claiming as it spread into the intimate mix of blood, saliva, man, woman. At the same time his body surged into hers, convulsing in ecstasy as she made her claim. His expression went savage, his mood primitive, snarling as he pulled her closer, demanding more. She gave it. While the violent culmination drove everything from his mind except the pleasure of the bite, the joining of their bodies, only one wild thought consumed hers.

Mine.

"**THAT** wasn't quite the way I planned it."

Nowhere in his imagining of the moment that Miri claimed him had Jace planned on losing control like that.

Her hair whispered against his shoulder as she looked up. "Why? What did I do wrong?"

He touched his finger to the softness of her cheek. "I'm the one who didn't last long enough to see to your pleasure."

She tapped the center of the bruise. "I was pleased."

His breath sucked in as erotic pleasure spilled over him again. His cock hardened as if he hadn't just come. "I'm sorry."

He caught her hand before she could pull it free. "You didn't hurt me."

"I didn't . . ." Those big golden-brown eyes of hers dropped to his groin and then back up. "You're sensitive."

From the smile on her lips, he saw she liked that. "Don't go getting ideas."

"Why not?"

She wiggled until her other hand was free and then brushed it over her mark. The sensation shot straight to his gut. His muscles clenched and the smile on her lips widened. She hitched herself up and hooked her soft thigh over his. The brush of her lips was heaven and hell. "This makes up for your not being ticklish."

"I think I've unleashed a monster."

She snuggled back into his shoulder. "In that case you'd better look afraid."

"I'm vampire, I *am* the monster."

Instead of teasing, her expression grew serious. "Not to Brenda Lynn."

"No, not to her."

"What do you think she meant when she said she'd prayed for someone?"

So she'd been thinking on that, too. "I don't know, but I intend to find out."

"Do you think someone's threatening her?"

"Maybe, or she could just be worried Travis will be coming back. She's awfully young. She might not understand the concept of death."

She nestled her cheek into the hollow of his shoulder. "Maybe."

"He could put quite a scare in a little girl. Especially if he was using her to get her mother's cooperation in his bed."

She covered his mark with her palm. "It's hard to believe an Alpha could behave so to his pack."

With a hitch of his arm, Jace pulled her in. She'd lost a lot of illusions this year. The hardest might have come last. Pack were as susceptible to failure as vampires and humans. "There's good and bad everywhere, princess."

"Well, Travis apparently gathered up more than his fair share."

"No arguing that."

The mark burned and itched. The stroke of her fingers soothed the irritation but created another deeper burn. He pulled her up so she draped across his chest. She propped her chin in her hands. The points of her elbows dug into his chest. He hated to kill the hope in her eyes but hiding from the truth wasn't going to save her. "Not everyone's going to accept me right off."

"You'll win them over."

"Some of them might never accept me."

"Then they can leave."

"Some of them might even have strong opinions about my staying on."

She frowned down at him. "What are you trying to say?"

"I'm not always going to be able to be the nice guy. There will be challenges. And it won't be like with the McClarens. These boys could be serious."

She leaned in. "Will you promise me something?"

He knew what was coming. She had a soft heart. A woman's heart. And she wanted this pack to like her. Her tempting lips came closer. Full and red, still swollen from his previous attentions. The mark she'd given him burned at the sultry lure of her scent, her heat, her energy; it throbbed with the need to experience the liquid heat of her passion again. "Anything."

"If anyone challenges you"—she fitted her lips to his, top to bottom, edge to edge—"kick their asses."

❧ 20 ❧

HE was going to have to kick some ass. Two hours out from the compound, at the end of another fruitless rumor-chasing search for Faith, standing in a phone booth waiting for Caleb to pick up, watching the sullen-faced weres take up protective positions, Jace felt the gnawing of doubt. What the hell good did it do him to head up a pack of wolves if they couldn't find what they were hunting for? With every day that passed, Faith was getting farther away. And with every failed mission, the hope he harbored that he could bring their daughter home diminished. Staring into the shiny metal of the phone front, he saw his reflection, felt the weight of his responsibilities. His mind's eye superimposed the image of his daughter's face, as Miri had given it to him, over his reflection. Tiny, round, red with fury over her introduction to the world. An introduction he would have had be so different. She had the Johnsons' square chin, he realized. He reached out, touching the squared bottom of his/her chin, imagining she felt the contact wherever she was. Imagined it gave her comfort. Tried not to hear the cries he couldn't soothe. He wanted his daughter, damn it. Wanted to hold her and let her feel his love. He couldn't bear the thought that she didn't know how much she was loved by her father. That she might grow up not knowing the families she belonged to, who waited to welcome her home. The phone rang with pointless insistence. He pressed against the image. Cool metal greeted his touch rather than petal-soft skin. Her image fell away and he was once again staring at nothing more than his reflection. Jace let his hand drop to his side. His fingers curled into a fist. *I'll find you, little one.*

"No answer?" Brac asked from his left.

Jace blinked, brought back to the present. The phone crooked between his shoulder and ear was still ringing through to Caleb. "Not yet."

"We don't have all night."

They had as long as they needed. The insolence in Brac's tone was an indirect challenge he was soon going to have to address.

If he needed more proof, if the lip the guards had given him before letting him through the last checkpoint wasn't sufficient, the assessing looks his two "guides" were giving him now practically begged an ass kicking.

One Jace wasn't averse to giving. The same restlessness that plagued the weres gnawed at him. He was tired of waiting, tired of everything feeling beyond his control. He might have to wait for Faith, but there was no reason he couldn't have things out with the Tragallions. If they didn't make a move soon, he was going to make it for them. Their resentment of his leadership couldn't be allowed to fester. It needed to come to a head. This needed to be settled. Not only for the pack's sake, but when he found Faith, he needed the pack unified. Frankly, he'd expected to be jumped way before now, but for some reason the weres were holding back. There was almost an aura of waiting. Shaking his head, Jace turned his back to the wolves. He was beginning to think Miri was right. He didn't understand weres.

The ringing abruptly stopped. Caleb came on the line. "Hello."

"Hey, Caleb."

"Jace?"

"None other."

"Why aren't you calling in on your cell?"

"Dead battery."

"You let the battery run dead?"

He couldn't blame Caleb for the shock. It wasn't something he normally did, but Brenda Lynn had brought a new friend around. One of the five children on the compound. The boy had been roughly her age. A cute boy with hair that went every which way. In his hands he'd had a toy car. In his eyes there'd been the conviction Brenda Lynn had given him that Jace, as Alpha, could work miracles. It'd been the kid's birthday. Three hours later Jace had adapted the charger to run the toy. The kids had been happy. And his cell phone had been living on borrowed time ever since. "There were extenuating circumstances."

"Damn it, Jace, we have got to get you out of the dark ages. I don't like you being out of touch."

"The storm coming in should lay a base for the snowmobiles to get through with the supplies."

"If it doesn't, I'm hiring choppers," Caleb growled.

"This is too dangerous."

"I don't care."

Jace sighed. "I'm fine."

There was a pause in which Caleb communicated his skepticism eloquently with his silence. Finally he asked, "The Tragallions make their move yet?"

"No."

"What in hell are they waiting for?"

He wished he knew. "Could be they're not the hurrying type."

"And pigs fly."

There was another silence. Jace could easily picture Caleb running his hand through his hair as frustration ate at him. His brother had a sense of responsibility that didn't quit and no matter how old

Jace got, how mean he proved himself to be, in many ways Caleb couldn't see him as anything other than his little brother that needed his protection.

He changed the subject. "How's Joseph doing?"

"He's holding his own."

"What exactly does that mean?"

"It means I wouldn't say he's thriving."

Jace didn't need telepathy to feel his brother's anguish. He glanced at the weres. They were still standing where he'd left them, no doubt listening. "Damn, I'm sorry. But Slade will figure something out."

"I know." Caleb took an audible breath, the only betrayal of the pain he and Allie had to be going through. "How's Penny doing?"

It seemed wrong to answer with the truth.

"Jace?" Caleb prodded.

"What?"

"Allie and I would kill for good news right now."

Jace sighed. "She's thriving."

"Thank God." Another pause and then, "Are the Tragallions treating her right?"

"She's everybody's darling."

"Maybe they aren't all bad."

No. They weren't. "They've got their good points."

"I still don't understand why you didn't just tell Ian to go to hell. Miri would have been happy with the McClarens."

Jace wasn't so sure about that. Lately he'd sensed the same need for challenge in Miri that prowled in him. The McClarens were safe and settled. Life there would have been as routine for her as it was for him. He would have been getting itchy feet within a month. He had the sense she would have, too. The current situation with all its ups and downs suited both of them much better. Somehow, Ian had known that.

"What can I say, the man is a shrewd negotiator."

* * *

JACE made it home just before dawn. He paused outside the door and glanced at the weres.

"Sure you boys don't have something you want to get off your chests?"

Wind blew as the two men looked at each other. Jace glanced up at the dark sky. The storm was coming. It was going to be a big one, big enough to solve a lot of their issues. He could feel it in his bones. He was even looking forward to it.

The more vocal of the men smiled, showing even white teeth and sharp canines. "Maybe another time."

Jace nodded and opened the door. "I'll look forward to it."

It wasn't a lie. His temper was fraying under the stress of waiting. He wanted to do something besides run in circles chasing his tail. He wanted his child. He wanted to move on to the future without the past dragging him down. He wanted normal. Jace entered the house and closed the door, breathing in the welcoming scents of home. Wood polish, Miri, and charred steak. The latter brought a smile to his lips. Miri must have lost another battle with the woodstove.

He found her in the kitchen, over a paper plate on the floor, cutting away on one very black on the outside, very rare on the inside steak with a plastic knife and fork. She wasn't making a lot of headway. She looked up as he came in the room and smiled a welcome while her eyes coursed over him from head to toe, looking for signs of injury.

He motioned to the plate and plastic utensils. "That looks like a challenge."

"It is."

"So why are you smiling?"

"Brac's mother sent over some sheets and blankets."

"And this makes cutting a steak with plastic utensils easier how?"

"It doesn't help a bit."

"But you're still smiling."

"It was a peace offering."

"Maybe she was just appeasing a guilty conscience."

Miri raised her eyebrows. "You so do not understand weres."

"So I'm beginning to believe."

He took off his Stetson and sat down beside her, putting his hat on the floor. Leaning back against the wall as she sawed through the last bit of fat, he rested his hand on his knee. She offered him the piece she finally succeeded in cutting off.

"No, thanks. I had a snack when I was out."

She wrinkled her nose at him, staring at his face as if checking for confirmation that he'd fed.

"My momma taught me how to use a napkin, you know."

For two heartbeats she didn't get his meaning. "That's gross."

He pointed at the meat. "When I'm done eating, my meal gets up and goes about its way. Yours has to cock up its toes. You tell me which is grosser."

She didn't bat an eyelash. "Yours."

Putting his arm around her shoulder he tugged her across the distance between them and smiled. "Uh-huh."

It must have been as strained as it felt because she set the plate on the floor and scooted along, with his encouragement, until she was all but sitting in his lap. The scent of her shampoo drifted up. Wholesome and sweet, a cleansing balm for the sickness of his fear. When her cheek touched his shoulder he confessed, "It was a dead end, princess."

She nodded. "I know."

He guessed his coming back empty-handed made that clear. "I will find her, though."

There was no condemnation in the stroke of her hands down his chest.

"I know that, too," she whispered, nothing but trust in her gaze.

Shit. He didn't deserve it. He rested his head against the wall and closed his eyes, weariness dragging at him. There was no guarantee he could deliver Faith to her. Despite his best intentions his promise might just turn out to be so much hot air.

Paper slid across linoleum. "Your promises are gold."

Shit again. He'd projected. "You're getting good at reading minds."

Denim rustled as she came up on her knees. His senses flared to absorb the heat of her body as it rose along his. Nerve endings strained for the culmination of anticipation. It came in the brush of her lips against his neck. The shiver then snaked down his spine and lodged in his soul.

"No. Just yours."

He cracked an eyelid. She was staring at him with all the conviction she felt inside shining from her eyes. It was a hell of a lot. Her hands settled on his shoulders, hesitantly, as if she debated, and then firmed as she came to a decision.

"My feelings for you don't hinge on whether we find Faith tomorrow or ten years from tomorrow, Jace."

She didn't have to tell him that. "I know. Mating's not a choice."

Miri shook her head, her hair tumbling about that piquant face he loved so much, casting her eyes in shadow, but nothing could disguise the emotion within. That blazed out at him. Not with the frantic energy that he expected, but with a calm certainty. "When I said that, it was a cop-out."

"Yeah?"

"Yeah." Her hand connected with his shoulder in a small slap. "I gave you my mark, Jace Johnson, because you're the only man who could wear it. I gave you my heart because there's no other man I would—I *could*—trust it to."

He didn't know what to do with his hands, what to do with the storm of emotion her statement created in him. He settled for cupping her face in his right hand and her shoulder in his left. "You've got lousy taste in men."

If anything, her expression grew softer. "I guess it's up to you then to improve it."

"Like hell. If you're insane enough to think I'm the shine on your Sunday best, then I'm keeping you crazy."

"You do that, and I'll keep you from taking on too much responsibility."

A tilt of her head to the side and her mouth was at the perfect angle for his kiss.

"I'm sorry about Faith."

It just slipped out. Against his will, a confession for the guilt gnawing him alive, an outlet for the grief he struggled to contain.

"It wasn't your fault."

"If I had stayed with you—"

She put her hand over his mouth, stemming the flow of words, tears welling in her eyes. "You wouldn't be the man you are, and nothing would have changed. I was betrayed, Jace. There's no preparing for betrayal."

She would know. The emotion grew as her tears welled. He'd failed her, brought this upon them. If he'd just asked questions, found out what mattered to her. If he only hadn't assumed he knew best. Pain and understanding flowed in the wake of the what-ifs, filling the space between them. A space for three that only held two. It was so easy to imagine Faith in Miri's arms. So easy to picture wrapping his arms around them both, smiles gracing the moment instead of the heartbreak of tears. Easy and impossible at the same time. Goddamn, he wanted his daughter.

Miri's lips brushed his, then lingered in a kiss that shared so much more than passion. Her arms came around his shoulders, slender and fragile, but so strong in ways that had nothing to do with muscle. "We're in this together." There was nothing he could do but pull her closer as her energy slid along his, finding the pockets of grief, sheltering them in the grace of comfort. He wanted to pull her beneath into his skin, soak in her comfort. "Our little girl is missing. No matter how much you pretend, I'll always know you hurt. Hiding it doesn't help either of us."

The simple statement, laced with truth, made him want to do nothing more than absorb her into the shelter of his body where nothing could ever hurt her. His fingers fisted in her hair as he struggled with control. Nothing was supposed to hurt either Miri or Faith, yet both had suffered. "Showing it doesn't help."

The little hesitation the words evoked was reminiscent of the one she'd made all those months ago when he'd told her he was going on a mission.

It was simple to tug her face up. Not so simple to decipher her carefully blank expression. "Talk to me, princess."

"If you don't share with me, I'm all alone in my pain. And it hurts so badly, Jace."

She was killing him, ripping the shields from his soul. Not looking away, not granting either of them a reprieve, just letting big tears flow down her cheeks. With brutal honesty she whispered, "I need someone who grieves as I do, to hold me. Someone who longs as I do, hopes as I do." She licked her lips. "The only person that could be is you."

Catching a tear on his finger, Jace couldn't be any less honest. "I'm not a man for showing weakness, Miri."

"I know that; the world knows that." Another pass of her tongue across her lips. "I just need you to be strong enough to hold me and let me cry."

Why didn't she just ask him to carve out his heart and hand it to her? It would be a lot less painful than watching her cry. "I don't think you know how much I hate seeing your tears."

"I know." She didn't say anything more, just sat there staring at him, asking silently for him to share the pain. Her pain, his pain. "Ah, hell." He could at least try.

Enfolding her against his chest, cradling her in his lap on the kitchen floor of their new home, Jace dropped his cheek to the top of her head and said, "Then cry, baby. For both of us."

She sniffed, her tears already wetting his shirt. "You might not want to give such blanket permission. I can really wail when there's a need."

Their daughter was out there somewhere, hunted by Sanctuary, held hostage by unknown Renegades, her future uncertain, her tiny life at risk. Linking his energy to hers, he murmured, "Wail away, princess."

A half hour later, Miri stirred. "You must be cramped."

He was getting a pain in his thigh. "I'm fine."

She wiped at his sodden shirt. "You're damp."

Soaked. "Do you feel better?"

She nodded. "How about you?"

Linked as he had been to her, there was no way he couldn't have shared somewhat in the expenditure of pent-up grief. "A little damp around the edges but functional."

He lifted her off his lap, as always struck by how light she was. And he'd interrupted her dinner. As soon as she settled beside him, he reached for her discarded plate. Handing it to her seemed such a normal thing after the last half hour of pure emotion, he couldn't resist.

"So, darling, how was your day?"

She took it. "Surprisingly, not that bad."

"So things around here are picking up?"

"This is a good pack, Jace. They've just been driven to desperation and suspicion by bad leadership."

There was no way he was letting that pass.

"I think you've been looking at things through rose-colored glasses again."

"With enough time, we can turn things around."

"It's the time between now and then that worries me."

The Tragallions were a very tight pack. Because they were wolf they hadn't risen against their leader, but they might rise against him. No doubt there was a whole different set of rules that applied when a vampire usurped a pack. And that worried him. He didn't like the thought of what could happen to Miri if they organized a revolt. "This pack's a hairbreadth from full rebellion."

Miri went to work on another piece of steak. The knife scraped across the paper. "There's no doubt they're a bit hair-trigger."

"That's the understatement of the year."

Her grip went white-knuckle on the utensils. "I just don't want you to write them off."

"What makes you think I'm planning on doing that?"

"They can be difficult."

"In case you haven't noticed, so can I."

The glance she cast him from under her lashes was assessing. "I think you're going to be good for them."

"Even though I'm a vampire?"

Miri shrugged. "You're more wolf than vampire."

"Only in your eyes."

With a shake of her head, she said, "In everyone's eyes."

"I'm a Johnson," he corrected. "First and foremost."

She kissed his shoulder. "That is absolutely going to work for us. And while the pack is coming to realize that, we'll make sure that they're warm and fed and have some outlet to earn money." She went back to sawing on the steak. "Remind me to talk to Ian about that, by the way."

"What? There's suddenly a demand for bad attitude?"

She pointed to the ornately carved wooden bowl in the center of the floor as if it were the place of honor. "Have you seen the artistic talent this pack has? When the modern world gets a look at pieces like that, poverty will no longer be an issue. Heck. All they need is a Web page and a shopping cart."

"There's no doubt they can turn wood, but, Miri, you're talking battle-scarred warriors with a stubborn streak a mile long that are used to action."

"Oh, you'll have to make sure they don't get restless." She said that as if keeping the edge off a hundred prowling weres was nothing. "But I think you'll be surprised how fast they'll take to being family men."

"Family men? Last I checked the majority of the men don't even have mates."

The plastic knife scraped the paper plate again. "Of course they don't have mates." She waved the piece of meat on the end of the fork as she made her point. "When would they have time to find mates, and even if they did how could they convince them to want to live here? There isn't even modern plumbing in all the houses."

"I've got Slade working on some energy sources to change that."

"I know, but being single with little hope of being seen as a viable prospect by a woman of the more modern packs has got to be wearing on their nerves."

Jace could think of another part of their body it would be wearing on.

"It's one of the reasons they're so tense," Miri finished.

"You're saying being single is making them crotchety?"

"Didn't it make you crotchety?"

He wasn't touching that with a ten-foot pole. "I've got to admit I'm a lot happier now that I have you."

Her smile was knowing. "Good answer."

He inclined his head. "Thank you. Still, princess, no matter how positive the changes, you've got to know there will still be some that balk at them."

"They'll be in the minority."

"That minority can still be pretty deadly, and just so you know, at the first hint of danger, I'm pulling you out of here."

"We can talk about that if it becomes an issue."

Straightening, he corrected, "That was a statement of fact."

She put her plate on the floor and shifted up on her knees. "If there's real danger, I'll leave, but not just a pack dispute."

"What constitutes a pack dispute?"

"There's a possibility I may have to put a couple weres in their place. You can't interfere in anything like that."

"I'll interfere whenever I see a need."

"That's not good enough."

"Which one of us is Alpha?"

She didn't look away and he liked that. Some men liked their women intimidated. He liked Miri just like this, ready to back her point of view with argument. Even against him.

"How about I promise that as long as the situation doesn't seem to be life threatening, I'll let you handle it?"

"I can live with that."

She set the plate on the floor. He reached over and picked it up. "Are you all done?"

"Yes." Getting to his feet, he dumped the rest of the steak in a plastic container and put it in the refrigerator. All the while she watched him, her dark-gold eyes deepening to burnished brown with interest. Her gaze dropped to his groin. His cock twitched and, when her tongue touched her lips, filled. "I like the way you think."

She blinked and grinned, all innocence. "And how do I think?"

He bent and scooped her up in his arms. "Like my woman should."

She wrapped her arms around his neck. "And how is that?"

He hitched her up. "All wild and eager."

The nails of her right hand stung the nape of his neck while the left went to work on the buttons of his shirt. "I like that you can carry me so easily."

He grinned down at her. "Turns you on, huh?"

The look she shot him from under her lashes was hot enough to singe his short hairs. "Absolutely.

She spread his shirt open, her nails scoring a sizzling path from his breastbone to the point of her mark. And paused.

"What?"

"My mark." She traced the outline, sending chills of anticipation down his spine. "It's almost gone." She frowned up at him as if it was all his fault. Which it probably was, since he was a vampire, with a vampire's self-healing metabolism.

Hot and thick, desire surged through his blood, slowed and deepened his drawl as he realized what that meant. "I guess that means you'll just have to mark me all over again."

Her smile proved as wicked as his thoughts. She pressed her index finger to the center of the faded mark. "Hmm, and I might just have to take my time about it, too."

The tip of her soft pink tongue rolled over her full lips. She held his gaze as she slowly, so slowly leaned forward. His breath stuttered to a growl. She didn't move forward or backward, just hovered there taunting him with the promise of her kiss. "Son of a bitch."

"What?" She touched the spot with her tongue, igniting the flames that burned straight to his cock.

He slid down the wall, holding her mouth to him. "We're not going to make it to the bedroom again."

TWO weeks later the Tragallions weren't the only ones spoiling for a fight. Two weeks of sidestepping challenges and chasing shadows and Jace would give his eyeteeth to sink his fist into something. If he was back at the Circle J, he could have counted on Jared to say something provoking and give him cause to vent, but here he was surrounded by fight-at-the-drop-of-a-hat Tragallion males who seemed determined to wear out his good nature with cool smiles and endless patience. And he was reasonably sure they were doing it on purpose. The bastards.

Jace glanced around from the rooftop where he was replacing shingles. Hammer thuds reverberated in the cool night air as the men worked, in a rush to beat the warm weather and the early spring rains predicted for the next day. He glanced at the near-depleted bundle beside him and the roofs that still needed repair. Damn, he wished they'd been able to bring in more.

He took off his Stetson and rubbed the back of his hand across his brow. The move dragged the material of his shirt across the mark Miri had replaced that morning. He sucked in a breath as the sweet burn pierced his composure with the memory of the night before. The woman had a wild side for sure.

"We're going to run short," Marc said, following his gaze across the rooftops and their obvious state of disrepair.

"Yeah." He rubbed at the spot on his chest, forgetting about the hammer in his hand, rapping himself on the chin with the claw.

"Damn it!"

Brac shot him a look, hammer poised over a nail, a smirk on his lips. With a clean smack he drove the nail home. Jace considered walking across the short expanse and kicking his ass.

"You got something to say, were?"

"Nope."

Jace pulled a nail out of his pocket and lined his shingle up under the one above. "Too bad."

He would have enjoyed kicking Brac's ass. The man was a walking irritation.

"If things are too peaceful around here for you, vamp . . ." The hammer drove another nail in. "You can always go home."

"And leave you children alone to play unsupervised? I don't think so." He nailed the shingle down. "Miri would never forgive me."

"We don't need supervision," one of the men growled from the adjacent rooftop. "Especially from a candy-ass vampire whose only claim to fame is mating to one of our females."

Jace set his hammer down and stood. Slowly. At last. "I bet that just stings, doesn't it?"

The man, Brody, was big and, to judge from the way he leapt across the space between the two houses, agile. Jace grinned. It'd be a good fight.

Brody's answering smile was a slow, easy expression of confidence. "As a matter of fact, it does."

Jace stepped away from the debris and shook the stiffness out of his arms. "Good."

Brac stepped forward. "Not on the roof."

"Worried your pretty boy is going to get hurt?"

"No, more like I'm worried shingles we can't replace will get ruined and when the rain pours in, Maura will blame us and there won't be any blueberry pie this summer."

Brody grumbled. "Good point."

He walked to the ladder. Jace waited until he was halfway down before levitating past him.

"Asshole."

Tipping his hat, he continued on, taking off his coat and throwing it on the step when he reached the bottom. Jace rolled up his sleeves as he waited the minute it took Brody to clear the ladder. Aggravation laced the other man's steps as he approached.

"That little trick isn't going to save your ass."

"And running off at the mouth isn't going to save yours."

Weres poured off rooftops and skimmed down ladders. Silently, they formed a circle around Jace and Brody until they made a solid wall of muscle and hostility. A sense of familiarity came over Jace. Unlike the cat-and-mouse games he'd been playing the last two weeks with whomever had Faith, he appreciated this confrontation. This was familiar, played out so many times in his past that it had the feel of an old friend. Nothing like a good fight to clear the air.

He wiggled his fingers, inviting the were to make the first move. When Brody did, Jace met it head-on, the teeth-jarring impact of Brody's body centering his focus. Pain exploded in his gut as Brody landed a blow. Jace twisted away, kicking out, catching the were on the side of the face. Brody shook his head, stunned for a second. Jace didn't move in. He had a few more demons to work out before he let this fight end.

Ten minutes later, Jace wished he'd reconsidered. This wasn't Brody's first fight and the way he took blow after blow while delivering some nasty ones of his own proved he was in this for the long haul.

A very long haul. After thirty minutes neither man was a clear winner, and the fight was nowhere near done. Jace ached from head to toe and Brody didn't look like he was faring any better.

Jace wiped the blood from his mouth as the other man circled. Brody's greater size gave him impressive endurance, enough so it compensated for Jace's enhanced strength. But not his vampire powers, if he wanted to throw that into the mix. That wasn't going to happen. This had started out as a fair fight and it was going to end as one. "Ready to give up, vampire?" Brody growled, wiping the blood from his eye.

"Ready to call it quits, were?"

"You can't win."

"Well, I'm sure as shit not losing."

He jumped back as Brody lashed out. His talons caught on the pocket of Jace's shirt. Material tore with a soft hiss as he spun away. The cool air on his mark made it burn. When he turned back, Brody just stood there, staring at him, a strange expression on his face. A glance around showed everyone else doing the same.

Crooking two fingers, he invited Brody forward, back into the fun.

It was Brac who stepped forward, frowning. "You didn't tell us she marked you."

Jace kept his fists up. "Probably because it's none of your damn business."

"When did this happen?"

"Which time?"

Brac's head snapped up. "What do you mean, 'Which time?'"

Jace made his smile as patient as he could. "I'm a vampire; I heal, remember?"

"Son of a bitch."

Brody stepped back, his hands dropping. "How often?"

"What?"

Lifting his hand, Brody indicated the mark on Jace's chest. "How often do you go through marking?"

"About every couple days."

Another "son of a bitch" rose out of the crowd.

What the hell did his mark matter *now*? "Do I need to remind you we were in the middle of a perfectly good fight?"

With a wave of his hand, Brody put an end to his fun. "We're done with that."

"The hell we are." Jace still had a load of aggravation to work off. "C'mon."

Brody didn't put up his fists. "No."

"It is against pack law to fight a man in the midst of marking fever," Brac interjected.

"Marking what?"

"The emotional upheaval a male goes through after his mate marks him."

"Why the hell not?"

"They're not rational."

Sweat stung the mark, reminding Jace of the sting of Miri's sharp white teeth. His cock stirred, riding the rush of adrenaline from the fight.

"As Alpha I'm abolishing that law."

This time it was Brac's turn to look patient. "The law was set by the Enforcers. It's beyond your reach."

Another look around showed the Tragallions were convinced of what they were saying. "Figures." Jace walked over and grabbed his coat off the step and drew it on in short jerks, grunting as the blows he had taken to his torso made their locations known.

"What are you going to do?" Brody asked.

"Since you've put an end to our fun, I figured I'd finish the roof."

He climbed the ladder rather than levitating, annoyance demanding more aggressive movement than a soft drift. The ladder rattled as someone else climbed on. A look over his shoulder revealed Brac following.

Jace wiped the blood from his cut lip, wincing at the sting. "Whatever it is, Brac, this isn't a good time."

"Tough."

Jace cocked an eyebrow at him. "You say 'tough' to your Alpha?"

Brac shrugged. "When he needs to hear it."

"What in hell makes you think I'll listen?"

"You are not an unreasonable man."

That made him blink. "What? No qualifying that with 'for a vampire'?"

"You can't fit with the pack if you don't understand the law."

He subdued the pulse of victory and contemplated how much it was going to hurt clearing the top of the ladder. "I didn't realize you thought of me as a permanent fixture."

"You grow on a pack."

That surprising tidbit came from above. Marc. Jace swung his leg over the top of the ladder.

"Like a fungus," Brac grunted.

"You heard?" Brac looked pointedly at Jace's chest.

"Yeah." Marc sighed. "That could be a problem for some."

Jace winced as his ribs screamed a protest at the need to straighten, once he stood on the roof.

Marc noticed the betraying movement. "Brody's got a hell of a punch, doesn't he?"

"He's a one-man battering ram."

"You did well against him."

"I'd rather have finished it."

Brac shook his head. "That won't be allowed."

"Because Miri marked me?"

"Pretty much."

Jace crossed to where he'd left his hammer. He didn't bend down, though. No sense faking what no one believed. Probing his ribs for breaks, he asked, "Either one of you plan on telling me why Miri's marking me is putting a damper on my fun, or should I guess?"

The two men exchanged a glance and then a nod.

"Marking is a highly erotic event," Marc began.

"No shit."

"It leaves a man off balance for days while the hormones work through his system."

"Hence the law," Brac interjected. "Too many battles turn deadly when men are in marking fever. It's never been a problem before, as it's a onetime thing." He eyed Jace with a combination of disgust and awe. "Or it used to be."

"I've got to admit, with the usual Johnson contrariness, you've carried marking fever to a new extreme," Marc added.

"I hate to break it to you, boys, but I am not the contrary one."

"Shit, if you weren't my Alpha, I think I'd have to kill you," Brac muttered. "I haven't enjoyed the experience once and you're indulging on an almost daily basis." He grabbed up a hammer and a handful of nails.

Jace smiled, showing all his teeth. "Eat your heart out."

"Trust me, I am, but you're wearing on my nerves."

"That just breaks my heart."

Jace's cell phone rang. He checked the number before flipping it open. "Caleb."

"How's life going as lord of the weres?"

He checked the bruise on his belly. "It's a real blast."

His sarcasm got through. Two thumps came clearly over the line. Caleb's feet hitting the floor. "Are you having problems?"

"Nothing twenty years or so of building trust won't take care of."

"Are the Tragallions turning nasty?"

Jace glared at Marc and Brac. "Apparently, I'm immune to nasty."

"How the hell did you manage that?"

"Miri arranged it."

"She's a resourceful little thing, isn't she?"

Jace's fingers drifted instinctively up to his mark. It burned just at the mention of her name. He flipped Brac off when he smiled knowingly. "She's just full of surprises."

"Why do I think there's more going on than you're telling me?"

"Probably because I'm still working out the kinks."

"Anything I can do to help?"

"You could tell me there's news on Faith."

Caleb sighed. "Nothing concrete."

Jace tucked the phone between his shoulder and cheek, blocking the spread of sound. "What exactly does that mean?"

"There's been a lot of chatter where there shouldn't be and none where there should."

"Shit."

"That was pretty much my response."

Silence reigned for a heartbeat. Caleb wasn't telling him the whole story. "What else?"

A heavy sigh and then, "Tobias has gone missing."

"On purpose?"

"No one knows."

"Who the hell are these Enforcers?"

"You mean besides being a law unto themselves?"

"Yeah."

"I have no idea."

"Do you think Tobias is mixed up in Faith's disappearance?"

"To his eyeballs. I'm just not sure which side he's going to come down on when the smoke clears."

Jace knew. "Tobias may be Enforcer, but he's were. There's no way he's siding with Sanctuary."

"I hope you're right."

"Weres are real big on standards."

The ladder rattled as men began returning to their job. While they gathered their equipment and got back to work, Jace was subjected to many strange looks. And Brac was still studying him with that inscrutable something on his face. Another silence. Jace checked his watch. "If we don't want the Sanctuary tracing this, we need to hang up."

"I know." Caleb still didn't end the call, his worry stretching across the distance. "Jace?"

"Yeah?"

"Watch your back."

"You've got it."

⋇ 21 ⋇

THE call came from Tobias two hours later when Jace was between the garage and the house.

"Yes?"

Without any preamble, the Enforcer broke the news. "I found Faith. They want to make a trade."

The pain in his bruised abdomen was nothing compared to the pain of hope. "Who are they?"

"The only thing I know is they're wolf, not vamp."

That was a plus. "What do they want in trade?"

"Brenda Lynn."

"Why?"

"That mystery is going to have to be solved at a later date."

Which translated to they didn't have much time. "When do they want us to make the exchange?"

"Tonight."

"Not in any rush, are they?"

"It gets better."

"Why am I not surprised?"

"They want you to come along to the meeting place. Just you

and Brenda Lynn. If they hear any rumors of this or they see you bring anybody else, they'll kill Faith."

Weres were beginning to look at him funny. He started walking again, faking a calm he didn't feel. "Are you sure they have Faith?"

"They described her rescue from the Sanctuary to a T."

"They risked their lives to save her and now they're threatening to kill her?"

"I know. It doesn't make sense. Could be she's no use to them anymore."

Which she wouldn't be if she were sickly like Joseph and struggling to hold on to life. The sense of urgency inside him increased. If Faith was doing poorly, time was even more of the essence. Jace kept his voice as even as possible. "Does this mean that you found your rogue Enforcer?"

There was a pause and then an equally careful "I'm getting closer."

"Now, why doesn't that give me a warm fuzzy?"

"It shouldn't. Nothing about this should give you a warm fuzzy, but there is the upside."

"Yeah. We finally found Faith."

"And she's alive. That's a hell of a lot more than we had last night."

And it was going to be a hell of a lot less than he had tomorrow, because tomorrow he was going to give Miri back her daughter. "Yeah. Where's the meeting place?"

"The cave's sixty miles south of here."

That would put the meeting place between the Tragallion lands and the Circle J. Jace could use that.

"Thanks."

"Whatever plan you come up with, be careful who you confide it to. We don't know who to trust, Jace. They've got to have somebody on the inside for them to know as much as they do about the Tragallion situation."

Jace glanced up at the sky. Dawn was starting to push out the night.

Tobias continued, "I also don't like the fact that somebody knows more about Brenda Lynn than we do."

"She's just a little girl."

"A little girl that Travis kept close. There has to be some significance to that."

"Whatever it is, you know it's wrapped up in power. Everything Travis did—keeping the pack in the technological dark ages, driving out dissenters—it all fed into his love of power."

"In werewolf culture, power comes through the females."

"I thought of that, but Brenda Lynn does not have the D'Nally golden eyes."

"What does her scent tell you?"

"That she's overly fond of the scent of lilacs."

"Lilacs?"

"The kid smells like she bathes in the stuff."

"Interesting."

The kid's daily choice of stench took on new meaning as Jace glanced across the compound to where Brenda Lynn's house resided. Only one light was on, in one of the bedrooms. As he watched, it went out. Werewolves had very sensitive noses. They wouldn't wear such a strong scent unless they were trying to cover another scent. He remembered Brenda Lynn's complaining once of itchy eyes. Too dry contacts caused itchy eyes. "I'll get back to you, Tobias."

"What do you want me to tell our little party of kidnappers?"

"Tell them I'll be coming for them at the appointed time."

"With Brenda Lynn?"

"Tell them I'll be coming with what I need to get my daughter."

Jace pressed the off button and snapped the phone closed. They'd found his daughter. He pulled up her mental image, stroking her little cheek in his mind. *I'm coming for you, baby girl. You just hold on and tomorrow you'll be back home with your momma.*

He didn't include himself in the promise. Odds were he wasn't going to get out of this alive. The caves were the perfect place to set up an ambush. Lots of dead ends, lots of hiding places. Too many for one man to manage. Maybe not for two. He crossed the compound, heading for Marjorie's house and the answers he needed. If he was right, Marjorie was more than just another pack member and her daughter possibly more to the Tragallions' future than just another little girl.

He flipped his cell phone open as he crossed the street. Before he did anything else, he needed to make a call. He hit the send button. Caleb answered on the second ring. "I need your help."

LYING to Miri was the hardest thing he'd ever done. Jace could feel the probe of her energy against his, searching for what he wasn't telling her as he checked his weapons before loading them into the SUV.

"Why won't you tell me where you're going?" she asked for the third time.

"Because it's not important."

"It's important enough for you to turn yourself into a walking arsenal."

"I'm a cautious man."

"You're an evasive man."

"For a reason you should respect."

Her arms folded across her chest. The gold of her eyes heated with her frustration. The same gold of Marjorie's and Brenda Lynn's eyes when one removed the contacts. The D'Nally eyes that Travis had planned on exploiting through a biddable Brenda Lynn once it became clear that Marjorie wouldn't play along with a man who would sell out his female Alpha to the Sanctuary. Brenda Lynn would be Travis's ace in the hole to finagling ascension once he succeeded in getting rid of Miri and Marjorie.

"I don't respect what I don't understand."

He cocked an eyebrow at her. She didn't melt like she usually did. "Some things have to be taken on faith."

He realized it was a poor choice of words as soon as he said it. Miri's brows snapped down as puzzle pieces fell into place. "You're going after Faith, aren't you? That's why you won't give me any details."

Jace slid his revolver into his hip holster before reaching for the knife harness.

"I told you I'm not talking about it." Not to her, because if she got an inkling Faith was near, she'd be all over it regardless of the danger. And she was too important to him and her pack to be anywhere near the mess this rescue was going to become.

On a "Stand back" he hauled the energy shield cover off the SUV.

The material was heavy with the energy it had absorbed from the vehicle. Too heavy for even him to lift. He let it slide to the ground, jumping back before it could crush his foot or leg. It would be a couple minutes before it would lose the energy it had absorbed and become light.

"I love you, Jace."

The words encompassed him with the softness of her energy, the underlying edge of desperation not diminishing the impact. He absorbed both, her love and her fear, relishing the former, working to diminish the latter as he turned to face her.

She was so achingly beautiful in his night vision. The stark black and white highlighting the purity of her features, the rich black of her hair, the tempting fullness of her mouth, the thickness of her lashes over those incredible eyes.

He'd always imagined the first time he heard those words from her would be in bed, when she was drawn past her inhibitions by the force of their passion, but here was okay, too, seeing as it might be his last chance to hear them and if things went bad, he was selfish enough to want the memory to hold on to when he passed to the other side.

"Thought you were saving up those words."

"I thought you were going to share with me."

She rubbed her hands up and down her arms and took a step closer. "Why aren't you taking anyone with you?"

Jace nudged the shield with his foot. It was still too heavy to move.

"Because bringing someone along would complicate things."

"We're in the middle of a war, Jace. No one leaves the compound without reinforcements." She took another step closer, close enough that he could see the sheen of tears in her eyes. "That's your own rule."

He took the step that closed the distance between them, cupping her cheeks in his hands, rubbing his thumbs over the fine skin of her cheekbones, calluses rasping on the scars. He'd rather tear his heart out than see her hurt again. "You know I'd do anything for you, right?"

"Yes."

There wasn't an ounce of doubt in her voice. "Good. I want you to remember that. Right along with the fact that I love you. Have since the moment I saw you and that won't ever stop."

Fingers encircled his wrists like delicate chains that made him want to forget everything happening later that day. "That sounds like good-bye."

"A good-bye would imply I'm not planning on coming back."

Her gaze met his and held it. "Are you?"

"Always." No matter how remote the possibility, he would do his damnedest to make it back to Miri and his daughter.

A flicker of sensation along his consciousness alerted him to an intrusion. Miri was attempting to read his mind. He snapped his mind closed. Had he closed it in time? Nothing in Miri's expression changed; nothing showed she'd slipped past his guard.

Jace glanced out the window of the garage. It was full dark without even a hint of moon lighting the black. Prime hunting time for vampires. The lack of light would give him an advantage over the werewolves, as their vision would be compromised. It was a small advantage, but he chose to take it as a good omen. He gathered up the shielding material and tossed it into the back of the SUV.

Miri came up behind him and put her arms around his waist and squeezed tightly, her cheek resting against his back. "Don't do this, Jace."

He turned in her embrace, cupping her head in his hand and pressing her to his heart.

"Whatever it is you're going to do," Miri whispered, "whatever it is you're planning on sacrificing yourself for, it's not worth it."

He rested his cheek on the top of her head, memorizing the feel of her in his arms, relishing the way her heart beat in synch with his, feeling her strength, her determination, knowing the pain of loss that ate her alive. Pain he'd created. Pain he could heal. "I'll keep that in mind."

He tipped her face up, allowed himself one last look into her eyes, one last kiss, one last "I love you."

Then he turned on his heel and got in the SUV.

JACE waited until he was out of sight of the compound before taking the dummy he'd built and buckling it into the passenger side of the front seat. From the distance, he figured it would do to make whomever was watching think he had the little girl with him.

He sensed a presence and looked up. Tobias stood beside the car. Jace blinked. The powers the Enforcer wielded were impressive. Almost as impressive as the determination illuminating his cold eyes. Jace rolled down his window. "Nice of you to make it."

The door locks on the SUV popped open. Tobias glanced over at the dummy then back at Jace. He raised his eyebrows and opened the back door. "Do you think that's going to fool anyone?"

"As long as no one gets up close and personal, it will do the job for as long as I need it to." Especially since no one expected a vampire to have a moral code and therefore wouldn't expect him to have any compunction about sacrificing a child for something he wanted.

The door closed. "Got a minute to talk about what exactly the job is?"

"Getting my daughter back."

"I figured that. The question is in the how."

"I'm counting on luck."

"Funny, I got the impression this was a suicide mission."

"I'm not suicidal."

Tobias leaned back in the seat. "Just reckless."

Jace shrugged. "Only a little."

"I know the goal is to get Faith back to Miri, but did it ever occur to you that without you, that's not going to be enough?"

"It'll be enough."

"Miri's right. You don't understand weres. Miri will never accept your death. She'll follow you to the grave."

That was not part of the plan. "Slade will find a way for her to live for our daughter."

"Uh-huh." Tobias motioned to the road. "Shouldn't we be going?"

"I believe I was told to come alone."

"You were. But I told them the cost of bringing me in to broker a deal is they get to have me there when the deal took place."

"They didn't object."

Tobias smiled a cold smile. "I think they're planning on killing two birds with one stone."

Jace met his gaze in the rearview. "You've got to admire their efficiency."

"Yeah. You do."

"So what do you think this is going to get them?"

"Brenda Lynn, because for sure they aren't going to think you won't bring her to trade."

"I considered it."

"No, you didn't."

"Don't tell me you've suddenly decided I have scruples."

"I've always thought you had scruples. Who do you think suggested to Ian to let your mating to Miri stand?"

"I wondered why no one just took me out."

"You can thank me by not getting killed now and upsetting Miri."

"That's not in the plan."

"As far as I can see there isn't much of a plan."

Jace put the SUV in motion. "If you don't like it, you can get out."

"There's always plan B. I'm just going along for the ride, to protect were interests."

"Which would be?"

"The Tragallion Alpha."

"I'm thinking there aren't too many that would be sad to see me go."

"Miri would. She loves you."

"And I love her."

"And it's definitely coloring your thinking."

Jace steered the SUV around a rut in the road.

"What? You believe vampires can feel love?"

"I believe the Johnsons are capable of a lot of things most vampires aren't."

There was a series of clicks. Jace glanced in the rearview. Tobias held a cell phone in his hand. He glanced at the screen. A small smile touched his stern lips.

"Why are you smiling?"

Tobias put the cell phone away.

"Just a touch of optimism."

He leaned back in the seat and closed his eyes. "Wake me when we get within five miles of the exchange site."

JACE parked the SUV at the base of the caves. He glanced in the rearview. He could feel Tobias's presence, but couldn't pinpoint it, hadn't been able to since the Enforcer had gotten out of the car five miles back. He'd just disappeared into the trees like a shadow conjured from his imagination. Jace shook his head. The man was good.

Tugging the energy shield with him, he got out of the car. With a smooth arc, he threw it over the car. Immediately the mechanical energy reading winked out. Hopefully, anyone scanning the area would assume the shield blocked Brenda Lynn's energy, too. Otherwise, his plan was dead in the water.

The path to the caves was on the right. No weres dotted what he could see of the dirt trail before it disappeared into the heavy wood, but he could feel their presence as soon as he entered the forest. About twenty-five in all, soundlessly pacing him in the woods. A hundred feet up the path they came out, encircled him. They were all young, all heavily armed.

Jace stood, hands at his sides, his vampire rising at the threat.

"You were supposed to bring the girl."

He jerked his chin over his shoulder. "She's in the car."

"Get her."

"Not until I see my daughter."

The speaker, a handsome were with young energy, motioned with his gun to two others, who immediately headed back down the trail.

Jace met the leader's gaze. "They touch that SUV and that kid in the car is going to be bits and pieces all over the landscape. Along with your pack mates."

The leader's eyes narrowed. "You'd kill a child?"

Jace smiled. "I'm vampire, what do you think?"

"I think someone should take you out."

"Bigger men than you have tried."

The kid didn't rise to the bait. Just hooked his teeth over his lower lip and let out a short whistle. The two weres stopped and looked back. He waved them in.

A rifle muzzle dug into Jace's back. "Get moving."

Jace looked over his shoulder. "Is this the part where I'm supposed to say, 'Take me to your leader?'"

"This is the part where you get your arrogant ass in gear, or I'll blow it off."

Jace glanced over his shoulder. "You do that and you'll lose your ticket to pack status."

The were stared at him. Surprise tinted his scent.

"You didn't think I'd find out about Brenda Lynn's parentage. The little Alpha female you're counting on for ascension? The one tied up in my booby-trapped SUV? The booby trap that only I know how to disarm?"

The were snarled again and shoved him forward. Jace went, sheer force of will keeping his breathing regular and his heartbeat slow as their destination became clear. The third cave on the left. That was where Faith was.

Caleb? You here? Caleb had been the only one of his brothers he could summon because only Caleb could manage the exposure to sunlight to get here in time. It seemed to take forever for him to answer. In reality it was about five seconds.

About thirty feet on your right.

The third cave on the left.

I've got it.

Remember, no matter what, you get my daughter out.

I'm getting you both out.

Worry about Faith.

I'll worry what I want.

Jace ground his teeth as Caleb severed the connection. He needed to know Caleb would put Faith first. A man appeared in the cave entrance. Long dark hair blew away from his face. Even from this distance Jace could make out the eerie silver of his eyes. Tobias's supposition had been right. There was an Enforcer mixed up in this. The man had something in his arms. He came down the path with an easy grace, meeting them twenty feet from the cave entrances.

"Jace Johnson?" he asked.

Jace couldn't take his eyes off the baby, wrapped in a khaki blanket. She had the sweetest face, was actually the spitting image of Miri. He touched his energy to hers; it meshed perfectly. His daughter. His knees almost buckled. This was his daughter.

Caleb's energy immediately bolstered his, sliding along their private pathway. *Steady.*

Jace blinked, tearing his eyes away from Faith's rosy cheeks and the wild tuft of hair on the top of her head that just begged to be smoothed down. His apparently healthy daughter. God, he wished he could transmit that fact to Miri.

"Is this her?" he asked the rogue.

"Didn't you just get that answer for yourself?" A spill of energy accompanied the question. So the rogue could sense energy but not control it. Jace could use that.

"Just verifying my suspicions."

"Where's the girl?"

"I told you. In the car."

The wolf who'd brought him up the mountain sneered, "He threatened to blow her up."

The rogue studied him. Jace felt the probe of his energy. He was skilled, and probably could be lethal, with training, but he wasn't trained now.

"You endangered a child?"

"I did what I had to in order to get *my* child."

The rogue glared at the men. "Duncan, you left a child bound in a car rigged with explosives?"

"There wasn't anything else to do until he saw his daughter. He's a damn vampire, Broderick. We believed him when he said he would blow her up."

Broderick grunted.

Interesting that the rogue's scent changed at the thought of a child in danger. He might not be as rogue as Tobias feared.

"You've seen your daughter. Let the other girl go."

"I'd like to hold my daughter."

"I'd like the last ten years back. Neither is going to happen." Broderick motioned with his hand. "Let's go."

"Hand me my daughter now, and I might just be persuaded to forget all about your holding her hostage."

Duncan poked him in the back with the gun.

Glancing over his shoulder, Jace warned, "Do that again, son, and you're going to be eating that thing."

"Brave words from a man who's outnumbered."

"Dumb words from a man who hasn't studied his enemy."

Broderick's laugh was more of a growl. "One thing's for sure, the rumors of your arrogance are bearing out."

Jace pinned him with his gaze, letting his vampire roar beneath the flames. "The only reason you're still alive is you saved my daughter's life, but be advised, you endanger her again, and I'll take you out." He paused and added, "Slowly."

The rogue didn't flinch. "And you be advised the only reason you're still alive is because of the way your mate sees you."

"And how's that?"

"Worth something."

Jace chewed on that. Even when she'd thought he'd left her in the labs, Miri had believed in him. Damn, the woman didn't know the meaning of the word "quit."

It was faster going down than up. They approached the spot where he'd left the SUV. It wasn't visible.

The rogue stopped studying the area. "Your brother found a way to shield it."

"You know of my brother?"

"Everyone knows of Slade Johnson."

That was not good news. "Yes, Slade found a way."

He glanced over at Jace. "It doesn't leave a trace?"

"Not a bit."

Broderick frowned again, studying harder, unconsciously jostling Faith when she squeaked and fussed in the blanket as he did so. The latter was totally instinctive. Jace wondered if the rogue knew the damage holding the little girl did to his macho image. He doubted if Broderick understood that he'd just saved his own life with that betraying gesture. Johnsons didn't repay a debt with betrayal. And like it or not, they owed the rogue a debt that could never be repaid. His daughter's life.

The rogue Enforcer isn't to be hurt, he told Caleb.

Jesus, Jace. Why don't you just tie my hands?

He's the reason Faith is alive.

Son of a bitch!

He felt Caleb shift positions. There still was no sign of Tobias.

Pointing to the copse where Caleb lurked, he ordered, "Get my daughter out of range."

Broderick's chin snapped up. "You're not in charge here."

"I'm the one who created the bomb, and I'm saying my daughter will be safer over there."

The rogue snarled, revealing sharp canines. His energy whipped out. "Disarm the bomb. Now."

Jace blocked the wild thrust of energy and smiled inside. The rogue had the weres' love of children combined with an enhanced need to protect. It explained a lot, most especially why he'd risked everything to save Faith.

Jace jerked his chin in the direction of the woods where Caleb waited. "Take Faith back."

The rogue handed the baby off to another were with young energy. Jace frowned. All the weres had young energy.

"Where's your pack?"

"We have no pack."

"Travis saw to that," someone else muttered.

Which explained the interest in Brenda Lynn. These were Tragallion weres. Members of his pack. Killing the group wasn't going to be the clear-cut joy that he'd been looking forward to. Damn it. Either he was getting old or life was getting complicated.

He walked toward where he'd left the SUV, relying on memory

as the vehicle wasn't visible. He reached for the cover. The rogue pulled him back. "I'll do it."

Jace shrugged. The man leaned forward. There was a hiss of sound and the cover slid off the SUV. Jace leapt back, reflex saving him from being crushed under the fabric. Broderick wasn't so lucky. Breathless curses came from under the cloth. Tobias seemed to appear out of thin air beside the fallen man. In his hands were two nasty-looking weapons, on his face a smiling invitation to the cursing rogues to join his party.

Another curse came from the edge of the woods where Jace had sent Faith. A quick glance showed the were down and Caleb holding the baby, but he was surrounded and going nowhere. With a snarl, Jace dove into the wolves. In slow motion he saw the muzzles turn, heard Tobias's shout, Caleb's warning. He paid no mind, surging forward to the weaker corner, his only goal to create a route through which Caleb could escape with Faith. Snarls came from the woods, blending into the mix. The fucking rogues had reinforcements.

Guns fired in rapid succession. Jace leapt into the hail of bullets, grunting as they tore through his flesh, ripped open his organs, not caring, his total focus on gaining those precious few seconds that Caleb needed to get Faith out. He just needed a few more so his brother could get her to safety. *Please God, a few more.* A rogue lunged for Caleb. He went down in a slash of Caleb's talons. Another appeared behind him. Two more to the left. The snarls grew louder, collided. Men hollered. A rogue reached Caleb. Grabbed for Faith with bloody claws. With the vicious skill he was known for, Caleb sliced off his hand. The next rogue pulled up, staring at the severed appendage and the spray of blood. Caleb leapt into the hesitation and broke free, a blur of motion heading east.

Jace fell into the gap, snarling and whirling around, filling the space with all the aggression inside. Any son of a bitch that was stupid enough to try was going to die here and now. He threw back his head and howled his challenge. The Tragallion battle cry roared over the other sounds of battle.

All around, were voices picked up call, echoing it off the mountains. Over and over the cry swelled as voices reinforced the challenge. Tragallion voices lifted in the Tragallion war cry spilled into the clearing, came closer. Blood dripped in his eyes and poured down his side. Jace swayed, wiping at his face, clearing his vision. Ready for the next wave.

Except there wasn't anyone coming. The clearing was filled with the hard-eyed faces of men he recognized. The reinforcements hadn't been rogue, they'd been pure pack Tragallion. Only one person could have arranged that. Miri must have given instructions for them to follow him.

He spotted Brac, knee planted firmly in another man's back, ruthlessly tying up a rogue. As if feeling his gaze, he looked up. Jace ignored the black edging his vision. He nodded his thanks. Brac got to his feet.

To Jace's right someone called his name. Sweet and feminine, he'd recognize that voice anywhere. *Miri.* He closed his eyes, struggling to maintain his balance as blood soaked the ground at his feet. She shouldn't be here to see this.

"Jace!"

Her footsteps were light on the ground, soft punctuations to the touch of her energy. It wrapped around him in a desperate hug two seconds before her arms came around him. As he swayed, she gasped and widened her stance, her shoulder wedging under his in a too-short support. "Don't you die on me, Jace Johnson."

He licked his dry lips, striving for strength. "You shouldn't be here."

"What I shouldn't be, is here this late. You should have told me about this, not forced me to read your mind."

Her grip slipped through the blood. She gasped again and then her hands were all over him, checking wounds, sobbing when she found them. "Oh, God." She patted his chest. His cheek. "Oh, God."

"Caleb!"

It was a high-pitched shriek that reverberated in his head and his ears. Jace's knees buckled. She tried to catch him. He had just enough strength to throw himself backward to avoid falling on her. The pain was intense. "I'm okay, Miri."

"You're bleeding out." She tore at her shirtsleeve.

There was no bleeding about it. He was about out.

She held her wrist to his mouth. "Feed, Jace."

He reached for her hand, missed the first time, caught it the second. He brought it to his mouth, pressed a kiss to her palm, then shook his head. "I'd drain you and bleed out anyway."

She pressed harder. "Caleb will be here in a second."

Even Caleb's blood wouldn't be able to keep him alive long enough to recover from this. That would take a lot of blood. A steady supply. "It's okay, Miri."

Tears dripped off her face onto his.

"No, it's not."

"Don't cry, princess." He raised his hand to her cheek. Blood smeared through her tears. "I hate to see you cry."

She wiped at her cheeks, smudging the blood into larger blotches. "Don't tell me what to do."

He felt the faint vibrations of approaching footsteps. He struggled to get up. It was a measure of how close to death he was that it only took one of Miri's hands to keep him down.

The darkness was calling. He didn't have much time. "I saw Faith, Miri." He stretched his fingers to touch her cheek, only realizing then that she was holding his hand. His voice was a dry rasp. "She's beautiful—healthy. Looks just like you."

"Shut up."

"I love you."

"I said, shut up."

A shadow darker than the night appeared beside them. Brac.

The Tragallion stared down at him, assessing his wounds with a soldier's objectivity. "You're seriously fucked up, vampire."

"I've had better days."

"You were foolish to try and do this alone."

"I can see that."

"You deserve to die for that stupidity alone."

"Probably." And he was right, for a lot more reasons than that.

"But not today." Brac rolled back his sleeve.

Jace blinked, not sure he understood. "You don't have enough blood."

Brac eyed him and his injuries. "Probably not."

Across the field, Jace saw Caleb appear out of the woods. He still had Faith. Jace forced a smile. Caleb didn't smile back.

Brac knelt beside him, bellowing, "Tragallions! To the Alpha!"

There was a murmur and then footsteps approached. Jace looked up. He was surrounded by hard-faced, cold-eyed Tragallions. Just what he wanted. To be encircled by high-handed weres at his death. To his surprise, they began rolling back their sleeves.

"You're not going to give him blood, are you?" one of the rogues snarled in disgust. "He's a fucking vampire!"

The sound of a blow interrupted the silence.

Brac's eyes burned with werewolf intensity as they met Jace's. He sliced his claw through his wrist. His life-giving blood dripped into Jace's mouth in a potent wash of power. "Yeah, but he's *our* fucking vampire."

Jace frowned, forcing back the darkness sweeping in. "What the hell is this?"

Miri's hand was gentle on his forehead. "You, Jace Johnson, are being claimed, Tragallion style."

"This mean I'm stuck with you?" he asked Brac.

The big were scowled. "Until we kick your ass out."

The were's blood filled his mouth. Jace swallowed, gathering the last of his strength as he absorbed the deeper meaning.

"Well, hell."

❧ Epilogue ❧

THE music was too loud, the attendees out of control, and there was no room to escape, either.

Miri, holding a happy, smiling Faith, came up to Jace's side where he stood leaning against the doorjamb fulfilling his role of chaperone at Brenda Lynn's first party. Her gaze never left the heavily guarded rogues' awkward attempts to re-establish bonds. She clearly wasn't ready to drop the discussion that had been interrupted by Faith's need for a diaper change.

"You can't adopt them, you know," he told her, watching the rogues mingling under close supervision with the other Tragallions.

Miri leaned into Jace's side. "Why not? You adopted Penny the minute you saw her."

And that was working out well. Penny and Marc were building their relationship, but, true to his word, the were shared Penny liberally with Miri and Jace. As often as not both could be found at their house.

"In case you haven't noticed, those boys weigh well over two hundred pounds and are packing a ton of attitude."

"They have no pack."

"They can find one elsewhere."

"They belong here. They're Tragallions."

Broderick glanced over, met Jace's gaze, and didn't look away. The pup, too bold for his own good, reminded him of his brother Jared in attitude. All hard edges and aggression, covering a sense of responsibility that wouldn't quit. There was no doubt Broderick had potential, but Jace still thought Tobias had bit off more than he could chew when he'd offered to recommend him for Enforcer training. Then again, offering the rogues shelter here didn't make much sense. Except, as Miri said, they were Tragallions. That made them his, and he didn't let anything go easily. "They'll cause all sorts of havoc," he warned.

"You like havoc."

He kissed the top of Faith's head, the happy touch of her energy to his a wonder he'd never get used to. He wrapped her in a mental hug, felt Miri's energy blend with theirs. He looked up and caught Broderick still looking at him, at the world Jace held in his arms. There was no mistaking the devastation in his silver eyes. In the next second it was gone, replaced by the defiance Jace was more used to seeing. "They won't thank you for it."

Miri shrugged. "Maybe not at first."

"Maybe not at all."

"They'll find their place eventually."

"Or not."

"Jace."

He looked down. Miri leaned her cheek against the fresh mark she'd given him that morning, rubbing gently, love and amusement deepening the gold of her eyes as his breath caught.

"What?"

"Think of it as a challenge."

He glanced around the room at the faces of the people he'd sworn to put above all else. People whose blood now ran in his veins. People whose lives he'd promised to make better. Little changes had already been made. Fresh clothing had been brought in, sprinkling the room in flashes of bright color. Toy cars whirred between the adults' feet; ray guns flared as kids played werewolf and Sanctuary. Bigger changes needed to occur, but this was his pack. He'd make them happen. One at a time.

Wrapping his fingers in Miri's hair, Jace tilted her head back for his kiss, finding a smile on her lips and all the love in the world in her eyes.

"In that case, it's a good thing I understand weres."